KALAHARI

KALAHARI

JESSICA KHOURY

razOr
bill

An Imprint of Penguin Group (USA) LLC

razOr
bill

A division of Penguin Young Readers Group
Published by the Penguin Group
Penguin Group (USA) LLC
345 Hudson Street
New York, New York 10014

USA / Canada / UK / Ireland / Australia / New Zealand / India / South Africa / China
Penguin.com
A Penguin Random House Company

ISBN: 9781595147653
Printed in the United States of America
1 3 5 7 9 10 8 6 4 2

TO MAMA,
WHO TAUGHT ME TO
SEEK ADVENTURES

ONE

The lions were napping on the runway again.

I held up a hand against the blazing African sun and stared at the small silver plane that was just minutes away from touching down. I'd have to move the pride before it landed.

"Theo!" I called. The Bushman was sitting on the hood of the Land Cruiser, and when he looked my way, I pointed at the three lionesses and two cubs sunning themselves on the hard-packed sand. Laughing, he leaned backward and honked the horn of the truck, his way of saying we'd have to chase them off. I nodded and ran back to the Cruiser, tossing my folder of papers in the backseat.

In a moment, I had the engine roaring and we were off, rattling down the runway toward the sleeping lions. They yawned and chuffed at me in a lazy attempt to scare me off, but I bore down on them. I recognized the pride; the lionesses were sisters, used to us rambling around the bush. They barely opened their eyes as the truck trundled up to them.

I stopped the Cruiser, leaving the engine running, and climbed onto the hood. From there, I shouted and waved my arms, to the amusement of the cubs, who rolled and yowled and stretched. At last, their mothers lifted themselves up huffily and ambled off the runway. They were soon lost in the waving golden grass, their tawny coats blending into the dry savanna. Just the black tips of their tails showed, flickering slyly above the foliage, and then those too vanished.

I drove the truck back to the other end of the runway and parked it, then grabbed my folder out of the backseat. The plane was dropping lower in the sky, lining up with the runway.

Theo glanced at me sidelong. He was part Bushman, with the lovely golden skin characteristic of his nomadic ancestors, and though he was older than my father, he was no taller than I was. He had found a praying mantis somewhere, and the insect was crawling over his hands, from one to the other. As soon as it crawled onto one hand, he lifted the other and placed it in front, so that the mantis was continually crawling forward but getting nowhere. Theo could charm any creature that walked, crawled, flew, or slithered.

"You look like you got a toothache, girl," he said.

"Two weeks," I murmured, my eyes still on the plane. "What are we going to do with five teenagers from the city for two weeks?"

"You're a teenager." He grinned, taking far too much delight in my dismay. "I am sure you will have a grand time."

"Yeah. A grand old time." I sank lower in my seat and flipped open the folder, riffling through the documents inside. "I went to school for three months in the States once, did you know that? The kids in my class called me Mowgli and threw bananas at me during lunch."

"What is the problem? At the end of the day, it was you who ended up with all the bananas." Theo turned in his seat, and though he was still smiling, his dark eyes were serious. "Tu!um-sa, it will be good for you. You cannot live your whole life with only animals for friends."

"I can try." I sighed and shut the folder. "Here they come."

The plane touched down in a cloud of dust, its silver sides reflecting golden grass and blue sky. It taxied down the short length and then turned, the propeller whipping up a whirl-wind of sand. Theo and I got out of the truck and walked toward the plane, and I held my scarf over my mouth and nose to keep from breathing in the dust.

After the engine died and the propeller wound down, the pilot ran around the front of the plane and opened the passen-ger door. I drew a deep breath and put on what I hoped looked like a welcoming smile.

"And here we go," I muttered through my teeth.

An Asian boy with a bright red baseball cap cocked side-ways over his long, shaggy hair tumbled out of the plane. The pilot, a young Frenchman named Matthieu, was standing at the door and tried to help him out, but the kid ignored him and fell to the ground, where he promptly puked onto the hard-packed sand.

I winced and consulted the papers I was carrying, quickly putting a name to our first guest's greenish face: Joey Xiong. From California. Seventeen years old, Hmong American. Listed Sasquatch as his favorite animal. I hoped his sickness was due to the plane ride and not a sign of something worse.

The last thing we needed was flu or malaria in our camp. The nearest hospital was an hour's flight away.

Next out was a tall, graceful girl with springy dark hair. She paused in the doorway, half bent over, and stared at the spot where Joey had deposited his breakfast. For a moment it seemed as if she would turn around and go back inside the plane, but Matthieu offered a hand and she gingerly stepped down, her expression a mask of disgust. While Joey lurched to his feet, she pointedly stood a few steps away from him and stared in the other direction. Avani Sharma, her profile paper read. Canadian, of Indian and Kenyan heritage. 4.0 GPA. The list of her academic achievements, recorded there for no apparent reason, was long enough to put some college professors to shame.

I let out a little breath, trying to force my thoughts to stay positive, as the next two guests exited the plane: a boy and a girl so entangled with each other that it was hard to see where one ended and the other began. They were both dark haired and pale skinned. They had on khaki from head to toe, but they wore it as if they'd just arrived for a Burberry photo shoot—his shirt was partially unbuttoned, her beige scarf was arranged in a complex knot, and they were both sporting manicured, immaculate hairstyles. There was no denying they were both drop-dead gorgeous and deeply obsessed with each other.

They could only be Miranda Kirk and Kase Rider of Boston, Massachusetts. They had come together and they were both seventeen. Other than that, the profiles they had filled out were scant on information. The space asking why they were here at all—*Please state what you hope to gain from this experience*—was blank on Miranda's, while Kase's form said only *wildlife photography portfolio.*

They jumped to the ground without taking their arms from around each other, then stood between Avani and Joey, whispering in each other's ears and regarding the surrounding wilderness with suspicious looks.

Last out of the plane was a boy who must have been, by process of elimination, Sam Quartermain, our final guest: shaggy dark blond hair, a plain white tee tucked messily into his jeans, carrying a tattered Adidas duffel bag. The moment his shoes hit the ground, his head was up and his eyes were wide, scanning the trees around us and finally settling on me.

"Hey!" he called out, the first of them to even acknowledge my presence. "Sarah, right? I'm Sam!"

"Hi, Sam."

"Mind if I take a picture?" said Kase, pulling out a camera roughly the size of a lawn mower engine.

"Um, no?"

"Sweet." He held up his camera and the shutter clicked. Then Kase cursed and fiddled with the dials. "Crap. Settings are all screwed up."

Miranda shielded her eyes from the sun as she whipped out her phone, her fingers a blur as they navigated the touch screen. "Ugh! No service? Are you *kidding* me?"

I suppressed a sigh and nodded to Matthieu. "*Salut*, Matt. *Bon vol?*"

He grunted and began unloading the boxes of food and necessities I'd ordered from our supplier in Maun. "*Je ne t'envie pas vraiment dans cette situation. C'est aussi amusant qu'un panier de serpents.*" *I don't envy you with this lot. They're about as much fun as a box of snakes.*

Easy for him to say. I was the sort of person who, upon arriving at someone's house on a social visit, ended up making friends with his or her canary instead. I'd take a box of snakes over these five any day. But as Dad was fond of saying, "We must soldier on, eh?"

"Hello, everyone," I said, clearing my throat. *They're just people. Get it together.* "Um, I'm Sarah Carmichael and this is Theo. Welcome to the Kalahari."

Beside me, Theo flashed his brightest smile and said, "Hello, hello," in his soft accent. I was glad I'd brought him along to meet the plane, because he immediately began putting everyone at ease, shaking hands, taking Miranda's and Avani's bags and pretending they were too heavy for him. Avani smiled a little, but Miranda rolled her eyes. Only Sam and Joey laughed, and Theo gave them a grin and a shrug as if to say, *Girls, eh?*

"Climb aboard," I said, waving at the battered green Land Cruiser. "It'll be a tight fit. You'll have to hold your bags. We're about a ten-minute drive from the camp."

As the group climbed into the Cruiser, I made a quick check of the supplies Matthieu had brought and then left Theo to stand guard over them until I returned with the car to load them up.

The Cruiser choked to life as I turned the key, and the whole thing began vibrating like it was about to fall apart. I heard a little shriek from behind me but couldn't tell who it was.

"This is Hank," I shouted over the engine, slapping the dash. "He sounds like a trash compactor, but he's the only thing that'll get through this terrain."

I turned the Cruiser around and rumbled down the track to the camp. The sides were all open and the canvas roof was rolled back, allowing the passengers a 360-degree view of the Kalahari semidesert.

A dry wind blasted my face, pulling my hair out of its messy braid and nearly sucking the wide-brimmed sun hat off my head. All around us, the graceful acacias and stocky *Terminalia* swayed and rustled, and a lone chanting goshawk cut the air above, hunting for mice in the tall golden grass. Behind us, Matthieu's plane grunted to life, and moments later I saw him climbing into the sky ahead of us, destined for Maun and his next group of tourists to ferry through the cloudless Botswana sky.

When I looked down again, I realized there was a face hovering beside mine and I jumped, gripping the wheel harder and biting back a curse. It was the one named Joey. His baseball cap was now backward, and a sprig of his black hair sprouted over the Velcro strap.

"I'm Joey," he said. "Nice wheels. Very rugged. I like a girl who can drive manual. And on the wrong side of the car too."

In response, I kicked the Cruiser into third gear and gave him a tight smile.

I desperately wished we didn't have to do this, but my dad's conservation research needed all the funding it could get, and in return for babysitting four American (and one Canadian) students on a conservation exchange program, we'd receive a research grant from the Song Foundation. We might even be able to buy another vehicle, which we sorely needed. It wasn't a good idea to be this far out into the Kalahari bush with only one form of transportation readily available, not with the way the terrain around here destroys cars. We'd had a second car, until Mom's accident.

I turned to Joey and smiled a bit wider. "Have a good flight over?"

"Ugh! Dude, did you see me hurl?" He laughed and elbowed Sam. "You totally shouldn't have let me eat all those sausages in the airport, man."

"You guys know each other?" I asked.

"Nah, met on the plane from JFK. Totally bonded though. We did a *Die Hard* marathon on the flight over, but my man Sam here conked out halfway through number three. Yippee-ki-yay!"

Joey's chatter continued, most of it blasted away by the wind, but I nodded and pretended to listen as I navigated the Cruiser through the treacherous sand. There's not a single stone to be found in the Kalahari, just endless deep sand, white in the north and fading to red in the south, the nemesis of every vehicle that attempts to cross it. I'd lost count of how many times Dad, Theo, and I had had to dig this thing out. It was the reason why I had "muscles like a rugby fullback," according to my dad. He's from New Zealand, and in his view, everything on the planet can be analogized to rugby.

We startled a pair of tall gray kudu, and they froze in front of the car, their huge dark eyes fixed on the great gray-green monster that had interrupted their grazing. At once, everyone behind me was leaning forward, and I stopped to let them get a better look. Kase's zoom lens extended over Joey's shoulder as he snapped a ream of photos. Avani suddenly spoke up, identifying the "two young female kudu, called cows, scientific name *Tragelaphus strepsiceros*" and rattling off a stream of kudu-related information as deftly as any safari guide.

As the car approached them, the kudu leaped into fluid motion, disappearing into the brush in three steps. They weren't called the "gray ghosts of the bush" for nothing; despite their size—they stood as tall as horses—they could vanish in moments into the dry vegetation.

The group let out a collective sigh and then they all fell silent, now on high alert for more animal activity, but we reached the camp without seeing anything more exciting than a few sparrows and fork-tailed drongos.

My dad was waiting. He stood with a warm smile and an armful of bottled water, outfitted in his usual khaki gear, rugged and faded like a worn photograph that's been handled too many times. He looked older than he was, tanned and leathery from spending all his time underneath the suns of a dozen wildernesses, from the Burmese jungles to the Australian outback and now the Kalahari savanna, charting migratory patterns and documenting the myriad ways humans were destroying the natural world. His long graying hair was tied in a ponytail at the back of his head, though a few wispy strands had escaped.

As soon as our guests' feet touched the ground, my dad introduced himself, his strong Kiwi accent booming across the grass. "Welcome to our little corner of the Kalahari, boys and girls! My name's Ty Carmichael, and I'm the head researcher here at Camp Acacia."

You're the only *researcher here,* I thought, shaking my head a little.

"Camp Acacia" wasn't much of a camp. There was my tent, Dad and Theo's shared one, and then there were the two new ones we'd put up that morning to accommodate the guests—one for boys, one for girls. The tents were large enough. You could stand up straight if you were right in the middle of them, and they kept out rain (for the most part), if not bugs and the occasional snake or wildcat. There was a fire pit in the middle of the camp, surrounded by logs for seating, and a portable shower was set up in the trees nearby. It was about as crude a camp as you could ask for, but it had been my home for the past five years, more or less, and resembled every other camp I'd lived in as my family moved from one remote location to the next.

"Where's the lodge?" asked Miranda.

Silence fell. We all stared at her. She took off her designer sunglasses and gave my dad a bewildered look through mascara-laced eyelashes, then turned to her boyfriend.

"Uh . . . Mir . . ." coughed Kase, looking a bit pale.

"You said there would be a lodge," she replied to him, quite loudly. "You *distinctly promised* there would be a lodge! The only reason I agreed to come on this—"

"Miranda, listen, I might not have mentioned . . ." Kase reached for her hand.

She slipped her shades back on and folded her arms, resisting his touch.

"Baby, don't—" Kase kept whispering apologies.

"I'm sorry if there's been a misunderstanding, mates," my dad interjected, looking only slightly rattled as he started handing out the waters, "but you'll soon see that staying in a tent brings you closer to nature than any lodge could. Now, girls will be there in the blue tent, and fellas, you'll be there in the green. There's an outdoor shower behind that tree—don't worry, we'll put up a privacy screen. We're close to an old borehole, luckily, so there's no end to freshwater." He kept casting anxious looks at Miranda, who glared back at him as if being "closer to nature" was synonymous with "closer to hell."

Dad's description of camp life and its scant luxuries continued as I fired up Hank for the return trip to the runway. By the time Theo and I had loaded all the supplies and arrived back at camp, the girls had disappeared into their tent and the guys were beating around in the bushes, Kase busy photographing every leaf and spider within a hundred-foot radius with his massive camera. Dad met us and started unloading boxes before I'd even properly parked.

"God help us," he said in a low voice as I helped him carry a cooler of meat into my tent, where we kept most of the provisions. Above us, the shadows of the trees danced over the beige canvas, like the reflection of rippling water. "What did we agree to, Sarah? Why are we doing this?"

"Just keep smiling and think of all the fancy equipment you can buy with that grant money."

Dad groaned. "Your mother would have known what to do with them."

The blood drained from my face. For a moment, I couldn't move, couldn't breathe. In an instant, frost crackled over my heart. It had been four months, and still the simple mention of her crushed me.

Dad's hand went to my cheek, the warmth in his rough palm shattering the ice inside me.

"Chin up, love," he said softly, and he kissed my forehead. "We must soldier on, eh?"

I couldn't talk about her, not even in passing. Every time her name rose in my throat, I choked on it and fell apart. Dad knew that, and so he didn't press me but held me to his chest for a moment while I pulled myself together. His rough cargo shirt smelled like all the things familiar to me: gasoline, campfire smoke, the lavender-scented laundry soap I used when I washed our clothes under the pump. I used that scent and his quiet strength to steady myself.

"All right, then?" he asked, stroking my hair, and I nodded. "Good girl. Because I don't think I can manage this lot without my Sissy Hati."

Oh, now he was really fishing for a smile, pulling out that old name. When I was three, I'd thought the Bengali term for a baby elephant was Sissy Hati. Close, but not quite the right words. The village we were living in had turned the mispronunciation into a pet name for the little white girl who ran wild through the jungle with their own children, stripped to the waist and without a care in the world.

Another kiss on the top of my head and Dad was gone, striding back to the truck.

It took me a minute to catch my breath, and when I stepped outside again, I saw Sam helping to unload the truck. Kase had disappeared into his tent, and Joey—it took me a moment to locate him—had climbed to the top of an umbrella thorn acacia, which was a remarkable feat considering the two-inch thorns that covered it. I watched him for a moment, incredulous. Sam caught my eye and gave an exaggerated shrug, shaking his head at Joey's antics.

"You should have seen him on the plane," he said. "I think the flight attendants were plotting to sedate him."

I showed Sam where to put the box of muesli he was carrying and held open the tent flap for him to duck inside.

"This your place?" he asked.

"Home sweet home."

He set the box down at the front of the tent with the others; my cot and the sum of my worldly possessions were at the back, behind a wall of boxes and crates. I had a shelf made of crates and boards, and it was cluttered with Bushman artifacts and crafts I'd bought from the children in the village markets. A worn stuffed elephant I'd had since I was three sat on my bed, alongside a stack of Agatha Christie books I was reading through for the third time. The mosquito net draped around the bed was decorated with tiny beads I'd painstakingly sewed on.

I felt a sudden flare of embarrassment at this invasion of my privacy. Everything in my tent suddenly seemed shabby and odd. I moved between him and my "room," feeling far too exposed.

We didn't normally get visitors, and though I used to love seeing new faces around to break up the monotony of my remote life, lately it seemed as if every new face I saw only reminded me of the one face I loved most, the one face I would never see again. *She would have known what to do with them.*

Sam brushed his fingers over a delicate dream catcher hanging from the poles that crossed at the apex of the canvas roof. "Nice place."

"Thanks. We can handle the rest of the boxes," I said.

"Nah, I don't mind." His smile was easy and quick, like a strike of lightning. He picked up a book from my small folding desk and stared at the cover; it was a copy of *Dreams of Afar*, the memoir my mom had written about our family's travels.

His lips twitched as if he was about to say something; then he put the book down and moved on.

As he slid past me and back outside, I pulled the papers out of my pocket and scanned his file again. Sam Quartermain, from Pittsburgh, Pennsylvania. Age: seventeen. Favorite animal: wolf. His statement for being here simply read *Keeping a promise*. There wasn't much else, besides his medical needs (none) and allergies (peanuts).

When I reached the Cruiser, I saw that Dad had stopped unloading the boxes and was occupied with the radio on the dash. The incoming voice, fuzzy with static, could only be from Henrico, the South African warden stationed south of us. He was the only human within communicable distance of our camp, unless we used the heavy, awkward satellite radio that was currently gathering dust in the back of the truck.

Dad's face was thunderous; whatever Henrico was saying had gotten him unusually riled. My dad was normally as easy-going as they came.

"Theo, what is it?" I asked. The Bushman made a shushing noise. He was also listening in. I stepped closer, trying to overhear Henrico's words, but at that moment Dad said into the speaker, "I'll look into it and let you know. Give a call if you hear anything more." He dropped the radio onto the seat of the car and turned to me, his face flushed.

"Sarah. There are reports of poachers in the area. A white lion's been spotted just west of here, and Rico thinks they're after it." The mere mention of poachers sent my dad into a blind rage. I didn't know how many times I'd fallen asleep at night listening to him rant about the declining rhino population, the uselessness of antipoaching NGOs, the apathy of the world toward the cause. Only my mom's death had elicited a stronger emotional response from him.

My heart dropped. "Dad. Dad, no—"

"It might be the same outfit who slaughtered those rhinos up in Chobe last year. They slipped past us once—we can't let them do it again." Dad had spent the better part of that month helping Botswana's antipoaching unit track the poachers, only to lose their trail in the end. The poachers had cut right through the area we'd been researching, and Dad had been angry about it for months, swearing that he wouldn't let it happen again.

"Dad, *please*," I said, leaning into the word, "you promised you wouldn't do this. Not after—We had a deal, remember? We stay together. Always."

Dad paused, the crusader's fire fading from his eyes. "I remember, kiddo. You're right. But if this is the same crew . . ."

I sighed, seeing the anguish in his eyes. I'd been the one who'd drawn that promise from him, terrified as I was that the past would repeat itself and I would lose him too. But letting the poachers slip away again would wreck him.

"Promise me," I said slowly, wilting beneath my own sense of guilt, "you won't get involved. You'll just find them and send their location to the government. If you don't see anything by dark, come home, okay?"

Dad's face relaxed into a grateful smile. "I swear. Cross my heart." He drew an imaginary X on his chest, then took my shoulders and quickly kissed my forehead. "Thanks, sweetie. I'll be back tonight. Everything will be fine. It's just a few hours, and I have the radio. Got yours?"

I tapped the radio clipped to my belt. Dad sighed at my expression of unease. "If you really want me to stay—"

"Just hurry," I said. "And don't do anything stupid or heroic, all right?"

His grin did little to soothe the constricting knot of worry in my gut. He climbed into the Cruiser and cranked it. "You can look after these guys for a few hours, honey. You'll be fine," he said. Sam stood a short distance away, watching solemnly, and I could see that even from up in his tree, Joey had heard what was happening. The tents behind us opened, and the other three emerged curiously to see what the fuss was about.

Dad leaned out far enough to grip my shoulder. He had that look in his eye, the one that could stop a lion in midcharge. "Love you, Sissy Hati."

Theo returned with bottles of water, jackets, and my dad's old shotgun, and he jumped into the passenger seat.

"What? You're taking Theo?" I grabbed hold of the windowsill, standing on the footstep below the door.

"Hey, now!" said Theo. "Can't keep me out of the action!"

"He's the only one who can track them," said Dad. "We'll be back before dark, I promise!"

He stomped the gas, forcing me to jump back from the vehicle. Hank seemed to have caught my dad's anger, chugging like a locomotive. Theo threw me a wide smile and a cheery wave. You'd have thought he was going on a picnic.

"Be careful!" I yelled, but he was already gone, churning up a whirlwind of dust and sand, massive tires crunching over the dry brush as Hank hungrily devoured the land in his path.

Sound travels extraordinarily far in the rolling Kalahari. A minute later, I was standing in the same spot, still hearing the Cruiser's roar. Then I turned on my heel and froze. Five pairs of eyes stared back at me.

For a moment, my brain went blank and I had no idea what to say or do. Dad was supposed to have taken the group out on a drive to spot the nearby animals while I made a light lunch. That was The Plan. We'd been working on it for days—sectioning these two weeks into carefully premeditated activities designed to give our guests maximum exposure to the gritty, unglamorous face of conservation fieldwork, so that they could return home with their cameras loaded with shots of themselves saving the planet.

Instead, there I was in the middle of the Kalahari wilderness with no Dad, no Theo, no Hank, and no Plan—with four Americans (and one Canadian) wholly unsuited to this place and this life. I looked at them, they looked at me, and I think we all came to the same realization:

This had been a bad idea.

TWO

An hour before dark, I sent them all out to gather firewood. Joey and Sam took off like a shot, eager to explore, and Avani wandered off with a bit less zeal. Miranda promptly sat on one of the logs around the fire pit and began buffing her nails, looking not the least bit ashamed, as if the request to scrounge firewood couldn't possibly have been directed at *her*. Kase looked from her to the bush, then settled for something in between, picking up tiny twigs around the tents. I stared at Miranda, who ignored me, then sighed and gave it up.

In minutes, the first three returned with armfuls of wood. In this waterless scrubland it was easy to find dry kindling. They piled the wood by the pit, and I knelt in the sand and began stacking the pieces together, stuffing dry grass beneath them to catch the flame. Kase deposited his handful of twigs beside me, then sat with Miranda, who cuddled against him.

It took one match to light the wood, and it flared up instantly. I'd seen entire stretches of land go up like that—all at once, bone-dry wood almost instantaneously combusting. Bushfires were common out here but still dangerous. Our camp was surrounded by a firebreak, but there had been two or three times when it wasn't enough, and we'd had to pack up and drive to Ghansi until the fires had passed. Then there would be the fallout—animals my parents had been studying had moved on to find better grazing, and we'd have to move after them, roaming the wilds of central Botswana like the nomadic Bushmen who'd lived there for thousands of years. Even they had gone now, moved on to the towns and cities, and though its edges were being gradually eroded by cattle ranches, this land was still a vast wilderness where nature, not man, reigned supreme.

As the fire settled into a steady, flickering blaze, my five visitors sat around it. They'd all fallen quiet, even Joey. I glanced at each one and found varying levels of worry and discomfort in their eyes. I wondered what had brought each of them here, what they were expecting, and how disappointed they were. According to the schedule, this was the time Dad would start a discussion about conservation and wildlife management, since that was technically what they were here to study. That would be followed by a San dance by Theo, who'd insisted that no visit to the Kalahari was complete without a display of Bushman culture. He'd even got out his traditional outfit made from animal skins, ostrich feathers, and caterpillar cocoons filled with bits of twigs to make them rattle when he danced. My primary job for these two weeks was to cook, clean, and take notes on how it all went for the Song Foundation, which planned on expanding its teen wildlife ambassador program if this trip went well.

Dad had asked me to also be in charge of the "teenybop-per fun stuff," meaning games and what he called a "bush party," or a night of music, dancing, and talking. I'm pretty sure this was his roundabout way of trying to get me to hang out with kids my own age. He always worried that I didn't get enough age-appropriate social interaction, despite my insistence that I was just fine, thank-you-very-much. Between him and Theo and the abundant wildlife that found its way around and even into our camp, I had a more than sufficient social life to keep me busy. I barely found time each day to do my schoolwork.

"I've got loads of friends, Dad," I'd said.

"Monkeys," he returned, "do not count."

At which I'd poked my tongue out at him and proceeded to split my orange with one of the vervet monkeys who some-times hung around hoping for scraps.

Reluctantly, I pulled out a wadded paper from my pocket on which I'd scribbled a few halfhearted activities just to appease Dad. Now that I looked at them, they all seemed stu-pid. But anything was better than sitting in awkward silence. I sighed and picked one at random.

"Want to play a game?" I asked, pitching my voice into a high, bubbly tone.

Their heads lifted, and I was reminded of a row of giant eagle owls by the way they blinked at me.

"Okay," said Avani uncertainly.

"Wait right here," I said. I jumped up and ran into the bush, searching for the spot where I'd seen a kudu earlier. After a few minutes of scouting through the underbrush, I found what I was looking for, then stopped by my dad's tent.

I grabbed his canteen of whiskey and poured a small portion into a cup, then returned to the fire.

"I learned this from some kids in a village near Gaborone," I said. I held out my hand and opened it. They all stood and came over, peering at the contents of my palm.

"Is that . . ." Sam began.

"I think it is," said Avani, holding a hand over her mouth.

"Kudu droppings!" I said brightly. "So what you do is, you just drop one into the whiskey—that kills any bacteria and also helps with the taste—then you put it in your mouth like this, and—" I demonstrated, popping one of the brown pellets in my mouth, then shooting it out. It sailed an impressive distance, and I was pleased. A yearly dung-spitting championship (the Afrikaners called it *Bokdrol Spoeg*) was held in South Africa, and I'd seen some of the best contestants do worse.

"So basically," I said, "the object is to see who can shoot them the farthest, and . . ."

My voice died as I took in their expressions. Each one was gaping at me with a mixture of shock and horror. My heart quailed.

"It . . . it's not gross. See? It's just grass, really." I broke apart one of the pellets to demonstrate, but they turned away, making retching noises and cursing. Only Sam was left staring at the droppings in my hand, and then he looked up at me as if he wasn't sure what language I was speaking.

"Okay," I said quietly. "So maybe a different game?"

I tossed the droppings back into the grass, and when I turned around, they were all seated at the fire again. Kase, Miranda, and Joey had their smartphones out and were either playing games or listening to music. Avani took out an electronic reading device and was soon absorbed in a book. Their faces were all illuminated by soft blue light that seemed otherworldly out here in the wilderness. Sam was writing in a journal, stopping in between words to chew on the end of his pen.

I stood and watched them for a minute in silence, then tossed out the rest of the whiskey and went to make dinner.

There was still no sign of Dad and Theo. A seed of anxiety had settled in my gut, and now it was growing, a toxic vine that wrapped around my nerves and my heart. Every time he left, even for a little while, a part of me was certain that he wouldn't return. I even dreamed about it, a regular nightmare that had plagued me since Mom's death. It was like my subconscious had reasoned that by always expecting the worst, I could somehow blunt the pain before it struck.

The others noticed me haul a stack of pans out of the supply tent and looked over curiously.

"Dinner?" asked Joey hopefully, and I nodded.

"Where's your dad?" asked Avani.

"He'll be back by dark," I said, in a tone far more confident than I felt. The light was already beginning to fade, turning the sky murky gray. "In the meantime, I'll get some burgers going."

"Miranda's vegan," said Kase. His girlfriend sniffed and gave me a challenging look.

Well, of course she was. "All right. I've got beans."

"Are they organic?" asked Miranda.

"Oh my *gawd.*" Joey flopped backward off his log, landing with his arms spread in the dust. Miranda gave him a venomous look.

"Yes," I said. I had no idea if they were organic or not, but honestly, it wasn't like there was a grocery store down the street.

It didn't take long to cook up burgers and beans on our portable propane grill. Avani handed me the burger buns and passed the finished ones out on aluminum plates. I wondered if Dad had even stopped to think that he'd driven off with most of our supplies still in the Cruiser. We'd unloaded only the cooler and a few boxes of muesli before he'd taken off. Other than that, our supplies were pretty low.

I stirred up a quick pot of lemonade and served it in tin cups. Having smelled the food, our local vervet monkeys came sauntering into camp. Normally, the monkeys wouldn't have stayed out here through winter; they would have followed the elephants north to the Okavango Delta after the summer rains were gone. But thanks to our borehole, there was usually a large puddle under the pump, which sustained the monkeys and enabled them to beg at our table year-round.

One of them broke into a loping gallop, and before I could cry out a warning, it scurried up to Miranda and snatched a handful of her beans. Miranda let out a bloodcurdling scream, scaring the monkey witless. It sprang away with a loud shriek, then bucked and flung dirt at Miranda while she scrambled away. Everyone was on their feet now, shouting excitedly. Recognizing a familiar face, the monkey scurried to me and leaped onto my shoulder, sitting with his paws on top of my head and his tail curled around my neck. I reached up and stroked his back to calm him.

"He didn't hurt you. See?" I held up a piece of bread, which the monkey snatched and gobbled up. In thanks, he began grooming my hair, making me laugh; his tiny fingers tickled.

"They're really quite friendly! You were lucky; they usually don't let strangers touch them. Do you want to pet him?"

She gaped at me as if I'd been speaking gibberish.

"She could have gotten rabies!" Kase snapped.

"That's ridiculous! The monkeys aren't rabid."

"What is *wrong* with you?" Miranda sobbed. "It attacked me!"

"No, it just wanted—"

"Leave her alone," said Kase. "You're only making it worse."

Ears burning, I turned and walked away, while the rest of them stared from me to Kase and Miranda as if they were spectators at a Ping-Pong tournament. The offended monkey screeched at them in reproach. When I drew near the edge of camp where the rest of his troop was waiting, he took a flying leap off my shoulders and vanished with them in the bush, with only one backward glance. People who say that animals don't have emotions have never seen the expression on the face of an insulted monkey.

I took my time washing the dishes under a small pump rigged over the borehole, which was one of the few working ones left in the area and the only reason we were able to stay out in the field for such long periods of time. There is no permanent surface water in the Kalahari, not this far south, and the borehole was our lifeline.

"You're not going to eat?" asked a voice.

Sam was standing behind me, his hands in his pockets. He'd put on a gray fleece and a raggedy knit cap against the quickly falling temperature.

"I ate while I cooked," I lied. Truth was, I didn't have an appetite. My stomach was too full of worry over my dad.

"Don't you have a radio or something? Some way to reach him?"

I studied Sam thoughtfully, wondering how he had guessed my thoughts. "I tried earlier. He's either out of range or he turned it off. Or the batteries are dead." I picked up the stack of clean dishes and turned off the pump. "There could be a hundred reasons for him to still be out there, and ninety-nine of them are nothing to worry about."

"And the one reason left?"

I started to reply, then found I couldn't.

"Sarah, should we be worried?" His voice was soft enough that the others couldn't hear, and I could tell he was already worried but didn't want to upset the group. He met my gaze, and I was the first to look away.

"The poaching has been getting worse lately," I said. "The fewer rhinos and elephants there are left, the higher the price of ivory and horn gets on the black market. Which means higher competition to bag the animals." I set the dishes down again and looked Sam squarely in the eye. "When I say poachers, I don't mean a few guys with hunting rifles. Selling illegal animal goods is one of the most lucrative crimes in the world. These poachers operate like military strike teams. Tactical gear, assault rifles, helicopters, you name it. They're often working for terrorist outfits that operate in central and North Africa, and even in the Middle East. The ivory and rhino horn they take goes to fund people like the Lord's Resistance Army in Uganda. That's why my dad was so upset. It's not just that they're driving species to extinction—they're sending the money to slavers, warlords, and terrorists."

Sam's eyes went wide as he digested this. "And he's going

to take them on by himself?"

"He'll just get their location, and then he'll send that to the government."

Sam nodded.

But I really didn't know what Dad would do once he found them. In India, he'd chased a pair of poachers for miles through the jungle all by himself. He'd shot up the foliage and raised as much noise as he could to make them think there were a dozen of him. That time, it had worked. But out here? There wasn't enough ground cover for that kind of approach. If they saw him . . . I swallowed the thought, but it stuck in my mind like a splinter under a fingernail. Once I'd have shared his reckless heroism, even begged to come along.

But that was before Mom.

I carried the dishes past Sam and to the small folding table I had set up by the grill. Sam grabbed the towel on the table and began to dry the dishes, handing them to me so I could stack them in a crate.

"He's brave," Sam said. "I'll give him that."

"A brave idiot," I muttered.

Sam's lips twitched. He rolled up his sleeve in order to reach into the bucket of water for the clean plates, revealing a muscular arm dusted with fine blond hairs. His hands were large, his fingers long—ideal rugby hands, Dad would have said. I realized I was staring a bit long and jerked my gaze away. I reached up to tuck a stray wisp of hair behind my ear, and Sam's eyes followed the gesture.

"Nice tattoos," he said. "What do they mean?"

I paused, a plate in my hand, to look at my arm. "This one I got last year. It's for Bangladesh, where I lived from the time I was three until I was eight." The stylized Bengal tiger stalked over my left shoulder, teeth bared and claws extended. I tapped the skin behind my left ear, where a spiral was inked in black. "This is a Maori symbol from New Zealand. My dad's country. It's called *koru* and stands for new beginnings."

"And your mom?"

"She's from North Carolina. This one is her." I turned over my left wrist; on the delicate skin, still pink around the edges from the recent inking, was a simple black bee. "She loved bees." Loved them to death, as it had turned out.

He nodded, looking very serious, then pulled up his sleeve farther to reveal a yellow star inked on the inside of his arm. "That's for Adam, my older brother," he said softly, his eyes going distant, and then suddenly he yanked the sleeve down again and grinned. "So when are we going to see lions?" His tone was light and casual. I suspected he was trying to distract me from Dad, and though it wasn't really working, I appreciated the effort he was making.

"Tomorrow, maybe. There's a pride not far from here." I said, my eyes lingering on his arm. I tore them away and dried the last pan. Somewhere out in the bush, an eagle owl let out its first piercing whistle of the night. The nocturnal Kalahari was beginning to wake, and still there was no sign of Dad. "I'm going to try Dad again. I'm sure everything's fine," I added.

He didn't look convinced, and I felt his stare on my back as I hurried to my tent.

THREE

I unclipped the radio from my belt loop and pulled on a ratty gray sweater that used to be my mom's, covering the tattoos Sam had been so interested in. Then, sitting cross-legged on my narrow little bed, I gripped the radio with both hands and pressed it to my forehead, drawing a deep breath. Visions danced through my mind, memories from the day Theo and I had found Mom with her neck broken and her head dented in from crashing the Land Rover into an umbrella thorn acacia. She'd been missing for a week before that, but when we finally did find her, she'd been dead for only a few hours, her skin swollen with beestings. In my fevered imagination, I saw Dad posed exactly the same way, his skin cold and his eyes open, unseeing, the way hers had been when I'd lifted her head from the steering wheel.

My fingers shaking, I pressed the talk button.

"Dad. Dad, come in. Theo, are you there? Hello? Anyone?"

No answer.

I tried Henrico next, getting no reply, and went back to searching for Dad.

"Dad, please. *Please.* Where are you? Pick up the damn radio!" Heat flared through me, and I hurled the radio at the side of the tent, where it bounced off the taut canvas and fell to the floor. Then I sat with my head cradled in my hands, staring wide-eyed at the lacing on my worn hiking boots. All the panic, all the boundless terror came pouring back, my thoughts running wild with images, possibilities. *They shot him. He found the poachers and they shot him.*

No. I had to keep myself under control. I had to think about the five outside, who were—except for Sam, maybe—oblivious to the panic blossoming in my skull.

He's just running late. He got caught up tracking with Theo, and now they're hurrying back, probably driving too fast. That's it! He got the car stuck, and they're trying to dig Hank out of the sand.

I picked up the copy of my mom's book and stared at the cover. It featured a photograph of her sitting on the back of an elephant somewhere near the border of Nepal, with me—just four years old, my hair wild and my face smudged and smiling—sitting in front of her. Her arm was around me, and she was looking down at me as I waved my hands above my head. Holding my breath, afraid I'd shake loose emotions I'd been keeping at bay for months, I brushed my fingers over her face. Then I cracked open the book and read the words scrawled across the title page in my mom's messy cursive: *My Sarah, the wonder of my life.* I hugged the book to my chest for a moment, then set it aside.

I'd left my guests too long by themselves. Joey might have wandered off to God knows where. I picked up the radio, brushed it off, and clipped it to my pocket before going back outside.

Sure enough, there was one face missing from the circle around the campfire.

"Where's Joey?" I asked, feeling the edge to my concern returning.

They all swiveled to face me and gave a unified shrug.

"He went that way," said Sam, pointing toward the darkening bush.

I cursed under my breath and grabbed a flashlight from my tent before trudging in the direction he'd indicated. To my surprise, they all got up and followed.

"Maybe something ate him," said Kase, and I could have sworn he sounded hopeful.

I found Joey's tracks leading out of camp and followed them. The sun was sitting just on the horizon ahead, and light beamed through the trees and brush, giving the illusion that one of the infamous Kalahari brushfires was sweeping toward us.

The others clustered around me, probably feeling safer with the group. Sam gallantly held aside branches for me to pass through, while Avani plucked leaves from the bushes and pressed them into a notebook. There weren't many around; it was winter, and few plants had retained their leaves.

In the distance, a haunting, almost-human howl rose from the bush. Avani grabbed my arm and Miranda and Kase came together like magnets.

"Easy, everyone. It's just jackals," I said.

"I thought they laughed," said Kase.

"That's *hyenas*, you idiot," said Avani, letting go of my arm.

"Oh, well ex*cuse* us," said Miranda. "It's not our fault we spend more time in the *real world* than in a library."

"Why are you even here?" asked Avani in a heated tone. "You obviously don't care about the environment."

"Whoa, whoa, *whoa. I* don't care about the environment?" Miranda put a hand to her collarbone, looking supremely offended. "Excuse me, Aveeno or whatever your name is, but *you're* the one who heartlessly wolfed down that *burger* tonight. I'm vegan, you know!"

Avani rolled her eyes. "Eating a burger doesn't—"

"Sh!" Sam held up a hand. "Be quiet! Did you hear that?"

While Avani and Miranda exchanged toxic glares, I strained to hear what Sam had: a voice. Joey. He was . . . *crying?*

I broke into a run. The others jogged close on my heels; the camp was out of sight now and I knew they didn't want to be left alone out here, so I slowed just enough for them to keep up. Joey's voice grew louder. He wasn't crying, I realized. He was laughing.

When we got close, I sprinted ahead, weaving through the thick bushes and startling a tiny steenbok out of hiding. The delicate antelope, no bigger than a cat, sprang away with its tail flashing white like a rabbit's.

When I saw Joey, I skidded to a halt, sending up a spray of sand, but not in time to avoid crashing into the porcupine he'd been feeding.

I've run into a lot of things in the wild, but I've never smacked full tilt into a porcupine that stands as tall as my waist. I managed to turn enough that I hit it with my back and not my front, shrieking as the quills stabbed into the skin just below my right shoulder. I twisted aside and landed roughly on my stomach in the sand. The porcupine skittered off, minus a dozen or so quills, which were now protruding from my back. I moaned and pushed myself to my knees as the others arrived.

Miranda shrieked as the porcupine ran past her.

"Sarah!" Sam yelled. "What happened? Are you okay?"

Joey stood with a look of shock as Miranda squealed and Sam and Avani rushed to me. They helped me stand, and I winced as the movement made the quills stab me more. I pulled most of them out with one grab, but Avani had to carefully extract the ones that had punctured deeper, her touch surprisingly gentle.

"My parents are both doctors," she said, as if that meant they'd magically transferred their skills and training to her. "And you, honey, need an antibiotic of some sort. Some of these cuts are deep."

"Neosporin at the camp," I gasped out.

I leaned on her as we made our way back. Darkness was falling quickly, and Joey led the way with my flashlight, taking care to hold aside any branches in my path, trying to make up for getting me impaled, I guessed.

Back at the fire, Avani smoothly applied the Neosporin and a few bandages, decided I was going to in fact survive, and then proceeded to instruct me on how often to change the bandages. I thanked her for her help, and she began to arrange and categorize the leaves she'd been collecting.

"Sorry," said Joey, though he didn't really look it. "I could have told you to stop if you hadn't come charging in like that."

"Dude, you were feeding the thing," said Kase. "You're an idiot."

"Yeah, I know." Joey stretched his arms and grinned. "I was just taking a walk, minding my own business, and he came right up to me! I gave him the rest of my burger bun."

"Theo's been feeding a pair of them," I said. "He's got a soft spot for them. I guess you found one of his tame ones."

"You feeling all right?" asked Sam.

"Sure. I've had worse." Still no sign of Dad. I radioed again, this time with everyone watching, their eyes round and worried, but got no reply. I don't think I even expected one.

"What do you think happened?" Avani asked softly.

I shrugged. "Most likely a tire blew, or the truck got bogged down."

"Is he lost?"

"Not with Theo, no." The Bushman could track a leopard for miles through the bush; he'd never lose his way, not with the Cruiser's tracks to follow.

"What do we do if they don't come back?" asked Kase.

I shrugged again, then sighed and said, "He'll come back, don't worry." I looked around at their faces, saw the weariness there, and added, "You guys must have jet lag. You should sleep. I'll stay up till Dad gets back. When you wake up, everything will be just fine. I promise."

They nodded, and one by one they rose and wandered off until only Sam was left. He watched me with solemn green eyes, his mouth pursed into a frown.

"Sarah," he said. "You're worried."

"You talk like you know me," I said, attempting and failing at lightness.

"Well." He looked down at his hands. "I guess I should tell you—"

He was interrupted by a shriek from the girls' tent. We both jumped up as Avani and Miranda tumbled out of the tent, Avani in her bra and underwear and Miranda in a skimpy nightgown despite the cool night air.

At once, Kase was there, taking Miranda in his arms, and Joey seemed ready to do the same for Avani but she smacked him when he got close, screeching at him not to look at her.

"What was it?" I asked wearily.

But before they could reply, I saw it for myself. A small warthog sped out of the tent, grunting and squealing and looking more frightened than the girls. It trotted around the fire and veered right, vanishing into the shadows.

"Oh. My. *God.*" Miranda was trembling head to foot. "I *hate* Africa! I hate this desert!"

"*Semi*desert, you mean," said Avani, looking shaken but more composed. She slipped back into the tent, shooting a dark look at a grinning, dazed Joey.

"Okay, move on," I said, waving my hands at him. "Get out of here."

He ambled off, still grinning to himself, and I let Kase deal with his traumatized girlfriend. Sam walked me back to the fire, seeming reluctant to go to bed.

"Is it always this exciting around here?"

"Not hardly." Then I considered. "Well. I guess it might be, if you're not used to it."

"And you are?"

I shrugged. "This is my life. I've woken up to chimpanzees staring me in the face, or to elephants ripping up my tent. When I was three months old, we spent a few months in the Congo, and one of the gorillas my parents were studying picked me up in the middle of the night and carried me off."

"No way. Really?"

"It's true." Granted, it got only a few yards before my parents woke up and stopped it. I'd always loved to hear my mom tell that story, about the time the gorillas kidnapped me. I hadn't thought of it once since she'd died. I felt a small, genuine smile on my lips and, surprised to find it there, I pressed my fingers to it.

"So why are you here?" I asked him.

"What do you mean?"

"Why did you come on this trip?"

He crossed his arms and frowned at the fire. "My brother—"

"Adam?"

"Yeah. He always wanted to come out here, you know. It was his big dream. He used to read *National Geographic* to me every night when I was little, tell me stories about Africa, India, Australia. He always promised me we'd travel all over the world."

I noted his use of the past tense, and my heart clenched. Sam's eyes had gone distant, his tone flat—the same way mine did when I talked about my mom.

"What happened to him?" I asked softly.

"He did go overseas, but not to explore." He sat down on one of the logs and leaned over to toss another stick into the flames. As he did, a chain slid out of his collar, and the metal tags on it flashed in the firelight. He caught them and dropped them inside his shirt with practiced ease. It was then that I realized I'd seen the star tattooed on the inside of his arm before: It was the star used in the U.S. Army logo. It all fell into place then. His brother had been a soldier.

"Sam—"

The radio on my hip suddenly crackled to life. Instantly I unclipped it and held it to my ear, my heart skipping a beat. Sam lifted his head, his eyes widening.

"Dad?" I said into the radio. "Dad, I can't hear you. Hello? Is that you?"

Crackling white noise, then *"Sarah."*

"Yes! Dad, I'm here!" Dizzy with relief, I clenched the radio as if I could squeeze his voice out of it.

"Sarah . . ." More fizzling and crackling.

"Dad? Hello?"

". . . fifteen miles southwest of camp . . . are you there?"

"I'm here! Dad?"

It was nearly impossible to make out his words between blasts of static. ". . . ambushed us . . . trying to lose them . . . if I don't make it back—"

The relief I'd felt began to turn icy. *"Dad.* What's going on? Hello!?"

". . . can't reach anyone, bad reception . . . I'm sorry, sweetie. I am so sorry. I—"

I'd turned up the volume all the way in order to hear him better, so the sudden round of pops that cut him off hit my ear with almost physical force.

"Dad?" I turned up the volume, which only resulted in louder fizzling bangs. *Is that . . . gunshots? No, it couldn't be—it's just static.* "Dad!"

Then the noise cut off and the channel went dead.

FOUR

immediately tried every channel on the radio, in case he'd somehow switched. I got nothing. I tried Henrico. Nothing. As a game warden, he often went on weeklong trips to survey the land. Chances were he was out of range.

I met Sam's eyes speechlessly, beseeching him to make sense of what we'd heard. He returned my look grimly.

"What do you think happened?" he asked.

I didn't know what to think. I *couldn't* think. My mind was transfixed, as if the static had invaded my brain and pushed out all other thought.

It took Sam's repeated question to pull me out of my stupor.

"He must have caught up to the poachers," I said. "Or they caught up to *him*. He said he was trying to lose them. They must have seen him and Theo." I ran my hand agitatedly over my hair, tangling my fingers in the ends. "We need to call someone. The military, the emergency center, *someone*.

But the satellite radio is in the Cruiser with Dad. The nearest road is thirty miles away, but since most of the villages around here are abandoned, vehicles are rare as rhinos in these parts. You could stand on that road for days and not see a single one. *Sam*. What if . . ." I squeezed my eyes shut and inhaled sharply. "What if those were gunshots? What if he — What will I do?"

"Whoa. Don't jump to the worst conclusions. Not yet." He was rattled too. I could tell by the way he knit his fingers together, his knuckles white with tension. I gazed at him in a silent plea for answers. "Let's think this through, okay? What do we *know*?"

I nodded shakily. My nerves crackled like electric wires, making my entire body buzz with anxiety, and I clung to his question as if it were the only thing keeping me grounded. "He's fifteen or so miles southwest of here. The poachers know he's onto them. He's being chased and . . . and it sounded like he was being shot at." Those last words stuck in my throat. *Don't panic*, I told myself. That was the first rule for dealing with trouble in the wild: *Don't panic*. I almost laughed aloud. It made as much sense as telling an antelope *don't run* when faced with a hungry cheetah.

Sam nodded, encouraging this line of reasoning. "So what are we going to do?"

I shut my eyes, striking off the first dozen ideas that spasmed through my thoughts, ranging from *Find the bastards and shoot their faces* to *Run screaming into the bush*. "We either stay here and wait," I said, "or . . . *don't*."

Sam nodded thoughtfully. How *did* he stay so composed?

"Can you track him?"

My heart was beginning to pound at the thought. "Yes. Theo's been teaching me bushcraft for years."

Sam's green eyes burned into mine. "I trust you, Sarah."

Well, that made one of us. I tried not to think about the fact that the Kalahari is larger than the state of Texas, that if I got us lost, we could walk for weeks out here without finding another person. Sure, I knew the *general* direction of civilization, but even our most thorough emergency evacuation plans always included some form of transportation, either by land or air, and I never expected to be out here on my own, with five people depending on me.

I forced a lid on the hysteria before it could boil over. This wasn't like me. I was underestimating myself, wasn't I? I'd spent my entire life in the woods, in the jungle, in the desert. This was my element.

"I can't sit here and wait," I confessed. "I just can't. He and Theo could be out there injured"—*or worse*—"with no one to help them. It's too dark to track now, but if I leave first thing in the morning, I could go see what happened and make it back here tomorrow night or the next morning. Would you look after the others while I'm gone?"

"I'd rather go with you. I'm not the sit-and-wait kind either."

"Okay," I said. "But only you and me. As a group, we'd be too slow."

Sam nodded. "We'd better tell them."

I called to the others, and they poked their heads out of their tents with irritation on their faces—most of them had been nearly asleep, I guessed. They threw on some clothes and came to the fire, shivering in the cold and demanding an explanation. When I told them what had happened, the fatigue in their eyes turned to horror.

"*What?*" Miranda screeched. "You mean we're *alone out here?*" Immediately she whipped out a smartphone. "I'm calling nine one one. There's *got* to be some kind of coverage out here." She stood up and began pacing around the camp, holding up her phone in what I already knew was a completely futile search for a signal.

"I want a straight answer," said Kase. "Are we in danger?"

I paused, weighing my words. "There's always danger in the wild. So . . . yes. But if we stay calm and—"

"Why am I even talking to you?" he said. "You're not an authority here. Let *me* talk to your dad."

"I can't even reach him!" I said. "Look, I don't want to be in this position any more than you, and believe me, I wish my dad were here to call the shots. But right now, I'm all you've got."

"How do you know your dad will be there when you go looking for him?" asked Avani. "What if he was taken hostage?"

"I don't know," I confessed. Secretly, I hoped he *was* a hostage—it was better than the alternative. "All I know is that I need to find out what happened. He and Theo could be hurt."

"You said yourself that you could barely hear what he was saying. Maybe you're wrong. Maybe everything is fine." Avani said it as if she were trying to convince herself more than me.

I didn't tell her that that was exactly what I was counting on, that somehow the situation wasn't as dire as it seemed and that any moment, Dad would radio again to explain it was all a mistake.

"I was there when her dad called," said Sam. "She's right. He's in trouble."

"Look," I said, "I can go and be back the day after tomorrow at the latest. I'll go after my dad and find out what happened."

"Isn't that dangerous?" asked Avani.

"I know the bush," I replied, hoping I sounded more confident than I felt. "Anyway, I can't sit here waiting without knowing what happened. You don't understand. I just—I can't." Because the last time this had happened, the last time someone went missing out there, I did wait. I told myself everything was fine, that she'd be back, that it was all just a misunderstanding. Only she didn't come back, and if I hadn't waited, if only I had *gone looking*, maybe she'd still be alive.

I wouldn't make the same mistake twice. Dad would understand. Dad would *have* to understand. He had been the one to assure me Mom would be fine, that she could handle herself out there, when I began to get nervous about her prolonged absence. I knew that deep down, I still blamed Dad for her death. If he had let us go looking for her earlier . . . Well. He'd been wrong then, and maybe he'd been wrong to go after these poachers. Once I'd have believed unwaveringly in my dad's judgment. But after Mom, he seemed to shrink in my eyes. Maybe I didn't trust him like I used to, but I still loved him. He was all I had, and I wouldn't sit idle while he was in trouble.

"I have to look for him," I said. "Sam's coming with me. Avani, you can be in charge till I get back."

"Uh-uh," said Avani. "You are *not* leaving me in charge of the prom queen or *that* one." She tossed a sour look at both Miranda and Joey. "I'm coming with you."

"Me too," said Joey.

"We should all go," said Avani. "Separating now will just be worse. We're safer together."

"Babes, no!" said Miranda, pressing herself against Kase. "Tell her I want to go home!"

"This is ridiculous!" said Kase, his face reddening. "We can't just hike off into God knows where! *You* are responsible for our safety, so *you* need to arrange transportation for us to go home! Not all of us came here on scholarship"—at this he threw a derisive look at Sam—"and my parents paid a hell of a lot of money for this trip. Miranda and I will not be treated like hired grunts, hauling junk all over Africa!" He kicked at a sleeping bag.

I shut my eyes and tried very hard to keep my breathing steady.

"There's nothing she can do," said Sam. "We're all in this boat together."

"No one asked *you*," Kase snapped.

"It's not like there's a bus stop nearby!" Sam replied.

Kase turned to me and I winced under the heat of his glare. "My parents can sue you for all you own. Not," he sneered, "that that's much." He gave our camp a contemptuous look that set my blood boiling.

"I'm trying my best," I said hotly. "I don't know what else to do. Look, just give it one night. Like Avani said, it could be a mistake. Things might be back to normal in the morning."

Kase exhaled loudly and waved a hand as if dismissing me. "Whatever. But don't think you'll get out of this without all kinds of legal hell coming down on you. And you're *not* leaving us out here on our own. Wherever you go, we go. I'll be watching you. This is all your fault—yours and your irresponsible dad's."

"I've about had it with you," Sam growled.

"Yeah, man?" Kase stepped forward aggressively. "What're you going to do about it?"

Sam's eyebrows shot up. "Oh, you want to play *that* game?"

"Stop!" I said. "Just—just let me *think*!" I pressed my hands to my eyes and ground my teeth together.

They'd slow me down. I'd have to spend twice as much time foraging for things to eat, and I'd waste valuable tracking time watching for snakes and other dangerous creatures that might bite them or sting them when my back was turned. We could very well run into the poachers. On the other hand, leaving them by themselves was no guarantee of safety either. I looked at Sam.

"We all go together, then. We'll track my dad and Theo, see what happened, and then decide what to do from there."

He shrugged. "It's a free country."

"This is the Kalahari. It's *deadly* country."

Miranda whimpered.

"This *is* what we came out here to do," Sam pointed out. "'Wildlife ambassadors' is the name they put on the website for this thing. Up close and personal with nature, that's what they promised us."

"Fine!" I looked them each in the eye to be sure I had their full attention. "But if we see even a sign of the poachers, we have to hide. Got it?"

They nodded, except for Kase and Miranda, who seemed intent on ignoring me now.

"Good, then. We'll leave at dawn. Pack light. Water is the

JESSICA KHOURY

most essential thing—once we leave, what you carry is what you get, and that's it. There are no boreholes, no streams, not so much as a puddle."

"I can't," said Miranda faintly.

"Babe?" Kase squeezed her arm.

She shook her head and sagged against him. "I can't do this. I can't. I want to go home!"

"We will, babe, just hang in there," Kase murmured. "These people are under *legal* obligation to keep us safe." He gave me a pointed look, and I wondered at the fine print on the safety waivers they would have signed before coming here. *Could* he sue us for everything?

"Why did you bring me here? We're all doing to *die!*" Miranda's voice pitched upward hysterically, and she slammed her fist into Kase's chest. The rest of us watched, silent and embarrassed, as Kase tried to calm her. Avani was the first to sneak away, and the rest of us followed. I figured it was best to let Kase deal with his panicking girlfriend alone.

My stomach was in knots as I went to my tent. I felt jittery, as if hyped on caffeine. My hand went to the radio on my belt, but I didn't dare try reaching Dad. If he was hiding from the poachers, then my voice could give his location away. I'd wait a few hours and maybe try then.

I didn't sleep. I sat cross-legged on my bed all through the night, cowering as a thousand different scenarios ran through my thoughts like a herd of stampeding wildebeests. The words I didn't dare say aloud pounded against my skull: *Dad could be dead. Theo could be dead. What if I've already lost them? What if it's already too late?* I tried reaching them every hour but got only silence in reply. Never had I felt so alone.

44

When the first pale hint of dawn gleamed on the horizon, I was already moving, preparing for the hike into the bush. The first thing I grabbed when I went to pack was my mom's pump-action shotgun. She'd never used it and had refused to carry it with her. Sometimes I wondered if things would have turned out differently if she'd taken the gun with her on that final day. I hated the thing, but I did know how to use it, and out there in the bush, on foot, there was just no telling what we'd find—or what would find us. And if we did run into the poachers, I didn't want to be totally defenseless.

I tied my hair back into a low ponytail and checked my gear. I had on a beige cargo shirt beneath a dark green jacket, and I grabbed a kaffiyeh to tie around my neck. It would come in handy if the wind picked up and gusted the sand around. I had on a pair of loafers and changed these for my sturdy brown hiking boots, which I laced over my cargo pants. Then I tossed a few muesli bars, some bottled water, and a flashlight into my backpack. After a moment, I added the multipurpose knife my parents had given me on my thirteenth birthday, and a few other survival essentials: parachute cord, a map of central Botswana, a box of matches plus a flint and steel, spare batteries, some glow sticks, and a notebook (this last out of habit; I never went anywhere without some means to record what I saw). As I dug through the food crates in the front of my tent, I realized with a plummeting heart that our supplies were even lower than I'd thought. We had enough muesli bars and kudu jerky to last us a day or two out in the bush, but the rest of what we'd unpacked of the new shipment had to be kept cool in the icebox. It did us little good unless we stayed at the camp. This trek would have to be fast—or we'd be stuck in the middle of nowhere with nothing to eat or drink. We wouldn't last long.

I roused the others and urged them to pack. Their eyes widened at the sight of the shotgun, but they said nothing. Miranda whined a little, but she seemed more stable. She must have reconciled with Kase, because she was pressed against his chest with her hands gripping his arm so tightly I wondered if his fingers would turn purple.

After checking to be sure they all had water and food and sleeping bags, I tightened the straps on my backpack and looked them each in the eye, trying to measure their resolve. What we were about to do was no easy thing, and these five were, as Dad would have said, "babes in the wood." Well, maybe we'd locate Dad quickly. Maybe we'd never have to find their limits, because it could all be over soon. At least I hoped so, because I didn't think we'd last long as a group. We were already falling apart, and we hadn't even started.

FIVE

For a while we walked only to the sound of grass crunching beneath our feet, but as the sun rose higher, the birdsong swelled around us. Shrikes and sparrows twittered in the low brush, while hunting goshawks, their pale bellies flashing in the sunlight, cut the sky above. We came across the tracks of aardvarks, honey badgers, antelope, and a lone leopard, but whatever creatures lay ahead of us, they must have heard us coming and disappeared. I was used to walking silently in order to get close to the wildlife, but the five behind me walked with all the stealth of an elephant herd. Not that I minded. The fewer critters we met, the fewer bites and scratches and stings we'd have to deal with.

The Cruiser tracks were not too difficult to follow. They led west, curving now and then to avoid the larger trees but plowing straight over the smaller bushes, which the vehicle's bumper would have crushed as it hauled itself forward. The resilient plants simply sprang up again, but the broken twigs around them were a sure sign that Dad had gone this way.

About an hour into our hike, Sam went still and held up a hand. The others froze. My heart leaped into my throat and I scanned the way ahead, dreading that I'd see poachers armed to the teeth bearing down on us.

But Sam only pointed to a stand of camel thorn acacias that had retained their dry brown leaves through winter. A pair of giraffes were grazing there, their long, graceful tongues stripping the leaves away regardless of the thorns.

Kase began snapping pictures. Sam turned to me with a wide, goofy grin.

"Giraffes!" he said in a loud whisper.

"Ya think?" Avani muttered behind us, but he ignored her.

We stood for several minutes watching the pair. Everyone—even Miranda—stared with wide eyes, mouths open, expressions alight. Sam most of all. You'd have thought he was seeing angels fly out of the clouds.

"Come on," I growled, and the others stared at me. My surliness was completely undeserved and probably rude, but we weren't here to sightsee, not anymore.

"I've never seen a giraffe before," said Sam distractedly.

"Not even at a zoo?" asked Avani, looking askance at him.

"Never been to one." He looked caught in the midst of a dream.

As we neared the giraffes, they picked up our scent and reeled back in alarm, taking off at a run. Their long legs and loping gate made it appear that they ran in slow motion, and despite their height, they disappeared quickly into the bush. It was as if they'd never been there at all.

"Wait!" said Sam, throwing out an arm to stop me. "There's one more."

A bit belatedly, a small calf trotted out of the trees and stopped dead in front of us. Its long legs—it was already taller than any of us—splayed wide and the calf snorted, its thick fringe of eyelashes quivering over huge brown eyes as it studied the six creatures who had interrupted its family grazing.

Sam let out a breath, and his face lit up with that loopy grin again. Even Miranda was smiling, her hands pressed to her lips. Joey, like an idiot, began clucking and calling to the calf, which only startled it into motion, and it raced off to join its parents.

"Moron," said Avani in a low voice.

"Oh, come *on*. What's the matter, Canada, did they confiscate your sense of humor at the airport?"

"You're *so* not funny."

The giraffe incident seemed to have shaken the silence out of them, and they began chattering like a troop of baboons. What had begun as a risky trek into the wilderness was feeling more like a glorified field trip, with me as the overly stern teacher. I think the others had lost the sense of danger, perhaps unable to believe they were really threatened by anything worse than warthogs and porcupines. Except for Sam, they hadn't heard the tone in Dad's voice that had made my blood turn cold; they couldn't understand that my fear stemmed not only from the gunshots I thought I'd heard, but also from my memory of Mom's death. It had been one thing to imagine Dad in danger; to *know* he was in danger was a whole new level of dread.

The day was comfortably warm, and I could have walked

for hours fueled only by my concern for Dad and Theo, but the others began to lag. First Avani, then Kase, then everyone was stopping to catch their breath. Reluctantly, I called a halt.

"Where are we?" asked Sam.

We were in a spot that looked like nearly any other in the Kalahari; the landscape out here could be dangerously monotonous, devoid of landmarks by which you could orient yourself. I had a map in my backpack, and I pulled it out and spread it on the ground.

"We're west of the camp," I replied, circling an area on the map. "And a little bit south."

"How can you tell?"

"The sun. And the nests." I pointed to a nearby Terminalia tree, at the pod-like nests of woven grass that hung from the branches. They looked like Christmas tree ornaments, some of them messy globs woven by the younger birds, others tightly knit orbs made by the expert weavers—the latter were more likely to attract females. "They indicate the compass points, and I've been keeping an eye on them while we've walked."

"What are they?" asked Sam, holding up a hand against the sun as he stared at the nests.

"White-browed sparrow weaver nests," said Avani, before I could say a word.

I frowned. "No, actually. The sparrow weavers make those bushy nests, pushed back into the branches. Like those over there." I pointed to a nearby wattle tree, its branches thick with bundles of grass. "The hanging nests are made by southern masked weavers."

"Um . . . pretty sure you're wrong," said Avani.

"Pretty sure I'm not," I muttered. As she consulted her

guidebook, I continued, "They build them in the lee side of the tree, safe from the wind. The wind here blows from the east, so the nests are on the west side of the tree."

They considered this thoughtfully for a moment.

Then Joey said, "They look like balls."

"You can't be serious," Miranda sighed, burying her face in her hand.

"Dude, don't they look like balls?" Joey looked to Sam for support, but Sam just looked away, shrugging.

"I'm just saying," said Joey, "I mean, we were all thinking it, right? Right, guys?"

We walked on, and he gave up badgering us for a response. I glanced at Avani and noticed she'd shut her guidebook and was pointedly avoiding my gaze, her lips pinched together.

I watched carefully every time someone took a drink of water or ate a muesli bar. I hated to be a tyrant, but we couldn't afford to have anyone run out. I'd made each of them take as many bottles of water as they could carry, and we'd split the muesli bars between us. We each had five—enough for one, maybe two days. But it was the water that worried me most. The Kalahari climate was so dry you could almost feel the air sucking the moisture from your body, and our bodies each needed at least a gallon of water a day to stay hydrated out here.

The sun rose; the sun fell. As it began to sink toward the horizon ahead of us, the trees turned into black silhouettes. I took out the radio from time to time to call Dad, but I heard nothing in reply. The silence did little to soothe my nerves. I didn't say it to the others, but I knew we should have found *something* by now. Dad had said he was fifteen miles from the camp. We were approaching that fifteenth mile now if we hadn't passed it already, but there was no sign of Dad, Theo, or the poachers besides the monotonous tire tracks. Dismayed, I began to rule out the possibility that he was on his way back to the camp, safe and sound. If he were, we'd have met up with him by now. *He could have gone back by another route,* I told myself. But my hope was soon swallowed by my mounting dread. My thoughts spiraled like water down a drain, circling and circling only to inevitably end at the same conclusions: He and Theo were either injured and unable to radio, captured . . . or dead.

As evening grew closer, I knew we would have to stop soon to set up camp, but I pressed on, telling myself, *Just a few more steps, just to that tree, just a little farther. . . .* Then, right when I was about to call it a night, Dad's tracks changed.

At first, my heart leaped with relief: The tracks had doubled, almost as if Dad had turned back and driven toward camp. But when I bent down to look closer, I saw that both sets of tracks led in the same direction—and the second, fresher set did not belong to the Land Cruiser. I traced it back until I found where it branched away, leading north. This must have been where Dad found the poachers.

Or . . . no. This is where the poachers found Dad.

My skin turned to gooseflesh as a chill ran through me. *They were following him.* I hadn't been certain of it from his garbled message the night before, but seeing it written so plainly in the sand was like dreaming about a monster only to have it later appear in the flesh. It gave physical form to my worst fears. I realized I'd still been holding out hope that Dad's message had been a mistake, and that even now he'd be back at the camp wondering where we were. Now I knew it was a lie I'd been clinging to, and that he'd definitely run into trouble.

"Sarah?"

I turned to see Sam making his way toward me.

"What's wrong?" he asked, his brow furrowing.

I pointed to the tracks.

"See these prints?" I circled a small, almost imperceptible line of impressions with my finger. "These are korhaan and sparrow tracks from this morning, when the birds come down from the trees to look for food. Under those are these brown hyena prints, crossing over and under the tire tracks. The hyenas are nocturnal, so that dates the vehicle at late last night, about the time Dad called."

Sam looked up at me. "You can tell all that?"

"Bushmen are the best trackers in the world," I said. "I learned from them." I bent low to the sand, squinting at the faint impressions. "There aren't any tracks between my dad's truck and the one following him, which means they were close on his tail, but not so close that he'd see them yet. They were following slowly, maybe waiting to see where he was going before . . ." I stopped, shook my head.

"Before they caught up to him?" Sam asked gently.

"And when they did . . . Sam, what if those *were* gunshots we heard?"

"Do you really think they'd try to kill them?"

"To protect themselves, yes." Though that was an extreme measure, even for poachers. "Or maybe they only wanted to scare Dad off. The shots could have been to threaten him, nothing more, like an elephant flapping its ears to scare away a predator. It's just for show."

"Makes sense. We'll find him. Look how far we've come already."

"Not far enough."

Sam said nothing, just studied my face with his green eyes. His hair—the same color as the golden Kalahari grass—was tangled and windblown, shaggy like the mane of a young lion coming into his prime.

The others grumbled at having to resume our hike so soon after we'd stopped, but I pressed on relentlessly, doubling our pace. With the spoor of two vehicles to guide me, it was easier to track, so I focused on speed. With each step, my dread grew until I felt like I was dragging it behind me. I replayed his leaving in my head as though somewhere in the memory I could find a sign that everything would be all right.

I noticed another set of prints had picked up the trucks' tracks and followed them as relentlessly as I was. These prints confused me: They belonged to an adult male lion. He was alone, and his prints were deep and elongated, accompanied by a spray of sand behind each one, which told me he had been running, and had been following the vehicle tracks yesterday. Strange. Male lions are notoriously lazy, and if they aren't hunting or mating, they're almost always sleeping in the shade. This one wasn't pursuing prey—there were no other animal tracks in front of his. Why was he following the vehicles' tracks, and with such haste? It didn't make sense.

I remembered what Dad had said when he'd taken off after the poachers—they were hunting a white lion. Was this the lion? The tracks would make sense if the poachers had been pursuing the animal, but I was certain that the lion had come *after* the trucks, as if *he* were pursuing *them*. It should have been the other way around: Dad following poachers following lion. Instead, it was lion following poachers following Dad. No matter how I looked at it, the order of prints just didn't seem to add up to any reasonable explanation.

Reluctantly, I stopped just as the sun began to drop in the sky. It hung above us as if tempting us onward, a prize that would always be out of reach.

But as the others sat down and groaned in relief, I called for them to get up again. My eyes had fixed on the ground, and my pulse sped from what I saw written in the sand.

"You're a machine," complained Joey. "How are you not dead from exhaustion?"

"*Look*," I said, pointing at the ground.

They all stared at me blankly. Frustrated, I knelt and pressed my hand to the tracks.

"My dad finally realized they were following him. Right here, do you see it? He accelerated and so did they." I stood up and jogged ahead, eyes scanning the sand. "He began swerving, probably trying to go head-on with them, but they stuck close to his tail."

I wove in and out of the brush, my eyes reading the prints as easily as if they'd been words on paper. "Look at this! He tried reversing into them, but they swerved around and—" I froze, my eyes fastened on a *Terminalia* tree. Woodenly, I put out a hand and touched the trunk, rubbing my thumb over a jagged scar in the bark.

"This is where they shot at him," I whispered. The bullet hole was too neat to have been from my dad's gun. This looked like the mark of something deadlier, something intended to kill people, not animals—maybe an assault rifle or a pistol. I remembered the popping sounds that had come over the radio to drown out Dad's voice—gunfire after all, and not static as I'd hoped. This must have been where Dad called me.

"But they missed," said Sam. "Right?"

"I don't see any blood," I said, my voice shaking.

"Let's keep going," he said.

The lion's tracks were everywhere too. It seemed confused by the tangle of car tracks and had padded this way and that.

"So weird," I muttered. "It's tracking them like a bloodhound."

I grabbed my flashlight, though I wouldn't need it for another hour or two, and set off after the tracks, telling the others to wait and keep an eye out. The possibility of us finding the poachers instead of finding Dad was becoming a growing problem. If they'd caught up to Dad—I didn't want to consider it, but I knew for our own sakes I had to—where would they go next? Would they suspect us to be out here, or would they think Dad and Theo were alone? If they suspected Dad had radioed someone, would they go so far as to search for us? The thought made me feel sick. But I couldn't imagine them wasting more time out here, so far from the rhino and elephant herds they no doubt were hunting. They could be a hundred miles away by now, across any of four different national borders, if they weren't still hunting Dad and Theo. No, the greatest danger to us now was the bush itself, and that at least was a danger I felt somewhat qualified to handle.

Sam caught up to me, panting, and wordlessly stayed by my side as I zigzagged through the bush, my eyes pinned to the ground.

"I figured two pairs of eyes were better than one," he said genially.

He was right. He saw it before I did and grabbed my arm, stopping me in my mad rush, and said my name so softly I almost didn't hear it at all.

"There," he said, nodding ahead.

He was right. There was the Land Cruiser, sitting silently in the grass, silhouetted against the scarlet sky.

My heart nearly exploded with conflicting relief and dread. I broke into a sprint, kicking up clouds of sand.

"Dad!" I yelled, my voice hoarse. "Theo!"

When I reached the Cruiser I vaulted inside, noting the bullet holes ripped into the metal panels. The canvas roof was bundled in the back, and the cab was empty. The keys were still in the ignition; the engine had been left on but must have stalled at some point. The front bumper was pressed against a tree, and mounds of sand behind the wheels told me it had run nose first into the trunk and was left with its wheels churning for some time afterward.

My head roared as time seemed to collapse on itself, back to the moment I'd found my mother in the Jeep. It was a familiar scenario: the car smashed into a tree, the keys in the ignition. The only difference was that she'd been in the car. I scouted around the Cruiser and climbed onto the spare tire on the back to look inside. It was empty. No Dad. No Theo.

I was vaguely aware of Sam opening the door and catching me as I fell out of the cab. He lowered me to the ground and held my trembling shoulders as I mumbled, "No, no, no," over and over again.

He said my name softly, insistently. "Look at me, Sarah.

Sarah, please. I'm here, I've got you, just calm down. *Sarah.*"

Gradually, my eyes, feeling feverish and raw, focused on his.

"He's not here," I said.

"I know. That's a good thing, Sarah."

"It is?" My mind felt slow and dull. Thinking was like wading knee-deep through sand.

"Yes. Listen, if they'd shot him, they'd have left him here, right? There'd be blood, there'd be something to tell us he was hurt. But he isn't here, which means either they took him alive or he escaped into the bush. Don't you think it's more likely he and Theo ran off? Lost them on foot? When he called you, he said he was trying to lose them. That would have been easier on foot."

I thought about it; it seemed to take ages to slog through the facts as Sam laid them out. "Maybe. Maybe they tried, and the poachers caught up with them and—"

"Stop it. You're a researcher, right? You work with facts, not conjecture."

I stared at him dumbly.

Sam took my face between his hands. "Think about the facts, and only the facts. What you can see, what you can *know.* Your dad and Theo *were* here, but now they're not."

"So I have to find them," I whispered.

"Right. And I'll help you."

I pulled away from him. "Why are you doing this? Why are you so . . . calm? So nice to me? Why aren't you back there with the others?"

He opened his mouth to answer, then shut it, looking conflicted. "Just let me help you, okay?"

I nodded reluctantly, unsure whether to be suspicious or glad for his steadying support.

"Can their tracks tell you anything?" Sam asked.

Pulling myself together, I focused on the ground. I could almost see the scene happening around me, like a ghostly reenactment. "Dad hit the tree and then . . . Here, see these deep tracks, and the way the sand was pushed away? The poachers skidded to a stop, probably to avoid hitting the Cruiser. And there! Footprints!" My heart began to race as I processed the clues in the sand, sorting the impressions into a pattern I could read. "Dad jumped out here and took off to the west." I circled to the passenger side. "And Theo went east. They split up, trying to lose the poachers on foot. It's easier to disappear that way than to try to outrun them in the truck."

Which left me in a dilemma. Follow Dad or follow Theo? They had a twenty-four-hour head start on us, and as more time passed, their trails would only get fainter.

If I were a bloodhound, this was where I would have whined and run in circles, chasing my own tail. Racked with indecision, I spread out and followed each trail a bit farther before doubling back, just in case Dad and Theo had met up somewhere nearby and taken off together. They hadn't. And I noticed that the poachers had pursued Dad, not Theo. A closer look at the surrounding foliage revealed why: The brush through which Theo had passed was dotted with blood.

SIX

Theo," I said, my voice coarse as gravel. "It's Theo's blood."
I broke into a run, as fast as I could go while still keeping
an eye on his footprints. He had staggered along, dragging
one foot. Broken branches on the dry bushes showed where
he had grabbed them for support, leaving behind bloody
fingerprints. Left by any other person, these signs would be
normal. But Theo, my graceful, delicate Theo, could move
through the bush in a way that left no hint of his passing. He
could be harder to track than a leopard. Seeing these otherwise obvious signs told me more about the gravity of his condition than I could bear. My eyes began filling with tears as I
feared the worst. By the amount of blood he'd left behind, he
could already be dead.

I found him sitting under a shepherd's tree, slumped over,
so still that I nearly missed him altogether in the deepening
darkness. My stomach turned inside out; I couldn't breathe.
I fell to my knees beside him and gently took his face in my

hands, barely able to see him through my tears.

"Theo?" His eyes were shut, but he was breathing shallowly. "He's alive," I told Sam. I took out my flashlight and clicked it on, searching for the wound, gasping when I found it. He had been shot just above his left hip, and again in his right rib cage. How he was still hanging on, I had no idea.

"Help me," I said to Sam. "We have to carry him back to the truck. There's a medical kit inside."

"Are you sure we should move him?" Sam looked deeply shaken, standing over us with his hands clenched into fists and his eyes wide.

"We don't have a choice."

Sam carefully lifted Theo into his arms. The Bushman groaned but didn't open his eyes. I hovered anxiously at Sam's elbow.

"Hurry," I said. "Don't jostle him too much."

"Trying," Sam grunted. "He's heavier than he looks."

I hurried back to the Cruiser, leading the way with the flashlight. Once there, I pulled down the canvas roofing and laid it on the ground. Sam set Theo down gingerly as I rummaged for the medical kit. To my dismay, I found the boxes of supplies had been torn apart by wild animals. The food had all been damaged or taken, likely by jackals and hyenas. I found the med kit and went back to Theo, but the contents of the little box were woefully inadequate to treat Theo's wounds. I stared at the small bandages and bottles, wondering where to start and if it would make any difference at all.

"I can get Avani," said Sam. "She might know what to do."

I nodded numbly. "Bring them all here. We should stay together."

After he left, I sat beside Theo and buried my face in my hands.

"Tu!um-sa."

My head shot up. "Theo!"

His eyes were open and he managed a weak smile. "Are you well?"

"Am *I* well? Theo, you've been shot!"

"Ah, just so." He shut his eyes briefly, and I could see a tremor of pain beneath his gentle smile.

"Does it hurt a lot?" I asked quietly. "Theo, what happened?"

He sighed, his smile flickering out. "We split up . . . tried to lose them on foot . . . Too late for me now. Your father did not know they had got me, or he would never have . . ."

"Theo! Stay with me!" He was slipping back into unconsciousness. I dribbled some of my water into his mouth, which roused him again.

"Stop it, girl!" he said. "Don't waste your water on me!"

"You're going to be fine," I said. "We'll get you out of here and to a doctor."

"Make me a promise, Tu!um-sa."

"Theo—"

"Promise you will bury me here in the Kalahari, yes? In the towns, the sky is small. How can I see God through such a small sky?"

"Stop talking like that. I won't let anything happen to you."

"Out of earth we come, into earth we go," he murmured dreamily. "You cannot stop the sun from setting. Now hold my hand, child. I must tell you . . ."

I took his hand in both of mine and willed my strength

into him, blinking hard to keep my tears from falling. He looked at me and smiled, and for a moment my heart lifted as I saw his eyes fill with his usual mischief and joy. The skin of his face, golden brown and lined with years of laughter, crinkled happily. I smiled back through my tears, squeezing his hand as if I could anchor his soul to the world by sheer willpower.

"I saw . . ." His smile drooped. "I must tell you. Something . . . is out there."

"Theo, don't talk," I whispered. A tear slipped loose and trickled down the side of my nose. "Save your strength."

"Did you see it?" he groaned. "A spirit, perhaps, come for this old soul . . . So beautiful, so strange. All silver, like the moon . . ." He shut his eyes.

"Theo!" I shook him very gently, wild with terror. "Theo, come back!"

He grunted and his eyelids lifted just slightly, eyes staring up at the darkening sky. "The hunter becomes hunted. Keep watch, Tu!um-sa. Watch for silver eyes. The lion is hunting. . . ."

He coughed once, then sighed a long, long breath, his eyelids falling shut, his facial muscles slackening.

Just like that, he slipped away.

"Theo? No, no, *no*. Theo, look at me!" Wildly, I patted his cheeks, called his name, tried to shake him from his stillness. I pressed my head to his chest and felt a jolt of alarm when I could not hear his heartbeat. "Theo! Wake up!"

"Sarah . . ." I looked up to see Sam and the others standing over me, their expressions shocked and horrified. Kase cursed while Miranda went white as a sheet. Sam knelt beside Theo.

"Oh God, Sarah. I'm so sorry."

"He's just unconscious," I insisted.

Sam glanced up at me, and I refused to read what was written in his eyes. He held his fingers to Theo's neck, then his wrist.

"Sarah—"

"No." I looked away, my jaw set. "No, no, *no*. He needs a doctor. Avani?"

She backed away from my pleading look, averting her eyes. Sam just stared at me, full of sadness.

"Don't look at me that way!" I snapped. "Here, let me do it!"

I began pumping Theo's chest with my hands. His blood was slick and warm beneath my fingers. I breathed into his mouth, pumped his chest, breathed, pumped, breathed, pumped. . .

Finally Sam pulled me away. I fought him, struggling to get back to Theo.

"Sarah! Sarah, stop! He's gone; there's nothing you can do. It's over, Sarah, *please*. . . ."

"I have to try!"

He took my face in his hands and pierced me with his gaze. "You can't save him. It's too late."

I went perfectly still, my face burning under his palms. His hands slid down to my arms, holding me upright. His eyes were uncertain and watchful, as if he couldn't predict what I'd do next. I slumped forward, falling against him. Tears leaked from my eyes but I couldn't feel them; my skin had gone numb.

"He's dead," I said tonelessly.

Despite his silence, I could hear Sam's heart hammering

at his ribs. Why was he so warm, while Theo was turning so cold? So still? So . . . *lifeless?*

"Are you okay?" Sam asked, looking at me as warily as if I were standing on a bridge about to jump.

"No." The question made me angry. "How the hell could I be okay? What about this is remotely okay?"

"Sarah—"

"What do you want, anyway?" I demanded. I felt as if the top of my head were lifting off and steam were pouring out of my skull. "You're always following me, always asking questions—what is your problem?"

"I just—"

"Shut up!" I screamed, jumping to my feet, Sam quickly rising with me. "He's *dead! Theo is dead!"*

I began sobbing and grabbing fistfuls of my hair, as if I could pull the pain out of my head. Sam gripped my wrists and held them so tightly that my fingers tingled. He twisted my arms away from my face as I thrashed, kicked, and sobbed. He managed to spin me around while keeping a grip on my hands and held me tight against his chest with my arms crossed in front of me, a human straightjacket preventing me from harming myself or him. My knees gave out and I sagged; Sam knelt with me, still holding me tight, staying silent as I hurled curses at him, not caring if I sounded unfair and maniacal.

He held me until I ran out of breath and collapsed into him, no longer fighting. I turned my face into his chest and sobbed silently, the way I had for my mother. I cried without making any noise, and perhaps that was the worst way to cry, because the noise was trapped inside me like a hurricane, blasting my mind, scouring my heart.

It's a dream, it's a nightmare, it cannot be real. If I opened my eyes I would be back at camp, in my cot, with my mother's dream catchers hanging over me.

"The bad dreams will get tangled in the strings," my mother used to say. "They'll hang there like flies in a web until dawn, and they'll evaporate in the morning, and you'll never have a nightmare as long as they hang over you."

She had lied. I was sinking into a nightmare that never seemed to end—first my mom, now Theo, and probably my dad too. I couldn't imagine finding him alive, like I had forgotten how to hope.

"Dad," I gasped out. I hurriedly wiped my eyes with my kaffiyeh. "I have to find Dad." I scrambled to my feet and took off, ignoring Sam when he called for me to wait. The others were leaning against the truck and stared at me as I brushed past, my eyes on the ground, searching for Dad's trail. When I found it, I took off like a bloodhound following a scent. His prints wound this way and that, zigzagging through the bush—until he seemed to have evaporated. The trail disappeared. Why? Had they taken him? Or had he begun hiding his tracks? He knew how to disappear without a trace, just as Theo did. Well, if that was what he'd done, then there was no chance of me tracking him down now. I stared into the darkening bush, at the silhouettes of the trees against the twilight. I told myself that he was safe, that he knew how to survive out here.

"Nothing," I murmured when I arrived back at the truck. "He's out there somewhere. Maybe he got away."

The others remained quiet. They all looked terrified. I knelt in the sand by Theo, exhausted and numb. Sam had followed me back but held his distance uncertainly, looking as if he wanted to help but didn't know how.

"Why would they do this?" I asked. "Why kill him? He was the gentlest person in the world. He was my friend."

Sam murmured, "I know, I'm sorry. I understand, Sarah. I do."

"How could you *possibly*?" I whispered.

He came forward then and knelt rigidly beside me, his mouth tightening into a thin line. "When Adam was killed, it felt like I'd been buried alive. I went insane for a while. I was just so *angry*, at Adam, at myself, at the army, at every person I met. For a long time, I just wanted to break stuff. Punch things. Make the world feel my pain, you know? No one could handle me. I'd grown up in foster homes since I was five, and it sucked, but Adam was always there, you know? He was there to promise me that we'd get out one day, that we'd just grab our bags and go see the world. He was all I had. The one constant thing in my life."

I thought of Theo, of my mom. Sam might as well have been describing what they had been to me. They were the steady center around which I orbited. Without them, I drifted aimlessly through an empty, broken sky.

"If he made those promises," I asked, "why did he join the military?"

Sam let out a breath. His eyes were hard. "We got into some trouble, ran with the wrong crowd. Ended up stealing a car when I was fourteen. Adam was eighteen, and he took most of the rap for it, saying it was his idea. I hated him for that, hated and loved him, you know? I got a hundred hours of community service. He got a jail sentence but dodged it by volunteering to join the army. He died on his second tour."

Instead of distracting me from my own grief, Sam's story sharpened it like one knife to another. My chest compressed, and I felt a sob welling deep inside me, growing like a tumor. He must have sensed it, because he quickly took my hands and held them. I hated my tears. Water was the most precious resource in this desert, and here I was pouring it out all over the sand.

After a few minutes, I felt my grief begin to change. It grew hard and metallic and sharp, as if it had been forged over a bed of coals.

"I'll find them," I said, hardly recognizing my own voice. "I'll make them pay. I swear to God I will make them pay."

"You told us no confrontations, remember?" Sam's brow lowered and he met my eyes. "You said we were only going to find your dad, that no way were we going after the poachers."

"That was before. Things have changed. They crossed a line." My voice was steel. "Anyway, there's no *we*." I pulled my hands from his, stood up, and lifted my eyes to the sky. The stars had truly begun to blaze, their light strengthening in the darkness. "We'll bury Theo, and then I'll drive us back to camp in the Cruiser. We'll get as many supplies as we can and then drive to Ghansi. You can go home, and I can go look for Dad."

"You can't go after him by yourself."

"I have to find my dad, Sam." I felt suddenly weary; the toll of a day of hiking coupled with the emotional trauma of Theo's death was nearly crippling.

"Then I'll come with you."

"No, you *won't*. I don't need your help."

He didn't press the issue but looked as if he wanted to. Instead, he stared at Theo and sighed quietly. "Does he have family?"

"No." Maybe a few distant relatives near the Namibian border, but no one close. He'd always said he'd been born in the Kalahari, and so he wanted to die in the Kalahari. It was his people's tradition to immediately bury their dead and then move on quickly, never returning to the grave unless absolutely necessary. Theo had held tightly to these fading traditions. When we'd first met him, he was living in a hut in the bush outside Maun, having refused to move into the city with the rest of his tribe. And anyway, it was his last request of me. How could I say no to that?

Sam left and I sat beside Theo's body, trying to keep my eyes on the Bushman's face and not the bloody cavity in his chest. I clicked on the flashlight and shone it on the area around me, dancing the beam over my dad's footprints. *Where are you now? Are you safe?*

As my light grazed the surrounding sand, another set of prints caught my eye. I crawled on my knees to a patch of sand surrounded by flattened grasses and inspected it with the light held at an angle, to better throw the shadows of the impressions into relief.

The lion.

He'd been here too. Now that I had his track identified, I saw it all around. He'd prowled around the vehicle several times and seemed to have stopped to sniff it. Had he smelled Theo's blood? Was that why he'd been following the Cruiser—in search of an easy meal? But his tracks turned to follow Dad's, not Theo's, which worried me immensely.

Those questions opened the way for a whole slew of new ones. Theo had said Dad didn't know he'd been shot, but even so, if Dad was free and able, he would never have abandoned Theo for so long. Why hadn't he returned or come looking when Theo didn't show up? Which told me Dad must still be on the run or . . .

I unclipped my radio and murmured into it, calling for Dad. I heard my own voice, muffled with static, coming from the Cruiser. My heart sinking, I went to the truck and searched, noting with a sick twist of my gut that the satellite radio was gone, no doubt taken by the poachers. It was too bulky for Dad to have taken if he was in a hurry. I found the smaller handheld radio on the floor of the cab. The batteries were almost drained, probably from me calling so much.

Sam managed to persuade Joey to help him begin scraping sand aside to create a grave. After a while, Avani helped, and Kase pulled himself away from Miranda to join the effort. Miranda was swaying a little on her feet, staring dully at the ground, her lips moving but making no sound. Her state of shock made me irrationally angry. She had barely known Theo. I knew my flare of anger was foolish and unjustified, but I had zero control over what I was feeling. My emotions shifted and changed as quickly as a bushfire driven by the wind.

I finally forced myself into motion, sensing that if I stayed in my cocoon of shock for much longer I'd never rise out of it. Avani and I wrapped Theo in the canvas that had been the Cruiser's roof. Her hands shook as much as mine, and I guessed that for all her talk of her doctor parents and her medical know-how, she'd never dealt with an actual corpse before.

"I'm sorry," she said. "He seemed like a nice guy."

Before we covered his face, I bent to kiss each of his cheeks and his forehead. They were cool and dry, so utterly lifeless that I had trouble believing those eyes had ever been open. This wasn't *my* Theo, my vibrant, laughing Theo who was forever cracking jokes and trying to make me smile, the Theo who'd distracted me after Mom's death with silly games and long, wandering treks through the bush. This was some kind of awful trick. This was a nightmare.

The boys placed Theo in the shallow grave of sand and helped me fill it in. After it was done, I tried to say some words of mourning, to describe what Theo had meant to me, all that he'd taught me and how much I'd relied on him after Mom's death, but the words wouldn't come. I choked on them, and Avani and Sam supported me on either side.

We stood there for a long while, until Avani's teeth began to chatter from the cold. I busied myself with making a fire beside the Cruiser.

Sam combed the truck, looking for any supplies the animals might have missed, and returned with nothing but a single bunch of bananas. "I found these. They must have fallen out of one of the crates. They're bruised but I think they're okay."

So we each had a banana for dinner. Mine tasted like ashes and I could barely swallow. My earlier hunger had turned to nausea. We all sat silent and motionless, wrapped in our own thoughts. The air around us was numb and flat, like a room that's had all the oxygen sucked out of it.

After the others eventually dropped off to sleep, I went to sit by Theo's grave.

"Want company?" asked a soft voice.

I hesitated, then nodded, and Sam joined me. He was like my shadow, but instead of getting angry with him like I had before, I was glad for his quiet presence.

"It was Theo who taught me how to track," I said. "He'd take me out in the early mornings, when the animals were all moving around, and he'd leave me deep in the bush. 'Find your way home, Tu!um-sa,' he would say. He called me Tu!um-sa because it means 'rain on the sand,' which is what he thought my freckles looked like. He would pretend to leave me alone, but he was always close by, watching out for me." I shifted, crossing my legs and resting my elbows on my knees. "After my mom died, he would try to cheer me up by doing some of the traditional San dances—you know, pretending to be an ostrich or an oryx or a giraffe and stamping around the fire, making animal noises. It was the only thing that ever made me smile."

"Sounds like a great guy," said Sam. He plucked a tuft of grass and began pulling it apart, tossing the stalks absently to the sand.

I stared with glassy eyes at the freshly turned earth. "It was a dumb move, killing Theo. The penalty for poaching lions here isn't that steep—they'd probably get away with a fine—but murder?" I shook my head. "They've taken their crime to a whole new level."

"You aren't serious about going after them, are you?"

I sighed. "Not alone. You're right. It's too dangerous. But there's an air rescue operation in Maun, and they can call in the Defence Force. . . ."

"If the poachers find us before then . . ." His fingers

tightened around the grass.

"We have to be careful." My mind was wrestling over what to do next. I was desperate to search for my dad, but I couldn't just abandon the group. "We'll go back to the camp tomorrow like I said, but we'll have to be quick in case the poachers are nearby." These were no ordinary poachers. They had more to lose now, and I doubted that they'd hesitate to commit other murders in order to cover up this one. "We'll grab more water and any other stuff we can use and head out again."

I sighed and rubbed my forehead. "We'll have to forage and hunt while we go." Which would slow us down considerably. "We'll go west. It's the shortest route to Ghansi, anyway, and that's the closest town. We can reach the embassies from there, and the police and everyone's parents. Once you guys are taken care of, I'll go back and look for Dad."

I think he wanted to argue, but the look on my face seemed to stop him short. He simply remained silent and sat by me until, hours later, I must have fallen asleep. I was woken in the night by a shout and sat bolt upright, dimly noticing that I was by the fire, some distance from Theo's grave. Sam must have carried me there, which made my face warm a little. He'd even taken off my boots and placed them neatly at the foot of my sleeping bag.

I looked around for the source of the shout. It was Kase, barely visible in the light cast by the fire's remaining embers. He was swinging a flashlight around the bush and calling Miranda's name.

"What's wrong?" Sam asked, clambering out of his own sleeping bag.

Kase spun, his flashlight beam hitting Sam in the face.

"She's gone! I was on watch and I—I fell asleep, and when I woke up she was gone!"

"Miranda's gone?" Avani asked sleepily. "Where'd she go?"

Immediately I was on my feet, my flashlight in hand. "How long were you sleeping?" I asked Kase.

"I don't know . . . maybe half an hour?"

"She can't be far. Spread out, but keep each other's lights within view. If you look around and see only darkness, head back. We get separated out here, we get separated for good. Got it?"

I scanned the sand around the campsite, but we'd been coming and going so much that it was impossible to tell which tracks were Miranda's. So we fanned out and began walking away from the campfire, calling her name into the night and swinging our flashlight beams in wide arcs across the bush. I was already imagining the worst—she'd run across lions, leopards, any one of the numerous poisonous creatures that stalk the Kalahari.

When I heard Avani's shout change to, "Here! Over here!" I nearly fainted with relief. I reached her just before everyone else.

Miranda was stumbling through the grass, shivering and muttering, looking as if she'd just been through a war. She was scraped and dirty and half-delirious. I stepped in front of her, but she just tried to push her way around me.

"Gotta get out," she mumbled through chattering teeth. "Can't stay here. I have to go home."

"Miranda, it's me, it's Sarah. You have to stop!"

Kase caught up to us, his face panicky. "Mir! Are you okay?"

Her eyes were unfocused and unblinking, her skin was pale, and her breath was flowing in quick, shallow bursts.

"Miranda?" Kase looked in her eyes and took her hands. "Your skin's so cold. . . ."

Avani took Miranda's hand, and when Miranda didn't react, I knew something had to be wrong with her.

"She's in shock," said Avani. "Her pulse is weak and her eyes . . ." She shook her head. "We need to get her back to the fire."

"She hasn't said a word since she saw the body," said Kase. "But I thought . . . I didn't think it was this bad."

We rushed her back to the campsite and built up the fire. Kase held her close, rubbing her arms and shoulders, trying to warm her up.

"I shouldn't have brought her here," he said, sounding close to tears himself. "I thought . . . She's had a hard year. I thought coming here would help take her mind off things."

"It's not your fault," I sighed. "It wasn't supposed to go like this."

"You're right, it's not my fault—it's *yours!*" Kase snapped.

"Enough!" Sam growled, and for once, Kase fell silent. I dropped my gaze, wondering if he was right.

"She'll be okay, I think," Avani said. "We should get some more sleep while we can."

Sam sat on his sleeping bag and rubbed his face, yawning. "I'll keep watch."

"You've already done one shift," said Joey.

"I'll do it," I said.

Sam blinked at me with bloodshot eyes. "You sure?"

"I won't go back to sleep anyway."

They dropped off one by one, Kase last of all. He lay on his side, one arm curled around Miranda, who still sniffed and whimpered in her sleep. I rested my chin on my knees and stared at the fire, losing myself in the memory of a hundred fires, a hundred starry nights that had been spent with my family, when we had learned the dances and the stories of a fading culture from one of its last and truest sons.

SEVEN

Hank wouldn't start in the morning. The battery was dead, and there was no way to jump it.

"Now what?" asked Joey, kicking the rear tire, as if that would inspire Hank to start up.

"Like my mom used to say, 'Elbow grease and a prayer,'" I said. "There is a trick we can try."

I had Avani sit in the driver's seat, since she was the smallest, and the rest of us lined up across the hood and pushed as hard as we could. I wedged dry wood under the tires since the sand gave zero traction and called for Avani to turn the ignition. The engine didn't start, but with a great amount of grunting and heaving, we got the truck to roll a few feet back, turned slightly away from the trunk it had crashed into. I did a quick check on the engine; everything seemed to be intact despite the deep dent in the front bumper and the buckled hood. I picked up the pieces of wood and placed them on the other side of the tires.

"Okay, now push from the back."

Miranda was quiet but much more present than she had been the night before. She joined in. Together we all threw our weight into the rear end of the Cruiser. Sweat poured down my neck despite the cool morning temperature, and my back and legs ached, but I pushed relentlessly. It would have been so much easier with a hill, but even at its most extreme, the Kalahari could be described only as gently rolling.

Once we got Hank moving, I yelled, "Clutch!" to Avani. We kept pushing, beginning to gather a small bit of speed, and then I called for her to press the gas pedal. At first, nothing happened, and my heart sank.

Then with a cough and a grunt, Hank rumbled to life, sounding grumpy, as if he were annoyed that we'd disturbed his rest.

The boys hollered and high-fived and strutted as if they were wholly responsible for the working vehicle, but no smile would touch my lips. I had to willfully bend my mind each minute to the task at hand, because otherwise it kept slipping to Theo. I had kept watch until dawn, not daring to go back to sleep; I had been too afraid of the dreams waiting for me in the dark. As soon as the sun rose, I went and sat by Theo's grave. I told him stories about the two of us, calling up memories I'd nearly forgotten, anchoring myself to his spirit. Not for the first time, I wondered if the dead could hear the cries of the living. I hoped that wherever he was, Mom was there too. She could make a fish feel at home on dry land, if she wanted. It helped a little, to imagine them together, to imagine they could hear me.

We were still a mile away from camp when I sensed that

something was wrong. I smelled it first—smoke in the air—but it took me a minute to process the scent and what it could mean. At first my mind leaped to the most probable conclusion: a bushfire. I'd seen dozens of them out here, and though they were dangerous, they were fairly easy to avoid if you knew what you were doing.

But this fire was different. It smelled wrong, like burning plastic, and my heart rate suddenly spiked. *They found the camp. Why would they go after the camp?* And what did it mean for my dad? Had they caught him? And if so, why weren't they in South Africa or Namibia by now, on the run, instead of hanging around the scene of their crime? *Oh God—what if we'd been here when they arrived?*

I slammed my foot on the brake and Hank fishtailed in the sand, throwing my passengers forward.

"What was that?" Miranda shouted, rubbing her head where it had slammed into the seat in front of her. The ride seemed to have pulled her out of her state of shock; perhaps the comforting sound of a running engine, and the tenuous thread to safety it represented, had finally reached her through her daze.

"Stay here." I shut off the engine and climbed over the door. Since crashing into the tree, both doors were jammed shut.

Sam looked unhappy about it, but he stayed in the car with the others while I jogged ahead. When I drew near the camp, I ducked into the grass and ran doubled over, stepping on patches of bare sand to muffle my steps, hissing softly at the pain that rippled from my porcupine-induced cuts.

At the edge of the clearing where our tents were, I dropped

to my belly and crawled forward on my elbows, startling a mongoose out of hiding. As it slunk away, I came to a stop and parted the grass in front of me for a better view.

The camp was in ruins.

The tents had been piled in the fire pit and were now nothing more than smoldering black fragments. Strips of charred cloth had been blown all over the place and were caught in the branches of the acacias. Twisted bits of metal that had been the frames of the cots stuck out at crazy angles from the remains of the bonfire, giving the scene an eerie, skeletal look. A piece of paper, half-burned, was stuck in the sand near my elbow. I picked it up and stared at it, my stomach twisting.

It was a page of handwritten field notes—my father's handwriting. It was dated just three weeks ago, from his work documenting a herd of zebras that had moved into the area. He'd been so excited when he saw them, because it could mean they'd found a permanent source of water, which in turn meant the door was opening for all kinds of species to move back into the central Kalahari: elephants, buffalo, monkeys, and baboons.

They'd burned all of our research. I was speechless, at a loss as to *why*. What threat did field notes on the social behavior of the local zebras pose to them? My parents' entire collection of work on the central Kalahari was gone, destroyed by fire. Sure, we had electronic backups of some stuff that we'd sent to the universities that funded the research, but so much of it had been irreplaceable—not least because some of it was in my mother's own hand, often including beautiful sketches of the wildlife and scenery. Both my parents had preferred to handwrite their notes, though my mom had also been fond of voicing her thoughts on a recorder, leaving me the job of painstakingly deciphering their messy scrawl and her meandering monologues in order to type their research into our laptop. Since Mom's death, I'd fallen woefully behind in transferring her notes to the computer, because it had been so difficult to look at her handwriting or listen to her voice.

I crumpled the paper in my fist and stood up—then dropped like a stone. Two men had stepped into view, not twenty feet from where I was crouched in the bushes. They were dressed in fatigues and carried assault rifles, but they didn't look like soldiers. Their clothing was too messy, their hair too long. One was blond and the other redheaded, both with beards and cigarettes hanging from their lips. They spoke to one another in Afrikaans, so they had to be South African. I knew enough of the language to decipher their conversation.

". . . they'll come back?" the blond man was saying.

"Not if they're smart," his partner replied. "But if anyone can find them out here, it's Abramo. God knows he's got the cash."

"I shouldn't have taken this job. It's getting too weird."

"For what they're paying, I can swallow weirder."

They paused to glance across the camp, where two more men had appeared. They must have had vehicles parked somewhere in the brush near the water pump. Of these two men, one was tall and black, the other white, gray haired, and likely in his fifties. The latter seemed to be in charge, because he started shouting orders. He was too far for me to make out his accent. At his words, the two Afrikaners took off at a trot, joining the others at the far side of the camp and out of my hearing.

I stared at the remains of the fire, a heap of white ash and black charred cloth. There was no telling what they had taken and what they had burned; everything was gone. I didn't have a house to go back home to where my family albums and mementos would be safely stored. All that I had in the world, I'd had right here, and that included my mom, my dad, and Theo. And now . . . now there was just Dad. *And maybe not even him.* My fingers turned into fists, digging into the sand.

Who were these people? They'd seen Dad before he'd seen them. If they were just poaching, why didn't they simply leave when they were discovered? They could have turned around and driven the other way, cleared out of the area with their identities still under wraps. They would have gotten away clean. It just didn't make *sense*. My parents' lives—and by extension, my life—were built upon finding the rationale driving behavior patterns in species. So what was driving these poachers to such extremes, in murdering Theo, pursuing my dad, and now destroying our camp? I needed more information, but it was too risky to investigate now. Drawing on what little I knew of these guys, all I could guess was that they'd followed Dad here—though I couldn't imagine Dad coming home if he knew doing so would lead the poachers right to us. But even if they *had* followed Dad here, why go through the trouble of burning everything? My line of questions, strung one to another like a chain of paper links, led me right back to where I'd begun: pretty much nowhere.

I was certain of one thing though: Something bigger than poaching was happening here. But *what*?

I was only glad that we'd been gone when they arrived at the camp.

Miranda, Kase, and the rest of the group were going to be irate. Their bags with all their extra clothes and belongings had been burned with the rest of the camp, and deliriously, I wondered how I could afford to replace their gear. Would the Song Foundation hold us financially responsible? Would we be sued for the ordeal these kids were going through? The program, which was supposed to boost our research, could very well destroy it once and for all.

As if my thoughts had summoned them, the others came walking through the bush. I heard twigs snapping and sand crunching and whirled to see them all making their way toward me. Frantically, I gestured for them to get down. Avani caught on first, and the rest followed suit, bewildered. When they reached me, I wordlessly pointed at the ransacked camp and the cluster of poachers standing across it, out of earshot but still visible. Their eyes all grew wide and their faces a bit green.

"Our stuff!" Kase whispered in a strangled tone. "They burned it! Those—those *criminals*!"

"Why would they do that?" asked Avani. "Sarah, what's going on? What do they want?"

"I don't know," I admitted.

"Did you see your dad?" Sam asked.

"No." Then I added thoughtfully, "But if they captured him for some reason, he might be in one of their trucks." If they'd caught Dad, would they have coerced him into giving away the location of the camp? *Surely Dad wouldn't do that.* But the thought left me shaken.

Sam gave me a knowing look. "It'll be dangerous, going after him."

"You know I have to try."

"Are you getting a weird vibe about these poachers?" Sam asked.

I was, but I wanted to know what he was thinking.

"What do you mean?"

"Well, isn't this a crazy lot of trouble to go to? I mean, why murder Theo and trash the camp if they're just after a lion? What if they're not poachers at all?"

"But who else would do this?" I asked. "It's not like we have enemies, and Botswana is one of the most politically stable countries in the world. If we were in Libya or Uganda or a place like that, we could chalk it up to terrorists or a rebel group or something, but not *here*."

Sam shrugged and turned to watch the men. I couldn't shake his questions. There was something wrong here, something I was missing. I felt a rush of guilt, as if my inability to understand the situation was causing it to spiral even more wildly out of control.

"Sarah."

I turned to Sam, blinking away the mist of my thoughts. He was holding out one of my dream catchers, the smallest one I'd had. It had gotten tangled in a bush, maybe while the poachers were piling all of my worldly possessions into a bonfire. Sam placed it in my open palm and I closed my fingers over it, a knot rising in my throat. After a moment, I put it carefully into my pocket.

It was time for me to stop mourning. We were in more danger than ever, and I had to keep myself together. I could fall to pieces after this was over. For now, I forced all my feelings into the back corner of my brain, trapping them like angry bees beneath a cup.

Kase, who'd been quiet and thoughtful this whole time, suddenly said, "I'm going to talk to them."

"What?" I stared at him, aghast. "Why would you want to do that?"

"It's not like we've got better options out here! No food, no water, no gear . . . Look, I know they shot your friend—and my sympathies for that—but they can't just shoot us! I mean, for heaven's sake, that's barbaric! I know how these guys work. All they care about is money. Well, I happen to have a lot of it. Or my family does, anyway. They'll pay whatever it takes for us to get out of here, and if I offer it to them—"

"*Kase.*" I spoke between my teeth. "They will *shoot* you. This isn't about money anymore; it's about hiding whatever they've done. They killed Theo and they know they can't afford to have any witnesses. The only things worth more to them than money is their freedom and lives, and they'll lose one if not both if we survive to tell what happened here. The punishment for murder in Botswana is death by hanging. They won't risk that, not on the chance your parents will ransom you."

His brow furrowed in uncertainty as he digested this. Surprisingly, it was Miranda who brought him to his senses.

"Don't go out there," she pleaded. "Kase, please. Don't risk it."

He looked irritated but nodded sullenly.

"We have to leave," I said. "And we have to move quietly. They know we're out here somewhere and they're definitely looking for us." I told them what I'd overheard the Afrikaners saying, and the faces around me turned even greener.

If there were any trackers among them, then it was only a matter of time before they picked up our prints. If we got enough of a head start, I could throw them off by obscuring our trail, the way Theo had taught me. The thought of the poachers roaming the bush, intent on finding and killing us, dulled my grief and sharpened my mind. I could feel my body growing stronger with adrenaline as my survival instincts kicked in.

"Go back to the truck," I whispered. "I'll meet you there soon."

For once, no one argued or complained. They nodded and turned, making their way back much more slowly and quietly than they'd arrived. I watched them go, then turned, drew a deep breath, and set off to my right. It took a solid ten minutes to circumvent the camp without attracting attention. I stayed just outside the bare sand of the firebreak and kept low, feeling like a rabbit sneaking past a sleeping lion.

When I found the row of Land Rovers parked on the firebreak, my heart sped up. Was Dad in one of them? The windows were damnably tinted, so there was no way of telling. A half-dozen more men were clustered around the vehicles, talking and smoking. I couldn't get close without being seen.

On a sudden whim, I crept away and then darted across the firebreak as soon as I was out of their view. I went as close to the burned camp as I dared, then turned and stepped deliberately back toward the bush, leaving enough prints to account for five or six people. Keeping a careful eye out for the poachers, I worked my way outward from the camp, leaving a trail that pointed in the opposite direction of the one I and the others would take. Once I reached the bush on the other side of the firebreak, I continued for about a quarter mile into the foliage before deciding it was as good a false trail as I had time to lay. Then, taking care to hide where I stepped, I returned to spy again on the men at the trucks, hoping for one last chance to find out what had happened to Dad.

"Hey, boss!" called one of the men, emerging from the camp, "I found their trail!"

My heartbeat suspended. *Which trail?* I couldn't breathe again until I saw the man point toward my fake tracks. Dizzily relieved, I allowed myself a small smile of triumph.

The leader—I figured him to be the Abramo the Afrikaners had spoken of—waved everyone into the vehicles. About six men, including the blond and the redhead I'd first seen, stayed behind—to ambush us, I supposed, if we returned.

I strained to see inside the Land Rovers as the men opened the doors and climbed inside. Dad could have easily been inside one and still escaped my view. It was maddening, to think he could be so close and yet so unreachable.

The Rovers took off eastward, following my false trail. When they lost the tracks, as they inevitably would, I hoped they'd continue in that direction, anticipating us to have headed for Maun or one of the Central Kalahari Game Reserve guard stations.

I lay flat as the Rovers rumbled past me, then began painstakingly creeping back the way I'd come. I was moving so quietly that I practically tripped over a mother warthog and her piglets who were napping in the shade. They squealed and darted away, their tails vertical, and when they crossed the firebreak the men who'd been left behind began shooting wildly. I dropped, hands over my head, as the bullets pinged the sand, but none of them came near me. The shots didn't last long, and by the disappointed murmuring, I took it they had failed in dropping one of the warthogs. Thankfully, they hadn't seen me—but it had been close.

When I reached the Land Cruiser, the others were frantic with worry, having heard the gunshots. After calming them down, I told them what I'd seen, then bent down and traced a circle in the sand. "This is us. And this is Ghansi." I traced another circle northwest of the camp, then a line leading south from Ghansi. "This is the nearest road. If we drive west, then we can take the road north to town. It's opposite the direction the poachers went, so we'll have a head start."

"How long will it take?" asked Kase.

"Depends on the conditions. There's not a road from here to there, so we'll be driving through total wilderness, and the trip will be over a hundred and twenty miles. We can make it in one or two days." I didn't tell them that that would require an inordinate amount of luck. It was inevitable that the Cruiser would get stuck multiple times, and there could very well be damage to the car I didn't know about as a result of the crash. In the likely event that something happened to Hank, we'd have to walk to Ghansi—which could take a week or more. The poachers could hunt for us at their leisure.

I had to keep them optimistic. So I forced a smile onto my face and assured them everything would be fine. None of them looked very convinced, Sam least of all. His face was grave and his eyes constantly searched the horizon. Miranda looked dazed, as if she'd mentally checked out of the situation, and I wondered how she'd hold up. If she slipped back into a state of shock, I wasn't sure I could keep her moving, and the others might follow her. They all looked as traumatized as I felt.

"We'll starve to death out there," Kase intoned, his gaze wide and distant. "We'll die of dehydration. Or we'll—"

"Stop it," I said sharply. "We'll make it."

He blinked, his eyes refocusing on me. "We're in the middle of a *desert*."

"Semidesert," Avani and I said simultaneously. Joey groaned.

"Look," I sighed. "I know it sounds bad. It *is* bad. But if we stick together and be smart about this, we can make it. Will you trust me?"

I looked at each of them, hoping none of them would see that I barely trusted myself. But they nodded reluctantly.

"Okay," I said. "Let's load up."

Everyone climbed into Hank and we set off. It was almost sunset by then, and we drove deep into the bush before stopping in a nondescript thicket far from the ruined camp. We decided the girls would sleep in the Cruiser tonight, and we'd switch with the guys the following night. The day after that— if we were lucky—we would reach Ghansi.

We were starving. I searched in vain for *tsama* melons, tubers, anything edible, but darkness fell quickly, and my efforts turned up nothing more than a handful of shriveled berries.

"Great," said Joey tonelessly, staring at his meager share.

"You're alive, aren't you?" Sam said.

"For *now*."

"Shut up, man," snapped Kase. "We're doing the best we can. We don't need your whining to make things worse."

"My whining? It's your girlfriend who's complained non-stop since the airport."

Kase, who'd been relaxing against a tree, stood up then. "Watch it, dude."

"What?" Joey shrugged. "Everyone's thinking it."

"Leave him alone," said Miranda. "He just wants attention."

"*I* just want attention?" He gave her an exaggerated look of offense. "Oh, the irony! This coming from our own Kim Kardashian. Here's an idea—why didn't someone bring a satellite phone with them? Huh? Geez, what I'd give for one right now. Why didn't your Daddy Warbucks send one with you, huh?"

Kase swore at him, but it was Miranda who jumped to her feet and slapped Joey full across the face. He staggered back, eyes wide in surprise, but then he blinked at her and laughed.

"You slap like a *girl*."

"Dude, you need to take a walk," said Sam softly.

"Oh, yeah, here comes Mr. Strong and Silent. Did you stop to think we might not be in this mess if it weren't for *your* girlfriend?"

"What?"

Joey threw out an accusing finger at me. "Your dad left us in this mess. Honestly, who runs off to God knows where and leaves a bunch of kids on their own in the wilderness with fricking lions and homicidal maniacs for company?"

In the distance, a chorus of jackals began their nightly howling. The sound was so natural that I usually didn't even notice it, but tonight, it made the hair on my neck stand on end. The others stared with shocked round eyes from Joey to me.

"You don't know anything about it!" I said. "If it weren't for you, I could have found my dad by now! But no, I have to babysit a bunch of incompetent city kids while my *dad* is hunted by a bunch of murderers and my only friend lies buried in the sand!"

I regretted the words even before I said them, but Joey had touched too many nerves tonight and I was burning with anger. How dare he blame my dad? I wanted to slap him myself.

"Guys, *stop*!" Sam said, standing up and holding out his hands. "This is ridiculous. We need to sleep so we can get started early in the morning. Look, I'll take first watch, okay?"

I said nothing, but turned my back and walked away, trembling with anger. It would make more sense for me to take first watch; I knew I wasn't going to sleep. My stomach was too empty and my brain was too full. We were all ticking time bombs, like kettles growing hotter and hotter with stress and fear.

I went back to the camp and told Sam to sleep, that I'd take the first watch. He didn't argue, but I didn't think he was sleeping either. None of them did, for a while.

It didn't help at all that about an hour into the night, somewhere in the darkness a lion began to roar.

EIGHT

We set out early the next morning but made it only a mile or two before the truck came to a full stop in the sand. Holding back curses, I climbed out and took stock of the situation.

The tires were half buried, all four of them sunk. It would take a while to dig the truck out, and from the look of the land ahead, it was just going to get worse. We were in an old dry stream bed; thousands of years ago, this area would have been a paradise of rivers and lakes and grass. All that remained of those golden days of the Kalahari were these dry depressions, like the skeletons of a lost world. The stream bed was a sort of natural road, leading us in the right direction with fewer bushes and trees to navigate around—but with the unfortunate side effect that it was composed of deep, soft sand that sucked at the wheels like mud.

I sighed and suggested that we begin scouting around for pieces of wood to lever the wheels out. Then I would have to drive out of the bed and follow it from above if possible.

A pair of stately giraffes watched me with disinterest as I beat through the bushes. The rest of the group spread out in all directions, halfheartedly searching, probably as distracted by hunger as I was.

When I returned to the truck a half hour later with an armload of logs and branches, everyone was sitting in the shade, close to Hank. Sam looked up apologetically. "We heard lions."

I sighed and dropped my armload of wood.

"Where?"

The chances of them attacking us were about one in a thousand—if we were in the Cruiser. But if a pride got curious about us and decided to settle within sight, then we would be trapped in the vehicle.

Sam pointed in the direction they'd heard the pride, and I nodded.

"We have to be quick," I said.

But it seemed the more we tried to dig Hank out of the sand, the deeper he sank. The wood we wedged under the tires simply snapped or was buried, and it wasn't long before I heard the roar. One lion, from the sound of it. I thought of the mystery male who'd been following Dad and Theo, and I wondered if it could be the same one. Was it the white lion? The one who'd started all this mess?

We worked feverishly while Avani and Miranda took turns watching for the lion. I wasn't too worried about it; if it was indeed a loner, it would almost certainly make a wide berth around us. I was familiar with three different prides in the area, and there was one male who roamed between each of them. He was skittish and shy, never giving us trouble, but if this loner was one of the younger males that had been pushed out by its mother, it might be desperate for a meal.

Still, I was more focused on getting the Cruiser unstuck, seeing it as our bigger problem.

That was my mistake.

"I think I saw it!" I heard Miranda call. Immediately Joey, Avani, and Miranda jumped into the Cruiser, and Kase whipped out his camera. Sam looked excited, and I didn't blame him. This would be their first real wild African lion.

I stood on the top of the tailgate, held a hand up, shielding my eyes from the sun, and scanned the bush. The lion's tawny hide was perfect camouflage in the yellow grass, so it could have been anywhere.

"Binoculars," I gasped, holding out a hand. "Somebody give me binoculars!"

"I have this," said Kase, offering his camera.

I took it and climbed back onto the Cruiser, bracing myself better this time. Pressing my eye to the viewfinder, I roved the bush. Then, my hand shaking slightly, I twisted the heavy lens and zoomed in.

My breath stuck in my lungs. I couldn't understand it. It was like my mind rejected what I saw, telling me it was too impossible, too strange. It had to be a trick of the light, or some kind of prank.

"Sarah?" Sam asked again. "What do you see?"

What do I see? I had no idea. I could have seen a ghost, and it would have made more sense than the creature hovering in the lens of the camera.

It was a lion. Or at least, it was something *shaped* like a lion.

But it wasn't tawny or golden or even white, like the one the poachers were rumored to be hunting. It was like no lion I had ever seen.

This lion was *silver*.

Not silver as in silver gray or silver white. It was *silver*, from nose to tail, as metallic and gleaming as mercury. It moved slowly through the bush, twitching its silver tail and shaking its silver mane.

I stared, but couldn't comprehend anything about it.

"Sarah!"

I jerked my eye away from the camera and looked down at Sam. He gave me an exasperated look.

"It's a lion," I said. "I think."

"You *think*? We heard it roar."

I nodded. I had heard it too. I looked through the camera again, but the lion was gone. Frantically, I zoomed out and searched the bushes—there it was. It was moving faster now, its nose lifted. Had it caught our scent?

"Sam," I said slowly. "Kase. Get in the truck. *Now*."

"What—"

"*Get in the truck.*"

They climbed up, using the wheels and roof supports to haul themselves into the back of the Cruiser. Everyone crowded behind me, straining to see. Still shaking, I focused on the lion and snapped three photos.

"Holy cow," said Joey. "Is that . . . is that it?"

So they could see it now.

"What *is* it?" Avani asked, looking doubly shaken that here was something she didn't know the genus and species of.

"It's a silver lion," said Miranda.

"No, *duh*," said Joey.

"It's impossible," I said.

"Is it covered in paint?" asked Sam.

It was the most reasonable explanation I'd heard yet—except that no paint I'd ever seen looked that much like metal. No paint could cover a full-grown lion without flaking or wearing off.

I turned the camera to display mode and zoomed in on the picture I'd snapped. Kase's camera was extremely expensive, taking higher quality photos than even my dad's professional gear.

Everyone leaned around me to look.

"That's not paint," said Kase, taking the camera and squinting at the display.

I knew he was right. The silver was too perfect, showing no bare spots, not so much as a single tawny hair. The individual hairs of the lion, caught in crisp clarity by the camera, seemed to each be made of silver strands.

All silver, like the moon. Theo's dying words. I had taken them for delirium, never imagining. . . *Keep watch, Tulum-sa. Watch for silver eyes. The lion is hunting.* I had been right: The lion—*this* lion—had been following the vehicles, and Theo must have seen it sometime after he'd been shot, thinking it was a vision, a spirit come to escort his dying soul into the sky.

"It's like . . . it's like . . ." Joey started, but he stopped and shrugged. "I don't even know. What the hell is it?"

"The silver lion," I said softly. "This is what the poachers are after. I thought—the rumors Henrico told Dad about—they mentioned a white lion, an albino, we thought, but this . . . This isn't natural."

"I think that's obvious," said Avani. "So what is it? Some kind of robot?"

We all stared at the creature as it made its way toward us. The hairs on my arms stood vertically, and I felt cold despite the mideighties temperature.

"It moves too naturally," I said. "Like a real lion. No robot could be so lifelike."

"Is it some kind of projection?" asked Sam.

I looked around, making a wide sweep with my hand. "From where? Outer space?"

Everyone looked up, as if the idea weren't so far-fetched after all.

"This is too weird," said Miranda, shaking her head. "I don't like it. Let's get out of here."

"No!" said Sam. "We have to get a closer look. This is incredible!" He looked around at our stricken faces, his eyes alight. "Don't you want to know what it is? This could be like, some sort of breakthrough! Some kind of huge discovery!"

"It's coming straight toward us," said Avani.

I nodded. "Stay in the truck and it won't bother us."

"How do you know? Maybe a real lion wouldn't, but this is obviously not a real lion! Let's go!"

"I want to see it closer," Sam insisted.

"Then be my guest. Jump on out and go make friends with the freaky silver robot lion." Avani glared at him.

"Settle down, everyone. Nobody's going out there. Just stay quiet," I said.

The lion was a stone's throw away now. It stopped, lifted its head, and stared straight at us. The sunlight played in gleaming patterns over it, the way it would play off a knife; I could see spots of light dancing over the grass where it reflected off the metallic hide of the animal. It looked like something animated for film, like a 3-D model that hadn't been painted yet. It prowled closer and stopped again, sniffing, watching, twitching its tail.

Its eyes were silver like the rest of it. They looked like the blank, staring eyes of a statue, but I sensed this lion was far from blind. It stared too keenly, its gaze resting directly on us.

"Please," Miranda begged, "let's just go. What if it attacks us?"

I almost repeated that it wouldn't, but suddenly I wasn't sure. I had no idea what it would do because I had no idea what it *was*.

"They're not poachers," Sam said, his voice low. "This is something else entirely. This is way bigger."

I nodded, having come to the same conclusion myself. This was no ordinary prey, so I doubted its hunters were ordinary poachers. Whatever this . . . *thing* was, the men who were hunting it would obviously stop at nothing to find it and . . . what? Capture it? Kill it? All of my certainty deserted me. I felt as if I knew nothing, as if all my years in the wilderness and in research had done me zero good. It certainly hadn't prepared me for *this*. Whatever it was.

The lion drew closer to the Cruiser, and when it was about ten yards away, it went into a crouch. My skin turned to gooseflesh. Was it about to spring? Would it really attack?

Lions perceive people in cars as a unified entity. They don't see us as prey and will go out of their way to avoid us— particularly ones in the wild where people are uncommon.

But would this lion see us the same way? If I made the wrong call, it could cost us our lives.

"Stay still," I said, my eyes fixed on the creature. Despite the danger and impossibility of it all, I was overwhelmed with fascination. I wanted to get closer, like Sam. If I'd had my dad's tranquilizer gun I could have knocked it out long enough to get samples of its hair and skin and saliva. Unfortunately, the gun had been at the campsite, to either end up burned or stolen. I had the shotgun, but I wouldn't use it—not unless I had to choose between a human's life and the lion's. But who knew if it would even react to tranquilizers? Or bullets, for that matter? It looked as if it had been *made* of melted bullets.

Still crouched, its eyes on mine, the lion crept forward, step by slow step. We all held our breaths. Only the wind in the grass made any noise at all—I realized with a chill that the birds, a constant source of song in the Kalahari, had fallen silent. They knew something was awry here, that some unnatural thing had interrupted their ancient cycle.

I could feel the others tensing around me. Without moving a muscle, my gaze shifted to Sam. Sweat beaded his forehead, and the silver lion reflected in the dark discs of his eyes. He looked more entranced than afraid, and I thought of something my mom had said to me once, when I'd encountered a wild tiger in the jungles of India. I was six years old, and to me, all animals had been friends. When I strayed too close and the tiger went into an aggressive crouch, my mom had snatched me up in her arms and whispered into my ear, "The most beautiful things are often the most dangerous." She carried me away, walking backward in order to keep the tiger in her sight.

That tiger, in all its magisterial wildness, hadn't been nearly as beautiful as this extraordinary silver creature in front of me. And so, with my mother's voice hovering like a ghost by my ear, I knew it could very well be the most dangerous thing I had ever encountered.

"Steady," I whispered, as the lion drew within five yards of the truck and Miranda let out a soft cry.

The lion stopped so close to the back of the truck that I could have leaned down and stroked its silvery hide. This close, I could see each silver hair on its mane. The blank, burnished eyes stared at me unblinkingly.

"*Steady*," I said again, sensing the others beginning to shrink away.

The lion settled down, seeming to rest, but I could see the muscles bunching, rippling like mercury. The grass and sky reflected off the creature; if you weren't looking right at it, it would disappear as if made of living mirrors.

I held my breath. I couldn't exhale, couldn't look away, couldn't blink, because I knew, I knew it would happen but I didn't know what to do about it, couldn't stop it, couldn't *think*—

The silver lion sprang in an explosion of refracted light.

NINE

S creams erupted behind me. Everyone fell backward as the lion's claws seized the top of Hank's tailgate. The screech of claws tearing through metal seared the air.

I found myself tangled in everyone else and slipped, ending up wedged between the backseat and the tailgate. The lion's head lifted over the back of the truck as its rear paws found purchase on the bumper. Its fine, silvery whiskers twitched as it sniffed the air above me, and then it looked down and bared its fangs—shockingly, they were yellowish-white, normal teeth. I think it was the teeth more than anything that sent a jolt of fear down my spine. Before that, I hadn't categorized the lion as *real*, as if it might still be exposed as some kind of elaborate prank.

Suddenly someone grabbed me, pulled me up as the lion made a snap at my face. Its jaws closed on open air, but only just.

Sam had me by the shoulders and stood with one foot

braced on the tailgate, the other on the wall of the truck. Straining, he helped me over the backseat, out of the lion's reach.

Everyone else was in the front of the vehicle, screaming like maniacs. Sam and I clambered to join them. I slid into the driver's seat and twisted the key, gunning the engine.

I floored the gas pedal but though the engine roared, the wheels only dug themselves deeper. It was useless.

"It's coming!" Miranda screamed.

I looked over my shoulder to see the lion had made it into the truck; now it was climbing over the seats, intent on reaching us.

"Give me that shotgun!" I yelled to Joey, who was standing on it. He tossed it my way and I caught it, pumped the fore end—*chunk, chunk*—and fired, all in one swift motion.

I didn't like using the gun, but that didn't mean that I couldn't.

The buckshot ripped into the lion's shoulder, and even then, with only my shotgun standing between the raging animal and five human lives, I regretted it.

I didn't realize I was apologizing to the lion aloud until Sam yelled at me to stop and took my hand, pulling me out the door and onto the ground. I was barely able to grab my backpack off the seat and sling it over one shoulder.

We were running now. I struggled to keep up, because it felt wrong. Anyone who knew anything about the wild could tell you that when you encountered aggressive animals, the *last* thing you should do is run. I'd been charged by lions before, and each time, I stood my ground—heart pounding, my entire body shaking, my mouth dry—and the lions had swerved at the last minute and charged away into the bush.

But someone had rewritten the rules without my knowing it. They'd sent this twisted, unnatural creature after me and given me no guidelines for how to deal with it.

And so I ran, clutching Mom's shotgun to my chest and feeling like a soldier fleeing from battle. I threw aside all of my training and experience, all of the warnings of my dead mother and my missing father, and I ran.

Joey took the lead. He was fast. Not fast enough to outrun a lion, but that bullet had slowed it down. Sam had pulled me away before I'd been able to see the extent of the damage wreaked by my one frantic shot.

When I looked back, Hank's engine was still running, and I could see flashes of silver between the seats. If the lion was dying, it was taking its time about it, and I felt a small, guilty twinge of relief. Could we all walk away from this, lion included? Was that too much to ask? But my shot had been point-blank, and the silver hide of the lion had proved to be permeable. I'd half expected the animal to shatter like a busted mirror into metal shards all over the truck, but the silver had parted like, well, like *flesh*. I'd even seen a burst of scarlet blood from the wound.

So the lion was alive, at least in some way. It wasn't made of machinery; it had blood and teeth and it could be wounded. I noted these facts as if I were recording them in an observation journal for my dad to go over later.

If we stopped and went back to Hank, would the lion's carcass be lying in the truck? If so, I could attempt to glean some kind of understanding from it. I wondered what my dad, with all his years of zoology, would make of it, if he'd be as dumbfounded as I was.

We ran for only a mile or two before we all collapsed, gasping, onto the ground. I was delighted to hear birdsong once more and hoped that somehow all of this would turn out to be a mistake, that there was no metal lion and we'd been tricked.

"What . . ." gasped Avani, "was that *thing*?"

"Sarah shot it," said Sam. "It's dead, whatever it was."

I wasn't so sure, but I said nothing.

"Now what do we do?" asked Joey. "I'm not going back there."

"We have to," I replied. "All our gear is in the truck."

There was that and, if I was honest with myself, there was also the fact that I wanted another look at that lion if it was indeed dead.

"I'm going back," I announced. "You all stay here and wait for me."

"I want to come," said Sam. His eyes still held that glow of awe, and I knew he also wanted a chance to take a closer look at the creature.

"Fine," I said. "The rest of you stay here."

They didn't argue. Miranda and Kase didn't even look at me. They were folded into each other's arms, leaning against a dormant termite mound, their foreheads pressed together and eyes shut.

Sam and I backtracked in silence, until we came into view of the Cruiser and stopped.

"Do you see it?" he asked.

I shook my head and wished for the pair of binoculars I'd carried with me for nearly my entire life. They hadn't survived the fire at the camp.

"Let's get closer," I said, stepping forward, but at that

moment, Sam grabbed my arm and pulled me back.

"It's coming!" he said.

And there it was, yes, creeping out from under the Cruiser. I dropped to a crouch, as did Sam, hiding in the tall grass.

Sam pointed wordlessly off to the left, and I turned to see a stately male ostrich stalking into the riverbed. Its glossy black feathers ruffled in the breeze; it hadn't caught sight of the lion by the Cruiser. The lion's head turned only slightly and its ears cocked toward the giant bird.

Hidden as it was by the Cruiser, the lion had escaped the bird's notice. It crouched in the shadow of the truck and tensed, just as it had earlier. Then, in the blink of an eye, it sprang, light flashing off its haunches, and the ostrich didn't even have time to attempt to flee. It went down with a screech, sending up a cloud of feathers. The lion ripped its throat with its jaws, raked the body of the bird with its claws, and then—amazingly—walked away.

"It's not eating," I whispered. "Why would it do that, if it isn't hungry?"

Sam shrugged. "You're the expert, not me."

The lion stopped beside the Cruiser, sniffing the air, perhaps trying to pick up our scent. I studied its shoulder, trying to understand how it was still alive.

"I *did* shoot it, right?" I asked Sam. "I'm not crazy?"

"I saw it with my own eyes."

"But the lion . . ."

"I know." He looked as puzzled as I felt. The lion seemed entirely unwounded. The skin of its shoulder was smooth and seamless and gleaming, reflecting the savanna. It began violently tossing its mane, as if trying to shake off an invisible collar, and then it swatted its own face with massive silver paws. I tilted my head, watching and trying to understand, trying to read its behavior the way my parents had taught me. When the lion began crow hopping sideways, twisting its body and sending up long, agonized yowls, I sucked in sharply.

"It's like it's been driven mad," I said. "Look at it—it's out of its mind."

"Do you think it might have been normal once?" asked Sam. "That someone did *this*, whatever this is, to it?"

I shrugged. The lion rolled on its back, creating a cloud of dust and sand, and then flopped over, nose twitching in the air. Its head turned in our direction and chuffed.

"We should go back," I said. "It's tracking us."

"How can you tell?"

"It's searching for our scent and . . ." How could I explain a hunch? I knew only that it *would* follow us if it could, just as it had followed my dad and Theo and the poachers or whoever they were.

"Do you think you could shoot it again?" He nodded at the shotgun I still carried.

I shook my head. "If I missed, he'd be on us in a blink. Let's get away quietly."

Sam and I began to move backward slowly, taking care to make as little sound as possible. The lion continued to pad around the riverbed, uninterested in the dead ostrich. My body hummed with urgency, but I resisted the instinct to flee—it would only draw the lion's attention and anyway, it could outrun me in a heartbeat.

When we were out of sight of the lion, we straightened

and hurried faster, passing a young male kudu who fled at our approach, his spiraling horns flashing in the sun.

When we reached the others, they all jumped up and flocked around us.

"Is it dead?" asked Avani.

"Did it follow you here?" asked Joey.

"It's coming."

"Are you sure?"

"Let's go."

I began walking, not looking back to see if they were following. I felt as if my brain were a balloon floating above me, tugged along by my body but disconnected from the present. Nothing made sense anymore: Theo dead, Dad missing and possibly also dead, and now a lion of pure silver tracking us through the bush. It had the nonsensical quality of a dream.

"Sarah."

The voice floated around me, and though I heard it, it didn't register.

"Sarah!"

I stopped and turned, still feeling strangely detached. Sam was pointing behind us, his face solemn.

"It's coming," he said. "It's far behind us, but if you watch, you'll see the sun reflect off it."

I cursed and looked around for a tree or something to climb. There was a copse of *Terminalia* ahead on the top of a small rise.

"Come on," I said, breaking into a jog.

"It sees us!" shouted Avani. "It's running now!"

My heart pounding, I burst into a sprint, the others drawing even with me. I looked back, brushing aside my hair, and saw the lion skimming toward us, reflections of light and sky streaking over its metallic form.

"Faster!" I yelled, knowing it was useless if we didn't reach the trees before the lion reached us. I'd seen it take down the ostrich in a second. Would it go for all of us, or would it settle for just one? I glanced around and saw that Avani was the slowest. I reached out a hand and she took it, and I pulled her along.

"Thanks," she gasped.

Suddenly Joey, who was in the lead, cried out and skidded to a halt, his arms pinwheeling. "Stop!" he yelled. He spun around and threw out an arm to shove Miranda to the ground, and Kase toppled over her, both of them shouting in anger at Joey.

I stumbled and stopped, dropping Avani's hand. Sam fell to his knees beside me, bent over and panting.

"What is it?" he gasped out.

I didn't reply; I was too stunned by what I saw.

It was a crack in the ground, a long, narrow chasm that split the earth like buckled cement. It didn't seem very deep—maybe four feet at most, and it was filled with sand.

"Is it supposed to be like that?" asked Miranda.

"No." What was going on out here? First the lion—now this random split in the earth's crust?

"Then what—"

"Just *run!*" said Sam. "It's almost here!"

I whirled to see the lion bounding toward us, and at any other time I could have stared in wonder at the beauty of the metal creature, but now was definitely *not* that time. I jumped across the crack and landed in a crouch on the other side—only to feel the ground beneath me shudder. *What the—?*

"Wait!" I yelled, throwing up a hand, but it was too late. Everyone jumped across the crack and landed beside me— and the ground shuddered again.

"You guys feel that?" asked Joey.

Then the sand slid around my ankles, poured into the chasm. I stood up slowly, my arms spread for balance. It felt like an earthquake.

I turned to see the lion crouched on the other side of the chasm, all silver and light, and then it leaped straight for me. I yelled and fumbled with the shotgun, knowing it was already too late—and then the earth vanished beneath me, collapsing as if we'd been standing on top of an aardvark's tunnel, only much, *much* bigger.

We fell into the widening chasm, sand pouring around us like white rain. The lion sailed overhead and landed on the ground on the far side; I caught just a brief glimpse of it as I dropped like Alice down the rabbit hole.

Screams echoed around me, but I was silent, the air frozen in my lungs from sheer disbelief. The sky shrank to a strip of blue and then, totally unexpectedly, I slammed into deep water.

Stunned and disoriented, I sank into dark depths, seeing stars and bubbles rise around me. Then I began to kick out, pushing for the surface. The sounds of the others' screams had cut off, interrupted by loud splashes. I hoped desperately that they could all swim. Despite my furiously kicking legs, I found myself sinking, pulled down by the weight of my pack. I wriggled it off my shoulders and let it go; it disappeared into the dark murky water along with my mom's shotgun, which I'd lost when I hit the water. Freed of the backpack, I was able to swim.

When I broke the surface, I gasped and looked up. We'd fallen probably fifty feet into a huge underground reservoir of freshwater. The sides of the narrow chasm pitched upward at a slant; the opening above was much smaller than the space below. This had been a hidden cavern for centuries, perhaps millennia, and I was certain that it would have taken more than just the weight of six teenagers to crack its roof.

The lion's face hovered over the edge, and I wondered for a moment if it would jump down. But then it lifted and turned, and I saw one flick of the silver tail as it walked away.

One by one, the heads of the rest of the group popped out of the water. I counted, my heart stopping when I reached only four.

"Where's Avani?"

Everyone was coughing and spitting out water, but they immediately began looking around. Sam dove under, as did Joey. I turned in a circle, treading water that sparkled in the sunlight. Undulating patterns reflected off the delicate calcite deposits above us.

"Avani?" I called. "Avani!" Our voices echoed eerily off the cavern walls as we called for her.

Suddenly Joey's head lifted out of the water. "I've got her!"

He had Avani in his arms, and she gasped and sputtered, her eyes shut. "I think she's okay," he said. "Just stunned. Hey, Canada? You okay?"

Avani's eyes shot open into huge circles, and she clung to Joey so tightly that he nearly went under.

"I can't breathe!" she screamed. "I can't breathe, I can't breathe, I can't *breathe!*" She half sobbed, half choked, and clawed desperately at Joey like a cat climbing a tree. He spluttered and struggled to keep them both afloat. In two strokes, Sam reached them and helped support Avani from the other side.

"Avani, calm down!" he said. "Look at me! Meet my eyes."

She was trembling so violently that she seemed to have trouble focusing on him.

"Panic attack," said Kase grimly. "My sister gets them sometimes."

"I c-c-can't breathe," Avani stammered to Sam.

"Yes, you can," said Sam calmly. "You're breathing right now. Listen. In, and out. In, and out."

I treaded water, at a loss, as Sam coached Avani, his voice low and soothing, the way I would talk to a frightened, wounded animal. My skills ended at practical survival techniques. When it came to dealing with people, I was as comfortable as a fish on dry land. I watched with no small amount of awe as he successfully calmed Avani. Her eyes had fixed on his with single-minded attention, and she soon settled down.

"We're going to be okay," said Sam. "We're going to get out of here. But we need your help. We need the Avani who always has the answers, okay?"

Avani nodded and drew a shuddering breath.

"Maybe you can tell us what all this water's doing down here, huh? I thought this was a desert."

"*Semi*desert," said Avani, her voice weak. "The Kalahari is sitting on top of a vast underground water system; you could drill almost anywhere here and find it."

Sam smiled and turned to me. "I think she'll be fine."

It's sort of cruel, really—so much water placed just out of reach in a land that is almost completely dry. This cavern had to be linked to the massive cave systems that begin in Namibia, many of which are still unexplored. I once went with my mom to the Dragon's Breath Cave, which releases humid air that makes it look as if some subterranean monster below is exhaling. We'd rappelled down walls as steep as these to look at the white, blind catfish teeming in the lake.

I'd known that in theory, these underground lakes existed, but they'd been unreachable except through the boreholes and wells scattered throughout the region. The question wasn't how this place existed, but rather how had we found it? What had weakened the crust of earth above, making it give way at our weight?

And even more important—how were we going to get out?

I think the others had reached the same question, because their eyes were round and terrified, just as mine were, I was sure.

"Sarah?" Sam said softly, his voice still filled with the faux hopefulness that had calmed Avani.

I gave him what I hoped was a steady, confident look. "It's okay. We can get out of this. We just have to . . ." What? Climb? Impossible. The walls of the cavern bent over us at such an angle that we'd have to climb nearly upside down. We were in no condition for that; even an experienced mountain climber would shirk at the sight.

"Swim around," I said. "Spread out and look for a way out. But be careful. Conserve your energy. No unnecessary movement, got it? Sam, keep Avani with you."

He nodded.

"Well, hey," said Joey, grinning, "at least we've got plenty of water now." To illustrate, he scooped up a mouthful and swallowed it with apparent relish.

I tried to smile in return, to keep the mood hopeful, but my lips betrayed me. The water did taste wonderful, though, and I swallowed several mouthfuls, feeling instant relief as it poured through me. Then I turned away and began swimming toward the shadows at the edge of the cavern. I kept my darkest fear to myself: that in the middle of one of the world's largest deserts, we could very well drown.

TEN

The cold water left my legs and hands numb, and the sound of my chattering teeth echoed off the cavern walls. I'd explored a good portion of the cave's perimeter, finding no places where we could climb out, and I didn't even come close to finding the bottom. From what I knew of underground lakes like this one, the bottom could be three hundred feet deep or more. The thought was even more chilling than the temperature.

My arms and legs ached as I stroked back to the place we'd fallen through. How much longer could I do this? I was in better shape than everyone else, so I knew they had to be struggling.

As if drawn by one mind, the others moved to meet me beneath the circle of sunlight. I turned my face toward the light, feeling its warmth. Sam was there, Avani beside him still looking dazed and terrified, and Joey quickly joined us.

"Where are Kase and Miranda?" I asked.

"Probably making out," said Joey.

"No, really—where are they?" My heart leaped in panic. Had we lost them? Had they drowned already?

"Kase!" I called. "Miranda!"

But for the rippling water and my own echoes, silence.

"Spread out," I said wearily. "Search for them."

Everyone's faces displayed the one thought we dared not speak aloud: that Kase and Miranda had sunk beneath the surface. I don't think any of us was ready to accept that answer, though, because it could only mean that we each had a timer hanging over our heads, and that our seconds were almost up.

We made it just a few yards away from one another when I heard a shout.

"Over here!"

The voice was fragile and distorted, but I pinpointed its location and waved to the others. Together we swam toward it, leaving the light behind.

"Kase," said Sam. "That way."

"Hurry, guys!" Kase said, his voice growing stronger as we neared.

He and Miranda were treading water, only the whites of their eyes visible in the gloom.

"We found something," said Miranda, sounding exhausted. "This way."

My heart lifting despite my better judgment, I followed them as they swam deeper into the darkness.

"What is it?" asked Avani. "God, let it be a ladder."

"Close," said Kase. "Maybe close enough."

I didn't know they'd stopped until I bumped into Kase, and then I felt Joey bump into me.

"Reach out," said Kase, taking my hand and lifting it into the dark.

My fingers brushed metal and instinctively closed around it: it was a beam of some kind, cold and smooth. I heard the others murmur as they felt it.

"It goes up," I said. I explored with my hands, utterly blind. The beams were arranged like a scaffold, about three feet wide and enclosing a pipe about as thick as my torso.

"An old borehole, maybe," I said, though I was doubtful. The metal should feel rusty or corroded by the minerals in the water, shouldn't it? This didn't seem old, not by the texture of it, and its construction was different. But I wasn't about to question it—any way out would do.

"We might as well climb it," I said. "See where it goes."

"I can't!" It was Avani's voice that rang out in the darkness, and I could hear the panic creeping back into her breathing. "It's too dark, and the water . . . please, let's find another way out!"

I heard a few noises of exasperation from the others. Avani's breathing was punctuated by tiny whimpers, and I feared she was close to a full-on panic attack.

"I don't think we're going to find a better option," I said. "You can do this, Avani."

"But—"

"You can do it, Avani. We'll all climb together. Just—"

"I can't! I can't!"

"Please, Avani!" Despite my efforts, my tone was sharpening as my frustration eroded my patience. "Would you just—"

"We're going to drown!" Avani wailed.

"Oh, for God's sake!" Miranda snapped. "If *I* can do it,

anyone can! Start climbing or I swear I'll drown you myself!"

"Hey!" Sam's voice reverberated off the walls. "Look, it's not that bad. We'll go slowly and stay close together. Avani, here—take my hand. Got it? Good. I'll be right here, every step, okay?"

"O-okay," Avani replied softly.

"Breathe, remember? In-two-three-four, out-two-three four."

I took the lead, leaving Avani in Sam's care once more. Using nothing but my sense of touch to guide me, I clambered up the metal bars and bit down on my tongue to keep my teeth from grinding together. Splashes and grunts echoed around me as the others fumbled with the bars, trying to climb in utter darkness.

"It's easier if you close your eyes," said Kase. "Feel the way."

"You do this often?" asked Avani, her voice tight. I could tell that even with Sam beside her, she was barely keeping a lid on the hysterics.

"We spent some time spelunking in Mexico two years ago," he said.

"Oh." I could hear the surprise in her voice, and maybe even a little respect.

We climbed in silence then, using all our energy to scale the configuration of metal beams. About twenty feet up, the cave walls began to loom in on us, and we had to wriggle through the beams and climb inside the scaffold, our backs pressed against the pipe. I could feel the pressure of the narrow space closing in on me like a vise, and I had to remind myself to breathe. Below me, I heard a muffled curse followed by a splash.

"Everyone okay?" I called down.

"My camera!" Kase called, his tone high with panic. "It was slung over my shoulder, but it just dropped!"

"Keep climbing, dude," said Joey. "It's gone."

"I have to go back down!" said Kase.

His declaration was met with a chorus of protests.

"We're all below you!" Avani growled. "My arms are shaking as it is! I'm not climbing all the way back down for your stupid camera."

"*Guys*," I said levelly, trying to keep them cool. This was not an ideal time to panic, but the tension of the tight space and the absolute darkness was like a corrosive acid, eating away at our spirits. "We have to keep climbing, Kase. I'm sorry."

Besides a low snarl of frustration, he stayed silent.

We climbed for what seemed an eternity. I'd worked out the pattern of the beams and was moving more quickly now, one limb at a time, reminding myself not to rush. To fall at this point would be deadly, and I'd take out whoever was below me in the process.

Eventually my head struck what felt like concrete, and I yelped.

"What happened?"

"Are you okay?"

"*Don't* fall on my head!"

"I'm fine," I said. "I found the top. I think it's some kind of cover. Hang on."

Bracing my feet on the slippery beams, I ran my hands along the concrete overhead, then caught my breath when they touched a metal hatch. I found a handle and gripped it tight.

"Here goes," I said. "Cross your fingers."

With all my strength, I pushed upward. My arms were shaking and my feet began to slip, and I cried out and let go to grab the beams before I lost my footing.

"Someone else will have to help," I said.

"I'm here," said Kase.

I felt his hand groping the darkness, and I grabbed it and placed it on the metal cover.

"Got it?"

"Yeah."

"One, two, *three*."

We pushed up until I thought my head would explode from the effort—and then, with a groan of its hinges, the lid began to lift. Light shot through the cracks and I nearly fell again when it blinded me, but I gritted my teeth and forced myself to hang on.

It swung open with a crash, and I looked down to see the rest of the group groaning and blinking against the assault of sunlight.

I climbed up and offered a hand to Kase, and together we hauled everyone else out of the hole. I couldn't even see the lake below, it was so far, only an inky depth.

Once everyone was out, I looked around.

We were sitting on a concrete box built around the top of the pipe, which had made a turn just below the hatch and ran into a large pump set on metal rails over the ground.

"What is this place?" breathed Sam.

I had no idea. It was a complex of some sort: several low, windowless buildings; a few collapsed tents; and what looked like earth-boring machines—hulking cranes with long, twisting drills. The buildings were made of the whitewashed, adobe-style construction common in Botswana, except these buildings had solar panels attached to their thatch roofs and massive generators lining their exteriors. Whoever was here, they needed a lot of electricity.

I saw no vehicles and no people, which was odd. No one would go to the trouble of building this place only to abandon it—the solar panels alone were worth a small fortune. Nor had it been sitting long, or the panels would have been stolen by now.

What was this place? Why had I never heard of it? I thought I knew every village, every airstrip, every abandoned hut in the central Kalahari.

There were signs that this place hadn't been here long— maybe no more than two years. Still, word traveled fast in Botswana, particularly between those of us out in the wilderness. We had to know who our neighbors were, because we never knew when our lives might depend on them or when we'd need to alert them if a bushfire sprang up. Surely Matthieu had heard of this place or at least seen it from the air, but he'd never mentioned it to us.

I sighed and stood up, my exhaustion weighing on me. We were all dripping wet, but it wouldn't be long before the dry air sucked all the moisture from our clothes. I pulled the dream catcher from my pocket and held it on my palm to let it dry out; the feathers were bedraggled and pathetic looking, but it was the only real possession I had left.

Kase began cursing and kicking the ground, sending up small whirlwinds of dust. I looked over in alarm and asked what was wrong. His head reared up and he gave me a wild glare.

"My *camera*, that's what's wrong! It's still down there!" He pointed down the hatch.

"So's my phone," Miranda wailed. "All my music is on it!"

They stared at me with their eyebrows slanting angrily. I looked from one to the other, then caught on.

"You want me to go back down there?" I asked in disbelief.

Kase's eyes slid haughtily away. "Well, unless you want to replace six thousand dollars worth of equipment . . ."

"No one's going back down there," said Sam. "Dude, it's ruined anyway."

"No, it was *waterproof*."

"My phone wasn't!" Miranda cried.

My temples throbbed painfully and I pressed my fingers to them, wincing. "I'm sorry about your camera and phone, really! My backpack is down there too, with my—"

"Did your backpack cost *six thousand dollars*?" Kase asked. "You dragged us out here with nothing to eat, nothing to drink, no tents, no gear, and now you want me to give up *this*?"

That did it. "*Everything* I *own* has been destroyed! My friend is dead, my dad is missing, and every possession I had is gone! So excuse me if I don't exactly feel sorry about your cameras and phones!"

His mouth clapped shut, while the others watched in dead silence. Miranda took Kase's arm and pulled him back, whispering in his ear. I let out a heavy sigh and pulled the band out of my hair, letting it fall loose and dripping. I twisted it between my hands, squeezing out the excess water. The movements calmed me a little.

"Sorry," I said.

"Don't be," said Avani. "You're right. You've lost more than we can imagine, and we haven't even asked how you're doing."

I slowly tied my hair back into its usual low ponytail. "It's just things," I said hollowly. "They can be replaced. I just want to find my dad." I looked toward the building. "Let's see if anyone's here. At the least, there might be something to eat."

Everyone brightened at that, except for Kase, who was either ashamed or still angry, judging by his red complexion. We trudged to the nearest building. The door was cracked and creaked ominously when I opened it.

Inside was a laboratory. What exactly it was for I didn't know—but the place was unmistakably some kind of high-tech research facility. Long, low counters were cluttered with beakers, microscopes, computers, minifridges, and cabinets. The room looked as if it had been evacuated while everyone was in the middle of their work: Vials had tipped over, spilling liquid onto the counters. A Bunsen burner was still going in the corner, though it had to be nearly out of fuel. One of the minifridges was hanging open, and the samples inside— collected in neatly labeled plastic and glass containers— smelled spoiled. Whoever had been here, they had left in a hurry. The lights were even still on, one of them flickering and popping. But most noticeable of all was the heavy odor of smoke that soon had us coughing and our eyes watering. I quickly found the source of the smell—several metal wastebaskets filled with ash.

"What do you think happened?" asked Sam.

"Looks like paper, mostly, and computer parts." I picked up a scalpel from one of the tables and stirred it through the ash, revealing melted microchips and bits of paper that weren't entirely burned.

"They were destroying the evidence," said Joey.

"What?"

"Oh, come on. You've seen *CSI!*"

I gave him a blank look, and he sighed. "Right, you're probably more of an Animal Planet type. Look around. There are no notes, none of the computers work, these bins are full of ash. They were burning their research. Getting rid of it."

"Until something interrupted them," said Avani thoughtfully. She was recovering quickly from her panic in the lake and had been mostly quiet since we had surfaced. "This isn't cheap equipment. Strange to leave it like this." She picked up a microscope that had fallen on the floor and placed it respectfully on a table.

I studied the room more closely. Joey was right. Anything that might have held notes, research documents, or data had been burned. I knew enough about research to know you recorded everything; our camp was—*had* been—flooded with notebooks and lists and loose papers. Whatever was being researched here, apparently someone had taken pains to hide it. And I suspected Avani was right, and that they'd been interrupted before they could finish the job.

"Did you know them?" asked Sam.

I shook my head. "That's what bothers me most. If they were out here doing research, they'd have surely sought us out. We know this area better than anyone around—so why hide from us?"

Because they were certainly hiding. I didn't doubt that for a minute. I also knew that everything that had happened to us in the past few days was somehow linked to this place: my dad, the lion, the poachers.

I turned to the others. They were all staring at me, as if waiting for an explanation.

"Look around," I said. "We might find a clue about my dad, or that lion, or *something*. They left in a hurry, so they might not have had time to burn everything."

Everyone seemed reluctant to touch things, but they spread out and began opening cabinets, looking through the samples in the fridges, and sorting through the detritus on the floor. There wasn't much to be gleaned from broken glass and dusty microscopes. I tried to focus on anything that seemed out of place or missing. I stood still and let my eyes rove the room, considering each detail.

"It looks like they were studying rocks," I said.

"I'm getting the same thing," said Avani. "Look at these." She dumped over a box filled with rough, porous stones.

"There are no rocks in the Kalahari," I said.

"Yes, but did you see those big drills outside? They dug them up from beneath the sand. This was some kind of geology project."

I nodded. "If they created a weak point by drilling, fissures could spread out from it and weaken the crust over the caverns. But what were they looking for? Water?"

Avani tapped her lip thoughtfully and picked up the empty box. Then she slammed a finger onto a small scribble on the side. "Look! W!"

I gave her a blank look.

Avani sighed and pointed aggressively at the page. "W! It's the atomic symbol for tungsten. They were gathering samples of it." She began moving around the lab, setting up microscopes and digging through boxes. The rest of us watched, dumbfounded but hopeful that she'd somehow find meaning hidden in the chaos. After a minute, she stopped and looked at us. "What are you doing just standing there? Look around! There have to be more clues."

Thus bidden, we began a methodical search of the lab, finding more rock samples but little else of significance.

"Whoever they were, they haven't been gone long," Avani noted. "There's hardly any dust on the counters and the mini-fridges are still cool, even though they were unplugged. This place was trashed two, maybe three days ago, I'd guess."

"Right around when my dad disappeared," I murmured.

"What confuses me—among everything else," said Avani, "is why scientists would destroy what was obviously a pretty expensive, well-established project like this one? It looks like they'd been here awhile; I mean, this place doesn't look brand-new. No matter what they were working on, even if it was illegal or dangerous, they wouldn't just burn everything. I'm not saying they'd be publishing their work all over the place, but at the least they'd save their notes."

"Maybe they did. Maybe they took stuff with them," I suggested.

"Or maybe it wasn't them who did this," she returned. "Maybe someone else deliberately destroyed their research."

"Then where are the scientists now?"

She shrugged. "We're just guessing in the dark, really."

"We should search the other buildings," I sighed. "Maybe they didn't have time to sweep them all."

"Or we could just *leave*," voiced Miranda. "Why do we

care what this place is? It's creepy!"

"If this place is linked to that lion we saw or my dad's disappearance, then I want to figure out why. Anyway, they might have a radio or a phone we could use to call for help."

The ordeal was almost over, at least for the group. I still had to find Dad, but with the help of some soldiers or police and a plane, I didn't doubt that we'd find him soon. My only worry now was what state he would be in when we did find him. *Please, just let him be alive.*

Everyone split up to explore different buildings. I headed for the one farthest away, which was about as large as two trailers placed end to end. I made it only halfway before I heard a scream. I immediately ran toward the building it had come from—the middle one—reaching the door at the same time as Sam and Joey.

Inside, we found Miranda on her knees, her face white and eyes stretched wide, her lips open in horror.

ELEVEN

The walls were lined with cages. Inside were the bodies of animals, most of them dead, and from the look of them, they'd been shot point-blank. Monkeys, squirrels, meerkats, smaller felines like caracals, lynx, servals, and more—almost every mammalian species of the Kalahari was represented, with the exception of the bigger animals like zebra and kudu. The stench was overpowering. I leaned over, my hands on my knees, retching. Toward the back of the room, hidden in the reeking shadows, the still-living animals screeched and howled and rattled their cages, raising a hellish racket. I didn't know which was worse: the stink or the sound.

Sam opened the door to let fresh air in, but it wasn't nearly enough. Kase helped Miranda to her feet and took her outside; she was sobbing. I heard Joey go after them, muttering, "I can't, I just *can't*. . . ." I could barely hear him over the racket.

"Sarah," said Sam. "Come on. There's nothing here."

I shook my head. I was a zoologist—or practically was one.

I didn't flinch at death, though it always turned my stomach. I'd seen a lot: piles of elephants slain for their ivory; dead rhinos poached for their horns; colonies of birds poisoned by polluted water; entire ecosystems thrown out of sync because of human waste, deforestation, and greed.

This was one of the most horrifying things I'd ever seen.

"You go," I managed to choke out to Sam. "I'll look around."

He stayed with me anyway, though he looked ill. Together we walked down the aisle separating the cages, and I held my collar over my mouth and nose to try to block out some of the stink.

"*Sarah.*"

"What?"

Sam was a few steps ahead of me and he wordlessly pointed. About halfway down the aisle, the animals began to turn silver in varying degrees. Some of them were half-normal and half-covered in a metallic sheen. One baboon had silver hands while the rest of him was brown fur; he'd been shot like the others. At the very far end of the horrible room we found the animals that were still alive, as if whoever had come in here to execute them had been interrupted before he or she could finish the job.

These last animals were entirely silver.

They looked like the lion, and some of them had died not from a bullet, it seemed, but from fits of madness, judging by the state they were in. There was a silver owl whose cage was littered with shining metallic feathers after it had beat itself against the bars. The animals who were still living reminded me of the lion, how they shook themselves and scratched and yowled and chattered and screamed as only animals can.

I didn't realize how close I was to fainting until Sam put his hand on my back to support me.

"It's some kind of infection," I said. "Some kind of disease."

"Have you ever seen anything like it?"

"Nothing even close. Who would do this? And *why?*"

"Look," he said, pointing to the largest cage. The door was hanging at a crazy angle, as if it had been ripped open. Silver hairs mixed with tawny ones were scattered around it. I bent to inspect the tracks in the dust on the floor.

"The lion," I said. "He must have escaped and chased away whoever did this."

"Maybe he chased away *all* of them."

My mind raced like a mouse in a maze, turning corners, hitting dead ends, doubling back, and struggling to find sense amid this nightmare. "Henrico said someone had reported poachers chasing a white lion," I said slowly. "So suppose instead, it was these scientists chasing the *silver* lion. They were in the middle of destroying their research—which includes these poor animals—when the lion escaped. They knew they had to capture or kill it before someone saw it. So they went after the escaped lion and instead they found my dad and Theo." The pieces began to fall together now, like a line of toppling dominoes. "After they found Dad and Theo, they found our camp and realized there were more of us."

"So now they're out looking for us," said Sam. "We're loose ends."

"Right."

"But obviously they're not finished here," he said, gesturing at the cages. "There's still more to clean up. . . ."

I met his gaze and saw my own horror mirrored in his eyes. "Sooner or later, they're coming back," I whispered. "To finish the job."

"We should hurry," he said gravely.

I nodded.

Sam sighed and scraped his fingers through his hair, then turned and slowly surveyed the room. I looked down to my left to see a porcupine scratching at the metal mesh of its cage, its quills as silver and gleaming as giant sewing needles. I knelt and—keeping my distance—looked at the pitiful creature with tears beginning to well in my eyes.

"Why would they do this to you?" I whispered. "I am so sorry."

I felt almost ashamed to be human at that moment, to look so closely at the pain that my species had caused its fellow creatures. Ashamed . . . and outraged. I wiped away my tears with the inside of my wrists and stood up.

"Sarah."

The edge to Sam's tone caught my full attention. I turned away from the cage and looked to the corner on the opposite wall, where Sam was staring. There was a body, a young Indian man slumped against the wall, his eyes open and his face frozen in a rictus of pain. He wore a lab coat and latex gloves, so I guessed he was one of the researchers. The wounds on his chest and neck spoke plainly of how he had died.

"The lion," I said grimly. Sam had his hand over his mouth, and he turned away, nodding his head.

There was a revolver locked in the man's hand. So he'd been the one putting the animals down, before the lion broke loose and killed him. Where were his colleagues, that they'd left him like this? He hadn't been dead long, but surely someone would have come back for him by now. I knew I should feel angry at him for what I was seeing, for the horrors this building contained, but I could only look at him with pity.

Whatever the metal substance was, it had infected these creatures—and it looked as if it had spread, cage to cage, from one end of the room. If the animals hadn't been killed, would it have spread all the way? Was that why the dead scientist had been shooting them, one by one?

"It's contagious," I whispered, and Sam nodded.

"Let's go," he said.

This time I didn't argue. I'd seen more than I could stomach already, and as soon as we stepped into the sunlight, I hit the ground, retching violently, but nothing except water came up.

I stared at my hands, trembling in the sand. Were we already infected? How did it spread? Had I killed us all by leading us here? Was there a cure? My head spun with questions until I could barely see straight.

I turned to smile weakly at Sam, who looked as sick as I felt. "Some trip, huh? Bet you wish you'd never left the States."

He seemed to mull that over, then said softly, "No. I don't."

"Guys!" Joey was standing at the next building, waving for us. "Over here!"

Great, now what? I couldn't possibly bear to see more infected, massacred animals or dead scientists. I reluctantly stood up and followed Sam to the next building.

"What is it?" I asked warily.

Joey opened the door and pointed inside. "There's food in here!" He whooped joyously and disappeared indoors.

This building was similar to the first, except that it was divided into rooms by curtains that hung from the ceiling. Miranda and Kase were sitting on two chairs in a small kitchenette, wolfing down a pack of vanilla crème cookies. The food made my stomach growl, but my curiosity was stronger than my hunger, and there was no way I could eat after what I had just seen.

"So the building with the animals," I said, "it's worse than we thought. Remember the lion?"

"No," said Miranda flatly. "I'd completely *forgotten* about the horrible metal beast that tried to eat me. Wait." She put down her cookie. "Oh, *God*, you mean . . ."

I nodded. "Many of them are silver, some covered more than the others. Like it's a disease or a rash."

Miranda looked at her cookie as if it had transformed into a spider and quickly set it down.

"Do you think we could be affected?" Joey asked softly. Everyone's eyes turned to me with such horror that I flinched.

"I doubt it," I said, more casually than I felt. "We've barely been here fifteen minutes."

Avani gave me a knowing look, seeing right through my flimsy deflection. I tried to signal her with a small flick of my eyes to go along with it, to soothe their fear.

Too late. "We've been breathing this *air* for fifteen minutes. If it's airborne, we're already infected," she pointed out.

"I did *not* sign up for this freak show!" Kase shouted. He stood abruptly, his chair sliding backward with a spine-chilling shriek. Miranda emitted a pitiful moan and lowered her face into her hands.

"Stop it!" I ordered. "Just *chill*, okay? Look, the animals may have been infected, but there's no reason to believe the—whatever it is—can affect humans. The men I saw back at our camp were just fine—none of them were, um, silver. So let's just all chill. Please?"

Miranda whimpered. "I want to go home."

"We all do," Sam said softly. "But Sarah's right. We need to stay calm and not invent worries that might not come up."

"Did anyone find a radio? A phone? Anything?" I asked.

"No, but we found doughnuts!" Joey said. "They're a little stale, but hey, I wouldn't say no to moldy bread at this point."

Avani had found a closet stocked with food: crackers, canned vegetables, instant soup, even a box of Twinkies. At the sight of it all, my stomach gurgled. Trying to put the dead and infected animals from my mind, I forced myself to eat some crackers, knowing my body needed nourishment. We ate and packed at the same time, filling plastic bags with bottled water and as much nonperishable food as we could carry. I found a crate of emergency supplies, including candles, matchsticks, and a black flare gun. I tossed some of the stuff in with the food, but turned the flare gun over in my hands thoughtfully before tucking it into the back of my pants.

Joey opened a large freezer and dug around inside, loudly expressing his disappointment that there was no ice cream. Then he paused and picked up a large plastic container. He studied it for a moment, then said, "Uh . . . Guys? Is this what I think it is?"

Sam took a look, then gave a low whistle. "Bees?"

"Sickos," Joey muttered. "What do they do—sprinkle them on their cereal?"

"This is a scientific facility, you idiots," said Avani. "They're probably just specimens. My biology teacher kept frogs and fetal pigs and stuff in her fridge at home when the power went out at the school one week."

"Let me see that," I said.

"Prefer bugs over Twinkies, huh?" Joey asked, handing over the container with a shudder. "I should have guessed. Talk about Girl vs. Wild. Do you eat grasshoppers too?"

I studied the contents of the container. It held a partially intact hive filled with golden honeycombs. Dozens of frozen bees littered the bottom, but I spied more deeper inside the combs. I held the box to my ear and listened, catching a faint buzz. The insects in the combs were still alive, generating enough heat to survive by huddling and vibrating against one another. I'd seen hives like this before, in the cold winter months, when I was out doing fieldwork with my mom. The bees fed off their honey reserves until spring, withstanding temperatures below freezing.

The hunger in my stomach turned to a cold lump as my thoughts strayed inevitably to my mother. Of all the things to have in their freezer, why did the scientists have *bees*?

"Sarah?" Sam paused, his hands full of canned Spam. "What is it?"

I looked up at him, startled out of my reverie, and murmured, "It's nothing."

Hastily putting the bees back into the freezer, I gave Sam a worried look. "We need to scout every building and then get out of here," I said. "The scientists could be back at any moment, and I don't think we want to be here for that."

Miranda lifted her head and spoke around a mouthful of

peanut butter. "You don't seriously think they'll just show up and start shooting at us?"

I gaped at her, wondering if she'd completely forgotten about Theo.

"I think that's exactly what they'll do," said Sam. "Sarah's right."

Joey snorted. "Aw, dude, you're just agreeing with her because you want—"

"I'm just *saying*," Sam interjected hurriedly, "that we should play it safe. We've already seen people killed in this mess."

"Yeah," said Miranda, "but no offense, Sarah, your dad and your friend did go *looking* for these guys. They kind of asked for it. And if they hadn't, none of this would have happened."

My eyes nearly bugged out of my head, and I didn't realize I'd stepped toward her, my fists clenching, until Sam interrupted.

"She just lost her *friend*, Miranda," he said. "Leave her alone."

"I don't need your help here," I snapped at him, while at the same time, Kase bristled and pointed at Sam.

"Dude. Don't talk to my girlfriend like that," Kase snarled.

Sam held up his hands defensively. "I'm just saying, we need to work together instead of blaming each other."

"Who are you to tell us what to do? You're nothing but a charity case delinquent."

Now Sam's face flushed and his tone dropped below freezing. "What did you call me?"

"Yeah," said Kase, lifting his chin. He had the same look in his eye as I'd seen in a bull elephant squaring off for a fight.

"That's right, Quartermain. You didn't think I'd come out here without knowing who was going to be around, did you? My lawyer checked up on all of you. I've been watching *you* since day one."

Sam's lips curled inward. "You don't know anything about me!"

"Whoa, okay!" Avani held up both hands, palms out. The tension in the room was stifling. "Why don't we make a plan, huh? Let's look at this logically. I think what we have here is a communication problem. We need to delineate responsibilities and identify our priorities—"

"I swear, Avani, you and your SAT mouth make me want to gouge my own eyes out," growled Miranda.

From there, we descended into chaos. Everyone was on their feet, hurling accusations, complaints, and insults like a troop of mudslinging baboons. Sam and Kase were nose to nose and seething, and Avani was holding a frying pan, looking dangerously close to whacking someone with it. I grabbed a spoon and a metal teakettle and began clanging them together until everyone fell silent, their hands on their ears.

"Enough!" I said. "This is ridiculous! We should be focusing on getting out of here, not fighting with each other! If we keep this up, we'll be dead before the end of the week!"

At that, they fell reluctantly silent but still exchanged heated looks—many of them directed at me.

Then Miranda's eyes filled with tears. "Do you really think we're going to die?"

I sighed and put down the kettle. "I'm just saying that we need to work together. *Please.* I'm trying my hardest, I really am, but I need your help. We have food and water now, see?

We're going to be fine. We just have to keep our heads."

Avani nodded, looking abashed. "Sorry, guys. I don't mean to be a know-it-all. I just want to help."

"We all do," I said. I took a deep breath and tried to get us back on track. "What's back there?" I peered down a corridor between the dark curtains that partitioned off the long building.

"Looks like dorms," said Joey. "Beds and stuff. Be my guest." He waved at the corridor.

Leaving the others to cool down, I went into the first little room and found a sturdy cot topped with an air mattress. A plastic drawer set yielded an assortment of men's clothing and toiletries. On top of it sat a framed photograph. My stomach twisted when I recognized the young man in the photo as the same one Sam and I had found in the menagerie. In the photo, he was hugging an older Indian woman who may have been his mother.

A quick survey of the rest of the rooms settled my suspicion that the scientists were still currently in residence of this place, even though they were nowhere to be found. They'd left behind clothes, shoes, shampoo bottles, contact lens cases, even a pair of expensive-looking earrings. Were they the ones out searching for us, then? From the contents of each room, I gathered that there had been three men and two women working here. There had been more people than that at our camp, so if any of them had been the scientists, they had backup. Any notebooks, computers, or other sources of information had either been taken or destroyed with the stuff in the lab. Besides the one photograph, there were no clues as to the identities of the researchers.

At the far end of the building, I found a door to the outside. A beaten track led to a small trailer nearby, and I noticed with a chill up my spine that the footprints on the track were very fresh, made as recently as that morning. I waited, still in the doorway, watching and listening for any sign of people, but it seemed clear. I didn't see any prints from our group, so no one had explored the trailer yet. It was the last place a radio or phone could be, so I had to check it out. I walked slowly toward it, alert for any sign of trouble.

The door to the trailer opened with a creak, and I froze for a long moment in dread, my hand wrapping around the flare gun in the back of my waistband, but nothing happened. Cautiously, I stepped inside and pulled the door shut.

Another lab. Unlike the others, this one seemed to be currently in use. A long counter held liquid in beakers, computer screens running streams of data, vials dripping substances into other vials. I tensed, listening carefully for any sound that might signal someone was here, but the only noise came from the experiments percolating, bubbling, and beeping. I'd have to get Avani in here to interpret the scene. The chemistry equipment made about as much sense to me as Joey's pop culture references.

I went to the computer and tried to find some means of communication, but I got only a flurry of windows streaming numbers and formulas. A dead end. So I yanked open the drawers below the counter, one by one, finding nothing of use—until I was interrupted by a loud thump.

I whirled to face a door that led to another room in the trailer, but it stayed shut. Certain that was where the noise had come from, I armed myself with a scalpel snatched off the counter and slowly crept to the door, the hair on my arms standing on end. When I tried the knob, I found it locked.

"Hello?" I said, tentatively. "Is someone in there?"

No reply.

I debated whether or not to leave it alone, but what if there was a radio inside? Putting down the scalpel in favor of a slender metal pick and a safety pin out of one of the drawers, I tried picking the lock. When it clicked, I held my breath and eased open the door—only to have it violently thrown open from the other side, as a metallic silver hand lunged out of the dark interior, reaching for my throat.

TWELVE

I yelled and threw my weight against the door, staying clear of those silver fingers' reach. The door shut, but barely. The person on the other side began to groan and push back. He or she was stronger than me, and the door eased open a few inches. Still pressing myself against it, I stabbed the reaching hand with the pick. It swiftly withdrew as its owner wailed in pain, and I took the chance to peer around the door.

There were three of them, two women and a man. They still wore their lab coats over dusty cargo pants and boots. Every bared part of their bodies—skin, eyes, hair, nails—was silver. They looked like the animals in the menagerie, like the lion that had chased us, but seeing *people* like this was worse, so much worse. The moment they saw me, they lunged at me savagely, fingers outstretched and ready to claw me like animals. Only the cracked open door kept them from touching me—for the moment. There was something both feral and pathetic in their movements, almost as if they were desperate for someone to save them, but in the way that an animal caught in a trap will react with snarls and snaps. Yet for all their desperation, they seemed weakened and unbalanced, like starved animals.

I looked into the eyes of the closest one, a woman with shoulder-length hair that shimmered like tinsel. It was her hand that I'd stabbed.

"Don't!" I cried. "You're sick! You need help!"

If my words registered at all to her, she didn't show it. She emitted a high-pitched squeal that was altogether inhuman and slipped her foot in the door, jamming it open. The hairs on my arms stood up again. Hers was the cry of a rabbit snapped up by a jackal, the death scream of an impala brought down by a lion. I slammed the door against her foot, and she shrieked again. The others took up her cry, until it sounded like a chorus of keening ghosts.

I felt like a monster as I stamped my boot on hers, crushing her toes. She drew her foot back into the darkness of the room, giving me a chance to slam the door. Even then, the handle started to jiggle as she worked it from the inside. I gathered they had retained a rudimentary knowledge of how doors worked, though they'd been stymied by the lock. I gripped the knob with a sweaty hand, my heart hammering and my mouth dry as I plunged the pick back into the lock. My hand was shaking so violently that I lost my grip, and the pick slipped out again.

Suddenly, Sam was there, throwing open the door of the trailer. "Sarah! What happened?"

"Help me!" I shouted. "It's the other scientists. They're infected!"

He grabbed the door handle so that I could focus on locking it again. It took longer than opening the door had, but I finally heard a click and when he turned the handle, it held in place.

I dropped the pick and sank to my knees, shaking enough to set my teeth chattering. Sam was saying something, but in my haze of horror and adrenaline I barely heard him. He kneeled in front of me, repeating his question.

"Are you okay?"

"N-no." Impulsively, I threw myself at him, grabbing him in an embrace. It was meant only to help me steady myself, the way you might grab a table or the wall in a spell of dizziness. He froze, surprised, and then his arms curled around me, firm and safe. I buried my face in his shoulder and we sat like that for several moments, before my trembling finally subsided. Even then, I didn't want to let go. I hadn't realized how starved I was for this kind of closeness to another human being after days of living on the edge of life and death. I lifted my face and met his eyes, half embarrassed, half curious.

"Sorry," I whispered.

He replied with a somewhat strangled, "No, no, it's fine," as his eyes fixed on mine, his expression a strange blend of astonishment and concern.

My arm was still around his neck; I could feel his pulse thundering. Slowly, hesitantly, Sam slid his hand over my wrist, my elbow, up to my shoulder, his grip gentle but firm.

"You sure you're okay?" he said, his voice a bit hoarse.

I am now, I almost said, but instead I just nodded.

At that moment, the door from the outside opened again,

and Sam and I jerked apart as if electrified, expecting Avani or Kase or one of the others.

But the person who stepped through the door was a stranger, a man in a dusty, filthy lab coat. He turned to stone when he saw us, his eyes springing wide behind wire-rimmed glasses. His hair, a receding cap of tight gray fuzz that puffed out over his ears, gave him the look of a startled koala bear. He had been holding a clipboard and a handful of glass vials, and when he saw us, they dropped to the floor, the vials shattering.

"Who are you?" Sam demanded, leaping to his feet. I clumsily followed, my neck still warm from our close encounter.

"Who are *you*?" the man stammered in a strong Scottish accent.

My eyes darted from his hands to his pockets, searching for any sign of a gun, but he appeared to be unarmed and just as surprised to see us as we were to see him. Instead of answering Sam's question, the man looked from us to the door behind us.

"Did you open it?" he cried.

I frowned. "Yes, but—"

"*Did they touch you?*" His voice came out in a thin squeal, like air let from a balloon.

"No. I don't think so. Who *are* you?"

He muttered something unintelligible, then looked over his shoulder, through the open door. While his head was turned, I grabbed the scalpel, just in case.

"Why are you—" he started to say, then stopped when he saw me holding out the scalpel. "What are you going to do with that? Scratch me?"

"Your *name*," I said.

He frowned, swallowing nervously, and scratched his ear. "I'm—"

At that moment, a loud *clang* resounded through the room. With a startled grunt, the man collapsed to the floor, unconscious, as behind him Avani stood in the doorway with her frying pan still held high. She gaped down at the scientist, her mouth hanging open.

"I got him!" she gasped out. "I really got him!"

Joey, Kase, and Miranda poked their heads around the sides of the door, their eyes all wide.

Joey whistled. "Out cold. Nice hit, Canada."

"What are you doing?" I asked, exasperated. "He was about to tell us his name!"

Avani lowered her frying pan, her eyes still wide and energized, as if she were on a sugar rush. "We saw him walking outside and followed him here. I thought he might be dangerous, so I—I whacked him."

"Is he dead?" asked Miranda.

At that, Avani let out a whimper. "I didn't mean to hit him that hard!"

"It's okay," I said, kneeling down and peering at the man's face. "He's still breathing."

Grimacing, Avani quickly set the pan on the counter and wiped her hands on her shirt.

"We must have missed him when we searched the compound," I said. "Maybe he was out in the bush."

"Do you think he's alone?" Miranda asked.

Sam picked up the frying pan with a grunt. "Let's wake him up and ask him."

Joey had a bottle of water in his hand, and he poured water

on the man's face until he came to, spluttering and coughing. Immediately he jerked up into a sitting position and scrambled backward. His skin was so pale that I could see the fine network of veins in his neck and hands.

"My glasses . . ." he groaned, his bloodshot eyes squinting at me.

I found the dropped glasses and pushed them toward him. After he pulled them on, he blinked around at us. "You're just a bunch of kids!"

"Kids with a whole lot of questions," I said. "For starters, who are you?"

He eyed us mistrustfully and touched a hand to the back of his head. "What did you hit me with?" he asked, hissing through his teeth. "God Almighty, that hurts!"

"Who are you?"

His hand dropped to scratch the back of his neck. "I'm Monaghan. Dr. Carl Monaghan. I wasn't going to hurt you."

"Do you know where my dad is? Are you with the guys who shot at him?"

"What? I don't know what you're talking about. You kids better get out of here!"

"Why?"

"Because—because this is private property! Highly off-limits!"

"Is there anyone else here?" asked Sam.

Dr. Monaghan's eyes shifted to him, and his hand moved to his wrist, scratching. He was starting to make me itch just by watching him. He must have noticed me staring, because he looked down at his hands and suddenly clenched them into fists.

"Listen here, kids, they'll be back any minute, and you don't want to be here when they arrive."

"Who? Abramo?" I asked.

He grimaced. "How do you know that name? And what *are* you doing out here in the middle of the desert?"

"Semidesert," whispered Avani. She still stood framed in the doorway, with the other three looking over her shoulders.

"My father, Dr. Ty Carmichael, disappeared three days ago," I said. "He'd heard reports of poachers in the area and went out looking for them, along with our friend Theo. Theo—he's dead. Shot. My dad's missing."

Dr. Monaghan's expression had gone vacant, and though he was looking right at me, I suspected he wasn't seeing me at all. "Carmichael, you say?"

"Yes—do you know him?"

"No, no . . ." He was scratching his wrist again. The sound was infuriating.

"Look," said Miranda, her voice shaking. "Have you got a phone or what? I need to call my parents."

"And the police," said Avani.

"And my lawyer," added Kase.

"What?" From the way Dr. Monaghan's eyes roved restlessly, I wondered if he was sick or feverish. "No, no, haven't got a phone. That was the first thing they destroyed—our phones and radios. Smashed them all, after Naveen tried to call for help."

"Naveen? Is he the one . . . in the menagerie?"

Dr. Monaghan blanched even further, his skin nearly gray. "You went in the menagerie? Did you *touch* anything?"

"No, believe me, we got out of there fast as we could.

What happened to those animals, Dr. Monaghan? What happened to the lion?"

"You saw Androcles?"

So our silver nightmare had a name. "He chased us until we fell through the ground into one of the reservoirs. We swam until we found your pipe and climbed it to this place."

Dr. Monaghan sighed. He looked around at each of us thoughtfully, then shook his head and motioned for Avani and the others to come inside. "Hurry. It isn't safe." Once they were all inside, stepping around him with mistrustful looks, he shut the door and leaned against it, his hand gingerly nursing the back of his head. "I told Strauss we needed to stop drilling. 'We've gone too deep,' I told her. But did she listen?" He snorted. "Does she ever?" Sighing again, the doctor moved his hand into his pocket, as if fingering something inside. I tensed, wondering if it could be a gun. "It's probably too late, anyway. The lion's escaped, God knows what it's infected. You lot, probably."

"Is it some kind of disease?" asked Avani.

"Not a disease," said the doctor. "Lindy called it a virus. That's closer to the truth, I suppose, but it's more than that. More complicated."

"But it's metal," Avani said. She slipped into the room, stepping around Dr. Monaghan in order to face him. "Metal can poison someone but not *infect* them. Not like a virus. It's inorganic."

"Not anymore," he replied.

Avani looked alarmed. "What does that mean?"

"Can someone please explain what's going on?" Joey said. "I am so lost right now. And I totally slept through, like, *all* of my chemistry classes, so you have to speak in kindergarten terms."

"He's saying he discovered some kind of metal that's . . . well, that's *alive*."

"I didn't discover it," he said. "I *created* it."

We digested this in silence, until Kase said, "This is the part where we all laugh, right? Because that is absolutely *insane*."

"Why are you telling us all this?" I asked him, my suspicion too strong to ignore. "Why aren't you calling your friends, telling them where we are? Shouldn't you be trying to, I don't know, shoot us?"

"Hey, genius, don't give him any ideas!" Joey protested.

Dr. Monaghan met my gaze levelly. "Because they're not my friends. And because I have to tell *someone*. They destroyed all my means of communicating with the outside. You are the only chance I have of warning the world. If I tell you what happened here, will you swear to do your best to tell the authorities? The government, Interpol, the UN—they must all be warned!"

I studied him more closely, and if he was lying, I was unable to read it in his eyes. "We'll do our best. Tell us what happened."

"Like, for instance," said Avani, "how you created a virus made of living metal."

"And *why*," I added.

"Don't you see?" Dr. Monaghan replied. "Inorganic life! The secret of the origins of the universe! Life on other planets! This discovery makes almost anything possible."

"First Frankenstein the lion," said Joey. "Now aliens?"

"You mean Frankenstein's *monster* the lion," said Avani. And then she graciously added, "Common mistake."

"How can something inorganic be alive?" I asked. "Aren't those things mutually exclusive?"

It was Avani who answered. I suspected she was already several steps ahead of the rest of us in understanding what Dr. Monaghan was hinting at. "Depends on your definition of *alive*. If it can reproduce, isn't that alive? If it has some sort of metabolism, or if it fights other life-forms for its own survival . . ."

Dr. Monaghan fixed his gaze on Avani. "Clever."

"What I don't understand," she replied, returning his look with equal intensity, "is how it affects organic animals. It would be like people being infected with *rust*, or a computer getting the flu."

"Unless the life-form in question invaded like the Trojans, hidden beneath a mask, slipping through the body's defense system," said Dr. Monaghan.

"How?" Avani whispered.

"Ah, see, that was the trick. At first, we thought we'd just created a new life-form—and well, we *had*, you see." From his pocket he pulled out a small glass vial. I flinched, still half expecting a gun, but when I saw what was in the vial, I didn't relax. It contained a small quantity of what looked like mercury, flowing like water as he swirled it around. We all watched it as if hypnotized. "You've already said it yourself—the basic criteria of life: Metalcium is inorganic, and yet it self-replicates. It has a kind of metabolism. It adapts to changes in its environment. We created *life*, however basic, however simple. Just little cells of metal at first, but I began to wonder. . . . What *more* could it do? I was on the brink of something, I knew it. It was when we began adding lead that its true potential was realized."

"That's its Trojan horse," said Avani. "Lead!" She turned to the rest us, who sat blinking and clueless. "People get lead poisoning because the body mistakes lead for calcium, letting it slip through the immune system. He's saying this Metalcium stuff works the same way—sneaking into an organism's system by hiding behind a mask of lead."

"I sure hope there's not a quiz on this later," said Joey, "because I have no idea what's coming out of your mouth right now."

"It doesn't just use lead as camouflage," said Dr. Monaghan. "It evolved on its own and began to copy DNA from the host organism. It can essentially create inorganic copies of organic cells. It's like . . . hm, it's like comparing a clay sculpture of a man to an actual man—but in this case, the clay can sculpt itself."

"And what on Earth about this is a good thing?" I asked. "*Why* would you create something like that at all?"

"Don't you see what we could do with it? We cut the tails off mice, gave them an injection of Metalcium—and the tails grew back made of silver and pretty much indestructible. Metalcium heals itself. Cut the metal tail off, it grows back again. Imagine it! Prosthetics is just the tip of the iceberg! Why we—"

"Why here?" I said. He gave me an annoyed look for interrupting his monologue. "Why are you in the middle of the Kalahari?"

His reply was hurried and impatient. "For one, this is a

remote location in a country where fewer questions are asked. It's safer for us, way out here where there are no neighbors. Second, there are large deposits of tungsten below us and since my employer already owns a controlling interest in a few diamond mines in the region, it was easy to use them as a cover operation. We drill for tungsten and the other minerals we need to experiment with, and if anyone asks questions, we show them diamonds from one of the other mines."

So they really were experimenting illegally. I'd hoped that the government might know what was going on, but if what Dr. Monaghan said was true, then no wonder his "employer" was so desperate to cover up the real purpose behind this place. Their drilling would have been the cause of the fault line we'd stepped on and fallen through.

"But it went wrong," I prompted.

His expression rearranged into a look of defeat. "About six months ago. The Metalcium began attacking its hosts instead of healing them. It's like it was *learning*, getting smarter, evolving in a way we'd never dreamed. It healed the wounds, but it didn't stop there. The Metalcium decided that *all* the organic cells were defective and began killing the original ones and replacing them. It starts with the skin and hair, and then it goes for the brain. At that point, the infected subjects began to go insane. You've seen them—the silver animals, part organic, part inorganic. Chimeras, we call them."

While the rest of us gaped at him with horror, Joey asked, "Wait—you mean, like, a lion with an eagle's head and a snake's tail, that, like, breathes fire and crap?"

Avani shook her head. "That's only in mythology. In biology, a chimera is any organism that's a blend of different genetic sources or tissues. Dr. Monaghan, why didn't you stop the research then and there, or look for a cure, or tell the authorities, or—or *something*? Once you saw it turn against its hosts, shouldn't you have stopped it *before* it got out of hand?"

"I did," he said flatly. "As difficult as it was, I knew we had to stop. It had to be destroyed—all of it—or we could unleash the greatest plague Earth has ever known. But you must understand, at that point, it was out of my control. The biotech corporation I work for refused to end the project. They wanted us to find a way to control the Metalcium, to explore all of its potential. I could have walked away, sure, but the research would have gone on without me."

He made a small, pained noise in the back of his throat. "I fought them, I did. They threatened to have me removed from the project, which I didn't want. Lindy, you see, my assistant . . . she was like a daughter to me. I couldn't leave her, couldn't leave the others to face it alone. It was my fault that it ever existed in the first place. I'm not much of a scientist if I don't take responsibility for my own creations. We took greater precautions. We minimized every risk. . . . But it wasn't enough.

"Lindy was the first to get infected, and the rest soon followed." He cast a pained look at the door that held the infected scientists, then dropped his gaze to his hands. "A week ago, we were all fine. Then in the space of a few days . . . Too late." His voice had dropped to a hollow whisper. "Too late."

"Dr. Monaghan," said Sam softly, "could we be infected?"

"Did you touch them?" Dr. Monaghan asked. "Did you touch the animals?"

"No," I said. "But we were in the room with them."

"It's transferred by touch—direct skin-to-skin contact. It seems to only affect mammals—insects and birds and such are immune . . . for now. Who knows what it will evolve into? If you're infected, you'll soon know. It starts as an itch, you see. . . ." He began scratching his neck again, and his chin and his cheeks. "An awful, maddening itch all over your body, like a great invisible rash. *Don't scratch*—that just makes it worse. Don't scratch, and you can last four, maybe five days. I was doing so well up till now. But the others, Lindy and Ian and Vera, they scratched and they went quickly, silver from head to toe, and at last they went crazy. Completely wild. *Don't scratch*, I told them. But did they listen? Well, what does it matter now? I'm almost done for. When Abramo and his men get back they'll just shoot me anyway. God! You don't know how much I've wanted to *scratch!*"

Before our horrified eyes, the skin beneath his nails began to peel off, as if it were a thin mask made of hot wax. Strips and flakes of it hung from his cheekbones, and beneath the gaping tatters, there was a smooth, shiny patina of silvery metal. When he pulled his hand away, his cheek hung in loose strips and strands from his jaw, some of the pieces falling away to the floor. The remaining metal of his cheek was so smooth that I could see my own reflection in it. I recoiled in horror.

Miranda turned away, retching, her hands fumbling on Kase's chest. We all stared aghast as Dr. Monaghan lowered his hand and stared at me with eyes already tinged with silver around the edges, his left cheek covered with the sheen of Metalcium. Now I knew why he'd looked so pale; his skin was dying, killed by the infection of living metal cells he had created himself. When he scratched, the dead skin came loose and was replaced by a skin of toxic metal.

Bile surged in my throat, but I fought it down.

I held out a hand, keeping a good three feet between us. "Tell us how to help you."

He shook his head and blinked as if trying to clear his mind. The skin hanging from his face stretched, pulling more off with it. I winced and looked away, my stomach clenching. It was like the face of a living corpse.

"I thought . . . I thought if I could find some way to save them, to find an antidote, but I haven't got any time. Not now." He glanced aside as if deeply ashamed. "I couldn't save them, and now Abramo will come back and kill them. He gave me three days, three days to find a cure, three days to save them and myself, but time is up. It's day three, and my pathetic attempts . . . Well." He waved silver-tinged fingers at the counter of vials and computers. "Useless. I found nothing. It would take years to find a cure, if one even exists. I told Abramo we had to burn everything, the infected animals, the ones that escaped, before it spread. But it's too late. He's more concerned with covering this up than actually fixing it. He dropped everything here and took off when the lion escaped—I suppose that's when he found your father instead. It's only a matter of time before they find him. They can't afford loose ends."

I shut my eyes briefly, trying to steady my whirling thoughts. *Dad knows how to survive out here. If anyone can disappear into the bush, it's him.* But doubt was a crippling poison, and I didn't know how much longer I could hold out against it.

"We need to get out of here," said Sam. "If he's right about his time being up, then they could show up any minute."

I nodded, but I still had a few lingering questions. I asked hoarsely, "Who are 'they'?"

He grimaced, and the next thing he said was so soft, I had to strain to hear it. "*Corpus.*"

"Is that the company funding your research? The ones who forced you to make Metalcium and now want to destroy everything?"

Dr. Monaghan nodded, glancing around nervously as if they might be listening.

"And they aren't messing around. They sent their best. He arrived three days ago, after Lindy called to tell them what had happened—that we were infected. Tony Abramo. 'The Custodian,' we used to call him, back when I worked at head-quarters. Because they always sent him out to clean up the messes." He made a sound that might have been intended as a laugh, but it came out as more of a choke. "Never imagined he'd come cleaning up after me."

"How far will he go?" I asked softly, though I feared I already knew the answer. I was still holding out hope that somehow this was all a big misunderstanding, and that my dad would be found safe. "To 'clean up,' as you say—what will he do?"

"Whatever it takes," he said. "If word got out about Metalcium and it was traced back to Corpus, it would destroy the company. They've covered up a lot of secrets, but a para-sitic life-form spread by touch, for which we have no cure?" He shook his head. "Even Corpus couldn't weather that." He laughed hollowly. "I wonder if they'll name it after me.

Monaghan's monster. The world will turn silver and men will curse my name as they die."

"Sarah!" Avani said urgently. "We need to get out of here!"

"I know!" I replied, but I couldn't help turning back to Dr. Monaghan in exasperation. "You can't just give up! There's still time to think of a cure!"

"You sound like her," he said. "You look like her too."

"Who?" I said sharply. "What are you talking about?"

He coughed and bent over, his head in his hands. "Oh, it hurts! Dear God, it burns!"

"Sarah!" Avani said again. "Let's go!"

"Just one more minute, please! Dr. Monaghan, I need to find my dad! Tell me how I can reach Abramo. Maybe I can make a deal with him—please!"

"You can't *deal* with Abramo."

He lifted his face and held out his hands; they were splotchy with silvery patches and sloughed skin. "Help me. . . ."

"I—I don't know how."

His eyes roamed feverishly and his teeth began to chatter.

"So cold," he whispered. "Where is Lindy? I have to get back to work. . . . Deadlines, deadlines . . ."

I stared at him helplessly, torn between pity and anger. Pity, because he was obviously in pain and dying. Anger, because I was certain he could help stop the virus if he really wanted to. Even if he failed, he had to at least keep *trying*.

"Sarah," Sam said softly, "let's go. He's insane. We can't help him if we can't even help ourselves. We'll send someone for him once we're in Ghansi."

"Yes," rasped Dr. Monaghan. "Go. For God's sake, get out of here. Don't you see? Someone needs to warn the world.

Someone needs to know the true story. I'm out of time, damn it, but you can still make it." He blinked, his eyes focusing for a moment on me. "If you don't warn them, millions will die."

I tried to swallow, my eyes held by his fevered, desperate gaze, but my mouth was as dry as Kalahari sand.

"Go!" Dr. Monaghan roared. He threw open the door, letting the room flood with sunlight—and the sound of a chopping engine. My blood turned to ice.

A helicopter.

Abramo.

We were too late.

"He's back!" Dr. Monaghan cried. "*Go! Go now!*"

THIRTEEN

We darted out of the trailer, bending low, and ran to the building where we'd found the kitchen. Somewhat hidden in its shade, we pressed ourselves against the outer wall and watched as a black, unmarked helicopter set down fifty yards away in the grass, whipping up a maelstrom of sand and sending the vegetation into a frenzy. A small fox sprinted out of the way and blurred past us. A group of men filed out of the chopper, all of them armed. One of them started shouting, giving orders to his companions to begin cleaning out the buildings and piling everything—even the animals in the cages—into one big heap.

"Go back," I said, turning away from the door. "Into the bush."

"But the food and water we found—" Avani started.

"No time! They're coming this way! We have to disappear before they see us."

I led them back toward the trailer, keeping the building

between us and the men. Beyond the trailer was another building, and then the safety of the tall grass. I felt like a springbok trying to elude a pride of hungry lions, my senses on highest alert.

But my caution slowed us down, allowing the men time to spread out. Ahead of me, an armed man stepped out from behind the next building and froze, his long face reminding me of an astonished hartebeest. I winced and let out a strained breath, still crouched low but caught directly in the man's line of sight. I held up a finger to my lips in a desperate attempt to get him to stay quiet, but it was useless.

"Hey!" he cried out. "It's the kids! Hey, boss—the kids are here!"

I moved instinctively, focused on the safety of the bush with single-minded determination, in full survival mode. I ran straight at him. His rifle was slung across his back, so I took it he hadn't expected to find us that easily. He reached over his shoulder for it, but Sam streaked past me and reached him first, catching him in a flying tackle. They both crashed into the sand, the man's gun sliding off into the grass. I started to reach for it but dropped when I heard bullets zinging around my ears.

The other men had arrived. They were shouting and spreading out, intending to surround us. I yelled for my group to drop and crawl, and they reacted instantly.

"Get to the grass!" I hissed. "Hurry!"

We scrambled the rest of the way into the bush. The tall grass hid us temporarily, but it would be only seconds before the men reached us.

"They're shooting at us!" Miranda screamed. She was

breathing so rapidly that I feared she'd start to hyperventilate. "They're actually *shooting at us!*"

"Where's Joey?" Avani called out.

I looked around, taking count—and coming up one short.

"Do we surrender?" Kase asked, his eyes wild. "They wouldn't just *kill* us. That's . . . that's illegal!"

Oh, Kase.

"Split up," I said. "Go deeper into the bush. Meet up a mile west of here."

"Which way is west?" asked Kase.

I pointed.

Sam winced as a bullet clipped the grass over his head. "What about Joey?"

"I'll find him. Just get away from here and wait. If I'm not there in an hour, keep going west. You'll hit a dirt road—well, more of a track, really. Follow it north to Ghansi. Got it?"

"But—"

"Go," I said, and I rose to a crouch and ran bent over through the grass. The gunfire followed me, thudding into the branches and sand. I kept my arms over my head as if they could somehow ward off the bullets and made a wide swath around the compound.

When the gunfire stopped, I realized the shooters must have lost sight of me. I chanced a look back, popping up from the grass like a meerkat from its hole, and saw no sign of Sam and the others. The Corpus men had spread out and were searching the bush. From what I could tell, they'd left the compound unoccupied for now.

I spotted Joey behind a generator, crouched in a pocket of shadow, where he must have been forced to hide but was now trapped by the men that were moving toward the bush. Keeping low, using the helicopter as partial cover, I tried to figure out a way to divert their attention, giving Joey room to run. But before I could do anything, Joey began to creep out from behind the generator, intending, it seemed, to go the other direction while the men's backs were turned. But what he couldn't see was that Abramo was standing just around the corner of the next building, talking on the phone. I immediately recognized him from our camp and wondered when he'd met up with the helicopter. If Joey darted out into the open, Abramo would see him for sure.

"Joey!" I whispered, waving to get his attention, but he didn't see me. There were at least twenty yards between us, and I didn't dare call out. I could only watch with dread as he dashed into the open—and right into Abramo's line of sight.

"Stop!" Abramo ordered, whipping out a sleek handgun from the pocket of his dusty khaki fatigues and directing it at Joey.

Joey froze in midstep and slowly lifted his hands. "Aw, c'mon! Don't I at least get a five-second head start?" Despite his joking tone, he watched Abramo's gun with frightened eyes.

Keeping his gaze trained on Joey, Abramo muttered something into his phone and then hung up, slipping the device into his pocket. He called to the other men, and they regrouped around Joey, surrounding him like a pride of lions separating a lone wildebeest from his herd.

"Whoa," said Joey. "I mean, it's like you guys stepped straight out of a Bruce Willis film. Seriously. Have you thought about doing any movie work? You know, my mom

works for a studio. I could totally introduce you—Hey! Easy!"
He cursed as one of the men shoved him in the back, forcing
him to his knees.

"We lost the others," said a tall African wearing a pair of
cowboy boots. "Want us to spread out, flush them into the
open?"

Abramo's gaze flickered from him to Joey, and then he
grunted. "Yes. Get rid of this one first, though."

I couldn't just leave Joey there. I was responsible for him,
for all of them. And on top of that, I was tired. Tired of running, tired of thirst and hunger, tired of watching the people I
cared about get hurt. Stubborn anger washed over me, and I
stepped into the open.

"Stop!" I yelled, whipping out the flare gun and aiming at
the men. They paused uncertainly, still too far away to see
that the weapon didn't, in fact, shoot bullets. "Let him go!
Or I'll—"

"You'll what, Sarah?" Abramo asked, spreading his hands.
If he was surprised to see me, he was good at hiding it. "Shoot
us all at once?"

"How do you know my name?" I demanded. "Where's my
dad?"

Abramo wasn't brawny or imposing. He looked like he
ought to be sitting on some European sidewalk, quietly playing chess with the neighborhood grocer. His calm gray eyes,
in wrinkled pockets of tanned skin, were blank as stone as
they returned my gaze. Had this man killed my father? I
searched his eyes for guilt or innocence and found only blank
indifference.

When he made no reply, I whispered, "You killed Theo.

You destroyed my home. *What about my dad?*"

"Enough!" Abramo sighed impatiently, cutting me off with a wave of his hand. "Shoot the boy, take the girl. She'll lead us to the others."

"No!" I shouted. One of the men lunged toward me, and as I stumbled backward, my feet tangled together and I fell. My finger involuntarily squeezed the trigger of the gun, sending the flare streaking toward my attacker. It missed him by just a hair but startled him enough that I managed to get to my feet and sprint to Joey.

"Don't shoot!" I cried, standing back to back with him. "Please—"

But they weren't even looking at us; their eyes were fixed on something behind me, their faces shocked. Joey elbowed me from behind.

"Um . . . Sarah?"

I turned around and saw the door to Dr. Monaghan's trailer was open. Dr. Monaghan stood in the doorway, looking on the verge of collapse, his face even more silver than it had been minutes ago. But he wasn't the reason the men around us were now cursing and redirecting their rifles toward the trailer—it was the trio of metal-skinned scientists stumbling toward us, their agonized cries shivering through the air like nails scraping across a chalkboard.

"Run!" Dr. Monaghan cried to Joey and me. "Get out of here!"

We jolted into motion as the men opened fire on the three scientists. I covered my ears to dull the deafening shots. We ran for the bush opposite the trailer, desperate to get away while Dr. Monaghan's horrific distraction lasted.

"Sarah!" Joey cried out. "Look!"

I lifted my head and gasped. The flare I'd shot had sailed into the tall grass, where it still burned too bright to look at—and hot enough to have caught the surrounding foliage.

A bushfire.

The blaze spread with almost liquid fluidity, sweeping from north to south with the wind and creating a fiery band ahead of us, trapping us inside the compound. Joey shouted and jumped from foot to foot as mice scurried over his shoes in an attempt to outrace the flames.

"Go back," I said. "We can't get through it. Everyone else is on the other side of the compound—we can cut through the buildings to catch up to them!"

There was no time to create a firebreak. If there was one thing I'd learned in my years in Africa, it was that you never underestimate the destructive power of a bushfire. All we could do was run.

We turned and ran back toward the compound and the carnage taking place in the clearing between the buildings. The silver scientists were still on their feet, despite the shots the men had fired. As Joey and I skirted the chaotic scene, I couldn't tear my eyes away. The first scientist reached one of the gunmen and raked her metallic nails across his face, before he shoved her with his rifle, knocking her to the ground. I felt sick as he shot her point-blank. It took several rounds before she lay still at last. Was the Metalcium bullet-resistant? I recalled the shot I'd fired at the lion and how he had seemed unharmed afterward. The other scientists attacked the rest of the men, who then turned on one another, gunning down their companions who had been touched by the infected.

Horror-struck, I wondered how they could so quickly betray one another.

"Sarah, come *on!*" Joey tugged at my sleeve, and I quickened my pace. We were almost to the safety of the bush.

"Stop!" I heard Abramo shout. He alone was still focused on the two of us, leaving his men to deal with the scientists. I looked over my shoulder and saw him take aim at the backs of our heads.

"Joey, *down!*" I yelled, and I tackled him from behind. We thudded roughly into the dirt as Abramo's shot whistled overhead. Immediately I rolled sideways, pulling Joey with me, and put the trailer temporarily between us and Abramo.

"This way!" a voice hissed.

I looked around, then spotted Dr. Monaghan standing in the doorway of the next building—the menagerie.

"Hurry!" he said, waving us toward him.

We ducked inside the menagerie just as Abramo rounded the side of the trailer; one of his bullets bit into the door as I pulled it shut. Dr. Monaghan toggled a switch and a row of bare bulbs along the ceiling flickered to life. Joey said something, but I couldn't catch what it was above all the screeching and howling of the caged animals.

"Out the back door!" Dr. Monaghan cried. "Go, go, go!"

"What about you?" I asked.

"It's too late for me. Get out of here!"

We sprinted down the aisle between the cages as the crazed, infected animals raged at us. I heard another shot, and then the door we'd entered swung open. I looked back and saw Abramo and three of his men run inside. Were they all that was left after the scientists attacked them?

"Monaghan!" Abramo roared. "Stop them!"

"Too late!" Dr. Monaghan cackled. He unlatched one of the cages, releasing a silver baboon. The animal streaked across the floor amid a flurry of gunshots and then leaped onto one of the gunmen's faces, sinking its teeth into his neck. Abramo dropped the man and the monkey with two precise head shots.

"Stop!" he shouted, but Dr. Monaghan moved to the next cage, unleashing an infected caracal. We reached the door, and Joey pulled it open.

"Come on!" he said, but I hesitated, looking back. The last two men were desperately trying to bring down the caracal, which hissed and lunged at them, while Abramo stood behind them, using them as a shield from the animal.

"Dr. Monaghan," I said, "come with us!"

He stood still a moment and met my gaze, looking more like a machine than a man, but the misery in his eyes was all too human.

"She was your mother, wasn't she?" he said.

"What did you say?" I gasped out.

"Jillian. Jillian Carmichael—you look just like her."

"You knew my—"

"Sarah, let's *go!*" Joey grabbed my arm and yanked me out of the building, and the last I saw of Dr. Monaghan was his sad face vanishing behind the door as Joey slammed it shut.

FOURTEEN

whirled on him. "He was going to tell me about my mother!"

"Yeah? Well, excuse me for saving your life!"

I snapped my mouth shut and stormed past him, not really angry at him but at Dr. Monaghan—why couldn't he have mentioned her sooner?

How did he know my mom?

What did she have to do with this place?

I broke into a run, hardly noticing if Joey kept up or not. The wind carried the scent of smoke, but it didn't worry me. It was blowing eastward, which would sweep the fire away from us. We were safe as long as we stayed west of it.

There was no sign of the others. I hoped that meant they'd gone ahead. There wasn't time to check for their tracks in the sand. We crashed through the bushes, tripping over roots and aardvark holes. I nearly stepped on a pangolin shuffling through the grass, and twisted to look back at it; a sighting of the reclusive creature was rare and something Dad and I always got excited about.

This is not the time for zoology, I reminded myself.

From the sky came a heavy *chop chop chop*, and I yelled at Joey to get down. We ducked beneath a thornbush as the black helicopter swooped overhead, barely visible in the cloud of smoke from the fire. Had the men made it out of the infected menagerie?

Perhaps this would buy us time. Maybe Abramo would want to regroup and find some new thugs to replace the ones he'd lost at the compound, giving us maybe a day's head start to disappear.

After the helicopter faded from sight, heading southwest, we continued trekking. A mile from the compound, I slowed down and began calling for the others.

"Sam! Avani!"

"Think they went back?" Joey asked.

I shrugged, then froze. "Wait. There they are!"

I jumped and waved, and saw a hand to the north wave in response. Joey and I hurried toward it and found Sam, Avani, Kase, and Miranda in the shade of a shepherd's tree. Avani threw her arms around me. When she pulled away, Sam was there. For a moment, I thought he was going to hug me too, but at the last moment he shifted awkwardly and grasped my arm instead. While the others talked over one another, asking what had happened, Sam whispered, "Are you hurt? We saw the smoke. I was about to head back when you showed up."

"I'm fine," I replied. "Shaken up, but we're not hurt. You?"

He just nodded. "I shouldn't have left you. I—"

"You should have seen it!" Joey interrupted. "She went all Tomb Raider on them, pulling out guns, setting fires!"

"Well, I don't know anything about tombs," I said. "But you weren't so bad yourself. He could have told them where you were, but he . . ." My fervor faded as I recalled the infected scientists falling under the gunfire. Suddenly my memory of our escape soured. I fell silent and let Joey pick up where I'd left off. He embellished some of the details, but the gist of the story was there.

Forcing my mind away from the massacre, I replayed Dr. Monaghan's last words to me over and over, hoping there was some clue I'd missed. I walked a short distance away, wrapped in my own thoughts.

Jillian Carmichael—you look just like her.

I sank to the ground beside a shepherd's tree. A hornbill hopped through the branches above, eyeing us excitedly. I watched him and fought to control my breathing, which had become short and shallow as if I were on the verge of hyperventilating. Then I looked down at my left wrist, sliding up my sleeve to expose the tattoo of the honeybee.

I realized the others had fallen silent and were watching me.

"Sarah?" Sam asked. "Joey said the doctor mentioned your mom. You . . . you okay?" Concern was etched in all their faces, and for some reason, it made me angry. This was something I hadn't cared to share with them. The scars were still too fresh.

"Sure," I said, shrugging, but then my heart sank and my voice gave out and I shook my head. I abandoned my defenses, lacking the strength to hold their concern at arm's length. "No. No, I'm not."

Sam knelt in front of me, his eyebrows drawn together.

His face was tan and dusted with freckles from being out in the sun each day.

"We have to keep moving," he said. "We don't know if any of the infected animals escaped, but if they did, they couldn't be far. And there's the lion. He could be anywhere."

I sighed and nodded, knowing he was right. He started to extend a hand to help me up, then hesitated.

"Sarah, in the menagerie, you didn't . . ."

I shook my head. "None of the animals—or Dr. Monaghan—touched me. Joey?"

"Nope." He held up his hands. "I'm clean."

I rubbed my fingertips against my thumb. "Still. We have to watch each other. Dr. Monaghan said that it starts with itching."

"Great," said Avani. "Because the surest way to start itching is to *think* about itching, and now we're all thinking about it."

Suddenly Joey yelped. "My nose itches! *Help!*" He began scratching his face wildly, and at first we all recoiled, horror-struck, but then Joey burst out laughing.

"Look at your faces!" he gasped between guffaws. "Oh, I got you good!"

"I *hope* you're infected," said Avani. "It would serve you right!"

"Well, if I am," said Joey with a sly look, "why not share the love?"

He lunged at Avani, arm outstretched. She screamed and kicked, her foot connecting solidly with his groin. Joey's maniacal laughter turned into a squeal of pain as he crumpled, clutching himself and wheezing.

"Not cool," he groaned.

We all stared down at him without an ounce of sympathy.

"We left all the food," I said. "We have no supplies, nothing."

"Not so fast," said Avani. I realized then that she had a backpack on, and when she opened it to reveal cans of soup and beans and a box of saltines, we all cheered.

"Nice work, Avani," said Kase.

"Yeah," Joey added, still on the ground. "Hope you grabbed a can opener."

Avani's face went blank. "I . . ."

Her voice died in a puddle of silence.

"Don't panic," I said, as much to myself as the others. "We all ate and drank at the compound. That'll get us through the rest of the day."

"And then?" Kase prompted.

And then . . . I shut my eyes and sighed. "We can forage. We can—"

"*Great*," said Joey. "More fermented berries. *Yum*. Exactly how long can we live like this, anyway?"

"We can do it," I said, my voice weak. Sure, we could do it—for two, maybe three days. It wasn't food that concerned me most. It was water. I thought of all the bottles of water we'd left behind at the compound and wanted to punch something in frustration. The supplies at the compound would have made all the difference—possibly the difference between survival and death by dehydration. I kept that to myself.

"Should we go back?" Sam asked, perhaps guessing the concerns I dared not voice.

"I'm not going back here," said Joey flatly. "That place is crawling with monsters."

I nodded. "Joey's right. Some of the men might still be back there, in addition to the animals Dr. Monaghan released. It's too dangerous."

No one looked happy with this decision, but they didn't argue either.

We walked in silence. We were all paranoid, watching one another mistrustfully for signs of scratching. Joey limped at the back, blessedly quiet. Though his constant chatter and poorly timed pranks were irritating, I suspected they were just his way of exhibiting his fear. It was the same with animals: Their personalities shined brightest when they were most distressed. The biters bit harder, the runners ran faster, the hiders dug deeper. Jokers made more jokes.

My eyes played tricks on me, making me see things disappear into the bush—a silver tail, a silver ear. Every gray termite mound we passed made my stomach lurch, because I kept expecting to see a Metalcium-infected creature. What if some of them had escaped, like Sam said? Would they follow us? I tried to remember what Dr. Monaghan had said about the infected animals' tendency to turn aggressive. It must have acted something like rabies, causing them to attack on sight, even if the animal was normally peaceful and shy. Certainly that had seemed true of the infected scientists. I shuddered. Well, at least they were out of their misery now.

I called a halt about an hour before sunset and instructed everyone to give me their shoelaces and to find firewood while I set traps. They gave me odd looks but did as I asked. I hunted through the grass until I found a few likely looking bird trails, then set up three traps using the shoelaces, which didn't work as well as the handmade twine the Bushmen used but would have to do. The work was good for me. It settled my mind and distracted me from the haunting images of the Corpus compound.

If the traps caught anything, it probably wouldn't be until the morning, so hopefully the food we'd eaten would last us till then. I paused, my hands filled with dusty shoelaces, to survey the wide Kalahari, wondering where Dad was, if he was okay, if he was as thirsty and hungry and desperate as I was.

"Be safe," I whispered into the breeze.

I found the others sitting around a pile of firewood, staring listlessly at the ground. Sam was attempting to open one of the cans of soup, to little avail. Maybe if we'd had a rock to hit it with, but the only rocks we'd seen had been in the lab. I wondered how long it would take for Abramo to gather a new team and return to the labs to burn the rest of the research. Would he go there first, or would we become his new priority?

I forced myself to focus on problems I could control.

Avani had the one box of crackers, which was better than nothing. There were four sleeves inside, all of them full, and she parceled out one of them. It was hardly filling, and the saltiness made us all desperately thirsty. I wondered if we'd have been better off not eating them at all, but I took one look at the others wolfing down the crackers and decided to say nothing.

Building a fire posed a problem. I was already beginning to shiver from the cold. But a fire could attract more Corpus gunmen. I posed the question to the others.

"Start it," said Avani. "We can take turns keeping watch. They'll have to have lights if they're searching during the night, so we'll see them coming. As dark as it gets out here, we'll be able to disappear into the bush."

I had no matches or lighters; they'd all been in my pack.

"Okay," I said, rubbing my hands together. "Let's do this Bushman style."

I picked two sturdy sticks from the firewood pile and looked around at everyone, my eyes settling on Miranda's hand.

"Miranda, can I have your ring?"

Her fingers closed into a fist, the square cut diamond on it probably worth as much as the Land Cruiser.

"Why?" she asked.

"I'm sorry, but it's the sharpest thing we have," I said, wincing a little. "There are no rocks out here. There's no other way to drill this wood."

"What would your precious Bushmen use?" she asked, tucking her hand under her shirt protectively.

"Knives made from giraffe bones, probably. Want to volunteer one of those?"

"Use your teeth."

"Just give her the ring!" Avani said.

"Give her *yours*!"

Avani held up her hands, showing all ten of her fingers were bare, and then she lowered all but the middle ones.

"That's *it*," said Miranda, jumping to her feet and glaring at Avani. "You think you're *so smart*, but what good do all your snotty facts do us now? You act like we're all so far beneath you because we don't know the Latin name for every blade of grass out here, when the truth is, *no one cares*, Miss Honor Roll!"

Now Avani was on her feet. "Oh no. You do not get to

talk about me looking down on people! *You!* Miss Debutante, with your ridiculous designer clothes and jewelry—we're in the middle of the wilderness. What do you need to look like a supermodel for? I'm surprised your daddy hasn't picked us all up in his private jet! Doesn't he have you microchipped or something?"

Miranda slapped Avani hard across the face and Avani reeled backward, her hand going to her cheek. While Sam, Joey, and I sat gaping, Kase leaped up and grabbed Miranda, who looked ready to pull out Avani's hair.

Avani fumed while Kase whispered to Miranda in an attempt to calm her down. Miranda seethed and glared at Avani but let her boyfriend lead her a little way off.

"Can you believe that?" Avani asked, looking at the rest of us.

I sighed and shut my eyes. "I need something to carve this stick with, or this fire is not going to happen." I eyed my nails reluctantly. They were blunt and unlikely to be much use. I tried anyway, and succeeded only in getting a splinter wedged under my nail. For a few minutes I stared at the stick, trying to think of a solution but getting lost in a mental fog. My lips felt like blocks of wood, my tongue parched. Thirst was a terribly distracting need; it pulled at me more and more. I was just about to begin gnawing on the stick like a beaver when I heard a voice say, "Here."

I looked up to see Kase holding out Miranda's ring. She was sitting on a termite mound twenty yards away, her back to us.

"She's not as bad as you think," he said. "And she's not a debutante, Avani. At least, not anymore." He paused, as if weighing his next words, then he said softly, "Her family lost everything two years ago. And I mean *everything*. Her dad went to prison for fraud, her mom's in and out of rehab all the time, and all her old friends won't even acknowledge she exists. She's not perfect, even I'll admit that. But I love her, you know? And I just want you know the truth. She's a good person, if you just get to know her."

He seemed embarrassed by his speech, which for him was pretty long-winded, and he turned abruptly and walked back to Miranda.

We sat in silence for a moment, nobody looking up. I remembered suddenly something my mom had told me years and years ago, something I'd completely forgotten until now: *Everyone you meet has a secret that would break your heart.*

My cheeks flushed with shame for the thoughts I'd had about Miranda, for the assumptions I had made about her. When I studied wild animals, I always waited until I had all the facts before drawing conclusions about their habits and lives—why couldn't I do that with people?

Silently, I stood up and went to Kase and Miranda. Miranda's face was smeared with tears; she looked five years younger. His hand was on her shoulder. She reached up and squeezed it. Looking at them, so close, so unflinching in their commitment to each other, I felt a part of myself I didn't even know existed curl up with envy.

"Here," I said, holding out the ring. "I'll find something else."

She looked at me suspiciously, then her hand reached out. The tip of her finger touched the diamond, but then withdrew.

"No," she said. "Use it. It's not a real diamond, anyway. It's just cubic zirconia. Fake."

I closed my hand around the ring. "Thanks."

"Are we going to die out here?" Miranda asked suddenly, her voice cased in steel. "Tell me straight. Don't dish me false hope."

Lists and numbers swirled in my head like debris whipped up by a hurricane: the distance to Ghansi, the dangers between us and safety, our dwindling strength as our bodies succumbed to lack of water and food, the cold nights, the relentless sun in the day, Abramo and his men . . . In the center of it all, where I wanted to find a seed of hope, I found only a pulsing knot of suppressed panic and uncertainty.

"I don't know," I said quietly. "I'm sorry, I . . . I don't know."

FIFTEEN

The ring wasn't as good as a knife, but I was able to gouge a notch about the size of a fingertip in one of the sticks. I laid it over a bundle of dry, fine grass and held it down with one knee. I held the other stick, its tip sharpened with the ring, between my palms. The pointy end went into the notch, along with a few grains of Kalahari sand. I rubbed my hands quickly back and forth, my tongue sticking out slightly the way it always does when I'm concentrating. It took several minutes, but eventually the sticks began to smoke, and a tiny red ember tumbled into the grass. Immediately I set the sticks aside and lifted the bundle of grass, blowing gently on the ember. It seemed to die for a moment, but I kept breathing on it, slow and steady, and then all at once a flame flared up. I dropped the burning grass and began feeding it with smaller sticks.

"Well. That was cool," said Sam.

Joey looked equally impressed. "I gotta try it."

I handed him the sticks.

He spent the next hour trying to start a fire, before at last giving up. His hands were raw and blistered, and he scowled when I asked what went wrong. By then, it was dark enough that we couldn't see anything outside the fire's glow, and Kase and Miranda rejoined us, but Miranda wouldn't look at anyone.

Sam was gazing at Miranda thoughtfully. After a minute, he stared into the fire and said, "My mom's in prison."

She didn't look up, but I saw her eyebrows rise.

"Been in and out for ten years for drugs," Sam said. He prodded the fire with a stick. Embers stirred and broke apart, sending up a shower of sparks that reflected in his eyes. "Me and my brother grew up in foster homes since I was five. Never stayed in one town more than a year." He settled back and kept staring at the flames. "When Adam turned eighteen he became my legal guardian, and we lived in Pittsburgh for a while. Till he joined the military, anyway." His face was set in hard lines; the firelight made him look older, sharper. "He was killed by a sniper in Baghdad last year."

"Sorry, bro," said Joey, looking as serious as I'd ever seen him. His knees were drawn up and his hands dangled between them, his fingers absently working a piece of grass. "My grandma died when I was seven. She raised me, practically, while my parents worked. You never really get over it, you know?"

"Yeah," said Sam, and his eyes flickered to me.

I looked at the fire, my chest aching. *Mom. Theo. Maybe Dad too.* The others could talk about their loved ones, but not me—it was too soon. It was too close, their faces still too fresh in my mind.

"My dad made me come on this trip," said Joey. He stuck the grass between his teeth, then flopped onto his back, his arms stretched wide. "He's on the board of directors for the Song Foundation—you know, the group who thought it would be a *great* idea to send five random kids into the middle of nowhere. He said it would 'straighten me out.'" Joey laughed, not his usual light, joking laughter but something deep and slightly bitter. "Isn't that ironic, though? Like, I might *die*. Bet he'd feel guilty then. I coulda been surfing in SoCal with my gang, picking up babes." He rolled onto his side, head resting on his elbow, and he grinned suggestively at Avani. "How about it, Canada? I kinda dig the whole nerd thing. Nerd is the new hot."

"Dream on," said Avani, rolling her eyes.

"Why are *you* here?" he asked. "Is this, like, the land of your people?"

"My dad's parents are from Kenya," she said, her eyes narrowed. "And my mom is from Delhi."

"Where's that?" asked Joey. "Arkansas?"

"*India*, you moron."

"Do you, like, sit down and memorize dictionaries every day?"

"No," she said. "Only on weekends."

Joey stared at her, looking perplexed, then suddenly his face split into a grin. "Wait a minute. . . . You made a joke!"

Avani's lips curled into a small smile.

Sam caught my eye, then traced a heart in the sand between us. My throat tightened and I blinked at it, then looked at him in alarm.

He pointed at the heart, then made an exaggerated glance

from Joey to Avani, and then wiggled his eyebrows at me.

I smiled at the thought of mortal enemies falling for each other and shook my head at him. He shrugged and smudged out the heart. I watched his finger, my pulse settling like a leaf that had been caught up in a dust devil.

Of course he didn't mean that for me. He doesn't even know me. No one does.

That last thought struck me unexpectedly, like an arrow, leaving me slightly breathless.

No one does.

No one except Dad, now that both Mom and Theo were gone.

I'd never really thought about it before, but now that I had, it invaded my mind: I was alone. I'd never been on my own like this before. Sure, Sam and the others were here, but in a few days they'd leave Africa and I'd probably never see any of them again. I'd just become part of a story they'd tell their friends.

What if Dad was really gone? What would I do? Where would I go? Who would even want me?

I'd end up like Sam, I guessed. I had another year until I was eighteen. Maybe I could go to college early. I could just stay in Botswana, find work as a tour guide or something in Maun or the Okavango.

Why am I even thinking about this? I had to believe he was alive. Had to, or there was no way I could continue.

"What about you?" asked Sam.

It took me a moment to realize he was talking to me. "What about me?"

"What happened to your mom?" He asked the question gently, without meeting my eyes.

My thumb immediately went to my bee tattoo, rubbing it absently. "She died."

His gaze lifted to mine. They all waited quietly, and it was the silence that probed deepest, like a knife wheedling open a clamshell, more effective than any spoken questions could have been. And suddenly, I wanted them to know. I hadn't told anyone this story, hadn't spoken of it in months. Now something inside me seemed to release, and the story poured out of me.

"It happened four months ago," I began. "She left on a short trip to study the local beehives. Bees were her special area of interest. She was the only person I knew who was actually fond of the 'killer bees' that infest this area in the warmer weather. Then last summer she noticed a big drop in the native population of hives. So she set off to gather some data in hopes of finding out what was going on. She was afraid that the same mass disappearance of bees that was plaguing developed countries like the States was now happening here. We knew that the hives she'd previously documented were spread across a wide area, so we didn't really worry when she didn't return for four days." My voice turned husky as I recalled the memories, pulling them from the deep corner of my mind where I'd tried to hide them. Now I realized that effort had been as pathetic and effective as trying to hide the sun behind your hand. "We figured she'd stumbled on some clue. My mom was perfectly capable of taking care of herself, and if there was an emergency, she had the satellite radio. When she didn't call after a few days, Dad guessed she left the spare batteries behind—something she was notorious for doing. My mom was brilliant but also very scatterbrained about practical things like batteries when she was focused on one of her projects."

Looking back, I wondered how much fault in her death lay with my and my dad's casual dismissal of her extended absence. If we'd gone looking for her sooner, would we have saved her? But then again, maybe we wouldn't have found her at all. Because maybe she hadn't run out of batteries but was actually at the Corpus compound. I recalled the bees we had found in the freezer. Suddenly it didn't seem possible that it was a coincidence.

"When Dr. Monaghan said her name to me, I realized she must have been there. I think that in searching for the bees, she came across the Corpus compound. Remember the hive we found in the freezer? There has to be a connection. Maybe she was studying a swarm that led her to the lab. She would have been furious by the cruel treatment of the animals there, and I know without a doubt that she would have done everything in her power to expose the project. We'd assumed she'd died in a car crash, after being attacked by a bee swarm—when we found her, she'd been stung hundreds of times. Now . . . I'm not so sure."

I had a lot of unanswered questions about my mom's final days. I'd unfolded the memory countless times, taking it out like an old photograph, reliving the details, asking the same questions, getting no answers or comfort in reply. Then I'd try to push it all aside, pretend somehow it had all happened to someone else, some other Sarah. I tried to sever the past from the present, but it always seemed to come drifting back.

For a moment, I shut my eyes, trying to quell the rising storm of pain and regret that rioted within me. When I opened them again, I drew a shuddering breath. "There was nothing to indicate where she'd been or what had happened. Only that she was covered with beestings, and she'd written some words on her arm. *The bees are a fail.*" I slid back my sleeve, exposing the honeybee tattooed there. "That was it. Just another field note. They decided she'd been attacked by the very bees she'd set out to save. Ironic, isn't it?"

The crackling of the fire rose to fill the silence. We all watched the sparks spiral upward in a funnel of smoke, rising as if they aspired to join the ranks of stars above. Purged of my story, I sank into physical and mental lassitude, wearied in every sense.

Miranda, looking lost in her own thoughts, idly reached up to scratch her nose. Instantly everyone locked horrified eyes on her.

"What?" she said, sounding confused. Then her eyes widened and she stared at her fingers. "No! No, it's not like that! I just—I've been thinking so hard about *not* scratching that it made me itch all over! I didn't touch anything infected, I swear!"

"I believe you, babe," said Kase, but I noticed he'd scooted slightly away.

"We're all paranoid," said Sam. "If any of us were infected, we'd have noticed by now, surely."

"Yeah, totally," said Miranda, attempting to be light, but her shaking tone gave her away.

The fire was getting low. I reached behind me for the supply of sticks, and my hand closed around something long and slender—and definitely not made of wood. It was cold and smooth and it writhed in my grip.

I yelled and let go, jumping to my feet. A sleek black snake slithered through my legs and around the fire. One by one, the others screamed and scrambled up. Avani tripped and fell on her back, her eyes wide as the snake streaked toward her.

"Mamba!" I said. "Don't—"

Suddenly Joey was there. He snatched the backpack full of cans and swung it at the snake, diverting its attention away from Avani. The snake whirled and hissed angrily, then slithered toward him. It reared, its mouth gaping open to reveal its fangs. The snake glittered like obsidian in the firelight, eyes cool and lidless, fixed on Joey. It rose higher, its head level with Joey's waist, as high as I'd ever seen a mamba go. When its head drew back, I thought with dread, *This is it.*

The snake struck like a flash of lightning, faster than the human eye could track—and sunk its fangs into the backpack Joey held in front of him. Then, so quickly it was but a blur, the mamba sank to the ground and sped into the grass, vanishing in the blink of an eye.

No one moved or spoke. I let out a long, shaky breath. Then Joey slowly dropped the bag, his face flushed. It clanked by his shoes. He was smiling inanely.

"That," he said, "is the coolest thing I have ever done."

"You idiot!" Avani yelled, rising to her feet. "You stupid, brainless *boy*! That was a *black mamba*, the deadliest snake in Africa! If it had bitten you, you'd be dead before morning! What were you thinking?"

Joey looked at her the way the rest of us had looked at the snake: healthy fear mingled with shock. "But I . . . *saved* you."

"I didn't *ask* you to save me!" she replied. "I didn't *ask* you to do anything! I didn't *ask* to be out here, starving and thirsty, chased by some crazy hit man! You want to share life stories? You want my sob story? Well, I don't have one, sorry! I have a mom and a dad and a baby brother and I may never see any of them again! I just want to go *home*."

She sobbed into her hands, tears winding down her arms and dripping onto her knees. We all stared uncomfortably at our shoes, the ground, anything except Avani.

I felt someone should say something, so I said gingerly, "You probably shouldn't cry. You need to conserve your water."

Avani lifted her head and stared at me as if I'd cursed at her, while Miranda said, "What is *wrong* with you?"

"Huh? I didn't mean—"

"Can you possibly be more insensitive?"

"I—I'm sorry."

Their lives were so different than mine. So far, everything I had said to them had seemed wrong or silly or odd. I was the one who'd dragged them out here. I was the one who'd nearly gotten them killed.

"I'm sorry," I said, and was surprised to hear myself say it aloud. "I'm so sorry. I shouldn't have . . . I don't know."

They stared at me, all except Avani, and my face began to burn.

"I'm going to get some grass, for us to sleep on," I said, rising to my feet and leaving the fire, ignoring Sam's call for me to wait. I didn't want his help. I didn't want him to see me cry.

*   *   *   *

We saw no sign of Abramo that night, to my surprise. I thought that surely he'd be after us while the trail was still warm, but maybe finding more goons would take longer than

I'd thought. I had the last watch of the night, and at dawn I woke everyone and built up the fire. It was still dark enough that the smoke wouldn't give us away. I'd dug up *bi* roots from around the camp, and I offered them to the others.

"It's all we have," I said. "You don't want to dehydrate out here."

I showed them how to scrape the white tuber with their nails to gather a handful of shavings.

"Hold it above your face," I said, demonstrating. "Point your thumb at your mouth and squeeze."

White liquid ran out of the shavings and down my thumb to drip onto my tongue. It was bitter and left my mouth feeling dry, but it was full of valuable nutrients and would ensure, at least, that we didn't dehydrate.

"Ugh," Miranda said, spitting it out. "It's disgusting."

"Drink, babe," Kase said. "It's better than nothing."

She made a face but squeezed more of the pulp.

"Mm!" Joey rubbed his stomach. "I love me some root juice in the morning. Enlivens the senses!"

The "root juice," as Joey called it, took me back to my first year in Africa, when Theo used to take me on long walkabouts and teach me the survival skills of his ancestors. His father's generation had lived off the land, using the same techniques the San people had been using for thousands of years. They had been the last living remnants of the Stone Age, hunter-gatherers untouched by the modern world. All of that had changed in the last fifty years, when the few remaining tribes of Bushmen were displaced to make room for game reserves in southern Africa. Now all that remained were scattered, fractured groups who made a living by demonstrating their ancestors' ways to tourists or, like Theo, by tracking game for researchers or hunters.

The bitter taste of the root left me with bitterer thoughts about my friend's death, and I turned away from the others so that they wouldn't see the tears stinging my eyes. I wiped them off and steadied myself by naming the birds whose songs I could hear from the bushes and grass: *guinea fowl, korhaan, pale chanting goshawk, crimson-breasted shrike* . . . It was a trick I'd picked up when Mom died, a way of distracting myself from my own thoughts.

The traps were empty, though one of them had been sprung by a mongoose from the look of the tracks around it—that, or the mongoose had made off with whatever the trap had caught. Disappointed but unsurprised—trapping was hardly a reliable source of food—I instead turned to more brutal methods. We had to eat. There was no way we could keep walking without sustenance, and we needed something more hydrating than crackers.

I found a bent stick about as thick as my wrist and tossed it experimentally into the air, then nodded to myself.

"Okay, guys," I said. "Here's how it's gonna go. Hear that chirping?"

"You mean the sound like a turkey?" asked Joey.

"It's a flock of guinea fowl." I pointed in the direction of the noise. "Two of you sneak up on them—don't worry, they're pretty dumb and they won't notice until you're right on them. Scare them into the air and then duck."

"Duck?" asked Sam.

"Duck."

He shrugged, and he and Joey crouched into the grass and

headed for the flock. I motioned for Kase, Miranda, and Avani to stand back. They did, watching warily and yawning. The morning was chilly enough that I could see my breath in the air. I bounced on my toes, trying to warm myself so that my arm would be steady enough to throw.

Suddenly the guinea fowl burst from the grass, their wings flapping frantically as they cawed and chirped in alarm. Joey and Sam stood and waved, scaring the last of them into the air, and I yelled, "Duck now!"

They dropped back into the grass and I slung the stick as if it were a boomerang. It whistled through the air in a beautiful arc that would have made Theo laugh with pride.

The stick took out two of the fat birds, stunning them out of the air. They fell near Sam and Joey, who ran and picked them up. The boys turned to me, each holding a dazed bird, and their mouths fell open.

"Holy McNugget!" said Joey. "You are badass!"

"That was completely barbaric," said Miranda.

Despite Miranda's jab, I couldn't help smiling a little. It was nice to be appreciated.

I could have sworn I heard Theo's laughter rippling through the grass—musical, wild, completely uninhibited, drawing profound pleasure from the hunt. The first time I'd successfully brought down a bird, my mom had lectured me for an hour about unnecessary slaughter of the wildlife and the destructive ramifications of sport hunting. All the while Theo had stood behind her, safely out of her line of sight, giving me thumbs-ups and smiles as he plucked the birds in preparation for roasting them. Such a wave of sadness hit me then that my satisfaction was washed entirely away.

Guinea fowl was monstrously tough meat. I'd have much preferred a korhaan or a nice, fat kori bustard, but guinea fowl were the easiest to hunt and they were found in abundance. I had to snap the birds' necks to kill them, a task I definitely did not relish, but I did it quickly and got it over with. Then I plucked the birds, wishing I had the tools to properly prepare them. Sam rigged a spit out of sticks over the fire, and soon we had the birds roasting nicely. They wouldn't taste great, but they smelled divine, like roast chicken, and soon we were all huddled around the fire salivating. Even Miranda looked at the birds hungrily, but she swore she wouldn't touch them. Instead, she had more root juice and some berries she found nearby.

"I've been thinking about the Cruiser," said Sam as he slowly rotated the spit. "Should we go back and try to get it out of the sand?"

I mulled it over, then reluctantly shook my head. "The bushfire's in that direction. It may have already reached the truck, and anyway, now that those goons have a chopper, it'd be too easy for them to spot us in the Cruiser. We'll have to go on foot from here."

"How long?" asked Kase.

I squinted at the fire, doing the math. "A week? Depends on how much food and water we can find, and if we stay in good condition."

Everyone groaned.

"We can do it," I said. "We just have to take it a day at a time."

I watched the sky, listening closely for any sounds of helicopters and trucks, and sent out a questioning thought: *Where are you, Dad?* If only he'd pop out of the bushes and yell "Surprise!" I might be able to believe my own positive assurances.

"Um, so guys . . ." said Joey, when the birds were almost finished cooking. He scooted closer to the fire and glanced at Avani; she was perched on a termite mound a short distance away, struggling to open one of the soup cans again. He dropped his voice to a whisper and leaned in conspiratorially. "So I have a confession. I'm kinda into Avani."

Miranda arched one eyebrow. "I don't know who I feel sorrier for, her or you."

"Do you guys think she likes me?" he asked. "I mean, I know she pretends she hates me and all, but girls are always doing that." He sighed. "They just like me for my . . ." He made a vague gesture at his torso. "My body, you know? I just wonder if she sees me as a *person*."

"Breakfast is done," I announced, and he brightened, his romantic woes seemingly trumped by the announcement of food.

"Canada!" he called, and then he lapsed into full-throated rendition of the Canuck anthem. "*Oh, Canada! Something, something-ish in French* . . . Time to eat!" To the rest of us: "How do you say 'time to eat' in French?"

But Avani didn't come. She was peering inside the box of crackers as if she'd lost something inside.

"Um, Canada?" Joey called uncertainly.

She looked up, her eyes fixing on me. "I found something."

"What?"

Walking over, she upended the cracker box. The remaining packages of crackers slipped out—along with something small and black.

"It was down at the bottom. I didn't see it last night, but I was going to open another pack and when I reached into the box, I grabbed this instead. What is it? And why was it in the cracker box?"

I barely heard her. My ears were roaring as if I were standing in a hurricane. I stared at the little device, no bigger than a cell phone, and swallowed.

"What is it?" Avani asked in a softer tone, staring uncertainly at my stricken expression.

"It . . ." I had to clear my throat in order to find my voice. "It's my mom's."

SIXTEEN

It's a voice recorder," I said. "She always carried one, to record her thoughts and observations." My voice grew thick as I spoke. Tentatively, I picked up the recorder and turned it over. It was hers, all right. There were teeth marks all over from the time she'd dropped it and a hyena had gotten hold of it. I'd been with her, and we were stuck in a tree when the hyena showed up. He'd settled in the sand and chewed on the recorder for half an hour, until Mom frightened it away by singing "Bohemian Rhapsody" and laughing so hard she'd nearly fallen out of the tree. The recorder had still worked, though it was a bit slimy and we'd had to take it apart to let it dry.

"So it's true," I whispered. "She *was* there, at the Corpus compound."

Somehow, it hadn't seemed real when Dr. Monaghan said it, but I couldn't deny what I held in my hand.

"Why was it in a box of crackers?" asked Avani. She and

the others were circled around me, their expressions cautious, as if they weren't sure what I'd do.

I mulled it over, my finger hovering over the play button. "She must have hid it there. Somehow."

"Sarah . . ." Sam's teeth ran over his lips; I was beginning to recognize this as a sign of him worrying. "Do you think there's something recorded on there?"

I did. And it terrified me. Why else would she hide the recorder? I could almost see it: Mom finds the compound, starts investigating, records her discoveries, and at some point before or after she was caught (it had to have come to that eventually, or she'd still be alive today; I couldn't believe her connection with Corpus and her death to be coincidental), she hid the recorder in the box of crackers. It might very well have been the only damning piece of evidence to have escaped the compound.

"Are you going to play it?" asked Avani. By the look in her eyes, she was poised on the brink of snatching it back and playing it herself.

"Give her space, you guys," said Sam. "Come on. Let's eat."

He corralled them away from me, giving me room to breathe. To think. To dread. I should have been overjoyed at the chance to hear Mom's voice again, to finally discover the truth behind her death. But my hand trembled with fear. What if the truth was too terrible? What if the recorder was empty?

With a jolt, I realized my life these past few months had been one long series of what-ifs. What if I'd gone with Mom on that last trip? What if Dad and I had searched for her sooner? What if we had refused to accept her death as an accident and had pressed deeper into the Kalahari to find the truth? *What if* wasn't a form of comfort or healing. It was a purgatory, a waiting place of self-inflicted guilt and torture. There was no rest in it, no peace. How much longer could I go on like this, balancing on the edge of regret?

I hit play.

Muffled static. Wind, perhaps, or rustling grass. My ears strained for the sound of her.

Her voice broke through like lightning from a cloud, striking my heart, leaving me gasping.

"This is Jillian Carmichael. Date is January 14, and it's about, oh, ten o'clock in the—"

I hit stop.

Forced myself to take a breath.

It had been four months, but the pain felt so fresh. I brushed away a few tears and pressed play again.

"—morning. I've been tracking a swarm of honeybees that have been moving in a strange pattern, flying directly west. It's completely abnormal. It's like they know exactly where they're going, as if they're on a mission. I'm nearly a full day's drive away from camp, and they've led me to some kind of facility. Looks like a drilling operation, but there are armed guards. Military, maybe? I need to get closer."

"Please don't," I whispered.

She left the recorder running as she moved. I could hear her soft footsteps, boots crunching in the sand. Snippets of birdsong were caught in the recording, and I recognized much of it to come from species found here only in the green summer months, when the rains swept across the Kalahari and left behind countless pools of water in the once-dry pans.

"Something's not right," Mom whispered.

My heart raced so quickly that my chest began to ache. As she moved, Mom described the compound, the guards, the scientists. I recognized Dr. Monaghan by her description. Suddenly her voice changed, grew excited.

"I've never seen anything like it! The bees are *attacking* the researchers and swarming around the buildings. Is there a hive inside? It makes no sense! They're running—the scientists and the guards—going inside . . . I think some of them were stung, but it's hard to be sure. I can see clouds of bees moving around the buildings, as if searching for a way in. I . . . I don't know what to make of it."

There was a pause, then a loud crackling of static and Mom swore. My eyes popped wide at that. I'd never heard her swear before.

"Ty? Ty, come in. Sarah? You there, honey?"

I pressed a shaking hand to my mouth. She was trying to call us.

She swore again. "Ty? Hello? Sarah? Theo? Is anyone there? Crap, still recording . . ."

With a beep, the recording cut off.

My skin was a carpet of goose bumps. I hurriedly clicked the next button on the device, and a second recording began to play.

"This is Jillian Carmichael. Morning of January 15. I spent the night finding a way into the buildings. Made it into one of the labs when the guard shift changed. I knew all those nights sneaking out of my bedroom window back in high school would come in handy." She laughed, but there was no humor in it. "They haven't caught on to me yet. I imagine they don't expect company, way out here in the middle of nowhere. I'm just outside the compound now, hiding under a fallen log, but I can see them coming and going. Here's what I've managed to learn so far. . . ."

She'd learned quite a lot, by waiting until the scientists went to sleep and then sneaking into the labs through the high, narrow ventilation windows. During the day she hid in the nearby bush, watching and taking notes. She described the silver animals (apparently at that time, there were only two mice who were infected), Metalcium's creation, its evolving threat, even Dr. Monaghan's fight to shut down the project and Corpus's insistence on further research. Mom had combed through the scientists' notes and even found her way into one of their less secure computers.

"I used one of their microscopes to study it," she said. "It replicated via mitosis, like an amoeba splitting into two. Almost as if— Wait." Several seconds of silence, then a whisper. "*Someone's coming.*"

My pulse quickened. I could see her, crouched in the grass, listening raptly, her heart hammering as fast as mine was now.

"Hey!" shouted a masculine voice. "Who are you? What are doing here?"

"*Crap,*" Mom hissed. I heard a flurry of disjointed noise— was she running? Fighting? The recording ended abruptly. There was only one more on the device. My hands had gone cold and clammy, my thumb freezing on the play button.

This was it. This was the last recording my mother would ever make. The last words I would ever hear her say.

"Sarah?" Sam's voice was soft, uncertain. The others were

still around the fire, doing a bad job of hiding their glances at me. "Sorry, I just . . . wanted to see if you were okay."

I lowered my face to hide my teary eyes. My hair was tied back, but a few strands had come loose and shielded me from his gaze.

"They caught her," I said, my voice muffled with unshed tears. "There's one more recording. I don't know if I can . . ."

"Do you want me to go?"

I lifted my face. "No. Stay."

Sam looked at me uncertainly.

"Please," I whispered.

He nodded and, without a word, sat beside me. I handed him the recorder.

"Could you . . . ?"

With another nod, Sam pressed play. The voice that we heard next was not Mom's.

"—in this closet until we decide what to do with you. You should have stayed away."

My gaze met Sam's, and though I had known it was coming, it still chilled my heart.

"That's Dr. Monaghan," I whispered. "She must have started recording after she was caught."

"I was only trying to discover what was impacting the local bee populations," Mom explained. Her voice sounded muffled. I suspected the recorder was hidden somewhere beneath her clothes, where the scientists wouldn't have found it.

"Dr. Carmichael, the guards found your notebook and all the information you'd recorded about us—and we found your radio. Who did you contact? Who are you working with?"

"No one! I'm alone! Like I said—I was studying the bees, and they led me here."

"Someone is coming from our HQ, Doctor, and he will not hesitate to wring the answers from you. I'm trying to give you a chance! Be honest with me now, or I can't help you! *Who* did you contact?"

"What do the bees have to do with this place? Why did the hives converge on your facility?"

A pause. I imagined Dr. Monaghan exhaling his frustration. "*I* will ask the questions."

"Tell me about the bees, and I'll tell you who I contacted."

Another moment of silence as Dr. Monaghan considered this. Then a noisy sigh. "We've been plagued by bees for weeks. We think they're attracted by some of the chemicals we've been experimenting with—must be pheromones or something. So now you tell me: *Who did you contact?*"

"No one."

I could easily picture Mom and Dr. Monaghan trading defiant stares, like twin poles of two magnets colliding.

"You have twenty hours until he arrives," said Dr. Monaghan. "And then there will be nothing I can do to help you. I . . . you must understand, there's *nothing* I can do."

"You could let me go." Mom's voice was a gentle nudge.

Dr. Monaghan seemed to shuffle a bit before replying. "No. No, I couldn't."

I shot to my feet in a burst of fury. Sam, still holding the recorder, looked up in surprise. He hit the stop button.

"You okay?" He asked. "Need a break?"

"To think I felt *sorry* for him," I said through my teeth. Overwhelmed with the urge to hit something, I grabbed a handful of dry grass and ripped it out of the ground, tossing it aside. Then I spun, found myself facing a tree, and punched it hard.

"Hey!" Sam lunged forward and pulled me away. "I'm all for punching something to release anger—trust me, I've done my fair share of it—but at least pick something softer than a tree!"

My knuckles were bleeding. I slumped to my knees and let Sam dab the cuts with the cuff of his sleeve. His touch was gentle, and I watched his face as it creased with concern. His lips were cracked and dry, his hair a shade lighter from being in the constant sunlight. When he let go of my hands, the memory of his touch still burned on my skin. A part of me longed to throw the recording away, to pretend the past didn't exist, so that I could focus on today, on Sam, on the curiosity and timid hope that his touch incited beneath my skin.

But I couldn't shake the image of Mom locked in the closet where we'd found the box of crackers, trapped in the dark, hours away from her death. I could never outlive the past until I knew the full story.

"Play it."

"You sure?"

"*Play* it. Please."

He sighed and the recording continued.

"You're only locking me in here," Mom was saying, "because you don't have the balls to kill me yourself—you have to hand me over to your hatchet man. Is that it?"

"Good night, Dr. Carmichael. If you should get hungry, well, there are crackers."

We heard the heavy slam of the door, then nothing but

Mom's rapid breathing. With a wrench of my gut, I realized she was crying. She sniffed and drew a deep breath.

"This is Dr. Jillian Carmichael, on January . . ." More sniffling, a deep inhalation. When she spoke, her voice was straining not to break, "On January 17. I . . . I've been captured by a group of scientists experimenting illegally in the Kalahari. They're holding me until . . . Oh God! I just wish . . . I just wish I knew what it was with those damn bees!"

The recording didn't end, but for several minutes we heard nothing but silence and the occasional crackle that must have been Mom moving around. It sounded as if she'd tried the door, and at one point she pounded on it with something heavy. I was beginning to think the rest of it would just be empty, meaningless noise, but suddenly her voice surged through.

"Well," she said. "There's one thing Dr. Monaghan doesn't know, at least. I'm—"

The recording cut short. I looked up at Sam in alarm. "It ends there?"

He winced and shook his head. "Batteries died."

For a moment, I could only stare at him in disbelief. "The *batteries died*?"

He handed me the recorder and I tried turning it off and on, but nothing happened. I clawed open the battery compartment and took them out, shook them, and put them back in, but it still wouldn't turn on.

"Of all the stupid things," I said softly.

Sam picked up one of the grass stems I had torn out of the ground and ran it through his thumb and index finger. His brow was tense as he asked, "What are you thinking?"

My skin felt like hardening cement, fixing my features into a numb mask. I unzipped my pocket and dropped the recorder inside. "I'm thinking that Mom's 'accident' wasn't so accidental."

He nodded, watching me worriedly. "Are you going to be all right? Wait. That's a stupid question. Of course you're not. But can I . . . can I do anything to help?"

With a sigh that began deep in my abdomen, I ran my fingers through the loose hairs over my face, pushing them behind my ears. "I'll get through it. I have to."

"No," he said. "You don't. Not right away. You can't just listen to something like that and get over it all at once. You're not supposed to."

"Well, I don't have much of a choice, do I?" I returned, a bit too sharply. "Sorry. Look . . . thanks. For listening, I mean."

His smile was sad. "Yeah. Sure. Just . . ." His teeth skimmed over his bottom lip, as he watched me with cautious eyes. "Just know you're not alone, okay?"

A defensive protest welled within me, as it always did when someone tried to offer me comfort, but when I met his eyes it faded, a shadow shrinking from the light. For once, I didn't want to curl up like a hedgehog, spines out, pushing everyone away. Instead something in my chest gave way, and I nodded slowly. "I know."

SEVENTEEN

The next morning, after kicking sand over the campsite in an effort to hide our tracks from any passing helicopters, we set off due west. My spine stung from sleeping on the hard ground, and what sleep I had gotten had been plagued with vague dreams about silver animals that appeared and faded out of the savanna. So I walked like the living dead, stumbling and bleary-eyed, each step heavier than the last. The others walked with similar exhaustion. We drifted slowly apart, with me in the front, Sam a few steps behind, Joey in the middle, and the last three lagging after him. When that happened, I stopped and waited for everyone to catch up. It would take just a moment to lose sight of one another, especially here where the bushes were growing thicker and the grass taller, and once that happened it would be difficult to find one another again.

"Can't we stop for a while?" asked Avani when she caught up. She bent over, breathing hard. "I feel like I got hit by a truck."

"Fine," I replied, hiding my frustration. At our current pace, it would take a month to reach Ghansi. We had to move faster; every delay only gave Abramo a better chance of finding us. I didn't doubt that once he'd regrouped from the skirmish at the compound, he'd begin hunting for us. And anyway, we couldn't keep going like this for much longer. We needed water desperately, more than the others realized. I wondered if they felt the signs of dehydration like I did: My muscles were cramping, my heart would randomly burst into a series of painful flutters that left me dizzy and weak, and I felt nauseated when I moved too quickly. I could see signs of it in the others: their gazes were growing vacant, their steps clumsy.

"We're holding you back," Sam said softly. I was sitting with my back against a shepherd's tree, and he dropped down on its other side. I couldn't see him, but I could hear his whisper. "If it weren't for us, you'd be in Ghansi by now, wouldn't you?"

"It doesn't matter. It's not your fault we're out here."

He was quiet for a long minute, and his next words were so soft I barely caught them. "I have a confession to make."

"What?"

I could hear him pulling up the grass, roots ripping out of the earth, and I didn't push him to answer right away, though I was curious.

"I didn't just come randomly," he finally said. "I didn't want to tell you, but with everything that's happened, I mean, we don't know if we'll even make it out of this—"

"We'll make it out of this."

"Right. Of course. But still, I just . . . I want you to know."

"What do you mean?"

"I mean, I came to Africa because I wanted to meet you, Sarah."

I turned around and stared at the back of his head. "Meet me? You didn't even know me."

He looked over his shoulder, not at me, but at the ground between us. "It didn't feel that way. I read your mom's book."

My mom's book. I remembered the day Sam had first arrived, when he'd picked up the book in my tent and lingered over it.

"Why didn't you say so sooner?"

"I don't know. I thought you'd be weirded out, I guess."

I turned away again, considering. "I don't think so."

"Yeah, but you don't understand. That book . . . it changed me. Adam gave it to me with a bunch of other travel books when I turned thirteen. I grew up surrounded by cement and noise and traffic, but it was your mom who kept me believing that I could escape all that one day."

He stopped, his voice cutting off as if his outpouring had left him embarrassed.

"It's okay," I said. "She would have loved to hear that. That's why she wrote the book in the first place. I didn't like it at first. I thought it would be embarrassing for people to read about me without knowing me, but she told me something I never forgot. She said, 'People are like stars, but it's stories that turn us into constellations. If we don't tell our stories, we burn alone in the dark.' I couldn't argue with that, mainly because I was ten and I didn't know how. It sounded important, so I told her to publish the book."

Sam was silent a moment, then said, "Adam and I had this map we used to circle places on, all the places we wanted to go. We circled all the countries you and your parents had been to, because there was something about your mom and the way she wrote. . . . She made each place feel as if it were the ultimate, you know? Like you hadn't lived until you'd been there."

She had had that effect. Not just for places, but for people, for experiences, for moments. She could make a boring afternoon seem like your life's brightest highlight, a day never to be forgotten. She had seen the beauty in the most common things—a bird building its nest, an ant carrying a leaf twice its weight, a sunrise, a moonrise, a meteor streaking through the night sky. There was never a dull moment with my mom. People had loved her, gravitated toward her like thirsty herds to a clear, cool stream. I used to love watching her take a photographer or a journalist into the field; my parents had often guided people into the wilderness to earn some extra money. Give my mom a jaded, sour-faced journalist and she'd return him or her as a different person, full of awe and wonder and appreciation for the world. I never got tired of seeing her transform people by opening their eyes to the wonders around them. My dad had loved her for it. He used to say to me, "Your mother has the mind of a genius and the eyes of a child. You won't find better than that."

And I knew it was true.

I stared at Sam with new eyes, and something inside me softened at his confession. We were linked together by Mom's spirit, as if she were between us, holding each of our hands.

"She would have liked you," I said.

"You think?" He sounded pleased. "I wish I could have met her."

I drew a sudden, deep breath, feeling my eyes burn as grief blurred the corners of my mind. It always came like a flood, seeping through the holes I was so sure I'd covered up with silly distractions: ordering more food for the camp, making sure Dad's notes stayed organized, keeping up with my studies (which, since Mom's death, had been left mostly up to me. I could have quit school altogether and I don't think Dad would have noticed). Every time the black waters of sadness poured into my thoughts, I rushed to throw up flimsy dams. They worked for a while but never for long. It was like trying to patch a boat with Scotch tape.

I leaned my head onto my knees and shut my eyes, my default defensive position, curling up like a hedgehog. My hand automatically went to my pocket and around the recorder. I didn't even notice Sam had moved until he was beside me. He didn't touch me or say anything, but I could sense him there, silent and unmoving.

After a few minutes I lifted my head, my eyes dry.

"We should keep going."

He stood up and offered me a hand, pulling me up. "Are you sure you're okay with it?"

I smiled and held his hand a moment longer than necessary. "I'm glad you knew her, in a way. Sometimes I wondered if anyone else missed her. It helps, knowing she was a part of your life, even without having met you."

He smiled back, and suddenly I was aware of how warm his hand was in mine, each of his fingertips making my skin tingle. I pulled my hand away, blushing.

"Come on," I said. "Let's get the others."

"The boss is back," groaned Joey when we walked over.

"Lunch break is over."

"It's not a lunch break without lunch," said Avani grumpily.

I looked around, studying the surrounding vegetation, searching for something—*anything*—edible, and I smiled.

"I can fix that."

The others watched doubtfully as I pulled up a thick handful of dry, golden grass. I held it up proudly.

"Great," said Joey with zero enthusiasm. "Cow food."

"Crowfoot grass," I said, giving him a hard look, "is a staple of any proper Kalahari salad. It's actually pretty good for you and makes a tasty trail snack if you're out tracking a leopard all day."

"I assume you're speaking from experience?" asked Sam.

"Multiple experiences. Joey! Stop!"

He'd picked a handful of the grass and was stuffing it in his mouth. He froze and looked at me, long stalks hanging out of his lips. I heard Avani giggle behind me; there was certainly a kind of amusing bovine quality to his expression.

"Just the seeds," I said, and to demonstrate, I nibbled the tip of one of the stalks, where the tiny seeds were clustered.

Joey spat out the grass. "Oh. Right. So, not like a cow. Like a *bird*."

"Like a bird," I confirmed.

"It's actually not bad," said Miranda, trying some. "Sort of like sand. But in a good way."

"*Vegetarians*," muttered Joey, sliding her a suspicious look.

"Hey, I think there's some more over here," said Sam. He was several yards away in a thicket, and he waved. "Yeah, I see it— What the—!?"

"Sam!" I ran toward him, but before I could get three

steps, a young bull elephant burst out of the bushes, headed straight for Sam. I read the signs in a heartbeat: ears pinned back, trunk curled inward. This wasn't a mock charge.

"Tree!" I yelled. "Quick! Climb!" There was no time for full sentences.

He made for the closest one, and I grabbed my hair in my hands and yelped, "Not *that* one!"

But it was too late. He scrambled up three branches before he realized his mistake. His yowls of pain made me wince in sympathy. The elephant reached the tree a second later, and to my horror, it didn't stop. It rammed its head into the trunk and threw its weight forward. With a loud series of cracks and pops, the tree began to tip, with Sam clinging desperately to its branches.

Joey, Avani, Miranda, and Kase had all scurried up trees, but they'd had the fortune of *not* choosing the wait-a-bit tree that Sam had found. There was no plant in the Kalahari as notorious as that one. You only had to brush against it, and it would grab you with its thorny branches that put all other thorns in the world to shame. Extricating yourself from a wait-a-bit tree required surgical precision and patience—hence the name.

But the greater danger was definitely the fifteen thousand pounds of angry elephant intent on trampling Sam. If I didn't do something fast, the tree would fall and Sam would be flattened by those massive gray feet.

"Hey!" I shouted, waving my arms and advancing toward the animal. "Hey, big guy! What do you want him for, huh? What'd he ever do to you? Gosh, you're a big fella." Keeping up a stream of chatter, I managed to get the elephant to turn

JESSICA KHOURY

its head my way. His ears lifted as he studied me, and then he lifted his trunk into the air and trumpeted.

"Oh, is that right? You don't say." Keeping my hands spread wide, I moved in a direction that would lead the elephant away from the tree. "What are you doing out here, anyway? All by yourself? The girls are all up north, dummy. You're not supposed to be here. Sam?" Without changing my cajoling tone or averting my eyes from the elephant's, I addressed him: "Don't try to climb down. Stay in that tree! I know what I'm doing."

He stayed put, looking chastened, while I turned the elephant around. The animal was watching me warily, his trunk searching the air like a fat, gray snake. He trumpeted again and took a threatening step forward. Every muscle in my body was tensed, ready to react. I tried not to look at his long, white tusks, sharp enough to gore me.

I now had the elephant's full attention. All I had to do was figure out how to chase it away before it saw the others, up in their trees off to my left like a troop of alarmed monkeys. But at that moment, the elephant shot forward in a burst of speed—it was charging me.

I looked around, but I knew I wouldn't be able to reach a good tree in time. So I spread my feet and my hands to make myself seem as large as possible and began shouting at the elephant, meeting him eye to eye. The ground underneath me shook from his heavy steps and the sun flashed off those wicked tusks, but I didn't move an inch.

I could barely hear the others all screaming my name over the roar of the elephant and the rush of my heartbeat in my ears. The world shrank away until all I could see was a gray blur thundering down on me like a tsunami, and I had never felt so small, so insubstantial, a pebble dropped into a rushing river. I braced myself, prepared to be swept away.

But at the last moment, when he was just a few feet away, the elephant veered. He trampled past me, so close that the coarse bristles on the end of his tale brushed my shoulder.

Away he ran, noisy as a freight train, and though he disappeared in moments into the bush, I could still hear him trumpeting his frustration to the sky, and a minute later, a loud crack as he pushed over a tree.

I shut my eyes and let out a long breath. When I opened my eyes again, the others had all gathered around me, talking excitedly, laughing, swearing, patting my back.

"No big deal," I said, but my voice was shaking. "Happens more than you'd think. How is Sam?"

We found him still stuck in the tree, which was leaning at a crazy angle after being partially uprooted by the elephant. The thorns had him securely trapped deep in the branches. It took a good half hour to extricate him from the tree, and Kase and I also got stuck in the process.

At last, when we were all free of the wait-a-bit tree, we collapsed onto the ground, panting with thirst. But my spirits had risen like a leaf gathered up by a warm breeze.

Because where there are elephants, there must also be water.

EIGHTEEN

"Take your shirt off," I said to Sam.

He tried, sucking air through his teeth when the cloth rubbed the lacerations on his chest. The cuts from the thorns were nasty enough, but worse was the deep cut across his ribs where a branch had gouged him when the elephant had rammed into the tree.

"Oh, here." I gently eased his shirt over his chest and he lifted his arms to let me tug it off. I tried not to stare at his smooth bared skin, but it was hard given that I had to clean the cuts.

"Last thing you need is an infection," I murmured as I inspected his chest and torso. "And the thorns on that tree were no joke."

Avani appeared with a handful of leaves from the shepherd's tree, which was pretty much the only thing out here that kept its foliage through winter. I used them to wipe the blood from the wounds, my fingers strangely clumsy and my ears burning. Sam made a gargled noise in his throat and winced up at the sky.

"Ouch," said Avani, squinting at the cuts. "Some of them are pretty deep. We need antiseptic."

"See that bush over there?" I pointed.

Avani nodded. "*Ximenia*, yeah."

Of course she knew the name of it. "The berries are mostly dried up, but there should be some seeds still in them. Look in the center of the bush, where the animals can't reach to eat them."

She gave me a skeptical look. "They're an antiseptic?"

"No, but they'll help the skin heal faster."

"Oh, I'm fine," said Sam, waving his hand in dismissal and pulling on the injured skin around his ribs. He winced and sucked in sharply.

"Sure you are," I said.

Avani hurried off to gather the seeds. I glanced over my shoulder to check on the others, and to be sure our elephant wasn't lurking around, waiting to charge again. Kase, Miranda, and Joey were standing glumly in the shade, nibbling crowfoot grass and talking.

"At this rate," I observed, "it'll take *two* weeks to reach Ghansi."

"Sorry. If I'd seen the elephant—"

"Don't," I said. "It's all right. Happens to the best of us. Porcupine, remember? Anyway, nothing you did could have stopped him from charging. The younger males are always wild with testosterone. They spend most of their time knocking trees over in fits of anger. It's all that . . . uh . . . sexual frustration. You know. Because they haven't found a female."

I'd descended into an embarrassed mutter.

Sam laughed. "I know a couple guys like that, back home."

"Yeah, well. That's elephants for you."

My eyes settled on the dog tags that hung between his pectoral muscles—which were, I couldn't help but notice, remarkably firm and defined. Pretty much like the rest of him. My eyes trailed down to his abdomen, the tight muscles beneath smooth skin. . . . *Focus, Sarah.* I snapped my eyes back to the dog tags, safer territory that didn't send fiery tendrils curling across my skin. His brother's name was stamped onto the tags, along with a line of numbers and medical information.

"Do you remember what he looks like?" I asked in a low voice, so soft I barely heard it myself.

Sam frowned, then his hand went to the tags. "Sort of. I mean, I have pictures. But it's different."

"Yeah. I know." I brushed away some sand from around one of his cuts. His skin tightened at my touch.

"Your mom?"

"I'm starting to forget. I think that's the worst part. I try not to. I try to picture her face every night before I go to sleep, but it gets fuzzier each time. I look at photos, but it's not her. The more I . . . forget, the more it hurts." I couldn't believe I was saying this to him; I couldn't even talk to my dad about her. But I felt like I could spill all of my thoughts to Sam and he'd understand, and the weirdest part was that I *wanted* to. "When I heard her voice on the recorder, I realized I'd even forgotten what she sounded like."

"The pain does fade, Sarah."

I looked up at him. His eyes were gentle and unwavering. "Does it?"

"It doesn't go away, but one day you wake up and find it's a part of you."

I nodded.

"I felt guilty at first," he added. "I thought it wasn't fair to him if I, I don't know, got better. Like the only way I could honor his memory was by torturing myself. Not letting go."

I scrunched my eyebrows together, feeling as if he were reading my thoughts. I hadn't even known I'd felt the same way until he spoke it.

Suddenly, his fingers brushed my temple as he tucked my hair behind my ear. It was a tentative gesture, as if he was afraid I'd pull away. But then his fingers lingered on my hair. My thoughts went a bit fuzzy, and I tilted my head slightly, leaning into his touch. "They'd want the opposite, I think. More smiles about the time we had, instead of tears about the times we didn't have."

I gave him a smile that fell away as quickly as it had come. "That's pretty deep."

He laughed. "I stole it from my school counselor."

Avani returned with a handful of seeds, and Sam yanked his hand away, coughing, while I blushed furiously. I took the seeds from her and crushed them between my palms. I squeezed some juice from the bit of *bi* root I had left into my hand and mixed it with the seeds to create a poultice. Avani watched closely as I spread it over the deeper cuts on Sam's chest.

"Feel better?" I asked Sam.

"Yes, actually," he said, looking down at his torso with his brows raised. "Feels better already. Okay. Let's go."

"He still needs antiseptic," Avani muttered to me.

I sighed. "We'll be in Ghansi soon. He'll just have to make it till then."

"Ladies. I'm *fine*," said Sam.

"Mm-hm," said Avani, her hands on her hips. "You be sure and tell me that when you wake up in the middle of the night and pus is leaking out of your stomach and your skin's turning green."

He looked a bit taken aback and studied his middle more closely.

"You'll be fine," I said. "At least for a little while."

"Or we could cauterize it," said Avani, her face lighting up.

"Cauterize?" Sam echoed, looking slightly panicked. "Like, with *fire*?"

"Yes!" She grinned even wider. "I've read how to do it. I definitely could."

"I should've let the sexually frustrated elephant rip my guts out," Sam muttered. "At least it had the decency not to *smile* while it contemplated my murder."

Avani rolled her eyes. "Sam, you gonna put your shirt back on? Before Sarah here starts to hyperventilate?"

Looking thoroughly chastened, Sam shrugged his shirt on. I hissed at Avani through the corner of my mouth as he walked away. "Hyperventilate?"

She shrugged and inspected her nails. "You were studying him like you were prepping for an anatomy exam."

"I was not!"

She gave me a patronizing look. "Whatever, girl. Can't say I blame you. Personally, I'd also prefer to have him walk around with his shirt off."

I sucked at my teeth. "It's not like that. . . ."

"Come on, you guys are always whispering, always rushing to save each other. Anyway, it's not like it has to mean anything. Soon we'll all go our separate ways and that will be that."

I turned to face her full-on. "How can you possibly think that at a time like this?"

She looked thoughtful. "I actually think there should be a name for it. Some scientific term that describes the crazy that people get when they're in mortal danger. You know, like in apocalypse stories—everyone's biggest wish is to get with someone before the asteroid strikes or the aliens blow us up, or whatever. Or how people will confess all their secrets right before they're shot or hanged. Maybe it's the adrenaline. I should research it when I get home."

She must have realized I was staring at her, because she finally broke off and shrugged guiltily. "What? So I do research for fun. You should understand, right? Of all people?"

"No, it's not that."

"What it is then?"

"There's a scorpion in your hair. *Parabuthus granulatus*, to be exact." I thought she'd appreciate the specificity. "Don't move. I'll get it."

But she ignored me and went berserk, batting at her hair and dancing in a circle, screaming.

"Avani! Stop!"

At once, the others jumped up and ran over, asking what was wrong.

"It's the most venomous scorpion in the Kalahari!" she yelled.

"I know!" I yelled back. "That's why frightening it is a *bad idea*. It'll sting you!"

She went still and I quickly flicked the scorpion with a twig. Avani had only driven it deeper into her wild curls, and it took several tries to get it out; it stabbed the twig once, and I was infinitely glad that I hadn't used my finger. I'd been stung by this little beast twice, and both times had left me sick and in pain for days, and that was *with* the antivenom, which we always kept stocked.

The scorpion landed harmlessly in the grass and disappeared in seconds, probably gone to its burrow to recuperate after its terrifying ordeal.

"Okay," I said, maybe too brightly, "so this was a great stop. Very productive. Let's get going."

This time, no one complained about walking again. They all seemed eager to outpace the elephants and scorpions, and I didn't point out that there were likely just as many ahead of us as there were behind us. One good thing might still come out of the encounter: the elephant's tracks, which had come from the west, could very well lead us to a water source. I didn't voice this to the others, in case it turned out to be a false trail, but my spirit stubbornly clung to the hope. We needed water, and badly. I could feel myself drying out like a dead leaf, shriveling beneath the sun. The others were no better, and their chapped, dry skin and cracked lips were, like mine, only minor outward signs of the more dire inward symptoms. If we didn't find water before tomorrow, the Kalahari would kill us as efficiently as one of Abramo's bullets. The elephant's trail was my only lead and perhaps our last hope. Mercifully, there are few tracks as enormous and obvious as an elephant's.

The whole incident had been like a splash of icy water, yanking me out of the stupor Mom's recording had left me in. There was nothing I could do about Mom now, but there was plenty I could do to keep us alive out here. I promised myself that I'd focus on the present. Another lapse like that, and next time I might not see the danger in time and someone could end up hurt or killed. We couldn't afford for me to wallow in regret, not now.

The day was, like every winter afternoon in Botswana, brilliant and blue. No clouds, a soft breeze, temperatures as balmy as a Tahitian beach. The weather out here was weirdly coastal, even though the country was landlocked.

People often talked about the Kalahari as a place of physical and emotional healing, and on a beautiful day like this, I could easily see why. It angered me that Abramo and his people had invaded this sacred place, first to exploit it and then to poison it. I felt the same prickling heat that always rose in my dad's face at the mention of poachers.

I had to do something. Had to get help, had to find Dad, had to warn the authorities about the Metalcium—all of it. This was more than just personal now. What I'd seen in that menagerie had frightened me not only because it threatened my life but because it threatened the entire planet.

My wandering thoughts must have been partly due to my overwhelming thirst, because I can't explain how else I didn't notice the helicopter until it was nearly on top of us.

NINETEEN

Miranda yelled for everyone to hide. It took me a moment to realize what was going on, but then I saw it: low and ominous and black, hovering over the savanna like a giant dragonfly. I could just make out the faint *chop chop* of its rotors.

I didn't think it had seen us yet, because it was moving slowly, sweeping back and forth in a methodical pattern that would spell disaster for us if we didn't find somewhere to hide. The problem was, the trees and bushes around us were mostly bare and offered no good cover. The chopper was so low that its occupants would have no trouble spotting us, even if we were crouched under the foliage.

I looked around frantically, trying to find a solution, walking back and forth as the others peppered me with questions.

"What do we do?"

"Should we run?"

"Sarah? It's getting closer!"

My feet found the answer before my brain did. I hadn't noticed the network of holes until I tripped over one, landing awkwardly on my hands and knees in the sand. I froze, blinking at the hole, as I weighed the dangers underground against the dangers above it. It took less than a second to decide which was more likely to kill us.

"Over here!" I said, waving. "We can hide in these holes."

The others stared at them, doubt plain on their faces.

"How are we supposed to fit?" Avani pointed out.

"The openings are small, but crawl in a few feet and you'll find a somewhat bigger chamber where the—" The roar of the helicopter began to drown out my voice. "Never mind! No time!"

It was Sam who stepped forward first.

"I hope you know what you're doing," he said to me.

He started to kneel down at the hole, but I held up a hand.

"Wait." I studied the ground around it, noting the aardvark tracks, the sliding marks of porcupine quills, and a lot of warthog hoofprints.

"Hurry . . ." Sam muttered, shifting from foot to foot and eyeing the approaching chopper.

The aardvarks dug these holes, but they were used by many creatures as hiding places. Diving in without first checking to see if the hole had any residents was just asking for trouble. I didn't want any of us to come face-to-face with an angry mother warthog three feet underground with nowhere to run. After confirming that all the tracks that led *in* also led *out*, indicating the hole was deserted, I stepped back.

"All clear. Hurry."

He drew a deep breath and shimmied into the hole. I

knew his cuts had to be stinging him, but he didn't complain.

Without waiting to see his legs and feet disappear into the ground, I turned to the others. "There are holes all around here. I can't check each one, so you'll have to do it. Look for tracks leading *in* but not *out*. That'll tell you if they're still in there."

"I can't tell that from a few scuffs in the sand!" Miranda protested. "You check it for me."

I cast an anxious look at the chopper. It was only getting closer, and we had less than a minute before it was right on top of us. Then we'd have no chance at all.

"Avani, can you read the tracks?"

She nodded uncertainly. "I think so."

"Good. Take Joey and go. I'll take Miranda and Kase."

We split up, searching for more holes. Kase found one and I checked it, and then he kissed Miranda swiftly before diving inside.

"Your turn," I said when we reached the next hole.

Miranda looked ready to cry. "I can't do this," she said.

"Sure you can. The Bushmen did it all the time, when they were hunting."

"Have you done it before?"

"Loads of times," I lied. "Miranda, they're almost here."

"I can hide under a bush or something!"

"They'll see! And if they find you, they find the rest of us." I resisted the urge to grab her shoulders and shake her. Why couldn't she understand that the humans in that chopper posed a far greater threat than any critters underground? The sound of the chopper was almost deafening now, drowning out all other noise. For all I knew, they'd already spotted us. We were bent low and dressed in camouflaging khaki, so I thought we might have a chance still, but I didn't want to risk it any further.

"Miranda," I said, looking her in the eye, "if they see you, they'll kill you. And then they'll kill Kase. Do it for him."

That must have struck a chord, because she nodded and squared her shoulders.

Dizzy with relief, I watched her wiggle into the narrow opening, and once her top half had disappeared, I sprinted to the next hole.

There was no time to check the tracks. I just had to hope for the best.

I crawled as fast as I could, knocking loose so much sand that I was afraid I'd collapse the tunnel and bury myself, but somehow it held. I choked on the sand, shut my eyes against it, and crawled blind. The space was so narrow that I had to wriggle on my belly like a snake, my hands stretched in front of me. I had no idea if my whole body was concealed or if my legs were hanging out for the guys in the helicopter to see. Half expecting someone to grab my ankles and pull me backward, I pressed on, feeling roots snatch at my face and hair.

The walls around me began to open, and I wiped the sand from my eyes so that I could look around. I'd found the small cave that had been dug out by aardvarks and the other furry residents who had used this space, creating a chamber just large enough for me to turn around in if I needed to. It was dark and dusty. Only the faintest bit of light trickled in from the mouth of the tunnel. I guessed I was about three feet underground, not very deep, but deep enough to hide me from the eyes in the sky.

I stopped crawling and lay very still, listening to the sound of my heart and my breath. Together they were almost as cacophonous as the chopper had been; the aircraft was still roaring above, but it was muffled. I couldn't tell if it was right above me or already moving off. I wouldn't make a move until it was completely silent.

Shutting my eyes, I tried to distract myself by summoning a pleasant memory. I went back ten years, to a sleepy village in Bangladesh. We'd lived there for a year before moving deeper into the jungles in search of tigers, and I'd attended the tiny school with the Bangladeshi children. It was one of the few times I could remember making real friends with kids my own age. At the end of the year, we'd moved on and I'd cried as we loaded our belongings onto the backs of the elephants and walked into the jungle. My mom picked me up and let me ride on one of the elephants, right behind the huge flapping ears that the villagers had decorated with earrings and paint, and she told me that it was okay to cry for the friends I'd left behind, if only I promised to smile when I was done and be glad for the time I'd had with them. I realized this memory had come to my mind because my mom's words seemed to echo what Sam had said.

In the darkness of my tiny hideout, covered with sand and roots, I smiled.

I could almost hear my mom whispering in my ear, soft and sibilant, like a . . .

Snake.

My eyes snapped open and my mind focused intently on the present.

I was not alone in this hole.

The hissing grew louder, and though I couldn't see it, I knew the snake was in front of me, slithering toward my face. My hands were at my sides but I didn't dare move them, didn't dare breathe, didn't dare *blink*.

The slightest movement could incite the snake to strike, and if it was a black mamba or a puff adder or a Cape cobra—all distressingly likely cases—then I was dead. No negotiation, no magical Bushman cure, no 9-1-1 call. I wouldn't live to see the sunset.

I held my breath and went so still I swear my heart stopped beating altogether. I might have been a corpse already for all the life I displayed.

The snake's hissing was my only indication of its position, and even as my other senses shut down, my ears sharped, honing in on the sound.

It moved past my left ear. *Sssss*, soft as silk over glass.

I felt its tongue flicker across my neck and my stomach heaved, bile rushing up my throat. I didn't move. I didn't scream. I didn't even think. I just waited.

I was blocking the snake's exit, but that didn't discourage it. It simply chose to go *over* me.

Cold, smooth scales slid across the back of my neck. I could feel the muscles beneath them working, bunching and releasing, taut and strong and smooth as liquid.

Not inside my shirt, not inside my shirt, not inside my—

It slithered under my collar and across my bare back, and I have no idea how my eyes didn't pop out of my head then and there. They were so wide they ached, but I couldn't shut them out of pure horror.

This snake was *big*. Seven or eight feet, I guessed, which

meant it wasn't a puff adder or a Cape cobra. Most likely it was a mamba. Maybe it was even the same mamba that had slithered through our camp two nights before.

Of course, black mamba was the worst possible option. One bite held enough venom to kill twelve men in under an hour. At least a puff adder's poison would give me a chance to crawl out of this hole and die with the sunlight on my face.

Thankfully my shirt was untucked, so the snake didn't get trapped inside. It slithered out the other end and worked its way down my leg, over my pants, which were scrunched up to my knees from crawling, and my bare calves. It moved slowly, unhurried, which was good because it meant it wasn't alarmed by me, and which was bad because it took it *ages* to traverse my length.

By the time its head reached my ankle and slid off onto the sand, the tail was just slipping inside my collar. I endured in silence, barely aware of the tears burning in my unblinking eyes.

Then finally, blessedly, I felt the tip of the tail slide over my leg and into the sand, and I was almost free. I'd stopped listening for the helicopter and now I turned my hearing back to the world above.

Silence.

It had moved on, and we were safe for another few hours. I didn't relax quite yet, not until I was sure my way back would be clear.

Gradually my other senses reawakened. I blinked, and the tears that had been balancing on my lashes fell down my cheeks. I tasted blood; I must have been biting my lip the whole time. A slow, cold shudder worked its way down my body, from head to toes, and still I waited another few long minutes while the others searched for me aboveground, calling my name over and over with increasing panic.

At last, I began maneuvering myself around in the tiny chamber.

I crawled out at a snail's pace: I wasn't taking any chances surprising the snake from behind. As I neared the tunnel's exit and the light strengthened, I could make out the long, thin track the reptile had left behind. Seeing it made me shudder all over again.

Sam was the first person to spot me as I peeped out of the ground. He ran to me and helped me out.

"You okay?" he asked. "We thought maybe they'd grabbed you. What took you so long?"

"Snake," I gasped.

Now that I was on my feet, I was trembling, on the verge of throwing up. I bent over and put my hands on my knees, sucking in air as greedily as I had when I'd emerged from the underground lake.

After a moment, I was able to recount what had happened. They made faces of disgust at the story, but I don't think any of them could understand just how horrible it had been.

"We're safe," said Sam. "That's the important thing."

"Yeah," I replied, my voice still shaking. "No problem."

He cocked his head. "You've, uh, got some dirt on your face."

I wiped at my cheeks, but he shook his head. "Here."

Gently, he brushed the pad of his thumb over my eyebrow and temple. I shut my eyes, letting his touch steady me, even as it sent a nervous thrill shivering over my skin.

"Better," he murmured. "Can you keep going?"

I nodded, dazed, starting forward, and picked up the elephant tracks once more. Avani caught my eyes, raising her eyebrows and pursing her lips smugly. I gave her a quick defensive look before striding past her, ignoring her soft laugh.

TWENTY

The encounter with the helicopter left me shaken and para-noid. Now I mistook every bird I saw in the sky for the approaching chopper. Any hopes of Abramo forgetting about us were vaporized, and the grim desperation of our cross-country journey left my stomach in knots.

We walked until the elephant tracks led us to a fat, lone baobab tree. A small troop of bored-looking baboons was lounging in the branches. They perked up as we approached.

I grinned. It was about time we had a win. "If there's still fruit in the tree, we can eat it. And if there are baboons, there must be water nearby. Spread out and look for it, but please, *please* watch out for snakes and elephants and lions." I paused, then added, "In fact, just watch out for *everything*." Better to be on the safe side.

They scattered through the grass, each of them moving with hyperawareness. I went to the tree and eyed the baboons.

There was fruit all right. The baboons had it, and I wanted

it. Baobab fruit is not only delicious; it's a superfruit, packed with all kinds of vitamins and iron and carbs that our bodies desperately needed after meager meals of grass seeds and *bi* root. If I could get my hands on some of the fruits and if the others found the water source, then we'd have ourselves a Kalahari feast.

But there was the problem of the baboons.

After a bit of hunting, I found a termite mound and broke off a piece of it. The dried dirt was nearly as hard as rock. I went back to the tree and picked out the baboon on the lowest branch. It was a male, and he was holding a beautiful whole fruit the size of a melon. I was salivating just looking at it.

I tossed the dried mud in my hand, then pulled my arm back and threw it with all my strength. The time I'd spent playing cricket with the kids in Bangladesh had given me a strong right arm and good aim, and the clump struck the branch the baboon was sitting on. He jumped up with a shriek, showing me his long, yellow teeth. Then he chucked the fruit at me.

I had to dodge aside to avoid being hit, and I shot the baboon a startled look. His aim was impressively accurate.

With a laugh of triumph, I picked up the fruit and bowed to the monkey. "Thank you," I called out. "Much appreciated."

"Talking to monkeys, I see," said Joey.

I turned around to find him twirling a finger beside his temple. He added, "Looks like someone's had one too many swallows of root juice."

Indignantly, I threw the fruit at him. He caught it against his stomach like a football and grunted, wincing a little.

"You're welcome," I said. "Now are you going to help me?"

"You mean you want me to throw rocks at a bunch of

monkeys in a tree in order to compete for food and prove that I, man, am the superior species? *Chica*," he said, clicking his tongue, "I've been waiting for an opportunity like this my whole life. Uh . . . they won't, like, *attack*, will they?"

"Unlikely. There are only six of them, and we're bigger. And look—their male is scrawny and young. He won't mess with us."

We gathered an armful of chunky dried mud from the termite mound and spent the next ten minutes lobbing the pieces at the monkeys. My mom would have been horrified to see such wanton zoological warfare, but the baboons were giving as good as they got, and twice I was struck by flying fruit. It was astonishing how quickly hunger could change you, making you forget the high ideals you'd once lived by. Only the fed could afford morals. Out here, it was jungle law: eat or be eaten. The strong survive; the weak become prey.

By this time, the rest of the our group had joined in with gusto. At some point it turned into a contest to see who could elicit the most fruits from the irritated baboons. I was in the lead but Joey was close behind. He had wicked aim. Miranda and Sam weren't half bad either, but all of Avani's and Kase's throws went wide.

Soon the baboons ran out of missiles and resorted to screaming at us and baring their teeth, and I called a stop to our little war.

Victorious, we carried our hard-won spoils a short distance away, where Miranda proudly showed us the water she'd found. It was in a wide pan of hard-packed sand and mud that, when the rainy season came, would be flooded to the brim. The water that was there was left over from the last season, so it had probably been sitting for months and there wasn't much left. The sand around the pool was riddled with all kinds of tracks: lions, hyenas, leopards, wild dogs, aardwolves, hartebeests, zebra, and the wide, wrinkly prints the size of my head that belonged to our lone elephant.

Joey made an immediate dash for the water, but I called for him to stop.

"That water's been sitting there for months," I said. "And hundreds of animals have been walking through it, slurping from it, and defecating around it."

Joey giggled. "You said *defecating*."

I lifted my eyes skyward and dug very, very deep for a scrap of patience. "The water must be boiled before we can drink it."

"We should do it now," said Miranda. "We can fan the smoke to keep it from giving away our location."

Everyone stared at her.

"What?" she said, shrugging. "I can have ideas too."

"And good ones," I said. "Let's do it. Make a fire now, then let it die, and keep the embers going through the night. It'll still be pretty cold, though."

We devoured the fruits we'd won in our battle with the baboons, relishing the tangy flavor, and filled the shells with water. After fifteen minutes of blistering my hands by rubbing one stick into the other, I placed the shells around the fire, near enough to heat the water but not so close that they caught flame. While we waited for the water to boil, we sat and stared at the shells like jackals waiting for a lion to finish its meal so we could sweep in and grab the leftovers. We took turns fanning the smoke with a branch in an attempt to dissipate it. Otherwise, it might as well have been fireworks that spelled *We're over here!* for Abramo to follow.

Finally, I pronounced the water safe to drink. It was still brownish, but at least any bacteria in it would be harmless now. Infused with the taste of the fruit from the shells, the water actually tasted like a strong citrusy tea. None of us waited for it to cool before gulping it down.

"Baobab," said Joey suddenly. "*Baobab*. Funny word." He said it again, drawing out the syllables in a deep, rotund voice, and then he began to sing it to the tune of a song even I recognized.

"Baobab," he sang, "bao-bab, baobab! *Bao*-bab!"

At that point, Kase unexpectedly jumped in with the lyrics, breaking out in a high falsetto. "In the jungle, the mighty jungle, the lion sleeps tonight!"

The rest of them exchanged looks and shrugs, and chimed in: "In the jungle, the mighty jungle . . ." while Joey kept up his "baobab" rhythm. Then, still singing in a deep bass, he jumped up and began dancing like a maniac around the fire, stomping his feet and shaking his hips. He looked so ridiculous that we had to stop singing because we were laughing so hard. I felt some of the tension between my shoulders ease; the laughter was like a balm to my weary and frayed nerves.

For the first time since we'd climbed out of the underground lake, my thirst was fully sated. I was still hungry, but it wasn't the pinching, maddening hunger it had been before. The rich nutrients in the fruit were already boosting my energy, and, obviously, the others' as well.

At some point, Sam rose and said he was going to look

around. He had been quiet through the meal, smiling but not really laughing. I watched him as he meandered through the grass and finally sat down on the edge of the pan, staring at the sunset.

While the others kept laughing and attempting to sing, I stood up and began scouting the area, just to see if the lion tracks I'd spotted were fresh or not. I determined that the pride had come through that morning, which was good news. They wouldn't be back again for another few days, so we were safe for the night. From lions, anyway. I figured we could handle any other animals that came through.

Pretty soon, I found myself standing near Sam. He was lying on his back, with all the colors of the Kalahari sunset reflected in his eyes.

"Mind if I join you?"

He looked up at me as if I'd startled him, but smiled and patted the ground.

I lay down next to him with my head a foot away from his.

"How are you feeling?" I asked.

"Not bad." His hand went to his abdomen. "The cuts aren't bleeding."

"That's good. We should use some of the water to clean them properly, though."

"In a while," he said sleepily.

We stared up at the sky in silence, watching a pair of hawks circle one another on a thermal, their pale undersides standing out against the darkening sky. I tilted my head back to look at the setting sun and held up a hand against the crimson glow. Light streamed between my fingers.

Sam's nearness set me on edge. Or maybe it was Avani's

words. *You were studying him like you were prepping for an anatomy exam.*

I yanked a piece of crowfoot grass from the ground beside me and vengefully nibbled at its seeds. *Was not.*

"Crazy couple of days, huh?" said Sam. "Is your life always this nuts?"

"You should know," I said. "You read all about it."

He said nothing.

I sighed and rolled over, propped on my elbows. "Sam . . . I'm sorry. I didn't mean that, really. I feel like I'm hanging over the edge and losing my grip. I keep seeing Theo and wondering about Dad when what I need to do is concentrate on keeping us in the right direction. . . ."

"No. It's okay. I get it."

"I just . . . I wish . . . I wish we had *time*, you know? Time when we're not running or hiding or worrying about what we'll eat or where we'll sleep. I wish we had time to talk. To . . ." I hesitated, torn between embarrassment and boldness. "To get to know each other," I finally confessed, glancing sideways at him nervously, hoping I didn't sound like a total idiot.

He tilted his head backward to meet my gaze. "What do you want to know?"

Unable to hold his stare, I looked down at the sand and idly drew a circle in it with my index finger. "I don't know. Like . . . what's your favorite color?"

He laughed, a soft, husky sound that made my heart leap. "Blue. But not, like, *blue* blue. Sort of a steel blue."

I nodded. "Okay. Favorite movie?"

"*Dead Poets Society.*"

"Never saw it."

"You've *never* seen *Dead Poets Society?*"

I spread my hands apologetically. "I don't watch many movies. Not much electricity out here, remember?"

He shook his head. "Man, that is tragic. About the movie. Not the electricity part. I could get used to the quiet out here."

"What do you do in your spare time?"

"Read, mostly. Nonfiction and history. I love studying ancient cultures—Mayans, Phoenicians, stuff like that. I always imagined I'd go into archaeology or something." He said it a bit sheepishly.

"You should do it!" I said.

"Really?" He looked pleasantly surprised. "I haven't told anyone about that yet. But I want to travel first. I'm almost eighteen, so the state will probably put me up somewhere for a few months, and then I'll find an apartment. Get a part-time job. I've got one year left of high school. After that, I'm going to travel."

"Yeah?"

"Egypt's top of the list. I want to see the pyramids. They're the only one of the Seven Wonders of the World that still exists. Kind of sad, don't you think?"

"I've never seen the pyramids."

"Really? I'd have guessed you'd seen everything."

"No," I said softly. "Not everything."

"Then we should go. You and me and the pyramids."

I blinked in surprise. "What?"

Sam cleared his throat, looking suddenly shy. "I mean . . . since neither of us has been . . . Never mind, that's a stupid thing to—"

"No," I interrupted. "We should go. It would be fun."

Sam stared at me as if somewhat amazed. "Really? Well, yeah, okay. So the pyramids. Then India. Then Mongolia. Have you been to Mongolia?"

"Once. Briefly. My dad was visiting a friend of his who's studying snow leopards up there."

"I want to see it all," he said. "Just got to find a way to pay for it."

"You could get a job as a research assistant with a field team," I blurted out. "My dad had an intern for a while from Boston. His name was Pete. Maybe Dad could—" My throat constricted. "I mean, if he's still—you know."

"That would be great," Sam said firmly, cutting me off before I could voice all my deepest fears about Dad. "I'd love that."

"Oh, Sam." My ribs seemed to shrink, squeezing my lungs and heart, making me choke. "What if it's already too late?"

Sam sat up and looked me squarely in the eye. "He's out there, Sarah," Sam insisted.

I smiled, but it was weak.

"You *will* find him," he said. "And I'm going to help you."

I raised an eyebrow. "No. In a few days we'll reach Ghansi, and then you're going *home*."

Sam's brow creased and he cocked his head, studying me as if I didn't add up. I lowered my gaze, suddenly shying away from how deeply he seemed to look into me. Then I felt his fingers in my hair, running down one of the tendrils that had escaped my ponytail. I held my breath, lifting my eyes to meet his. Sam gave me a slight, quizzical smile. "You don't honestly think I'd just *leave*, do you?" he said softly.

"I don't need protection," I retorted, bristling a little.

He raised his hands in defense. "I think it's obvious that out here, you're the one taking care of *me*. What I mean is, nobody should be alone through something like this, Sarah."

That left me at a loss. I felt as if a hole had opened inside me, sucking away all my words, all my defenses. He was right. I had no one. He'd seen right to the core of my misery, and I suspected it was because he knew exactly what I felt.

"Were you alone?" I asked in a whisper. "When you found out . . . you know. Adam."

"Yes," he said. His eyes turned to the ground. "I'd been in Pittsburgh for less than a month. I didn't know anybody. No one to call, no relatives." He lifted his eyes. "You don't want to go through that. Let me help you."

"I—I can't. It's better if you go." I was already too close to him. My eyes searched for him too often, too instinctively. I blushed too deeply when his voice turned soft and his skin brushed mine. I reminded myself that he would leave sooner or later, and when he finally did, I didn't want to be the girl left behind.

"Why?" Sam asked. The pain in his eyes made me look away. "Is it because you think I'm some charity case delinquent?"

"I don't think that!"

"Because it's true. I'm only here because my history teacher convinced the Song Foundation to grant me a scholarship. I could never afford a trip like this."

I blinked, absorbing this, then let out a small, soft laugh, which elicited a look of surprise and puzzlement from Sam. I explained, "The whole reason we agreed to take you guys on is because the Song Foundation promised to give us money. What do you think I live on? Every bite I eat is paid for out of someone else's pocket. Our whole operation is run on grant money and donations from zoological societies. If you're a charity case, then so am I."

He frowned, taking this in, then a slow smile made his eyes brighten. "So. One charity case to another: Will you let me stay and help you?"

Our eyes held, and I forgot about silver lions and black helicopters, and hunger and time and my aching heart, and whether we'd reach Ghansi or if we'd even live through tomorrow.

My eyes fixed on his, and it was like looking into the starry night and realizing for the first time just how deep and wide and impossible space is. His eyes went on forever, tempting me, drawing me toward him. I felt the pull of an urge so primal, so natural, that I didn't need to think. I only needed to act, to give in to that intoxicating impulse.

I leaned toward Sam, he met me halfway, and we melted into a kiss that made my thoughts shrink together into a nucleus of vibrating sensation before they burst outward like a thousand stars. As soon as I felt his lips, I realized I'd wanted it for a while, maybe since the day I first saw him. My skin glowing with heat and longing, I surrendered.

I reached up and grabbed his shirt, pulling him closer. His hand slipped around my neck, his fingers threading through my hair. His lips tasted of baobab fruit, sweet and tangy like an orange. I could feel his heartbeat against the palms of my hands, its pace as frantic as my own.

He drew me in to him, his other hand pressing against the small of my back, and my lips parted against his. He felt like fire and the cool Kalahari breeze, making my heart pound and my thoughts whirl like leaves in the wind.

The kiss felt like a moment, but it must have lasted much longer, because when we finally broke apart, breathing hard, our foreheads touching, the sun was already below the horizon and the sky blazed from scarlet to purple.

I looked back toward the fire, wondering if the others were missing us, but he caught my chin with his fingers and turned me back to him.

"Don't go," he whispered. "Please."

I studied his face, the freckles on his nose and cheeks, the cleft in his chin, the faint crease between his eyebrows. His sandy hair had fallen across his forehead, and I couldn't resist sweeping it back. My fingers lingered on his face, trailing downward to his jaw, which was rough with stubble after days out here without shaving. "Okay."

The crease vanished when he smiled. He reached up and pulled me into his chest. "Tell me a story."

"A story? What kind?"

"Something about you. Something not in the book."

We were talking in a hush, even though we far enough away from the others that they would have heard us only if we yelled. Sam's face was inches from mine, so close that I could see the dark flecks in his green eyes.

"Okay. Um. One time, in Australia, I stole a baby kangaroo."

"What? No!"

I laughed. "Yeah. It was just so cute! I was only, gosh, six, I think? Anyway, these roos were pretty tame, you know. Used to people being around. It was great, except for when they kicked you."

"Did they ever kick you?"

"Several times. They kick like mules, but it's the funniest thing to see as long as you're not the one they're kicking. But that's not the story."

"So you stole the baby."

"The joey. Yeah." I giggled, thinking of our Joey by the fire. "Baby kangaroos are called—"

"Yeah, Sarah. I know."

"Okay. So it was only nine months old, but it was almost too heavy for me to carry. It had gotten tangled up in an old rabbit fence, and it couldn't hop. So I thought, in my six-year-old brain, that I could help it get better. I stole it when the other kangaroos were sleeping and took it back to our camp to put Band-Aids on its injured leg. Then I knew I couldn't hide it in the tent or my parents would find it. So I . . ." I paused and ran a hand over my hair, laughing in embarrassment. "Um, I hid it in the toilet."

"Wait." Sam held up a hand, palm out. "You hid the baby kangaroo in the *toilet.*"

"That's what I did. It was this little portable toilet covered by this tarp hung on a branch. It was the perfect size for the little roo—and I made sure it was clean. At least, a six-year-old's idea of clean. It never occurred to me that my parents would actually *use* the toilet. So I went to bed and I remember crying myself to sleep because I felt so guilty about hiding it from my parents, but I couldn't tell them, and I was like this little pressure cooker of conflict and guilt and excitement at having a kangaroo in my toilet."

"So what happened?" He was watching my lips more and more as we spoke, and I found myself losing my train of thought. I looked away.

"Well, my mom went to the bathroom in the middle of the night and saw it. She screamed—oh, man, I'll never forget it—and I woke up and I knew right away that she'd seen it. I think she secretly thought it was funny, but she was pretty harsh when she told me we had to give it back to its mother. She said, 'Nature has a way of taking care of itself, if we only step aside.' She let me watch the roos from a distance, as the mother took care of the joey and eventually it healed and hopped like the rest of them. Still, as punishment I had to do fifty push-ups."

"Push-ups!"

"My parents had weird disciplinary ideas."

"Push-ups. I like it."

"I like *you*." He looked startled. I stopped, wincing. "Oh my gosh. Sorry. Was I not supposed to say that? I mean, there aren't many guys out here, so I'm not really—"

Sam touched his finger to my lips. "Sarah," he said with a smile, "I like you too."

This time, it was Sam who kissed me.

We never made it back to the fire. We lay side by side for hours, as the night deepened and the temperature fell. When I began to shiver, Sam held me closer, tighter, and we kept each other warm.

"Do you ever wish you could pull a moment out of time?" asked Sam. "So that you could live it again whenever you wanted?"

I nodded.

The Kalahari night sky is the most beautiful in the world. There are no artificial lights to dim the stars, no clouds or tall trees to block them, and the universe is displayed the way it was meant to be seen: unfathomably beautiful, taking my breath away. Stars upon stars upon stars, as numerous as the sand, some bright and twinkling, some dim and steady. Across the center of the sky stretched the Milky Way, a thick dusty band of stars and supernovas and galaxies and worlds we'd never touch, swirling in shades of blue, purple, and pink. It made everything else shrink away, seeming small and ephemeral in comparison. We didn't talk much after that, just shared the night in comfortable silence, our breaths frosting the air.

TWENTY-ONE

When I woke, I was lying on my side, my head resting on Sam's shoulder and his face so close to mine that I could see his eyelashes fluttering as he dreamed.

It was barely dawn; the sun had not yet appeared but a pastel glow spread across the eastern sky. The sparrows and larks were already tuning their songs in preparation for morning. I yawned sleepily, feeling a dopey grin spread across my face.

I rolled onto my back, careful not to wake Sam. His hand, which had been resting on my shoulder, slipped to the ground. I was freezing cold. It had been stupid to stay out here all night, but I had fallen asleep without realizing it. I sat up slowly. Sam made a soft, sleepy sound but did not wake.

The others were sleeping close to the embers of last night's fire. Kase and Miranda were pressed against each other, and Avani and Joey were buried in nests of grass. The embers appeared to be dead, but I knew if we stirred them they'd come back to life quickly enough.

Suddenly I realized we'd failed to post guards through the night. Had it been that easy to distract me from the most important job of keeping everyone alive? Trembling with cold and self-directed anger, I gently shook Sam awake.

"Come on," I said, "come down to the fire. You're freezing."

"Coming," he murmured, without opening his eyes.

I stared at his face for a moment, then brushed the hair from his forehead, leaned over, and kissed him once, briefly, on the lips.

At that, his eyes fluttered open and he smiled drowsily, his hand lifting to stroke my hair.

"Look at you. You're beautiful," he said, his voice husky with sleep.

I smiled and batted his hand aside. "Get up. I'm going to start the fire. You need warmth. Your lips are kinda blue."

"But not from the cold."

I rolled my eyes. "I'll meet you down by the fire."

First I hunted for some firewood, keeping an eye on the tracks around us to see what sort of animals had come spying on us in the night. A genet, a jackal, a pair of warthogs, several kudu. Nothing too serious. I carried my armload of wood back to the fire as the others began to wake. It took a few minutes to get the wood to catch—there was very little warmth left in the ashes—but once it did, it blazed up merrily.

"I'm going to see if there are any more fruits around the baobab," I said. "Keep the fire going."

I hiked the short distance to the lone tree and found the baboons had taken off during the night. The ground around the trunk yielded no fallen fruits, and the few I could see on the branches were out of my reach. I studied the trunk and decided it was worth a try.

I was an excellent tree climber. My dad used to say that I learned to climb before I could walk. The baobab was tricky, since there were no low branches and the trunk was too fat to shimmy up, like I would a palm tree. Instead, I had to use the vertical grooves in the bark, wedging my feet between them and slowly making my way up.

When I reached the first branch—which was thicker than I was—I lifted myself over it and crouched there, balancing where the baboons had been the day before. From there, it was easy to navigate through the thick branches, picking the last of the fruits that the baboons had missed. I stepped from branch to branch with sure-footed ease, not minding the height or the twigs scratching my face, arms, and legs. The outermost limbs were heavy with sparrow weaver nests—bunchy, twiggy fabrications bedecked with loose feathers.

I dropped the fruits I gathered to the ground and looked around one last time, spotting a single pod still hanging at the end of the highest branch. It would be harder to reach, but it was the biggest one I'd seen so far.

I decided to go for it. I climbed up and outward, shaking off a few ants that had ventured onto my arms. I sat on the branch bearing the fruit and scooted out, my legs dangling thirty feet above the ground.

The end of the branch was too narrow to support my weight, so I leaned out as far as I could and stretched out my hand, biting my lip in concentration. The branch creaked threateningly, but I ignored it. The fruit was almost within reach—*Got it!*

The branch cracked beneath me with a loud *pop*. My stomach turned inside out as I began to drop, and instinctively I reached out for the branches beneath me. I landed on one, and it knocked the wind from my lungs with a gasp. I clung to it rigidly as a shower of branches rained around me to the ground below. After a minute, when all was still again, I shakily pulled myself upright and leaned against the trunk. The close call left me trembling but relieved, and I laughed.

I cautiously began to climb down the tree, searching for secure hand and footholds. There was a dark hollow above one of the branches, and I reached for it to lower myself down. To my shock, my fingers touched not wood—but soft fur. I yanked my hand back and grabbed the branch below the hole to steady myself, as two round eyes peered out of the darkness while the creature to which they belonged remained obscured in shadow. I recognized them right away: There was no mistaking the huge, luminous eyes of a nocturnal bush baby. I'd woken him up, and he squeaked at me indignantly.

Smiling, I said, "Hey, little guy. Sorry to wake you."

In response he burst from his hole and perched on my hand, which I thought was odd—they're notoriously shy creatures.

And then I saw the reason for his abnormal behavior.

I froze.

The bush baby's enormous eyes grew wider and wider as his cat-like ears swiveled rapidly. His fur, impossibly soft, impossibly silver, caught all the pastel lights of the morning and reflected them onto the branches around us, but most brilliant were those perfectly circular eyes, which held my own image in them with startling clarity, like small twin mirrors.

Suddenly I came to my senses and shook my arm as hard as I could. The bush baby leaped to the branch above and disappeared into the upper canopy of the tree. My heart had resumed beating, but at a galloping pace. I began whimpering, louder and louder, as I rubbed my hand desperately against my shirt.

No, I thought. *No, please. Oh, God. No no no no . . .*

I abandoned caution and shimmied down the trunk so quickly that it left my fingers and knees scraped and bleeding. I bent over and furiously scrubbed my hands with sand, my entire body shaking.

It touched me only for a moment. Maybe I'm not infected.

I lifted my hands and stared at them, remembering what Dr. Monaghan had said about Metalcium. *It starts with itching.*

I focused on my hands, trying to determine whether they were itching or not, even though it was likely too soon to tell.

"Sarah!"

I jumped at the shout. It was Sam, running toward me from the camp.

"There you are," he said. "What are you doing? Are you okay?"

"I fell out of the tree." I stood up, my hands clenched at my sides, and put on a false smile. "Not hurt, just a little winded."

He looked up at the high branches, then at me, his eyes wide. "Are you sure?"

"I'm *fine.* Can you carry the fruit back to the others? I want to look around a bit more, see if there's anything else that's useful."

He nodded, but still watched me mistrustfully. "You're *sure* you're okay? You're pale."

I pressed a hand to my forehead, then yanked it away as if it had burned me. "A little shaken, that's all."

He bent to pick up the fruit I'd dropped, wincing a little and putting a hand on his injury, and kept glancing back at me. To avoid his eyes, I walked into the bush, pretending to look around for any edible plants. In truth, I could scarcely see where I was going. I felt like a time bomb, ticking down to an explosion. I needed to be alone to think.

I found a secluded spot out of Sam's sight and sat down, leaning against an acacia. Holding my hands out in front of me, I studied them intently, turning them over, flexing my fingers. My stomach was twisting inside me, threatening to spill the fruit and water I'd had the night before.

I couldn't be sure I was infected. Dr. Monaghan hadn't told us the specifics of how Metalcium spread. Sure, he said it was by touch—but maybe he meant you had to be bitten, or had to touch the infected animal for a long time. Like poison ivy. If you just barely brushed against poison ivy, you'd probably be fine. It had to rub your skin to infect you.

I imagined the silver bush baby running through the grass, its silver tail raised like a banner, as it spread Metalcium like wildfire through the bush. Suppose a jackal snapped it up? And what if a leopard caught the jackal? This was a poison that could contaminate the entire food chain as it spread, touch by touch, outward across Botswana. What could contain it? How would we prepare? If what Dr. Monaghan had said was true, then infected creatures would have up to a few days showing no signs but itching. In that time, Metalcium could quietly expand across the borders, leave on planes with tourists. Like the bubonic plague all over again—only worse.

I imagined floods of silver rats infecting entire cities, people by the hundreds turning into silver madmen.

This had to change nothing about our original plan. I would get them to Ghansi, and then I'd go back. I'd just have to do it as fast as possible, and without any of them touching me.

Slowly, I stood up, holding my hands away from my body as if they were already covered in a sheen of parasitic metal. I realized tears had spilled down my cheeks. I wiped them on my shoulders and began to walk.

I had sworn to get the others safely to Ghansi, and I would not break that promise. Maybe they'd never have to know about the silver bush baby. And even if I was infected, Dr. Monaghan had said you could go for days before it showed. They'd never find out, because they'd be home by then. Except for Sam, if he still insisted on coming back with me.

Oh, Sam. A wave of sorrow swept over me. I should have been spending the morning basking in the kiss we'd shared, in the night we'd spent in each other's arms. Instead, that memory seemed as distant and untouchable as the stars under which it had happened. There was no way I could touch him now and possibly not ever again. That had been our first and last kiss.

I circled the camp, staying out of sight, my eyes sweeping back and forth across the sand. I named every set of prints I saw in an attempt to pull my mind out of the chaotic panic into which it had descended. It helped, a little. Solid, tangible things had a way of stilling my thoughts, like a steady hand catching a rocking swing. I had to anchor myself in the present moment, to let the future and all its potential horrors slip away.

I don't want to die.

The thought surged through me, weakening my knees. I collapsed and huddled in the sand, my throat burning with tears I fought to hold back. Since Mom's death, I hadn't much cared what happened to me. The world had been covered in a gray veneer, tasteless and uninteresting. She had been the sun that lit the savanna, and when she died, I'd been left in darkness, not caring whether I stumbled forever through the night or fell over a cliff and was lost.

Now I looked back and realized how idiotic, how *selfish* that apathy had been. I'd cloaked myself in the shadow of her death and never once considered that I could be happy again. The world hadn't gotten darker—only my vision had. Now I saw that my sadness wasn't entirely to be blamed on my loss; I'd stolen my own happiness by refusing to search for it. In the moment it took to register that she was gone, I'd forgotten everything she had ever taught me.

And Sam—sweet, smiling Sam with his dogged optimism— had known it. Somehow he'd reached me through my fog and begun to draw me out, and last night for the first time I'd felt the light again. Realized that the sun *could* rise on a world without my mom. Recognized that I might even be happy again. I'd caught the spark of wonder from Sam's eyes and with it, I had begun to see the beauty that I had shut out.

But none of that mattered anymore. That stupid, impossible little animal with its mirrored eyes had shattered my future and my brief happiness with its gentle whispering touch.

I was wasting precious minutes out here, drowning in melancholy, when we needed to reach Ghansi faster than ever. Only time would tell if I was truly infected. Maybe I didn't have tomorrow, but I had today, and I'd be damned if I didn't make that count.

TWENTY-TWO

We reached the road that afternoon. It was hidden in the brush, so we didn't see it until we stepped right onto it. I stared at it, a bit stunned by its suddenness.

The "road" was barely that; it consisted of a series of sandy tracks that ran north to south, and over time, it had grown wider and wider as the passing tires had worn the ruts deeper into the sand, creating treacherous ditches a foot or more deep. Cars had begun to drive beside the road rather than on it in an effort to navigate around the trenches, resulting in even more ruts. What had started out as a one-lane road was now almost a dozen lanes wide, some of them zigzagging crazily around encroaching vegetation.

I crouched down and studied the tire spoor.

"A truck went through this morning," I said.

"When will the next one come?" asked Avani.

"No telling." I shrugged. "Could be five minutes, could be five hours. Could be tomorrow."

"How far are we from Ghansi?"

I considered. My wrist was itching, and the sensation yanked my concentration. I squinted, trying to focus my thoughts, telling myself it was just my mind playing tricks. I was focusing so hard on *not* itching that of course I did. But was it *just* my imagination? "Sixty miles, give or take."

Everyone groaned. Their initial excitement at finding the road faded visibly.

Except for Sam. He hadn't stopped grinning since he woke up.

"Hey, guys," he said. "We made it this far, didn't we? We can do sixty more miles. That'll take, what, two days?"

I winced. "Not if we're having to hunt for food."

"Okay. So three or four. And if we walk along the road, chances are a car will come by. And maybe the driver will even have a cell phone!"

That *did* cheer them up. They began talking about the first things they'd do when they got to civilization.

"Shower," said Miranda. "Followed by a bubble bath, followed by a swim in a pool—I don't even care if it's chlorinated! Followed by another shower."

"Buffet," said Joey. "Hands down. I'd rent the entire place and have the whole thing to myself, just rows and rows of steaks and mashed potatoes and tacos and those fried little squid things—"

"Calamari?" Avani offered.

"Calamari! I love calamari. What about you, Canada? What'll you do?" He sidled up to her. "I'll share my buffet if you ask nicely."

She shook her head. "Uh-uh. I'm finding some Internet. My grades from last semester were posted a week ago and I still don't know if—" She was drowned out by a chorus of groans and boos.

"I just want to sleep," said Kase. "In a hotel bed, where I can order room service until I'm sick."

"Mm, baby, count me in," said Miranda, slipping her arms around him and going in for a kiss. "I'm sick of this desert."

Avani cleared her throat. "You mean, *semi*—"

More groans and boos drowned her out.

This whole time, I stayed crouched on the tracks, staring at an ant that was traversing what, to him, was the Grand Canyon. I let them talk back and forth, unable to bear breaking the reality to them.

"Sarah," said Sam, kneeling beside me. "What's wrong?"

The others fell silent and looked at me. I sighed and stood up.

"We can't follow the road," I said. "We just needed to find it in order to get our bearings. We have to walk to Ghansi."

There was loud silence filled by chirping crickets and birds.

Then they erupted.

"What do you *mean*, we can't follow the road?"

"My feet are covered in blisters!"

"*More* walking?"

"No! I'm sitting here until the next bus comes by."

I waited in silence until their protests subsided. When they did, I pointed at the sky.

"They'll be combing the road for us," I said. "If they're

smart, they'll check every vehicle that goes through this area. This road is the most dangerous place we could be. Now"—I bent down again and drew a few quick lines in the sand—"if we cross here and make a wide circle north, we can approach Ghansi from the west. We have to get there without Corpus knowing, and it'll be hard to escape notice in a town that size."

"We can send in Canada," said Joey. "She'll blend in."

Avani looked as if she were about to punch him, then she paused. "Actually," she said, "that's not a bad idea."

Joey beamed at her.

"We'll worry about that when we get there," I said. "But we're still a few days out. Now, we're behind schedule as it is, and Matthieu should land at Camp Acacia in a few days. He'll notice something's wrong and alert someone." If Corpus didn't find him first. I didn't want to think about that possibility. Just how desperate were they to find us? They'd already proven they were capable of murder and sacrificing their own people to clean up their mess, but would they go so far as to eliminate every person who wandered into the area, just in case they'd met and talked to the six of us? Our continued survival put the whole population of central Botswana at risk if Corpus thought we might tell what we'd seen. Then again, if we were caught, who would tell everyone about the Metalcium outbreak? Either way, lives were at stake.

Putting that unsettling thought aside, I added, "Even if Matthieu does alert someone that we're missing, there's just as much chance of Corpus finding us as a search team. We can't sit around waiting to be rescued."

No one looked happy about it, but they nodded agreement.

I felt relieved; I'd expected more of a fight. That relief shattered as my wrist began to itch again. I stared at it, throat dry, willing myself not to scratch.

"Good," I said, my voice hoarse. "So first thing, we need to get away from this road. . . ."

My voice died as a new sound cut the air: an unmistakable *chop chop chop.*

"Chopper," I said. "*Hide.*"

We darted across the road and into the bush without looking back. I frantically searched for holes we could hide in like the last time, my heart thumping like a caged animal's. The chopper was coming from the south, following the road just as I'd predicted.

I began to panic as my search turned up no place suitable for cover. I called everyone together, keeping one eye on the helicopter. It was moving slowly, taking its time, the bulbous glass windshield like some giant all-seeing eye.

"If they see us, split up," I told everyone. "Stay low, stay in the thick brush, and follow our tracks back east, the way we came. We'll meet up at the baobab tree, got it?"

"I can't find my way back," said Miranda, her eyes large and serious.

"Then stay with Kase. Together your chances are better. That goes for all of us—stick with someone."

"Buddy system!" said Joey.

The chopper was almost on us. There was no more time to plan; I had to hope we wouldn't be seen. I wasn't at all confident we'd find one another again if we split up now, even though it shouldn't be hard to follow the only trail of six human footprints for miles around. What worried me more was that Corpus would catch up to one of us.

"Get down!" Sam shouted.

We rolled under the bushes, lying flat in the tall grass. I was very careful to keep a healthy distance between me and anyone else—I didn't want to accidentally bump into anyone. *Our chances are good*, I lied to myself. The cover might be thin, but animals managed to disappear into it, didn't they?

"Keep still," I said, as the helicopter began prowling over the stretch of road we'd just crossed. Its round shadow swept over us, making me shudder. It was close enough now that I could see the pilot, his face hidden by his helmet, and Abramo sitting beside him. He'd found a new crew; there were several men behind him. The aircraft looked capable of carrying half a dozen people at least.

The chopper slowed above the road and hovered so low that it whipped up a great funnel of sand. My heart stopped. Why were they stopping? What had they seen? Not our tracks—they'd destroyed them by stirring up the sand. Unless they had binoculars or something and had seen them from far off, but that would take a masterfully sharp eye.

Though every muscle in my body was on the verge of bolting, I forced myself to remain still, even holding my breath. My arm was itching terribly now, my skin crawling as if covered with scuttling spiders.

Don't scratch, Dr. Monaghan's delirious voice whispered through my thoughts.

My heart plummeted and I stared at my skin. *It's my imagination. It's the grass rubbing against it, or it's just the sand. . . .*

How quickly did Metalcium take effect? Dr. Monaghan had said that it could kill you within days, but how long did it take to actually set in?

A cry interrupted my grinding inner panic. I looked around. The chopper was slowly gliding away from the road—and toward our hiding spot. It was Avani who'd cried out, and Joey was shushing her.

Had they seen us? If they'd seen us, we had to run *now*. If they hadn't, we still had a chance. I was torn between staying and bolting, unsure which was more likely to get us killed.

"Oh, no," Sam said. "Miranda! Kase!"

They had begun to creep out from under their bush, apparently going to make a run for it. Sam urged them again to stop, and then he looked at me for support.

I stared at him with my mouth gaping. I didn't know what to do or what to say. Maybe they *should* run.

The chopper's wind rattled the grass and vegetation, blowing sand into my eyes. I winced and rubbed it away, and when I opened them, I saw that Kase and Miranda had dashed out of cover and were running north. Avani and Joey went next, heading south, and then Sam was in front of me, holding out a hand.

"Let's go!" he said. "They're confused about who to chase—now's our chance!"

I almost took his hand. Almost. At the last moment I snatched it back, horrified at how close I'd come to infecting him.

"Go!" I yelled. "I'm right behind you!"

But he waited until I was on my feet before sprinting away.

The chopper was roving in a wide circle above us, perhaps trying to keep an eye on all three pairs, but we were spreading too far apart. They had to choose.

They went after Sam and me.

We wove back and forth, sticking to the most overgrown thickets in an attempt to lose them. It was no good. Every time we thought we'd reached sufficient cover, they flushed us out again. It made me think of the old hunting techniques poachers once used to drive buffalo out here, chasing them with airplanes until they ran into the veterinary fence that stretched like a belt across the whole of Botswana; then the poachers would pick off the trapped animals at their leisure.

Were they trying to exhaust us, then grab us? What was the point of chasing us if they weren't going to shoot?

As we ran, I had to split my attention between the chopper and Sam—specifically, on not accidentally touching him. I kept a safe ten yards between us, and he was so focused on watching where he was going that he didn't have a chance to ask me why.

Suddenly we broke out of the thick brush we'd been dodging through and onto a wide flatland of grass and low thickets. There was zero cover. We turned around, intending to dart back into the tall bushes, but at that moment the side door of the helicopter slid open and a man crouched in the opening began firing at us with an automatic rifle so loud I could hear it even over the chopper's engine. He was spraying the bushes with bullets in a clear indication that he meant to drive us into the open.

We had no choice but to keep going. It was useless, really.

We couldn't outrun a helicopter. I realized they must have seen this flat area long before we did, and had been driving us toward us, herding us from the air. On the open grassland, we made for much easier targets.

"We have to split up!" I yelled to Sam.

He nodded but didn't look happy about it.

"Meet you at the baobab!" I called, and I veered to the left. Sam went right. All too quickly, he was swallowed up by the vast savanna, out of sight, and I was alone.

TWENTY-THREE

The helicopter hesitated once we split, then turned to follow me. I wondered if that was deliberate, and if Abramo had recognized me from the lab.

The chopper sped up and passed me, then slowed and turned to face me head on, intending to cut me off. I skidded to a stop and began to go back, but when I turned around, already sprinting, I halted so sharply that I fell forward onto my knees.

Three adult giraffes, each of them as silver as an American quarter, had broken out of the bushes and were running across the savanna, their long legs flashing in the sun. I was held enthralled for a moment, horrified and awed by the majestic creatures. The smallest of the three still retained some of its original coat around its legs, so that it looked as if someone had held it by the hooves and dipped it in a vat of mercury. They ran with their tails thrown over their haunches and their ears laid flat, as if they were running from predators, but I saw no lions or leopards chasing them. Likely they were trying to outrun the Metalcium itself, unable to comprehend what was happening to them.

I looked back at the helicopter, which had ceased firing at me. Abramo seemed to be focused on the giraffes now, perhaps trying to decide which was the greater threat—me or the infected animals. In the long run, it would be me—after all, I knew his name, his employer's name, and I had seen the lab—but on the other hand, the giraffes were too near Ghansi and its outlying villages to escape notice for long.

Go after them, I thought. *They're the ones you want.*

At first, I was certain the chopper would bear down on me anyway, but the giraffes were getting farther and farther away; already I'd lost all sight of them save for their heads above the trees in the distance.

Slowly, reluctantly, the helicopter turned and beat its way after the herd.

Panting, I slumped over with relief. After a moment, I lifted my head and called for Sam but heard no response.

I was desperately thirsty. It would take most of the night to hike back to the baobab and the meager supply of water, but it was the only choice I had. As evening approached, the chances of a car passing by shrank to practically nothing, so there was little point of waiting by the road. Anyway, it was almost certain that the chopper would return after the men destroyed the giraffes. I wondered what they would do—shoot them and move on? What happened to Metalcium when its host was killed? I could only hope they'd burn the remains; no carcass in the Kalahari stayed unspoiled. Maybe some animals would smell that something was wrong with the giraffes and leave them alone, but many others would try to take a bite anyway.

I dragged myself to my feet and began trekking east. The noise of the chopper had faded away, leaving the bush to its gentle symphony of birdsong and crickets. I walked quickly, wanting to disappear before the pursuers could return, but try as I might, I couldn't force my legs into a run. I was spent, dehydrated, hungry, and alone. In the quiet solitude, I began to fixate on my itching arms and back and the skin behind my ears. I knotted my fingers into fists so tight that my palms ached, but I held them there to keep from falling into a fit of furious scratching. The more I tried to ignore the itch, the more it spread, until simply *not* scratching drained my will-power as effectively as a hole punctured in an inflatable pool. How long could I hold out?

I needed to distract myself. I thought of my missing companions, trying to guess what they might be doing right now. I found I missed Joey's ceaseless chatter, Avani's matter-of-fact stream of information, and even Miranda's complaints. Never had the wilderness seemed so quiet or so lonely. For the first time in my life, the silence and peace I'd prized felt empty, as if something were missing.

I'd never made attachments to anyone, because I knew that sooner or later we'd have to say good-bye, but I suspected that if somehow we lived through this and they all went home, I'd miss them. More than I'd allowed myself to miss anyone in years, not since that school in Bangladesh. All of my carefully constructed defenses had been eroded and without meaning to, I had made four friends . . . and one relationship that might even be more than that.

I stopped myself there. I wouldn't think about Sam. I couldn't bear it. If I was infected with Metalcium, it wouldn't matter *how* many friends I had.

I walked in a daze, my pace slowing once I was several miles east of the road. I'd stopped once, to scout the sandy tracks. I found Kase and Miranda's prints heading east, and Sam's a short distance from those. I had to hope that Joey and Avani had crossed farther south. Surely with the sun setting on the western horizon, they'd be able to figure out that all they had to do was follow their shadows straight east. After the sun set, Avani ought to be able to keep them on the right track if she knew anything about the constellations in the Southern Hemisphere. Kase, Miranda, and Sam I wasn't sure about. If they got off track in the night, they could get lost for good. And even if they did keep their bearings, it would be so easy to pass the baobab in the middle of the night and never see it at all.

I followed Sam's tracks for as long as I could, and when the light faded, I stopped. I wasn't sure that even *I* could find my way back in the dark. When I had Sam, we could find the baobab. If anyone was missing . . . well, we would just have to search for them. It would be easy to continue to Ghansi and send back an official search party, but by that time, Corpus may well have found them first. I could imagine spending days out here just trying to find everyone, which made me feel sick. I didn't have that kind of time. Not anymore.

Do you ever wish you could pull a moment out of time? When Sam had asked the question, I thought I'd understood.

I hadn't then, but I did now. I thought of all the moments I'd have saved, moments that, even though I'd lived them, oddly felt as if I'd missed them. As if I hadn't taken the time then to cherish how sweet they were, and now they were lost forever.

I'll never get to see the pyramids with Sam. This thought, more than any of the others, left me more devastated than I could have imagined. I'd never been particularly interested in seeing the pyramids, but now that it was impossible, it seemed the most important thing in the world. How many places had I taken for granted, thinking I had my whole life to see them? How could I have been so shortsighted?

I plodded on, my feet dragging in the sand. My lips were chapped and sore. I began to fantasize deliriously about every drink I'd ever had, from chocolate milk to guava juice. I spent an inordinate amount of time trying to remember the flavor of each one, the sensation of cool wet liquid splashing over my teeth and tongue.

Night fell, but I kept walking. My body and mind had disconnected, functioning now on separate planes. The small section of my brain that had retained its sanity knew I should stop, that I had lost Sam's tracks and was wandering aimlessly through the bush, but it might as well have been sending signals to the moon for all the effect it had.

The only message that was circulating through me with any degree of success was *don't scratch.*

It was becoming an increasingly difficult command to follow.

My body was on fire. I was being bitten by a thousand invisible ants, and it took every ounce of willpower I had not to scratch till I bled.

I'd given up hoping that the bush baby had been a mistake, that I wasn't infected. Now hope was lost altogether and

Death was breathing down my neck.

I don't remember falling down or sleeping, but when I opened my eyes, it was dawn. I didn't know where I was or why I was lying with my face half-planted in the sand. Though it took a few moments, my thoughts did clear, and they were sharper than they had been during my hellish hike the night before.

As soon as my memory hit me, sliding into my skull like a brick, I sat up and immediately began inspecting my hands and arms. There was no sign of Metalcium yet, and the itching seemed to have subsided a little, though my wrists and elbows still burned. My nose itched, too, but I didn't dare to even rub it. Eyes watering from the effort of keeping my hands at my sides, I took stock of my position.

It was a stretch of Kalahari bush much like any other. Golden grass bent as if bowing to the rising sun, acacias with their bristling thorn, the white trunks of shepherd's trees rising above everything else, and . . . silence.

Silence.

I tried to remember what that meant. I'd heard it before, just days ago. . . .

The lion.

Or some sort of Metalcium-infected creature, anyway. It was morning; there ought to have been a chorus of birds rattling the savanna. Instead, only the hollow wind prowled through the grass like a ghostly predator, ruffling the backs of the thornbushes.

I heard a rustle off to my left and ducked behind a sickle bush.

The silver lion emerged from the grass to my left, moving

silent as a whisper on his huge silver paws. I caught my breath and shrank away, but not before he spotted me. Fear freezing my veins, I couldn't move, couldn't blink. His gaze held mine, utterly blank and terrifying. Time seemed to stand still, the world around us vanishing, as that long look bound us together with a force stronger than gravity. In those mirrored eyes I saw myself looking back at me, my hair wild, my eyes wide, my face dirty and scraped. Androcles stood as still as a statue and poured his stare into mine as if he could discern my very thoughts. And in that moment, my fear melted away, leaving behind a deep sadness and an odd wonder.

In that moment, I understood him.

His sorrow, his wildness, his pain. I felt them all, my own emotions reflected in those unblinking silver eyes. A sob welled in my chest but I suppressed it, feeling it press against my lungs.

Then Androcles turned away with a deep sigh that shuddered through his body, making his muscles quiver beneath his silver skin. He lowered his head and padded away, heading west, and vanished in his own reflection of the grass and trees and sky. I strained to hear his footsteps but there was only a glassy silence.

He knew I was infected. I don't know how I knew it, or if it was really true, but I felt it resonate deep inside me. He had looked into my eyes and seen it. Perhaps he thought it a waste of time to infect me, since I was already doomed. Perhaps he was just tired.

I let out my breath as my head sank onto my chest, my fingers burrowing into the sand. Behind me, I could hear a few reluctant sparrows whistle to one another, as if making sure their family was still accounted for after the unnatural interruption.

How far would this thing spread? How many would it kill?

Avani had described it as a new life-form, something alien to our world. Perhaps it was more lifelike than we knew. Maybe it could think, rationalize, plan.

Maybe it *wanted* to take over our world.

Berating myself for losing Sam's tracks, I followed my own, retracing my steps from the night before and wasting even more valuable time. I kept an eye out for the lion but didn't see another sign of him. I knew we'd have to be more alert from now on, since he was in the area.

It took me an hour to find where my prints deviated from Sam's, and I tried to make up for the lost time by moving quickly, my eyes speed-reading the sand.

To my surprise, his prints led me straight to the lone landmark I hadn't been sure even I could find: the beautiful, ancient baobab.

Sam was sitting in its shade.

TWENTY-FOUR

Sarah!" Sam jumped up and ran to meet me. He raised his arms to pull me into a hug, but I ducked it. His brow furrowed and he gave me an inquisitive look but said nothing about it.

"You made it," I said. "How did you find your way back so quickly?"

"Oh, ye of little faith." He grinned. "I remembered what you said about the nests."

"Huh?"

Sam pointed to a nearby tree covered with hanging sparrow nests. "You said they build the nests to face west, right?"

I couldn't help but smile, and for a moment I simply gazed at him, standing there in the morning sunlight with dirt on his face and tangles in his hair, grinning like a beautiful, proud lunatic. The urge to throw my arms around him pulled at me like Earth pulling at the moon, but instead I balled my hands into fists. My heart aching with longing, I nodded crisply. "Right. Well, we have to find the others."

"I know." He sighed, losing his grin. "Any ideas on where to start?"

"Let's give them another hour or two. They might still make it back. You did, after all, and you were on your own."

"Want some water while we wait? I've been here a few hours, so I had time to build up a fire and boil some more water. Took me forever to get the fire going. Thankfully some of the embers were still warm from when we camped yesterday."

"Yes! Oh, Sam, I could—" I stopped myself, choking on my own voice. I'd nearly said *I could kiss you*, but realized my mistake halfway through. My heart beat against my ribs like a fist punching me from the inside. "I could really use a drink of water," I finished weakly.

I followed him to the pan, where he had left some baobab shells filled with water near a small, smoldering fire. Barely letting the water cool, I gulped it down greedily, pausing only to breathe. I limited myself to only one shell of water; what had seemed a pool when we'd arrived was now more of a puddle, and I could tell from the tracks that a herd of kudu had passed through yesterday and drunk almost all of what was left. If the others made it back, they'd need water too. Though the edge was gone from my thirst, I felt far from sated.

Sam knelt and tossed a few sticks on the fire. "Close call, huh? I saw the chopper take off after the giraffes. Did they show up after that?"

"No. Of course, it got dark pretty quick. They couldn't have been flying at night."

"Unless they're really desperate."

I nodded reluctantly. "Unless they're really desperate."

Keeping distance between us, I sat down by Sam and tucked my hands under my legs to stop myself from scratching. The itch was maddening, almost blinding in its persistence. The more I tried to ignore it, the worse it got.

Avani and Joey appeared about a half hour later. Avani had her eyes on the ground, following my tracks, so she didn't see us until she was just a few steps away. Joey, who spotted us while they were still some distance away, had kept quiet and pranced behind her, laughing silently. When she finally realized she was standing two feet away from me, he burst out cackling.

Avani smiled sweetly and sat down, taking a shell of water that Sam handed her. "I'm gonna save those goons the trouble and kill him myself, 'kay?"

"Need a hand?" I asked.

I was more than impressed with both Avani and Sam for having found their way. All of them—even Miranda and Kase—had changed since I first met them. They were tougher, more capable—or maybe they always had been tough all along and I'd just been too blind to see it until now.

"I'm going to find them," I said, after an hour had passed with no sign of Kase and Miranda.

"I'm coming," said Sam.

"We all are," said Avani. "It's stupid to split up again."

I nodded. "We'll leave very clear tracks so that if they do come here, they can follow us."

Joey wrote a giant message in the sand that said *Gone 2 find U*, with an arrow pointing the way we went.

We walked side by side, instead of in single file, to leave a trail of footprints so obvious that it might as well have been lit in neon. It worried me a little. I doubted anyone in a helicopter would be able to see our tracks, but after what happened at the road, I wasn't sure.

Sam strayed closer and closer to me. Panicked, I sidestepped in what I hoped was a casual, thoughtless motion, not wanting him to accidentally—or purposefully—brush against me. *I have to tell him*, I thought. It was hard to put that distance between us, when what I really longed to do was hold his hand. The memory of our kiss rested in my thoughts like a fragile rose in the midst of a hurricane, the one bright and lovely thing I had to hold on to. I clung to it, using that kiss to distract me from the fiery itch burning on my skin, hoping somehow, *somehow* it wouldn't be our last.

We came across a patch of hoodia, a low-growing cactus-like plant, the meat of which can stave off hunger and thirst while giving one a boost of energy. The Bushmen had relied on it when they went on long hunting trips, to sustain them in the harsh conditions. It didn't provide any real sustenance though, so we'd need something more substantial soon. But it helped take our minds off our overwhelming thirst and hunger, and my thoughts felt clearer than they had in days.

The longer we searched, the more worried I grew. We were moving slowly, so if Kase and Miranda had reached the baobab and followed our tracks, they would have caught up to us by now. I knew that if we went back to the road and found their prints from yesterday, I might be able to track them from there. But time wasn't on our side. Between the wind and the animals roaming around, the tracks would be faint.

Since it was the only real lead we had, we made the long trek to the road for the second time.

"I have never," declared Avani, "been so thirsty in my entire life. And these don't help." She was holding another *hi* root I'd found. "They get nastier every time I drink from one. We can't keep going like this."

She was right. We weren't built like the Bushmen, whose small, hardy statures were suited for the harsh Kalahari. The hoodia suppressed our thirst; it didn't quench it or hydrate us much.

We were still a few miles from the road when Sam stopped and held up a hand.

"Do you hear that?"

I listened; the sound was faint, and at first I mistook it for a bird. But then the wind shifted slightly, pushing the noise toward us.

Avani heard it too. "Miranda."

I couldn't make out what she was yelling, but it was definitely Miranda's voice. We broke into a run.

We found her sitting on the ground with Kase's head in her lap. At first, I thought he was dead. His eyes were shut and Miranda was keening over him, rocking back and forth while her hands cradled his still face. I froze in shock, my abdomen turning icy cold. *No, please no . . .*

But then Kase's lips moved, though all he managed was a hoarse groan.

"He just collapsed," Miranda said. "I found one of those root things, you know, like you showed us? He made me drink most of the juice, said he wasn't thirsty! I—I believed him. How could I be so stupid?"

I knew immediately what we were dealing with. "He's severely dehydrated. He needs water now." I looked at Avani, but she wordlessly shook her head.

"I tossed the rest of the root away."

No one else had any, either. I began looking around, frantic. The roots belonged to a tiny, leafless shoot, and I scoured the area in search of one, down on my hands and knees. The others joined me in looking, as Miranda wailed and cried, her eyes dry from lack of water.

When it comes to surviving harsh conditions, you can generally go by the Rule of Three. Three minutes without air, three weeks without food, three hours without shelter in extreme temperatures . . . and three days without water. I didn't have to run the exact calculations to recognize that if we didn't find water—and *fast*—Kase wouldn't live to see the next morning.

I combed the sand with my fingers, using both my eyes and hands to locate the moisture-giving root, but I wasn't sure even that could save him now.

I froze, my hands having brushed something buried in the sand. Then, digging faster, I uncovered a rotting leather bag. It was the skin of a steenbok that had been tanned and cured, the legs tied together to form a strap. I picked it up and turned it over, and a jumble of items fell out: wooden arrows with tips made of giraffe bone, sharpened sticks like the ones I'd used to start the fire, a string of cocoons filled with bits of twigs and bone to make them rattle.

This was a Bushman's kit, buried here for decades. Often they would hide their stuff if they intended to get roaring drunk, so that their relatives wouldn't steal their gear. They usually forgot where they buried the stuff, and people would find these little caches all over southern Africa.

This had been Bushman territory. Which meant . . .

I looked around and spotted a shepherd's tree, its telltale white trunk and evergreen leaves standing out amid the dry, brown savanna. I ran to it and fell to digging furiously around its trunk, creating a trench around it. Nothing.

There was another tree a short distance away. I dug out the sand around it too, and around two more after that. I saw one last tree in the area and considered ignoring it. The chances of finding a *bi* root were much better anyway. But it was just one more tree. . . .

I dug with both hands, like a dog hunting for a bone. The sand shifted easily, giving way to yet more sand—there was no end to it out here. Around the tree I went, scooting on my knees, panting from the effort.

I'd nearly circled the whole trunk when I jammed my hands into the ground again—and struck something solid.

Heart pounding, I pushed the sand aside.

Nestled against the root of the tree, as white and pristine as the day it had been buried, was a smooth, round ostrich egg.

I picked it up and shook it, then let out a shout of glee.

The others gathered around as I ran back to them. I still had the Bushman bag, which I slung onto the ground. While they inspected the items, I pulled out the bundle of leather that had been used to plug the tiny hole in the top of the egg. Then I upended the egg over my mouth and a thin, sweet stream of water trickled onto my tongue.

"Water!" cried Miranda. "Give it to him!"

I didn't want to risk touching either of them, so I set the egg on the ground beside her.

She was so focused on Kase that she didn't seem to notice

the way I avoided her touch. She held open Kase's mouth and poured the water in, just a bit at a time. He swallowed, and his mouth spread into a weak smile.

"Come back to me, baby," Miranda murmured. "I need you. Don't you leave me here!" She looked up, her super-model beauty replaced by the face of a lost and frightened girl at the edge of her wits. Despite days of complaining, crying, and running for her life, she had never looked more vulnerable. "He's everything to me, you understand? *Everything*. He's always been there, through all the crap, keeping me together. I'll *die* without him! I—I love him!"

"Hey, angel," Kase murmured. His lashes fluttered but his eyes remained shut. "I love you too."

At that, a smile broke across Miranda's face and she bent over and kissed him.

With a little cough, I turned away.

"Spread out," I said to the others. "Look for trees with white trunks that still have their leaves, and dig around the root. In the rainy seasons, Bushmen would fill eggs with water and bury them under shepherd's trees for the dry season. There may be more hidden around the area."

"So *that's* where Easter egg hunts come from," said Joey, but his voice lacked its usual mischief and the joke seemed halfhearted.

Avani rolled her eyes. "Let's go."

They seemed invigorated by the possibility of finding water and vanished into the bush to search.

"Don't let him drink it too fast," I warned Miranda.

She nodded, and her breathing calmed. Her eyes were fixed on Kase's face, filled with a passion that left me oddly jealous. Their obsession with each other had annoyed me at first, but I was slowly coming to believe that they really did love each other as much as they said. Who was I to judge the depth of their relationship? I'd had only one kiss in my entire life. Maybe Kase and Miranda could barely survive a night in the wilderness—but they seemed to understand a much deeper mystery that I couldn't even grasp. Would maybe never grasp, I pondered morosely.

Kase would survive. They all would. The water-filled egg was a sign, I was sure of it. I'd never believed in signs, but my mom had, and she would have said this was a good omen, a "turning of our luck."

The others returned soon, one by one. Avani and Sam had both found eggs. Sam shared his with me (I made him drink first, just in case), and Avani split hers with Joey. We were far from being fully sated, but the water had restored our spirits. We were all together and we were alive, which was more than I'd expected twelve hours ago.

I was so overwhelmed with relief and satisfaction that I didn't even realize I was scratching my arm until I looked down and saw the small patch of silver just below my inner wrist.

TWENTY-FIVE

I immediately rolled down my sleeve, hiding the metallic patch. My chest felt as if it were being crushed. I mumbled something about looking for more buried eggs and hurried away, out of sight of the others.

Then, crouching beneath a tangle of branches, I pushed up my sleeve and studied the infected area, which had taken over the left wing on the tattooed bee.

The skin around the silver area was white and loose, and it itched like a bad spider bite. It would fall away at the slightest touch. Immediately I thought of Dr. Monaghan's pallid complexion and of how fragile the skin on his face had been.

Gingerly, trying to still my shaking hands, I touched a finger to the silver. I could hold it there for only a moment before jerking it away, my heartbeat racing. The metal was warm. I'd expected it to be cool, like a coin, but of course I'd forgotten that this wasn't just metal—it was *alive*. Maybe it wasn't quite an *entity*; that would require that it was able to think and reason. It seemed more like a bacteria, acting out of the purely biological impulse to replicate itself. Still, it was hard not to see it as being consciously malignant. It was *eating my skin*, after all.

I rocked back and forth in the sand, cradling my affected arm and staring blankly at the ground. Sure, I'd made myself accept that I was infected. But that was before I'd actually seen it. It was the difference between accepting that someone was going to die and seeing the actual body. This was a point of no return. My skin would melt off and be replaced with a coat of living metal. It would drive me insane and then I would die.

And what about Dad? Would I see him again? Even if he was still alive, out there somewhere in the deep bush, would I have time to find him? I longed for Dad so intensely that it hurt, a pain in my chest as if my ribs were pinching my lungs. I wished he was there to hold me, to tell me it would be okay, that I was his Sissy Hati and he'd never let anything bad happen to me. I wanted those silly, loving promises parents make. Wanted them so badly that I whispered them myself, soft as dandelion fluff, but it wasn't the same. They felt hollow and false, faint betrayals of my own breath.

With a mighty effort, I drew myself together and stood up. I kept my sleeves unrolled to hide my arms. The invisible counter attached to my life seemed to be ticking faster than ever.

"Find one?" Sam asked when I returned.

I blinked at him. "Find what? Oh. No, nothing. Come on, let's go. We're wasting time."

"Kase isn't strong enough yet!" Miranda protested.

"Too bad!" I snapped. "We're sitting targets out here, don't you get that?"

She gaped at me while the others exchanged silent looks. I sighed. "Sorry. Look, we should really get moving."

"What if we holed up during the day," said Avani, "and walked at night? They wouldn't see us, and we'd keep warm by moving."

"There are other dangers at night," I replied huffily. "That's when the lions are hunting and you wouldn't see a snake until you stepped on it."

"Oh," she said, dropping her gaze. Sam gave me a reproachful look, which cut my heart, but I forced myself to remain sharp.

"We can help Kase walk," I said. "It'll do him good, at any rate."

"I'm fine," he said, though he didn't look it. "Really."

Miranda glared at me but helped him stand up. He was a little wobbly, but I knew he would make it.

"What do we do with these?" Joey asked, holding up an empty ostrich egg.

"Leave them."

We marched on in silence, the others lagging a short distance behind me. I told myself that was best. I had to detach myself from them. Otherwise, I wasn't sure how I could say good-bye when the time came. As I walked, I tried to work out how I would tell them about my infection. I ran through a dozen different scenarios before my courage gave out. When the time was right, I'd tell them. But when was the time ever right to admit you were dying? How could you prepare for that?

We crossed the road before noon, several miles north of the spot where the helicopter had found us the day before.

Before crossing, we waited ten full minutes crouched in the bushes, listening and watching for any sign of Abramo's search team. Then we darted across together, leaping over the trenches in the sand.

The water and hoodia had given us an extra burst of energy, and coupled with my hardened drive to reach Ghansi in two days, we moved at a grueling pace. I found that the faster I walked, the easier it was to ignore the maddening itch that burned on my skin. I took extra care not to brush against branches or trees, and held my arms away from my body to decrease friction from my clothes. Several times the others called for me to slow down, and I would—for about five minutes. Then I'd slowly increase my speed until we were almost jogging again.

The edge came back to my thirst, sharp and knifing. My tongue was sticky and dry like a gecko's toes, clinging to the roof of my mouth, but I didn't stop to hunt for *bi* root. Joey had been stopping at every shepherd's tree we passed to dig for ostrich eggs, then running to catch up to us again, but he found nothing and soon gave up.

After a while, Sam jogged to my side.

"Sarah, what's wrong?" he asked sharply.

I stared ahead, not meeting his concerned gaze. "If we walk through the night, we might reach Ghansi by dawn. I know I said there were lions, but I think we can make it. They're less active near the villages."

"You're burning everyone out. Kase is about to faint."

I stopped so suddenly that he walked several more steps before realizing it. He turned to face me.

"That chopper really shook you, didn't it?" he asked.

I frowned, then seized on the excuse. "They were *shooting* at us. Of course it shook me."

"Me too," he said. "But we can't keep pressing on like this. We don't have the energy."

"They'll anticipate us heading for Ghansi," I said. "We have to stay ahead of them."

"We can't stay ahead of them if we collapse from exhaustion or die of thirst!"

It would be so easy to tell him the real reason I was rushing, but I couldn't stand for him to look at me the way we'd looked at Dr. Monaghan: with pity, yes, but also revulsion. I'd made up my mind to insist that he stay in Ghansi with the others. There was no way I could let him see me literally fall apart and turn into a metal monster.

"Okay," I said. "We'll take a short break. But then we *have* to keep moving."

"Thank you."

The others dropped to their knees when Sam told them we were stopping, and though they were too exhausted to say much, they all let me feel their indignation with heated glares. Ignoring them, I sat apart and dug up *bi* roots, which Sam distributed, as well as some chunks of hoodia that I found.

While the others scraped the roots and squeezed the pulp for water, Sam sat beside me and turned his tuber over in his hands.

"Are we going to talk about what happened?" he asked.

"What happened?"

He raised his eyebrows. "You know . . . the thing between us."

The kiss. I shut my eyes and sighed. I'd hoped he wouldn't bring it up.

"It was . . . great," I said, feeling completely lame. "But where is it going to go? You're going back to the States."

"Yeah. For a little while. But then . . . ?"

"What are we going to do? Be pen pals?" *If only.*

He shrugged. "I don't know. I just thought, you know, you'd want to talk about it."

I said nothing. I watched a hole under the bush in front of me, where a mongoose kept poking its head up, seeing us, and ducking down again.

"Sarah," Sam said as he shifted closer, "I really . . . like you."

His hand moved toward me; I jerked it away and stood up.

"You're a nice guy," I said, my voice shaking. "But I don't feel the same way."

The confusion in his eyes was a knife to my heart.

"But I thought . . . We kissed and you seemed, I don't know . . . into it."

Oh, that's putting it lightly. "I think that when we get to Ghansi, you should go home. You don't . . ." I paused and licked my chapped lips, glad that my body lacked the moisture to generate tears. "You don't belong here. None of you do. Just go home and leave me alone."

Sam was shocked. "Sarah!"

"I just can't deal with this right now. Between my mom and my dad and Theo and everything else . . . I can't deal with any more complications."

He stared at me as if I had tried to bite him.

I turned away and walked to the others, feeling his eyes burning into my back. My hands were shaking again. I thrust them into my pockets and blinked furiously to cool my burning eyes.

We didn't speak the rest of the day, and when evening fell, I reluctantly agreed to stop. I pointedly avoided Sam, but it was hard to do considering that everywhere I turned he seemed to be there, and when I closed my eyes to sleep, I saw his wounded gaze. He was sleeping by the others, all of them pressed shoulder to shoulder for warmth. I curled up on a grassy patch ten yards away and shivered in the cold, my teeth clenched to keep them from chattering.

It has to be this way! I told myself furiously. I couldn't put him or myself through what was to come. Maybe I could write him a letter or something and have it sent to him after I . . .

I cried silently, though I was unable to produce tears. I covered my mouth with the hem of my sleeve to muffle my soft whimpers, my abdomen clenched and aching from sobbing. I hated myself for being so weak. It seemed I didn't even have the grace to die with dignity. Instead I was wallowing on the ground, weeping like a coward. I wanted to fight somehow, to prove that I deserved to walk on this Earth a little longer, but my powerlessness ate away at my core, more devastating than the metal parasite wasting my skin.

My thoughts roamed to Dad, wondering where he was, what he was doing, if he was even alive. I found myself unable to summon any hope of finding him. He was gone, just like Theo. Just like Mom.

I am alone.

When I finally did fall asleep, I was haunted by nightmares. Creeping monsters with their skin hanging from them in ribbonlike tatters stalked through the savanna around me, animals with the faces of my friends watched me with shining silver eyes, and my parents and Theo ran ahead of me, always out of reach, and when I called out to them they turned to show their faces were made of metal. I screamed and clawed at my own face, and my skin tore away in my hands.

"Sarah! Wake up!"

I jolted upright, eyes flying open.

"Don't touch me!" I snarled.

Sam's hand was on my shoulder, our skin separated by thin layer of fabric, and he snatched it away, his eyes wide with worry. *Too close*, I thought frenziedly. *That was too close.*

"You were screaming," he said. "You woke us all up."

"Sorry," I muttered, pulling away from him. "Did you touch me?"

"What?"

"I said, *did you touch me?*"

His eyes went to my hand, then back to my face. "No."

"Go back to sleep," I said. "I'm fine now."

He watched me for a moment, his face unreadable, then he turned away and went back to the others. I heard them whispering to one another. It made me inexplicably angry.

"Go to sleep!" I snapped. "We have a long way to go tomorrow."

They fell silent and I lay back down, my eyes smarting. I felt rabid. Was it me or the Metalcium? Would it turn me silver first and *then* drive me insane, or was it the other way around? I tried to remember what Dr. Monaghan had said, but I couldn't seem to focus my thoughts.

It took me a while to fall back asleep. The whispering started up again, but this time I held my tongue. They probably already thought I was a monster, even without seeing my face turn silver.

I pulled up my sleeve and looked at my arm. It was hard to see, until I shifted it into the moonlight. Then the light reflected off the inside of my arm so intensely that it seemed to be emitting its own florescence. I quickly turned it over so the others wouldn't see.

The Metalcium had spread while I slept. My inner wrist was covered now, with just half of the bee tattoo still visible, and silver streaks ran down to my elbow. It was moving faster than I'd feared.

Awake or asleep, I was locked in a nightmare. The whole of the Kalahari around me, the vast, starry sky above, and yet I had never felt so trapped.

I remembered the dream catcher in my pocket and pulled it out. As I clutched it tight in my hand and held it to my chest, I felt a mellowing of my spirit. My weary eyes slid shut, and instead of the nightmare I expected, I saw Mom, her hands nimbly weaving dream catchers as we sat in a field of golden grass. Her hair was gusting around her face, blown wild by the Kalahari winds, but she only laughed when I asked if she wanted to tie it back. Instead she caught one of the wayward hairs and pulled it out, then wove it into the dream catcher. "There," she said, holding it out. The feathers danced in the breeze. "Now you'll dream of me." My memory of that day mingled with my imagination, until I didn't know how much of it was real and how much of it was spun by my own wishful heart. As that golden, windswept field faded away, Mom's playful smile lingered, and I fell into a dreamless sleep.

I woke when dawn was just a faint promise on the horizon, nothing more than a soft glow. Sam was the only one up, sitting cross-legged in the sand and scraping a *bi* root. He cast me a brief, blank look, then went back to scraping. He'd also gathered some crowfoot grass, which he portioned out.

I stood up and stretched, careful to keep my left sleeve pinched between my palm and my fingers so that the rash of metal wouldn't show. I felt a deep sense of calm in my spirit, an acceptance of the day and a resignation to my fate.

Sam stood up and brought me some grass and root shavings. I asked him stiffly to set them down, and as he did I saw the skin around those lovely green eyes wrinkle with hurt. Sam stood and stared at the ground between us for a moment, while I squeezed pulp from the shavings, and then he lifted his face.

"How long have you been infected?"

I froze. "W-what?"

"Sarah. I'm not stupid. When you told me not to touch you last night . . . I didn't want to believe it, but it's true, isn't it?" His voice was low and harsh, his brow furrowed in anger, not at me, it seemed, but at the ugly truth.

I drew a shaky hand across my forehead, briefly hiding the shame in my eyes. "It happened two days ago, when I went to get the baobab fruit the morning after we, um, kissed." I glanced at the others. They were still sleeping, oblivious to our conversation. "There was an infected bush baby in the tree."

Sam swore and threw the rest of the shavings at the ground. "I should have gone with you. I should have—"

"There's nothing you could have done."

"Why didn't you *tell* me?"

My hand moved automatically to my silver wrist, which was still covered by my sleeve. "I wasn't sure, until yesterday afternoon. I thought maybe . . . I don't know. Saying it out loud makes it *real*, you know?"

His eyes burned into me, his misery cutting me deeper than my own. "We have to get you to a hospital."

"Sam, I don't think—"

"How far to Ghansi?"

"Two days at least, and that's even if we hike without breaks from dawn till dark. It's not possible. You saw how quickly Dr. Monaghan went, after it started." I pulled up my sleeve and showed him the infected patch of skin. His face went white. "It's too late."

"We have to try!"

"Sam—"

"I won't let you die!" he yelled.

His shout woke up the others, who looked at us groggily and asked what was wrong. Sam exhaled bitterly and ran a hand through his hair, his eyes squeezing shut.

"Nothing," I said. "We should get going. There's some *bi* root if you want it."

While they roused themselves, I walked a short distance away, motioning Sam to follow. When we were far enough away not to be overheard, I whispered to Sam, "Don't make this harder than it is and blame yourself. Look. You're right. We'll get to Ghansi and I'll go to the hospital. They'll figure something out." My head spun suddenly and I stumbled. Sam's hand shot out to steady me.

"No!" I snapped, pulling away. "Don't touch me!"

"You're pale," Sam murmured. "Are you sure you can walk? I'll carry you if I have to."

"No, you won't. You'll lead the others to safety is what

you'll do. I can take care of myself. And please don't tell them. Not yet." I didn't want them to look at me the way Sam was, as if I were some kind of ghost.

The others were ready to go. They huddled together, stamping their feet to keep warm, their breath frosting the air. Avani watched Sam and me suspiciously. I sighed and stepped around Sam.

"We should go. Moving out, people," I said.

They groaned but nodded. Sam said nothing, but I could feel his concerned gaze burning at the nape of my neck.

I turned to face north, drew a deep breath, and then began to walk.

A few steps was as far as I got. Lights suddenly blasted from every direction, blinding me, and I stumbled back. The others cried out, equally disoriented. I blinked furiously, my eyes feeling scalded, trying to make out what was going on. Hazy shapes formed in front of me, like distorted reflections: a group of men in camouflaging khaki rising out of the grass, standing beside a trio of Land Rovers with their headlights on full blast. The lights centered on us, leaving me feeling almost naked, the beams so strong they seemed to hold us in place with physical force. My eyes foggily focused on the men. They all had guns, and they were pointed at us.

TWENTY-SIX

Lookee, boys," said the lead man, a tall African with a clean-shaven skull. From the French bent to his accent, I judged him to be from the northwest, perhaps Niger. "I think we found Mr. Abramo's missing kids."

Abramo himself was nowhere to be seen. He must have had more than one group of mercenaries scouting the Kalahari. It was a cruel trick of fate that we should walk right into this one, this close to our destination. There were half a dozen of them, big, tough-looking guys with dusty bandanas tied around their heads and necks, dressed in faded fatigues that might have been scavenged from a handful of different militias.

They cocked their guns and Miranda let out a sob. Our hands were all lifted, and I pushed mine forward as if I could stop the bullets with just my bare palms.

"Wait!" I yelled. "You really don't want to do that! I swear, you'll regret it!"

The men hesitated but didn't lower their guns. My mind

raced like a frantic gazelle trying to outrun a cheetah. My friends all looked at me with such desperation, such *hope* in their eyes that I felt nauseated. *Think, Sarah, come on. . . .* I snatched the first wild idea that drifted by.

"Where's Abramo?" I asked, in as stern and sharp a voice as I could muster.

The Nigerien man narrowed his eyes. "I am in charge now."

"I have information for him," I said to him in French. "Information he'll reward you for. You know about the Metalcium outbreak, right?" He nodded and spat, not taking his eyes off me. I drew a deep breath and, switching back to English, laid down a mighty bluff. "I know what the cure is."

"Ha!"

"What do you have to lose? Take us to Abramo, and if I'm lying, you can do what you will. But if you hurt my friends or me now, you get nothing, and when the infection takes over, which, believe me, it will, you'll die."

He considered me doubtfully as he clicked his teeth together. "Tell me what it is."

"I'm not stupid. I want to talk to Abramo."

The Nigerien sneered. "How could a girl know what these rich scientists do not? They cannot stop this silver poison—how can you?"

"I know that Abramo lied to you. He told you the silver poison is transferred by touch, right? Well, sorry, boys, but you've been duped. See, it's spread by the air, not by touch. You're all loose ends once this is over. Abramo's been using you to clean up this mess, knowing Metalcium would kill you for him."

A few shifted uneasily, but not the leader. He only bared his teeth in a scowl. "Lies!"

"Are you willing to bet your life on that?" I returned. "You might be infected already. Don't you know how it starts? With itching. Like a dog with fleas. Like a kid with lice." I saw a few hands leave their rifles in order to scratch beneath collars and sleeves, and looks of doubt and panic began to blossom around me. "The itching goes on for days before you start turning silver," I said. "It's impossible not to scratch. It's like ants biting you, like centipedes crawling up and down your—"

"Stop!" cried the Nigerien, not to me, but to his men, who were scratching furiously now.

"Man, I been itching for days!" cried one.

"Me too, brother!" added another as he clawed at his scalp. "What if he's lying? What if we all got the poison?"

"You are idiots!" snarled the Nigerien, but I saw his fingers twitching on his rifle.

"Are you *sure* you don't feel an itch?" I asked him. "An itch you just have to scratch?"

He swore as one of his hands flew to his neck. "Lies!"

I smiled. "Maybe. Maybe not. My friends and I went into that menagerie at the lab, the one with all the infected animals. Do we look silver to you? Are we scratching?" Out of the corner of my eye, I saw Joey snatch his hand from his shoulder to his pocket, apparently stopping himself in midscratch. My little speech must have infected my own group with the itch as well. But they caught my hint and stayed still.

"I was taught by a Bushman," I said quietly. "I know the secret remedies of the Kalahari. I cured us and I can cure you, if you will take us to Abramo."

I held the Nigerien's gaze. He fumed and bristled, but I hoped that I'd planted just enough doubt in his mind to save our lives—at least for another hour or two. Still, it was an hour more than we had now, an hour more to think of *something*.

"Take them to the trucks," said the Nigerien at last, with a look of disgust. "And stop that scratching! Idiots!"

I allowed myself one small, relieved sigh. *Now what?*

They marched us to the road, where there were three white Land Rovers parked in a line. None of us spoke, not even to one another.

We had been *so close*—just a few days' walk from Ghansi.

How had they tracked us? There had been no sign of the helicopter, and we hadn't lit a fire. Finding six teenagers in the dark in the middle of the Kalahari wilderness was like looking for a flea on an elephant. I decided it must have been more accidental, based on the men's reactions to us. They had seemed as surprised to see us as we were to see them.

I was put into the first Land Rover with Avani. The group's leader took the driver's seat, and a short, bespectacled man sat beside him. After hearing their accents, I identified about half of them as Nigerien, including the leader, while the rest were white South Africans, like the small man in the passenger seat.

"*Hoekom doen jy dit?*" I said to the latter.

He grunted but said nothing.

"*Taisez-vous,*" returned the driver gruffly.

"What did you say?" Avani whispered.

"I asked him why he was doing this. *He* told me to shut up." I murmured a nasty word in French, thinking he wouldn't hear me, but he did. He whipped around faster than I could have believed possible and slapped me across the face with the butt of his pistol.

"You will be silent, little lady," he said mildly, giving me a hard look before turning around and cranking the engine. "Or that smooth tongue of yours will get your lovely friend here shot." He gave Avani a cruel smile.

I stared at the back of his head, my cheek stinging. I could taste blood in the corner of my mouth where he'd hit me. Avani stared at me with wide eyes, and I shook my head slightly, warning her to stay quiet. She shrank down into the seat, shutting her eyes like she could wish all of this away.

After making sure that Avani wasn't looking, I pulled up my sleeve just an inch to inspect my skin. The Metalcium had crept inexorably toward my palm. I prodded it carefully. There was still feeling in the affected area, but it was like poking my skin through a layer of clothing. The sensation was dimmer, not like skin on skin.

With a shudder, I yanked my sleeve down again.

The Land Rover shook and bounced through the Kalahari, the Nigerien following the worn tracks of the road and at times making wide passes around the areas that had eroded into miniature canyons. My brain rattled in my skull from all the jerking and bumping, giving me a masterful headache. Through the pain, I tried to think of a way out of this dead-end trip. Ever since running into these thugs, I'd been pulling words and promises out of thin air. But what could I possibly say once we arrived at wherever Abramo was and it turned out I didn't actually know anything about a cure? I could light some grass on fire and do some kind of fake healing dance, mimicking the San rituals. Maybe I could fool some of the mercenaries for a short time, but I doubted Abramo would be amused.

After about an hour of rough driving, the Nigerien turned left and drove straight into the bush. It was slow going over holes and branches and brush. I could see that we were following a set of faint tracks, evidence of the vehicles' earlier passage. We drove like this for another hour, though we couldn't have gone more than twenty miles at the rate we were moving.

Finally we arrived at a bush camp set in a wide, flat pan bordered with hulking *Terminalia*. There were two rows of tents set up, as well as a fire pit in the center. Avani and I were forced to sit still until the mercenaries opened the doors for us. The Nigerien had my door, and at first I sat staring straight ahead, ignoring him. He then grabbed the back of my shirt and dragged me out.

"Where is Abramo?" I asked, wrenching myself out of his grasp.

He yawned in my face, his rank breath making me gag. "The boss will be here soon. Don't get any ideas, eh? These boys, they are very jumpy. Likely to shoot at anything, if you know what I mean."

Indeed, Abramo's hired men were watching us like hawks. They herded us into a group in the center of the camp, and several of them whistled and jeered at us girls in Afrikaans and Sesotho. I was glad that neither Avani nor Miranda could understand what the men were saying. I had met men like these before — often in connection to poaching rings. Many of them had grown up in the midst of violent wars, and some had been forced to kill while they were still children. Not many escaped that life.

I shivered, wishing I could hold Sam's hand for comfort. Instead I held my own, locking my fingers together as if I could squeeze an idea out of thin air.

"What do we do now?" asked Avani.

"I don't know," I whispered. "But if you've got any ideas, feel free to share."

"Better think of something fast," said Joey. "We're losing Ken and Barbie."

Avani cast a worried look at Kase and Miranda, who looked as if they'd fallen into a catatonic trance. Kase's arms wrapped tightly around his girlfriend. Both of them stared unblinkingly at nothing, their bodies trembling and faces ashen. Joey looked angry, glaring at our captors, while Sam watched me sidelong, his mouth a thin line of tension. He didn't even seem to notice the guns pointed at us, he was so preoccupied with my infection.

You okay? he mouthed.

I shrugged and started to give him a wan smile, then frowned instead, my gaze refocusing beyond him, past the mercenary leaning on a termite mound smoking, and on the bush beyond.

"Sarah?"

I ignored Sam's query and studied the grass. *Was that . . . ?*

The grass rustled in the cool breeze, sweeping against the thorny acacias in rippling golden waves. I narrowed my eyes, searching, probing . . . *There.*

"Kase," I said, my voice quiet and casual. "Miranda. I need you to focus."

They blinked and looked at me dazedly. I hoped they were tracking what was going on.

"What is it?" asked Avani worriedly.

"Trouble."

"What now?" squeaked Joey.

I shot him a shushing look. Our voices were too low for the mercenaries to hear, and I wanted to keep it that way. We had something they didn't—a warning—and I planned to use it to its full advantage.

"Wait for it . . . when I shout, be ready to run," I murmured, looking back at the bush. "Any second now . . ."

The silver lion sprang from the bushes with a wild roar that resonated in my rib cage.

"GO!"

TWENTY-SEVEN

Everyone yelled and several of the men fired involuntarily, spraying the sand at our feet with bullets. The silver lion landed beside the mercenary who'd been smoking, his paws sending up a spray of dust.

"Go go *go!*" I yelled. "Under the trucks!"

As the mercenaries fired at the lion, we darted toward the trucks and dove beneath them, wriggling across the sand and then maneuvering around to see if we'd been followed. I kept myself well apart from the others, Sam on one side, Joey on the other. . . . "Wait! Where are Kase and Miranda?"

"They went the other way, toward the tents," said Avani.

The lion had disappeared, presumably back into the bush, but I could still hear him roaring furiously from somewhere in the grass. He was moving fast out there, circling the camp. Abramo's hired men ran amok, shouting and shooting at the bush.

Avani's eyes looked wild. "How—"

She was interrupted by a deafening roar, and suddenly sand sprayed into our faces as four massive paws sprinted past the car—paws of pure silver. The lion bowled through a cluster of mercenaries, who scattered like pigeons. Gone was the regal, sorrowful lion I had met in the bush only yesterday. This Androcles was all fire and fury.

"—is it still following us?" Avani finished, wiping sand from her eyes.

"Bad guy, twelve o'clock!" yelled Joey.

One of the Afrikaner mercenaries had regained his composure and headed toward us, lowering his gun to line up a shot at Sam.

"No!" I shouted.

Before he could shoot, Androcles came galloping from behind a tent. I gasped as the lion sprung, and the man never even saw it coming. The giant paws, flashing with light, struck him at the base of his neck, and he fell face forward into the sand. Avani shrieked and covered her eyes as the lion's jaws closed on the man's head. The mercenary's screams pierced the air louder than even the shots being fired at his feline attacker.

I could see several of the bullets strike home, tearing gouges into Androcles's hide. From the wounds poured scarlet blood, but the lion wasn't slowed. I remembered what Dr. Monaghan had said about Metalcium's intended purpose in healing wounds, how it had taken a hailstorm of bullets to bring down the infected scientists. That must have accounted for why the lion seemed only slightly affected by the bullets. He shook himself, his tail curling and uncurling silver hair floating free of his shimmering mane. Then he snarled, showing rows of gleaming pearly teeth, and sprinted away in a spray of sand, at once terrifying and bizarrely beautiful.

"Now's our chance," Sam said. "While they're distracted, we can steal a car and get away. I'll go look for Miranda and Kase. See if you can get into one of the trucks."

He backed up and was off while Avani, Joey, and I crawled out and tried the doors.

"Locked!" Joey exclaimed. "Why would they lock them?"

Avani was already running to the next vehicle in the line, but when she reached the door, she shook her head.

"They're all locked!"

The gunmen around us seemed to hardly care what we did. They were too busy firing at every blade of grass that moved, calling to one another, "Over here!" or "There! There!"

"Look out!" called Avani. "Chopper!"

A helicopter set down in the grass just outside the camp, and before it even touched the earth, the door opened and Abramo, followed by a cluster of mercenaries, jumped out. They ran straight in Sam's direction.

"Sam!" I yelled, taking off at a sprint. I slipped between two of the tents, then froze. Sam was standing behind the tents with his hands spread at his sides, facing Abramo, who had a pistol aimed at him. I hadn't been seen, and I backed up just enough to conceal myself and get a partial view.

"Please!" Sam pleaded. "Sarah needs medical attention. Let me take her to a hospital and—"

"Where are the rest of you?" Abramo demanded, glaring.

"They—*Lion!*" Sam yelled suddenly, pointing behind Abramo, who spun and raised his gun. Androcles wasn't there, but Sam used the opportunity to disappear into the grass. Abramo turned back and cursed when he saw his quarry had vanished.

I needed to do something. There had to be another gun lying around somewhere—these guys had them coming out their ears. I backed up slowly, almost bumping into Avani, who had caught up. The close call made me dizzy, and I stepped hastily away.

"Search the tents," I whispered. "Find a gun."

She nodded and immediately ducked into the first tent, and I charged into the second.

When I opened the flap, someone jumped out at me and I shrieked and fell backward, almost toppling over.

"Oh, it's you."

"Miranda! Why'd you leap out at me like that? Never mind. Move."

I stepped around her and into the tent. Kase and Miranda blinked at me like a pair of owls.

"Are there any guns in here?" I asked.

"I don't know," said Kase. "But there's some kind of off-brand Gatorade."

He held up a bottle of blue liquid, and I'd never seen a sight more beautiful. I took it and drained it in seconds, feeling my body come alive, cell by cell.

When I lowered it, I saw the two of them staring in shock at my arm. In my haste to drink, I had let my sleeve slide back and the silver plate that stretched from my elbow to my palm was in plain sight.

"Oh," said Miranda softly. "Oh, Sarah . . ."

"Forget it," I said, shaken but determined to stay on track. "We're getting out of here while everyone's distracted. Go help

Sam and Avani look for guns or keys to the cars—anything that can help."

"How long have you been like that?" asked Kase, his eyes still fixed on my arm, even though I'd rolled down my sleeve.

"Just go!" I urged them.

There were still random shots being fired all around us, and I didn't like sending them out into the middle of that, but it would be worse if the men managed to kill the lion and turned their attention back to us.

I began searching through the tent. There was only one cot, against the far wall, and from the look of the place I imagined it was Abramo's. There was nothing personal about any of the items, not so much as a photograph or a souvenir. There was, however, a box of spare batteries, likely for their hand-held radios and other devices. At first, I tore my eyes away, but they were drawn back to the box as if magnetized. I grabbed two AAs.

In a quick, practiced motion, I popped open the back of Mom's recorder and replaced the old batteries. Then, my stomach in knots, I pressed play.

The noise outside seemed a thousand miles away. I barely noticed Kase and Miranda sneak out of the tent, hissing for me to follow. With my teeth clenched so hard that I could feel my pulse in my cheek, I held the recorder to my ear and listened.

Her voice crackled to life. "—one thing Monaghan doesn't know. I'm infected."

I forget entirely about the gunfight outside. The tent could have burned down around me and I wouldn't have noticed.

"I touched one of their silver rats. I didn't mean to—I thought it was dead, and I opened the cage. . . . I realized I was infected this morning. It matches the symptoms the scientists described in their notes: interminable itching. All over, like being covered in lice. I've half a mind to tell them, but then what'll they do? Keep me, that's what. They'll let me die in agony like their poor test subjects, while they take down notes. But if they don't find out, they'll simply get rid of me. There's a man coming, Monaghan told me, a professional. Abrams or Abramo or something." My blood turned to ice. My fingers locked like steel bands around the recording, as I hardened with cold rage. Mom's voice went on, "He'll want to stage my . . . my death like an accident, which means he'll likely leave me somewhere Ty . . . Oh. I can't believe I'm saying this." She let out a long, rattling breath. "He'll leave me where Ty can find my body. If I disappear without a trace, Ty will search deeper and deeper until he finds this place, which they don't want. So. They'll leave me somewhere in the savanna, but the joke will be on them." She emitted a dry, humorless laugh. "Because even if my skin hasn't turned silver yet, my autopsy will reveal the abnormalities that could lead the authorities back to Corpus."

Except that the autopsy had showed no such thing. Had she been mistaken? There hadn't been a spot of silver on her when we found her.

"I'm going to die either way," she said. "So I'd rather it be on *my* terms. If . . . if someone finds this recording, please take it to my family: Ty and Sarah Carmichael. They're camped in Acacia Valley, in the central Kalahari in Botswana. Ty, I have loved you ever since I first saw you plunge neck deep into the Zambezi River, running to rescue me out of a sinking canoe.

We've lived a wild and wonderful life, my love, and I have no regrets. And Sarah . . ."

I sank to my knees on the floor of my mother's murderer's tent, numb to my bones.

"My beautiful Sarah, so full of light. You are my life's greatest adventure. When you feel the wind on your face, smile and think of me. My heart is with yours. Keep it safe."

The recording ended with a short beep.

Keep it safe.

I turned over my wrist and stared at the plain black bee tattooed there, barely visible through the patchwork of silver that was slowly erasing it, the way it had erased Mom.

The bees are a fail.

Mom's last words. The mysterious sentence she'd thought important enough to write on her arm. Not *I love you* or *Remember me* or even *I'm sorry* but *The bees are a fail.*

She had been infected with Metalcium, and intended to keep it secret, so that even in her death, she'd be bringing the criminals responsible to justice. But her skin hadn't been silver, and the autopsy report had showed no signs of anything strange in her system. Instead, it had shown . . .

Keep it safe.

I saw her hands, her face, swollen with hundreds of stings.

The bees are a fail.

Abramo had known she set out to study killer bees. He knew we'd have no trouble believing the little creatures had killed her. After all, dozens of people died each year from these swarms. The scientists had been freezing hives in an attempt to quell the infestation of bees, so he had the murder weapon already on hand. All he had to do was leave Mom unconscious in the Jeep, throw in the angry, buzzing hive, and drive off, letting the bees finish the job. No wonder he'd gotten away so clean. It didn't take many stings from an African honeybee to kill you.

The tent flap suddenly flew open. I jumped, dropping the recorder, as Avani poked her head inside.

"Sarah! We didn't find any guns, but I got these." She tossed something through the air, which I automatically caught: a set of keys. "Let's go!" Her eyes dropped to the recorder, then to the box of batteries. "What are you—"

"Avani!" I jumped to my feet, waving the recorder. "I know what the cure is."

TWENTY-EIGHT

ere they are!" shouted a voice. Avani and I whirled around to see the Nigerien in the tent doorway, pointing his rifle at us. I dropped the recorder and the keys into my pocket and raised my hands.

"Get out here," he said, waving the gun.

Avani and I exchanged dismayed looks and walked outside. Abramo and his men were clustered around the collapsed form of Androcles the silver lion, staring down at the beast and muttering to one another. A little distance apart, Kase, Miranda, Joey, and Sam stood with their hands on the backs of their heads, with two armed men watching them.

It was over. We'd missed our window of opportunity. I cursed myself for giving in to temptation and listening to the rest of Mom's recording. If I hadn't let myself be distracted, maybe we could have escaped.

"I got them, boss!" said the Nigerien.

Abramo made no reply. He was busy studying the lion.

Avani and I were left with no choice but to walk grimly toward him. I averted my eyes from Androcles's grisly carcass; it had taken only the first glance to see that he was riddled with bullet holes. The shots must have finally overwhelmed Metalcium's healing ability, or else it was the metal parasite itself that had felled the poor lion, the very thing that had kept it alive ultimately killing it.

Instead, I locked my gaze on Abramo. My fear of him had been burned away by anger that swept through me hotter than a bushfire.

"You killed my mother." I strode toward him, hands clenched at my sides, crossing between his mercenaries and the lion; even the silver corpse frightened them, and they stood several feet away from it and made signs to ward off evil. "Not even having the guts to kill her yourself, letting a bunch of insects do your work for you."

I stopped only when Abramo raised his gun, the barrel planted on my collarbone, holding me at arm's length. He finally looked up from the lion and gave me a cold glare. I had to tilt my head back to look into his eyes. Sam was repeating my name, pleading with me to back off, but I barely heard him. I was too focused, too intent the wild plan that had popped into my head at the sight of the lion.

Abramo gave me a bored look. "It was one of my more creative jobs."

I slapped him hard enough to leave an angry red impression on his cheek. In return, he struck me with the back of his hand, knocking me off my feet so that I crashed into one of the mercenaries. My face stung and I tasted blood on my lips. I landed awkwardly in the sand, dazed but no less emboldened by my plan.

"And my dad?" I asked. "Did you kill him too, like you killed Theo? Where is he, you bastard?"

"Enough of this," he said, glaring at me. He made a sweeping gesture at his men. "Take them all, dispose of them and burn them with this." He kicked Androcles and turned away.

I was vaguely aware of Miranda sobbing, of Joey begging for his life, of Sam shouting angry threats that did little good.

"Abramo!" My voice was sharp and focused as an arrow aimed at his back. One of the mercenaries had grabbed me by my shirt and was pulling me to my feet.

"I'm infected!" I called out. At once, all of the men took a step back and began muttering in alarm, perhaps asking one another if they'd touched me.

And of course, one of them had.

Abramo froze, his back to me. All around us, activity ceased and my friends fell silent.

I stood, wiping blood from my chin with my sleeve, watching Abramo. His shoulders slumped slowly and then he turned around. His eyes looked more tired than I'd seen them yet. In fact, he looked ten years older than he had just seconds ago.

"Prove it," he said in a tone that told me he already believed me, but that he couldn't help asking.

Wordlessly, I slid my sleeve up and held my infected arm aloft. His eyes didn't even flicker to it. Instead, they fastened on mine. For the first time, I had his full attention. His hand — the one he'd struck me with, skin to skin — closed into a fist. Other than that, he made no movement. He looked like a toy whose batteries had run out.

"And now you are too," I said, unnecessarily perhaps, but

I wanted him to understand the full impact of that touch. My cheek stung from his strike, but I'd be lying if I didn't relish the justice that burned in that pain.

A part of me hated myself for holding this man, whatever his crimes, hostage against himself. I felt dirty and cruel having stooped to his level, drawing on manipulations I didn't know I had. Of all the truths I'd had to face about myself in the last few days, this was the hardest—that I was capable of such ruthlessness.

Abramo said nothing. He watched me warily, as one leopard might eye another that had wandered into his territory, sizing me up to see if I was worth the fight.

"I know what the cure is," I said.

"Let me guess," said Abramo drily. "You won't tell me what it is until your friends are safe?"

I nodded. "And not until the government has been alerted to the threat of Metalcium, and not until you tell me what happened to my dad. Not until we are assured that you and Corpus will have no reason to come after us."

He was already shaking his head, and the motion made my heart sink. Bluffing or no, I at least had to get his cooperation on this. Even if the "cure" failed, my friends would be safe. So why did I get the feeling Abramo was about to refuse me?

"If you don't do this," I said, "you'll die. Same as him." I pointed at Androcles.

"I could shoot your friends, one by one, until you tell me," he said musingly.

I tried to hide the panic that rocketed through me. "You'll do that anyway."

"I could torture them."

"Go ahead!" called Sam. "You stick to your guns, Sarah! Don't worry about— *Mph!*"

I spun to see one of the mercenaries clubbing Sam in the stomach with the butt of his rifle. Joey lunged sideways, going after the man's ankles like a rabid terrier.

"Stop!" I yelled, not to the mercenary but to my friends. If they kept that up, they'd get shot for sure, whether Abramo willed it or not. Joey went still, at least, and so did the mercenary. Sam was doubled over, gasping, but he lifted his head just enough to shoot me an anguished smile.

My heart hammering, I turned back to Abramo. "I'll tell you *only* if you meet my demands." It took every ounce of willpower I possessed to keep my voice firm.

But still he was shaking his head, looking like a cartoon with a repeating glitch. "You're just a kid poking a stick at a beast you don't understand."

I didn't like the look of resignation on Abramo's face. I'd expected him to fly into a panic, to reject my offer at first, but to ultimately come to some sort of arrangement with me. It wouldn't make sense for him not to. He knew what Metalcium did, how fast it worked, how inevitable death was—he knew that better than anyone, perhaps. So why wasn't he jumping at the one, slim chance of a cure? Even if he doubted it was real, he couldn't afford to gamble.

"You *will* die," I said, my tone taking a pleading edge. "I'm offering you a chance."

"The world is not so simple," he said. All the rancor was gone from his voice. Now he seemed only sad and wearier than ever. "I won't bargain my life for yours or your companions'."

My hopes popped like soap bubbles, leaving me bewildered. "But why? If there's a chance—"

"I have a job to do," he said, cutting me off. "And I will do it. I'm sorry. Really, I am. It's nothing personal." He lifted his gun, aimed it at my chest. A glimmer of movement over his shoulder drew my eye. Someone was in the bush, running toward us, camouflaged by khaki clothing. My breath caught in my throat.

"You see, Sarah," Abramo calmly went on, "there's only one thing I fear more than death—"

My eyes connected with Dad's for a heartbeat, and I saw his mouth open in a desperate shout.

"—and that's Corpus."

"DADDY!" I screamed. Too late. *Too late.*

Abramo fired.

TWENTY-NINE

The world toppled. I fell backward and must have hit the ground, but I didn't feel it. I felt nothing but colors, strangely. I don't know how else to describe it. I felt red, and black, and then blinding white.

The bullet had struck me in my left shoulder, squarely over my heart. And yet as I lay there in the sand, my eyes wide and my limbs twitching, feeling nothing and everything all at once, I realized I wasn't dead. Not yet. Not quite. Soon, I suspected.

Events unfolded dimly around me. I was set apart, as if watching a television screen with the sound muted. People ran past me, shots were fired, faces flickered in and out of view. All I could do was stare up at the sky like a broken doll.

I've been shot.

It seemed ridiculous. Almost like a joke. It couldn't be real, could it? Not for me. *I* wasn't supposed to get shot. Thoughts like these swam through my head, short bursts of brain activity that began in confusion and ended in bewilderment. I felt that strange detachment, as if my mind were a balloon drifting high above it all, attached to my body by only the thinnest of threads. At any minute, I was sure, that thread would snap and I would float away. The prospect was strangely calming. I wasn't afraid, I discovered—only annoyed. Getting shot was the most irritating thing that had ever happened to me.

Time flowed sluggishly, like a glob of golden honey. When the sounds began to fade back and the pain started to really hit me, only seconds had passed, but it felt like hours, as if my mind had been temporarily lost in time, moving at a speed much faster than reality.

Slowly I came back to myself—and the pain followed with a vengeance. It began in my heart and spread through my whole body, raging like fire, my flesh and bone screaming out. It was like needles and knives and burning coals, hot and cold together. I realized I wasn't breathing and hadn't drawn a breath since Abramo had shot me. So I sucked in suddenly, but the air hit my lungs like a torrent of nails and I cried out.

Someone was there. Chaos streamed around me—people running, shouting, shooting, falling—but a hand took mine, a body pressed close to me, and a face faded in and out of focus.

Sam. Don't.

I couldn't speak. I was broken and shattered. Nothing worked anymore, and even my thoughts were fragments, the splintered pieces of my mind.

"I'm here," he said, his voice watery in my ears. I fixed on his eyes like a ship casting its anchor, seeking some solid hold on the world. "Stay with me."

Don't touch.

He gripped me tighter and his other hand brushed over my face, pushing back the strands of hair that had fallen over my eyes and lips. He must have read the warning in my eyes, because he said, "Don't look at me like that. I've got gloves, see?" He held up a hand. "Found them in one of the tents. Better?"

I don't know if I succeeded in nodding, but I at least tried.

I had to shut my eyes because the pain was only getting stronger. It clawed at me from the inside out, shot through me in waves. I spasmed and coughed, tasting blood.

Dying.

"You're not dying," he said, and I realized I must have said the word aloud. "I don't know how, but you're not."

But that was absurd. Abramo had shot me in my chest—I had *felt* it.

". . . happening?" I mumbled, then I coughed on the blood in my throat. Sam lifted me up to a sitting position so I could spit it out. As I did, I looked down at my chest.

There was blood, a lot of it. I wanted to push the cloth aside, to see what had happened—had the bullet only grazed me? But my arms wouldn't move.

I looked around, my eyes reacting in delay, so that the world dragged dizzily around me. I saw mercenaries clustered behind one of the vehicles, their backs to me, firing at someone in the grass.

"Dad . . ."

"He's here. He's alive. Sarah, I'm going to move you. I'm sorry, but I have to do it."

He carefully lifted me into his arms. I whimpered at the bolts of pain this sent racketing through me and curled my hands against my chest, keeping my skin from brushing his. He strode quickly away, into the shade of one of the tents, where we were hidden from the skirmish.

There he set me down very gently in the grass, and he used his sleeve to wipe the blood from my lips.

"Right before Abramo shot you, your dad came charging out of the bush like a crazy person," he said. "He has a gun with him, and he starting shooting. Dropped two of the mercenaries before they got to cover. Joey and the others ran, and I'm not sure where they are. Your dad took to the bush." Sam went away, disappearing from my sight for a moment, and I lacked the ability to turn my head to look for him. Panic fluttered in my gut. *Don't leave me!* I wanted to call out, but my tongue was a hopeless lump in my mouth. Then Sam returned, hardly three seconds later. "He's pinned behind a tree," he said. "They're getting shots off at each other but not good ones. Seems to be a standoff. I don't see Abramo."

Sam's eyes traveled down to my heart. "Sarah. I need to look. Is that okay?"

"Yes," I whispered, my voice so faint I wasn't sure he heard me. But he nodded and gingerly undid the top three buttons of my shirt.

"Wow," he said, his face turning white.

I mumbled inquisitively. He propped me up so that I could see.

The bullet had struck just over my heart, and when Sam inspected my back, he told me it had passed clean through my shoulder. The skin over the wound was hard and silver, so smooth that Sam's face reflected in it.

"The exit wound is sealed over too," he said, his gloved

fingers gently probing the tear in the back of my shirt. "It must have spread over the hole right away."

I thought of Androcles, how he'd survived so many bullets, the Metalcium healing the wounds or maybe even deflecting the shots. And now it had done the same for me.

"Does it hurt?" he asked.

I nodded. Every movement felt as if I were being shot again in the same spot. The pain lanced through my shoulder like a scalding rod.

"Want to see," I said.

"See what?"

I couldn't summon my voice to reply, so I looked to my left, toward the center of the camp where the mercenaries were still firing at Dad.

Sam shifted me closer, so that I could see what was going on. Movement across the clearing, from the opposite row of tents, caught my eye. It was Joey and Avani, crouched in the grass. Behind them were Kase and Miranda.

"Sam," I whispered. "My pocket—there are keys."

He pulled out the set of keys from my cargo pants. "For the trucks?"

I nodded, then winced at the pain that sent rippling down my spine. But even so, I could feel myself recovering, regaining some semblance of strength. This wouldn't kill me. Metalcium might—but not this. "Get Joey's attention."

Sam waved wildly until Joey saw him.

"Throw him the keys," I instructed.

Sam's eyes widened in understanding. He showed Joey the keys, then tossed them through the air. They landed in front of Joey, who scooped them up. He caught on right away.

The Land Rovers were lined up between him and the mercenaries. Joey crept to the first one and tried the key, but it didn't work. He moved on to the next, staying low.

With a painful effort, I leaned out more to see if I could glimpse Dad. I only had to see where the mercenaries were shooting to spot him. He was pinned behind a stand of *Terminalia* and was firing at random back at the mercenaries. His shots were all wide—either because he couldn't see to aim or he was worried about hitting one of us—but not so wide that any of Abramo's men were willing to charge him. Their backs were to us, their attention focused on Dad. But then one of them started to split apart from the others, apparently to check on us prisoners.

Hurry, Joey, hurry!

Joey couldn't see the mercenary from where he was, but if they both held to their current paths, they'd inevitably bump right into each other—an encounter that would only end badly for Joey. Sam also saw it, and too late I realized what he intended to do.

"Hey!" he yelled, suddenly jumping out from cover and waving his arms like a maniac.

I don't know what Sam was expecting, but what he got was a spray of bullets that poked holes through the tents all around him. I tried to call out in warning—as if he wasn't aware of the torrent of gunfire—but it only came out as a strangled moan.

Sam fell backward through one of the tent openings, and for a moment I thought he'd been shot. I pulled back, ducking before the mercenary could see me, but not before I saw Joey open the door of the third Land Rover. With his concentration focused on Sam, the gunman didn't notice. Instead, he advanced toward the tent Sam had toppled into.

Still there was no sign of Abramo, which worried me.

I forced myself to my feet and found, to my surprise, that I was recovering more quickly than I'd thought. I still ached all over and my chest screamed with red pain, but I had control of my senses and my limbs.

There was a scuffle inside the tent. I heard shots, then a clatter, and the canvas walls shook and bowed outward as someone fell against it. The tent flap opened and Sam stumbled out, hotly pursued by the mercenary, who was calling to his fellows for help.

Sam tripped and fell, rolling over just in time to raise his hands in a mercy plea. From the look of the guy's face, I wasn't at all sure he would get a favorable response.

So I drew a deep breath and took a wobbly step into the open.

"Don't you dare," I said. "Don't you *dare* touch him."

"Sarah! No!" Sam yelled, but I knew what I was doing. At least, I hoped I did.

The man's rifle came up and he shot a single bullet at me. I was already throwing up my hands in involuntary if feeble self-defense. What happened next I could neither believe nor fully explain.

The bullet *melted* into my palm, striking the heel of my thumb on my left hand. This I registered with my eyes more than anything else; I barely felt it until a moment later, when the pain racketed up my arm and jarred my skull, driving me back two stumbling steps. But that first split second of impact was what stunned me. The bullet struck my palm but seemed to get stuck halfway into my skin. Then the flesh around it, which had been pale and pink before, flared into a spider's web of silver veins, emanating from the bullet hole. I turned my palm toward me and watched in shock as the Metalcium formed, pushing away my skin and ejecting the bullet. The little bit of twisted, flatted metal fell and dropped into the sand. I stared from it to my newly silvered palm, then at the mercenary. He too was watching in dumb astonishment.

Then Sam kicked savagely upward, his shoe connecting with the man's groin, and the man collapsed with a stifled grunt of pain. He lay writhing as Sam picked up his rifle. He trained it on the other mercenaries, who had begun to turn around to see what the commotion was.

By now, Joey had gotten Avani, Miranda, and Kase into the Land Rover and was attempting to start it. Two mercenaries noticed and headed toward the vehicle. To distract them, Sam leaned around the corner of the tent and shot off a few rounds in their direction, making them wheel and scramble for cover. I strained to get a glimpse of my dad, telling myself that if they were still firing at him, he had to be alive. Somehow I had to get to him, before it was too late.

"Get over here!" Sam yelled to Joey.

"I can't!" Joey shouted. "It's stick shift!"

"Oh, for crying out loud," I muttered. "Press the clutch!"

"What's a clutch?"

"Move over!" Avani suddenly commanded. Joey slid sideways and she climbed over him to take the wheel. The engine roared to life and the car started forward, stopped, and started forward again with all the elegance of a three-legged hippo trying to run. Avani seemed to be struggling with the gears.

Her eyes suddenly lifted and fixed on something ahead,

and she yelled at the others in the car. Heart sinking, I turned to see what had frightened her—and realized where Abramo had gone.

The Corpus helicopter, bristling with mercenaries and piloted by Abramo, had lifted into the sky and was swiftly bearing down on us all.

THIRTY

Sarah!" Sam yelled. He took me carefully by the elbow and pulled me toward the Land Rover. "Let's go."

"We can't outrun a chopper."

He stopped just long enough to spare me a madcap grin. "Is that a dare, Sarah Carmichael?"

Avani brought the Land Rover to a rough stop beside us. Everyone inside yelled at us to hurry, and hurry we did. Kase opened the door and offered me a hand, and Miranda and I simultaneously snapped at him to take it back. He did so, looking a bit pale and rubbing his hand on his shirt as if I *had* touched it. Sam lifted me up with surprising ease. Once he had a foot on the bar below the door, he told Avani to go.

Sam jumped in, shut the door, and dropped into the seat beside me. Kase gave us a healthy amount of space to ourselves, scrunching up to Miranda against the other door.

"I don't think I can drive this after all!" Avani called. "Sarah, can you take over?"

Gritting my teeth, I maneuvered into the driver's seat while Avani slid into the passenger seat, which meant she ended up in Joey's lap, leaving a dopey grin on Joey's face. Everyone was careful to avoid my touch. Once I had my hands on the wheel, I drew a deep breath and told myself I could do this. Never mind that I was infected with a lethal metallic parasite. Never mind that I'd been shot twice today. Somehow I managed to shovel all this aside and floor the gas.

"Gotta pick up Dad," I said. No one objected.

Sam pointed to a low-spreading *Terminalia*. "Behind that tree!"

"Guys," said Miranda, "I found this—"

"Everyone duck!" I yelled, cutting her off, my eyes fixed on the rearview mirror.

They all did, sliding onto the floor as the remaining six mercenaries on foot and Abramo and his buddies in the chopper opened fire on us. The glass in the back window shattered, and then the front windshield went. Avani shrieked as glass shards rained down on her.

I drove doggedly on, ignoring all obstacles in our path. As a result, the car bounced wildly as we crashed over termite mounds and shrubbery. At the same time, I turned the wheel sharply in all directions, trying to bob and weave to avoid as many bullets as possible. I sank down in my seat in an effort to shield myself from the gunfire, so I could barely see where I was going.

I drove in a circle around the outside of the camp, headed toward my dad. Keeping their gunfire on both Dad and us, the mercenaries moved to intercept me. I simply drove faster. Those who dared get in front of the Land Rover were forced to throw themselves aside or be run over. Their shots went wide for the most part, since we were moving too quickly to give them a chance to aim, but a few lucky bullets shattered the windows. Glass rained onto my lap and shoulders.

When I reached the trees sheltering Dad, I slowed just enough for Kase to throw open the door. "Dad! Get in!"

He was crouched between two gnarled roots, the trees around him gouged with bullets. As he hobbled to the car, I realized he was clutching his side—his hand covered in blood.

"He's hurt!" I yelled. "Help him!"

Kase and Sam took Dad's rifle and pulled him into the car He looked terrible. His clothes were dirty and torn, his hair untied and matted, and he had a week's growth of beard hanging shaggily from his jaw.

"Go, Sarah!" he yelled. "*Now!*"

"You've been shot!" I returned.

"We'll all get shot if you don't drive!" He winced and shut his eyes, pressing his head against the back of my seat.

Heart pounding with fear and worry for him, I hit the gas. "Where have you *been*?"

"Where have *I* been? Trying to find you! I've been tracking you kids for—" He cut off with a hiss of pain, his hand gripping the side of my seat and leaving bloody streaks on the leather.

The gunfire ceased. A glance in the rearview mirror revealed that the mercenaries were loading into the other two vehicles to give chase, but what worried me more was the helicopter.

We were driving straight toward it, and I spun the wheel,

turning us to the right. We moved in a cloud of dust that made it hard to see much of anything, so it was more dumb luck than my driving abilities that prevented us from crashing into a tree.

Everyone behind me was chorusing, "Faster! Faster!" which I ignored with clenched teeth. I was going as fast as possible, but we were in the middle of the bush and I didn't want to risk crashing or stalling. Every bump we hit made my dad gasp with pain.

"Chopper on our tail!" Kase reported.

Joey began whooping and laughing like a maniac, yelling, "Yippee-ki-yay, suckers!" to which Avani responded with a sharp pinch to his arm.

"Shut up, idiot! She's trying to concentrate."

"Are they firing at us?" I asked.

"Not yet," said Kase. "No, wait, they're opening their doors. Aaaaand . . . yeah. Those are guns. Really big ones."

"Guys," Miranda said again. "I really did find something—"

But at that moment we hit a massive termite mound head-on. We were all thrown violently forward. My head clacked against the steering wheel and I saw stars. I hurriedly reversed, then maneuvered around it.

"They're shooting!" Kase warned.

I cursed and began weaving again, my eyes working frantically as I tried to find the best route, aiming for the more open areas. But a strange thing was happening: Every time I blinked, my vision stayed dark for a brief moment, taking time to clear, as if there were a delay between my eyes and my brain. The corners of my thoughts were getting fuzzy. For a moment, I entirely forgot where we were and what I was doing. My heart fluttered in panic, and I didn't realize I was starting to hyper-ventilate until Avani asked me what was wrong.

I could almost *see* the Metalcium creeping over my skin, devouring my hands, my arms. My body was itching from head to toe. It felt like hundreds of tiny spiders scuttling beneath my clothes, biting me repeatedly.

The chopper didn't open fire right away. Instead, it passed over us and then dropped lower and lower until it was hovering directly in our path. When I tried to turn aside, it simply swooped to block me again.

"Can I reverse?" I asked Kase.

"No! The other cars are behind us."

I cursed again. We were trapped between the chopper and the mercenaries. Seeing this, the chopper set down, its rotors still whipping. I slowed, knowing we had just seconds to devise a plan. I turned in my seat.

"Dad?"

He lifted his head, his eyes bloodshot and his face creased with pain. "If they catch us, they will kill us," he said calmly. "We have nothing to lose."

I nodded. His words lifted some of the panic, replacing them with a strange calming recklessness. *Nothing to lose.*

Drawing a deep breath, I faced the chopper, steeling my will.

"Okay," I said. "Okay."

"Okay *what*?" asked Avani, with no small amount of alarm.

"Let's do this."

"Do *what*?"

I yanked the stick into third gear, alternating stomping the clutch and the gas, and the Land Rover responded like a racehorse let out of the gate. It roared forward, devouring the distance between us and the chopper.

"You're playing *chicken* with it?" Kase yelped from the back.

"Nothing to lose!" I replied, then realized I was laughing like a lunatic. "Might want to put on your seat belts."

"We're going to die!"

Maybe. But maybe was at least better than *definitely.*

Faster and faster we moved. The vehicle rattled like a space shuttle leaving orbit. It bounced and creaked and threw us every which way as it vaulted over holes and bumps. At one point, I think we were entirely airborne.

The faces of Abramo and his men came into view, looking shocked and talking frantically.

They would have to pull up. But they just sat there, the rotors whipping up a whirlwind of dust. I gritted my teeth and held the course in a kamikaze mania.

There is a bird in the Kalahari called the korhaan, which attracts females by flying straight up into the air, then tucking its wings to its sides and tipping beak down to dive-bomb the earth. It has to spread its wings at the last possible second or else smash into the ground—and they don't always succeed. I felt exactly like that korhaan.

The question here, though, was whether the chopper would fly, or if I'd kill us all.

At the last moment, the helicopter lifted just far enough for us to pass under it. The car erupted in cheers, which I thought was rather premature considering we were nowhere near safe yet. But I allowed myself one tight smile of triumph.

"*Guys,*" said Miranda. "Will you just look at the thing I found under the seat?"

"What is it?" Avani asked in exasperation.

I glanced in the mirror and saw the object in Miranda's hand. "Dad! It's a radio!"

He turned around and took the device. "This is brilliant, mates!" I could tell his tight grin was masking the agony of his wound, and I watched his reflection with mounting apprehension.

"Mir, *you're* brilliant," said Kase. He kissed her unreservedly, and they tumbled down, disappearing behind the backseat.

"Can you pick up anything?" I asked Dad.

He fiddled with the channels, raising a lot of static. "Nothing yet, but I'll find it."

"How do you feel? Are you okay? You—"

"Don't worry about me! Just keep us moving, kiddo."

That was easier said than done. The chopper kept trying to get around us, and every time they did I changed course before they could cut us off again. The other vehicles were having just as hard a time navigating the bush, so they worried me a bit less. What concerned me most was myself. My sight kept blurring and my head was pounding. Was it dehydration, fatigue, or Metalcium? Likely all three. I didn't know how much longer I could keep this up.

Through all of this chaos, I was trying to head more or less in the right direction. It was a bit like aiming a rock at a target while blindfolded, but I had to try. If I was going to be cured, then we had to reach Dr. Monaghan's laboratory. I figured we had about one in a hundred chances of actually finding it again. I looked over my shoulder at Dad. He knew the area better than I did; he might be able to point us the right way.

"Dad, there's this lab. We have to . . ."

But my eyes suddenly went out of focus, his face blurring. I blinked, trying to clear my vision, but still it was like trying to look through a glass of water. Everything was distorted and seemed to be slipping away, dragging downward and sideways so that I couldn't be sure what I was looking at.

Someone said my name, their voice coming to me as if from a vast distance. I tried to answer. If I did, I couldn't tell.

Have to tell them.

Have to tell them what?

The cure.

"The lab," I whispered. "We have to go back to the lab. I know the cure."

"What is it?" someone asked.

I couldn't find my tongue to answer.

"What's wrong with her?" I heard Dad ask.

"She's infected!" said Sam.

Dad swore, his voice fuzzy and distant. Everything was slipping—my vision, my hearing, my thoughts. I was standing on the side of a sand dune, the ground continually giving away beneath my feet. *The metal,* I thought vaguely. *It's the metal that's doing this. Eating me from the outside in.*

My stomach lurched sideways, as if I were falling, and I heard a dim chorus of shouting. Then I felt hands dragging me by my arms. Someone repeating my name, soft as a butterfly landing, lifting and fluttering, landing again. Dismay flooded me, so deep and greedy that it was like drowning in sand. I knew something was wrong but I couldn't reason what it was.

Silver butterflies. They swam in my mind. Silver butterflies, silver lions, a whole silver menagerie. The silver face of a man, half-flesh, half-metal, his cheeks melting from his bones like hot wax, his hollow silver eyes gaping at me. Silver people reaching out of the darkness, moaning and keening. I cried out and clawed savagely at them, heard a soft exclamation. Someone grabbed my wrists and held them tight.

For a moment I surfaced, my eyes settling blearily on Sam's face. His lips moved. I didn't hear what he said. *I am going crazy*, I thought. Then I slipped back under.

Dr. Monaghan's face leered at me, dripping with dead skin, his eyes blank and silver. *It starts with the skin and hair,* he laughed, *and then it goes for the brain.*

In and out of insanity I drifted. That hellish ride seemed to last for an eternity. I saw my own hands, both of them entirely silver, but I didn't know if it was real or not. I saw Dr. Monaghan's melting, metallic face. It haunted me whenever I closed my eyes. I saw the three silver scientists falling under gunfire. Voices mingled and warped, the words eluding me. At times I could hear nothing at all, and at others I heard too much: chattering voices, the rumbling engine, static and a heavy thumping drumbeat. Through all of it I was aware of his arms holding me, keeping my hands from scratching at his face or mine. Because the urge was there, whenever the Metalcium gripped my mind. I had to *fight*, had to claw my way free. I was seized with a feral desire to escape, to run, to hurt, to maim, to break free of this madness.

I didn't even realize we'd stopped until Dad and Sam lifted me out of the car. Dad carried me in his arms as if I were a baby and we rushed over the ground. He stumbled once, nearly dropping me, his arms trembling, and I wondered how he could even stand with his wound. I bounced and my teeth chattered. There was something important, something I had to say. . . . *Don't touch. Don't scratch.* The words wouldn't form. My voice was a sticky glob in my throat, choking me. He held me cradled against his chest, and I stared in dismay at where one of his hands wrapped over my bare arm. *No, please, not you too . . . Don't touch, don't scratch. . . .*

"Hush," Dad murmured into my hair as he ran. "I'm here, Sissy Hati. I won't let anything happen to you."

I smiled into the dusty fabric of his shirt.

They carried me into a building, a laboratory. They shut the doors, locked them, and shoved tables and cabinets against them. I wanted to help but I kept slipping away, as if this world were a dream I was trying to go back to. I smelled smoke, heavy and acrid, and thought of our ruined camp.

"It won't hold them for long," Sam said. "They'll shoot the locks and then shove their way through. How long before the rescue teams get here?"

Rescue teams? Had Dad reached someone on the radio after all? I tried to ask, but it came out as a groan.

"An hour at least," replied Dad. His face sharpened and then blurred, his skin pale, sweat beading his brow. He looked like he was about to pass out.

"Wake up, Sarah," my dad said. "You have to tell us what to do. We're here, at the lab. Now what? Sam?"

"She only said the cure was here. She didn't say what it was."

"Mr. Carmichael," Avani said, "you're bleeding! You can barely stand. We have to bandage that injury. Here, someone give me a shirt or something. Grab Sarah's scarf. . . ."

Their voices were like flashlight beams, probing the darkness of my mind. All the while, I huddled in the cold, shivering, not wanting them to find me, not wanting them to see. A terrible sense of shame overwhelmed me and I despaired that they would see what I had become. *Metal and madness and mirrors, that's all that I am.*

"Pyramids," I murmured.

"What?"

"Never saw the pyramids."

"What's the cure?" they asked. The word hammered at me. My heart picked it up and pounded it through my veins. *Cure, cure, cure . . .*

It was like being buried alive and trying to dig myself free. I reached, I fought, I struggled to push aside the insanity. *What is the cure?*

I knew what it was. I struggled to reach it. The answer was so high, out of reach. I stood on tiptoe and strained, strained. . . . I realized I was lifting my hands, stretching them toward the light above me. My wrist made of metal . . . My eyes latched onto the remnants of my tattoo, the one I'd gotten a month after Mom's funeral, the one to commemorate her death and her last mission and her final words. The tattoo that summed up the single greatest tragedy of my life.

The bees are a fail.

That's it. I have it.

THIRTY-ONE

B ee," I whispered.
    "Be *what*?"

"The bees . . ." I labored for breath. Was it in my throat now? Were my lungs petrifying too? "The bees are a fail . . . *safe*."

It had all come together when the word surfaced, hidden in Mom's final words to me: *My heart is with yours. Keep it safe.*

Fail. Safe.

A thing put in place to handle the damage should a crisis arise. The mechanism that put the system on shutdown, to contain the problem before it could spread.

That was what she'd been trying to write on her arm. At the very end, after Abramo's bees had stung her within an inch of her life, she'd realized what the cure was and tried to write it down. She had died before she could finish the word. *The bees are a fail-safe.*

"She always said," I whispered, my eyes anchoring on

Dad's face, struggling to stay afloat, "nature had a way of taking care of itself, if only we would step aside. Like the baby kangaroo, Dad, remember?"

He frowned. He didn't get it.

But someone else did.

"Wait a minute," said Avani. I couldn't see her but I could hear the excitement tinting her words. "Bees. Their stings inject apitoxin into their victims."

For the first time, I think she had everyone's full attention. I struggled to hold myself aloft from the roiling insanity that pulled at me.

"Go on," my father replied slowly.

"Don't you see?" she said, her voice rushing. "The apitoxin—the venom—contains a substance called melittin."

Silence and confusion. She exhaled noisily in frustration.

"Melittin breaks down cells and is used to destroy tumors and infective bacteria or viruses. They're even testing it against cancer. What if it works the same way against Metalcium, killing the cells like they were a tumor?"

"You're saying we should get some bees to sting her?" asked Sam doubtfully.

"Yes," she replied, but she sounded less sure.

Yes, yes! I wanted to shout, but I was sinking again, my voice powerless. Just like the bees that killed Mom. She *had* been infected, just like the mice in the lab, and the bees *knew* it. They were a fail-safe, nature's remedy standing by. I thought of how the birds all went silent when an infected animal appeared. They sensed the wrongness of Metalcium—and so did the bees, except the bees could actually do something about it.

"Guys!" It was Miranda, shouting from some distance away. "They're shooting at the door! Hurry!"

Dimly, I could hear the shots ringing out, the ring of bullets on metal.

"Kase," said Sam, "take the guns. You and Miranda guard the door. If it starts to open, just shoot in warning, okay?"

He handed over the two rifles, and Kase, pale but grim, nodded and dashed away.

"But it's winter," said Dad, ignoring the gunfire. "The bees are all dormant."

Which is why they stopped bothering the scientists. Which is why poor Androcles roamed freely for so long. I didn't know why I believed it so completely. I think it had to do with my strengthening insanity; what would have never seemed reasonable to me ordinarily now made perfect sense. Why *not* bees?

"There's some in the freezer," said Sam. "We found a hive filled with them last time. They were still alive. That's probably why Sarah wanted to come back here."

Yes! In the freezer! Hurry!

"It's no good!" said Avani. "They're dead by now."

"Maybe not," said Joey.

In the silence that followed, I easily imagined them giving him incredulous looks. *Tell them,* I thought to him. *Tell them what happens if you heat them up.*

"When I was a kid," Joey said, "we used to catch bees by sucking them up with a vacuum hose, then stick them in the freezer for like an hour. Then we'd take them out and tie a string around them, and when they warmed up they buzzed around on the string. Like little flying pets. What? Don't look at me like that! We let them go afterward! But don't you see? Maybe we could get the bees to revive."

"It is possible," said Dad.

"We have to try it," Sam said, his voice steely. "Someone get the bees."

"Hurry!" Kase yelled. "They're pushing open the door!"

"The burn pile is on the other side of the building," said Avani. "I saw it when we drove up—the freezer is probably there. If the bees are inside, they might have escaped being burned. Check the back door. If it's clear, one of us could sneak out there while they're still at the front."

I heard a shot from inside the building, and then Kase warning the mercenaries to stay back.

I drifted away again, falling into a memory that swirled around me like a living watercolor painting. Me, four years old, crying because I'd found a fat bumblebee lying in our freezer. My mom and I had been making homemade Popsicles, the kind where you pour juice into a cup and then put a stick in for it to freeze around. The bee must have crawled into the freezer while I left it open, then got shut up inside. It was in there for hours, and when I found it I was sure I'd killed it. I was upset because I knew bees were Mom's favorite, and now I'd killed one. "No, look," Mom said. She took it out and held it in the sun. After a few seconds, it began to buzz a little, then wobble, and then it suddenly zipped away, weaving a bit, but alive. My tears turned into a smile of awe and wonder. For years, I was convinced my mom had brought it back to life all on her own, with some secret magic. Maybe it wasn't a spell or some incantation she'd worked, but it had been magic all the same. Because she had taken something broken and made it fly. She had shown me that things lost could be found, and things dead could be reawakened if you believed hard enough.

I knew no amount of wishing could bring my mom back physically, but I realized at that moment that she *was* there. I'd never felt her presence so strongly since she'd died. After all, it was her words that had led me to this revelation. It was her hand, lifting that little bee to the sunlight, that had pointed the way. In this, she was present, holding me up to the sun in the same way, in a way I thought had been lost.

I clung to this with all my strength. It was the ledge that lifted me out of the flood. As long as I held on to it, I could breathe, I could see, I could make sense of what was happening.

They'd found the container of bees, and more buried under them. Thousands of them. Probably an entire hive that the scientists had found, smoked into senselessness, and then frozen for later experimentation. Likely they were curious as to why the bees seemed to be targeting them, but had never gotten around to actually figuring out what it was. They'd been so intent on destroying the bees that were attacking them, they'd never realized they were destroying the very cure they sought.

I'd heard of cases like this before, like with the oil spill in the Gulf of Mexico—the most effective force at cleaning up the methane wasn't humans, but a bacteria that emerged to break it down and digest it. Sometimes—not always, but sometimes—nature provides its own crisis managers, the same way the human body deploys certain types of cells to fight an invading virus. The bees were evidence of an intricate system, a system that rises up to defend itself when an alien invader appears.

"I can't believe it," someone said. "They're alive."

"The heat from the fire must have warmed them and woken them up."

"Angry little buzzers, aren't they?"

"Here, mates, hand them to me."

Dad pointed out that we'd have to limit the stings, because the particular bees we were working with was the notorious African honeybees, known also by another name: *killer bees*. They were responsible for many deaths all over the world, feared for their aggressive nature and tendency to swarm and sting whatever creature disturbed their hive. And they'd killed Mom. I could only guess that the venom from the bees, though powerful enough to counter the Metalcium, had been too much for her system. If it had been only a few bees, maybe she could have survived.

None of us knew how the bee's venom would work, and I think they all still doubted that it would work at all. But this was likely bigger than me. I was pretty sure Dad had touched me when he'd carried me inside. He wasn't showing signs of it yet, but he would. Maybe for him it wasn't too late. Maybe he could still reach a hospital and somewhere there would be an expert who would know what to do. For me, though? I doubted I had much longer. At the rate the Metalcium had spread and begun affecting my mind, I didn't think I'd last more than a day. It was a strange and unsettling thought. I contemplated my death with detached curiosity, as if it were a odd thing I'd found on the ground. I couldn't bear to bring it any closer, to consider what it really was.

A dozen bees slipped out of the container when Sam cracked it open. They shot upward, around, zipping through the air in a fury. My heart began to sink; they seemed uninterested in me. What if I'd been wrong?

"Help!" Miranda cried from the door.

Dad stumbled to them, taking the gun from Miranda and popping a few shots through the crack of the door. He roared at the mercenaries to stay back, then he shoved the door shut again and yelled at Kase and Miranda to push more furniture against it. Joey ran to help them. I fought to stay conscious, watching Dad worriedly; he was breathing hard and leaning against the door as if it were the only thing holding him up. Was his injury worse than he was letting on? The first sting took me by surprise. I hadn't noticed the one little bee that had, well, beelined for my exposed arm. I hissed through my teeth, wincing, and mutely shook my head at Sam's look of concern.

The first sting was quickly followed by others. The rest of the escaped bees converged on me, sinking their stingers into my arms. One of them escaped and buzzed away, harmless now that its stinger was lodged in my skin, or what was currently functioning as my skin.

The others all bent low over my arm, watching to see . . . something. Anything. Dismay began to flood me as nothing happened. I'd nurtured hope like a small ember in my heart, and now it began to cool. I whimpered, all my defenses falling away. *I am going to die.*

Then Avani breathed, *"Look."*

I held my hand up closer to my eyes, wishing I had a magnifying glass. But in a moment, I didn't need one.

The spots where the bees had stung were turning from silver to white. The Metalcium puckered around the stings, like tiny blisters, and then the affected area spread out. I began to whimper, then clamped my teeth over my lip as my hand began to burn.

It wasn't skin, I reminded myself. It wouldn't necessarily react the same way. And it didn't. It burned like acid corroding metal. The Metalcium began to bubble up, in just small areas around the stings at first, but then spreading as if the venom had created a chain reaction. Miranda turned away, looking ill.

My other hand gripped the edge of the table so hard I thought my hand would petrify around the edge. My body was rigid, and Sam must have sensed then how much pain I was in.

"What can I do?" he asked.

I just shook my head and closed my eyes. I couldn't watch anymore. All of my attention was focused on not screaming. If I had stuck my hand into the coals of a burning fire, it couldn't have hurt any more than this. Someone pried open my mouth and shoved a roll of cloth between my teeth. It was one of Sam's gloves. I bit down on it, tears bleeding from my eyes.

The bee venom had caused some sort of chemical reaction with the Metalcium. It lashed up my arm and across my chest, singeing the plate of metal over my heart like a brand pressed into my skin. I opened my eyes long enough to see faint wisps of smoke rising from the metal as it whitened and shriveled. I heard a bloodcurdling scream rise and I looked around to see who it was, only to realize it was me. The glove had fallen from my mouth and my lips were stretched in an inhuman cry that could shatter glass.

Then my voice cut off, blocked by pain.

The door flew open. My dad stumbled back, his rifle still raised and Joey behind him, holding the other rifle. Abramo stood in the doorway, flanked by his men.

"Drop your guns!" Abramo ordered. "It's over, Carmichael."

"Look!" Dad cried, his body slumping as he struggled to stay on his feet. "She's healing! It works—this cure, it works! Abramo, stop this! We can help you. Let us heal you!"

Abramo's eyes were already fixed on me. He looked shocked. His men seemed uneasy at seeing me in this state, and they backed away slightly.

"She's dying," Abramo said.

"No," Dad replied fiercely. "The metal is being purged, that's all. We can do the same for you—just put down the guns!"

Abramo shook his head in that slow, mechanical way of his. All the while he stared at me over Dad's shoulder, as if he didn't even notice the rifle my father was pointing at him. Then suddenly he whirled in place, his eyes focused on something outside.

"Hear that?" Dad asked. I could tell his voice was getting weaker. *He* was getting weaker. I forced my eyes to focus on him, noticed that he had bled through the scarf Avani had bound around his torso. "That's the emergency teams. I reached the government and now they're here. It's over."

When Abramo turned back around, his eyes were empty. "Do you realize what you've done?" he whispered. "You have made a failure of me."

"Let us help you," Dad repeated. His voice broke with

pain, and he dropped to his knees, using the rifle to brace himself. "Please . . ."

"I can't," Abramo said simply, staring vacantly over Dad's head. "It is better to die than fail them."

And then he put his revolver to his own temple and pulled the trigger.

Shock rocketed through me. The world reeled out of balance. My eyes rolled backward and I fainted dead away.

THIRTY-TWO

I woke to feel nothing at all, as if I'd been disconnected entirely from my body and were nothing but a consciousness in the air. I wondered if I was dead, if this was what came after.

Voices took shape around me, and then sights: the brown thatched roof, the lightbulb hanging from it, a dark blob that slowly materialized into a face. It was a stranger's face, but a kind one. She smiled in that particularly bright and cheerful way that the Batswana have and spoke to me in clear English. The words passed right through me, without comprehension, but they seemed to be pleasant and I smiled back. My thoughts were clouded, as if my skull were packed with cotton, mercifully dampening my senses. I was aware only that my mouth felt incredibly dry. I wanted to ask for water. I couldn't remember how.

The woman was wearing a white medic's uniform and blue latex gloves. She said something else, not to me but to someone across from her. I turned and there was Sam, nodding at her words. Then he looked down at me, and though he smiled, I could read deep concern in his eyes.

What happened? I wanted to ask. *Where am I?*

But they might have been speaking gibberish for all the sense I could make of their words. My sight blurred and faded, and I fell asleep again—into real sleep, not pain-induced unconsciousness. I slept deeper than I had in over a week, possibly since before Mom had died. I felt more refreshed when I opened my eyes than if I'd slept ten hours in a bed of silk. My head was clearer and though I still couldn't feel much, I at least had a grasp on the world.

The medic was gone, but soon after I'd opened my eyes, Sam appeared.

"Hey. How're you feeling?"

It took a moment to loosen my tongue. "Numb."

He nodded. "They gave you something. Morphine, I think."

"Who?"

"The medics. Your dad reached a game warden on the radio—Henrico, I think? Anyway, the guy called for help and gave them our location. They're all here. Medics, soldiers, some people in suits."

"Dad! Where is he? Is he okay?"

"Hey, easy! He's fine. Well, he did faint, just after Abramo . . . but the medics took care of him too. They said the bullet passed through him. He bled a lot, but he'll be okay."

I shut my eyes, letting relief wash over me like a cool breeze.

"Abramo shot himself." I said it with disbelief, wondering if I'd dreamed it.

But Sam nodded, his eyes grim.

Better to die than fail them. Wasn't that what Abramo had said? But why? What punishment could these people bring down on him that was worse than being consumed by a living metal parasite? What was so bad that he preferred shooting himself?

I shuddered, and the sensation unlocked some of the feeling that the morphine had been pushing away. My arms. My chest. My hands most of all. They felt raw and tender, and the smallest movement sent ripples of agony and pain through me.

Sam reached out and touched my forehead. "Be still," he said. "They're going to take you to a hospital soon. They won't let any of us leave until we've each given our side of the story, but I bet we get out sooner. Your dad's furious. He's talking to some government guy right now, telling him you need to be transported right away. The medics did what they could. They bandaged you up."

I looked down. My shirt was gone, and my arms and hands and my chest from my neck to my diaphragm were tightly swathed in bandages.

"Everywhere the Metalcium was, you have second- to third-degree burns," Sam explained, his voice gentle and his eyes serious. "The bee venom caused some kind of reaction, undoing the Metalcium, your dad said. Avani explained it too, but I understood only half of what she said. You were unconscious through most of it. It wasn't . . ." He chewed his lip, his eyes lowering. "It was good you weren't awake." Then he lifted his gaze, forcing a small smile. "They put on some kind of burn cream and these bandages, and they said it will take a couple of months to fully heal."

I nodded.

"Sarah?" He studied me closer, watching my eyes with intentness. "Are you okay with all of this?"

When I found my voice, it was hoarse. "I'll live?"

His brows furrowed, and then his eyes grew wide. "Yes! Yes, you're fine! The Metalcium is gone—all of it, that they can tell. Not that they know much about it. They want to run more tests, but it looks like you're in the clear."

"Just like Mom," I whispered. "Abramo killed her by setting a swarm of bees on her, thinking it would cover up her murder—and it did. But it also healed her of the Metalcium infection. She'd counted on us finding her infected and discovering the truth about the murder, but the bees' venom cured her before we did. It's like a weird, twisted circle." I sighed and looked up at Sam. "How's Dad? He touched me when he carried me inside."

"He got stung too. Some of the other bees escaped and they went right for him. They ignored everyone else, just stung your dad, like they knew he'd been infected. Your dad said it tingled, but it wasn't anything like what you went through."

I nodded. "He was barely infected, like my mom. That's why we didn't see burns on her—the infection must not have reached her skin yet. If it had, maybe Abramo would have seen how the bee venom healed her. Maybe then this could have ended months ago."

"But if it hadn't been for her, maybe the cure would have never been found at all," said Sam. "The whole world might have been—Sarah! Why are you crying?"

I didn't know. Relief, mostly. Happiness. Disbelief. Latent sorrow. The bandages were so tight I couldn't breathe deep enough to sob, so I just lay still and tried not to move while tears ran down the sides of my face. Sam hovered over me in distress, looking as if he wanted to hold me, not daring to move me. It was better that he didn't, though I'd have given my left arm if I could have only let him embrace me.

I'd held all hope for myself at such a distance the past few days that I couldn't bear the way it came crashing down on me now. I'd been so certain I wouldn't live, so resigned to going insane and dying like Dr. Monaghan, that the sudden turn of fate was overwhelming. I never knew that happiness could hurt so much.

I heard the door open and shut. I wasn't facing it, and it wasn't worth the pain of turning to look, so I had to wait until whoever it was came into view.

It was Dad, with an officer from the Botswana Defence Force, by the look of his crisp uniform. Dad was all concern and reassuring smiles for me. He looked much better. The color had returned to his skin somewhat, and he had a clean shirt on, with a slight lump on his side where the bandage was. The Batswana officer looked stressed, and I didn't blame him. I wondered how much he knew about what was going on.

Dad held my bandaged hand. "Sweetheart, this is Colonel Seretsi from the BDF. He'll have some questions for you."

"What's happening?" I asked.

Dad sighed and scratched at his hair, as weary as I'd ever seen him. "We let out the rest of the bees. They went straight after some infected animals that were in the area. We've already found a few silver rabbits and a duiker, dead from the venom."

"And we are bringing in more hives," said the colonel. "Importing them from South Africa and Namibia."

"So you're setting bees loose all across the central Kalahari? You trust they'll really be able to eliminate the rest of Metalcium?"

"Even if they don't," he replied, "we know now how to contain it. It's a simple matter of catching it early enough. Future treatments need not be so . . ." He raised a brow and his eyes roamed uneasily over my bandages. "So dramatic," he finished.

A soldier in a black beret trotted inside and snapped to attention. "Colonel, the president is requesting to speak with you."

The colonel nodded, gave me a tight smile, and excused himself. Dad studied my face; I didn't remember there being so many creases around his eyes.

"You doing okay, honey? It's good to see you awake."

"Better," I said. "Where have you been, Dad? We found where you'd crashed, and Theo . . ."

Dad's eyes lowered. He rubbed a weary hand across his ragged beard. "We were ambushed. Abramo must have figured out we'd been tracking them, then doubled back to wait for us. Theo and I split up, hoping to divide them. They chased me a whole day through the bush before I managed to lose them. Then I doubled back and found . . . ah, where you'd buried Theo." Dad paused to scrub at the tears in his eyes. "I shouldn't have told him to split off. We should have—"

"Not your fault, Dad," I whispered.

He sighed. "I tracked you back to the camp. Thought you'd got snatched there, so I jumped the two mercs they'd left behind."

"You *jumped* them?"

Dad shrugged. "All those years I spent playing rugby taught me a thing or two about tackling. You should have seen your dear old dad! I still have the stuff! Anyway, it became clear from those two thugs that you were still on the run. They told me about the Metalcium escaping the lab, Abramo hunting you, all of it. I tracked you from there until I found Hank swamped in the sand. I was already two days behind you at that point, and hoped to catch up. But then there was a bushfire—"

"Oh," I said slowly, wincing. "Yeah . . . I might have had something to do with that."

Dad raised a brow. "Hm. Well, you made things bloody difficult for your old man after that. The fire set me back another day, since I had to get around it, and by the time I picked up your trail again you'd been caught by the mercenaries."

"Did you see the lab?" I asked.

"Not until today. The fire forced me south, around this place. After I realized you'd been captured, I ran like a demon to catch up, but when I finally reached Abramo's camp . . ." He stopped, his voice going hoarse. "When I saw him shoot— Sarah, *Sarah* . . ." He gathered me into his arms, and though it made me ache with pain, I said nothing. The feel of his arms was too precious to let go. But then he must have realized how it hurt me, because he quickly put me down, muttering, "Sorry, sorry."

"I thought you were dead," I said bluntly. "I was taking us to Ghansi, and then I was going to come back and look for you."

He smiled sadly and ran his hand over my hair. "You did exactly right, sweetheart. I am so proud of you. Theo would have been, too, knowing how you used his teaching to stay alive. Your friends have been filling me in. According to them, you saved their lives a dozen times over. That none of them would have survived without you."

"They . . . they said that?"

I felt a few tears run down my cheeks, and Dad gently wiped them away.

"They've sent for a better equipped medical team, to take care of you. Shouldn't be long before they get here."

"And Sam and the others?"

Sam cleared his throat. "We have to stay until they decide we're not infected. A week, they're guessing, but it could be longer."

I grinned. "Can't get rid of you, can I?"

He smiled and stroked the hair back from my face. His fingers were bare now, and it made my breath catch in my throat. I caught my dad shooting a narrow look from me to Sam, and he scowled a bit before telling us he was going to go check on the medical team's progress.

When he was gone, I shut my eyes, feeling tired again and wondering if they could give me some more painkillers. Sam asked if I wanted water and I shook my head. I was thirsty, yes, but I didn't want to endure the pain of swallowing just yet. Anyway, I'd gotten very good at ignoring thirst over the past week.

"I want to sit up," I said.

"I don't think you should—"

"Please, Sam."

He didn't look happy about it, but he helped me up, propping me on some pillows that the medics had left for me.

I looked around, frowned, and turned to Sam. "They really burned everything?"

"Yeah. I guess after Dr. Monaghan failed to create a cure, they decided to get rid of the rest of the evidence. The ashes are still warm, so we're guessing Abramo had just finished burning everything when the guys who caught us called and told him we'd been caught. They found . . . Dr. Monaghan is dead. Abramo must have shot him, and had his body burned with everything else, including the rest of the animals that were in those cages."

The room was almost empty. There was only this table and a few bare cabinets left.

I sighed. "There was enough evidence in here to crack Corpus wide open. We saw it! We can tell them about Abramo, Metalcium, Corpus, all of it."

I didn't like the way Sam was avoiding my eyes.

"What is it?" I asked, dreading the answer.

"Sarah . . . Corpus doesn't exist."

My scalp prickled. "What?"

"I mean, you and I know that they do, but the name doesn't come up. We told that colonel guy everything, but there's no physical evidence. When they questioned the guys Abramo had hired, they said they'd never heard of Corpus and that they figured Abramo was trying to steal the research from this place. The helicopter—it's outside—and the cars they were driving were all registered in Abramo's name. They believe Dr. Monaghan was running this place on his own, since the funds they used came out of his private account. Besides us, no one who knew the truth is still alive to question, and they think we're all suffering from shock and dehydration.

If it weren't for us, the word *Corpus* would never have even come up."

"That's ridiculous!"

"That's what I said. What we all said." He shrugged. "Some people from the government are coming out here to talk to us. We'll just have to wait and see if they listen."

I couldn't believe that after everything we'd been through, the real criminals could get away clean. I hadn't even considered it a possibility.

"Sarah." He sat beside me on the table, took my bandaged hand in his. "Let it go. You're alive, we're all alive, and that's what matters."

I leaned against him, my head on his shoulder, and sighed. He was right. I decided to simply bask in the joy of my continued existence for the time being. After a few moments, I felt a calm come over me. I lifted my head.

"I want to go outside," I said.

He gave me a dubious look.

"I can't stand being in here another minute," I pressed.

That seemed to persuade him. He helped me stand, keeping an arm around my waist as I wobbled forward.

"Does it hurt?" he asked.

"Not too bad." But I winced and clenched my teeth as I took a step.

Outside, the sun was setting, and the people walking back and forth were silhouettes against the scarlet sky. No one seemed to notice us, for which I was grateful. I didn't feel up to conversation. I just wanted to sit somewhere quiet and feel the cool evening air on my face.

We went around to the back of the building, where we

found Kase, Miranda, Joey, and Avani sitting in the sand. They called to us, and we joined them. It took some very ginger maneuvering for me to lower myself to the ground, but managed it with Sam's help. I leaned against him and breathed in deeply, filling my lungs with the fresh Kalahari breeze.

"How are you feeling?" asked Avani.

"Better," I said. "Well, it hurts, but in a good way."

"I can't believe we made it," said Joey. "Can you say, 'best vacation ever'?"

We all groaned, but couldn't help smiling.

"Sarah." Miranda's voice was soft and uncertain. I met her eyes and found them unusually shy. "I just wanted to say, you know, thanks. For putting up with me. Keeping us alive. I was kind of a witch. . . ."

"We all were," said Avani. She took Miranda's hand and squeezed it, and the girls exchanged—of all things—a smile.

"For what it's worth," said Kase gruffly, "I've decided not to sue you."

"Um, thanks?" I said.

It may have been the medication, but I felt oddly at ease. Was it just a few days ago that I'd first met these people? I recalled the dread I'd felt that first day and of how I'd wondered if we'd make it through the week. In retrospect, it seemed silly. I felt I'd known them much longer. Despite the circumstances, I was glad we'd all met. Surprisingly glad.

I chanced a shy look at Sam, and found he was already staring at me. When our eyes met, we both blushed but didn't look away. His curiosity, his energy, his wonder for the world had reawakened the part of me I was so sure I'd lost.

"What now?" he asked.

I smiled. "Next stop the pyramids?"

He grinned, and impulsively I lifted my chin and kissed him. For a moment, the warmth of that kiss drove away the pain and the horrors of the last few days. I leaned into him as much as my bandages allowed, until at last I pulled my lips away and rested my forehead against his.

"The pyramids, the North Pole, the moon," Sam replied, his voice a bit hoarse. "Next stop anywhere, as long as you're there."

The evening cooled around us, soft and smooth as a black leopard stalking through the bush. High above, a few stars began their nightly vigil, lighting one by one, while the moon rose behind us. There is nowhere on Earth that the moon looks so huge or so near, like a great silver planet just out of reach. Only the far edges of the horizon still burned scarlet and orange, but the color was fading quickly. The few lean clouds that hovered in the distance caught those last vestiges of daylight, their edges burning gold. The sky was a dying fire, embers turning to ash, as night settled quietly over the great Kalahari.

ACKNOWLEDGMENTS

Special thanks to all those who helped make this book possible, providing support, inspiration, and advice. My editor, Jessica Almon—thank you so much for believing in this book! I can't imagine it coming to life without your insight and enthusiasm. Heartfelt thanks to Ben Schrank, Sarah Chassé, and everyone at Razorbill, for shepherding this book. Marisa Russell and the rest of the tireless publicity team at Penguin, thank you so much for spreading the word and making sure Sarah's story finds readers. And of course much love to Lucy; you are a lion among agents!

A huge thank you to all those who taught me about the Kalahari: Hank and the rest of the folks at Mabalingwe Nature Reserve in South Africa, and Jacobus and the team at Deception Valley Lodge in Botswana for answering my many questions and for the long, wonderful hours spent tracking elephants, lions, and leopards. Tsota and Xise, for sharing with me so much about Naro culture and survival skills; Sarah and the crew would never have made it out alive without you! Thanks to my translators—Sam and Christa for your help with Afrikaans, and Denise for your French.

Thanks to my family, particularly my dad, who read this first, and my grandmother, who lent her medical expertise. And my mom, who taught me to love animals and how to turn everything into an adventure. Love you all! And finally my Ben, for your unwavering support and for letting me drag you on this crazy adventure—even when it means ending up lost in the middle of the South African bush at midnight (totally my fault!). I love you.